LAST
BREATH

ALSO BY ROBERT BRYNDZA

THE DCI ERIKA FOSTER CRIME THRILLER SERIES
The Girl in the Ice
The Night Stalker
Dark Water

THE COCO PINCHARD ROMANTIC COMEDY SERIES
The Not So Secret Emails of Coco Pinchard
Coco Pinchard's Big Fat Tipsy Wedding
Coco Pinchard, the Consequences of Love and Sex
A Very Coco Christmas
Coco Pinchard's Must-Have Toy Story

STANDALONE ROMANTIC COMEDY NOVELS
Miss Wrong and Mr Right
Lost In Crazytown

LAST BREATH

ROBERT BRYNDZA

Bookouture

Published by Bookouture
An imprint of StoryFire Ltd.
23 Sussex Road, Ickenham, UB10 8PN
United Kingdom
www.bookouture.com

ISBN: 978-1-78681-145-5
eBook ISBN: 978-1-78681-144-8

For Veronika, Filip and Evie

'The scariest monsters are the ones that lurk within our souls...'

Edgar Allan Poe

PROLOGUE

Monday, 29 August 2016

It was three o'clock in the morning, and the stench of the dead body filled the car. The heat had remained unbroken for days. He drove with the air conditioning on full, but the smell of her still permeated from the boot of the car. She was decaying fast.

It had been two hours since he laid her there. The flies had been seeking her out, and in the darkness he'd had to wave his arms around to keep them off. He'd found it funny how he flapped and flailed. If she'd still been alive, she might have laughed too.

Despite the risk, he enjoyed these night-time excursions, driving along the deserted motorway, and into London through the suburbs. Two roads back, he'd shut off the car headlights, and as he turned into a run-down residential street, he cut the engine. The car freewheeled in silence, past houses, their windows dark, to the bottom of the hill where a small deserted print-works came into view. It was set back from the road with a car park. Tall trees lined the pavement, casting it in shadows, while the light pollution from the city threw a muddy orange glow over the surroundings. He turned into the car park, bumping and lurching over tree roots pushing up under the tarmac.

He drew up at a line of dumpsters next to the entrance of the print-works and turned the car sharp to the left, coming to a stop with less than a foot between the car boot and the last dumpster.

He sat in silence for a moment. The houses opposite were masked by the trees, and where the row of terraced houses met the car park it was just a brick wall. He leaned over to the glove compartment and pulled on a pair of latex gloves. He stepped out of the car, and the heat swelled up at him from the cracked tarmac. The gloves were wet inside within seconds. When he opened the car boot, a bluebottle buzzed out and found his face. He waved his arms, and spat it away.

He pushed back the lid of the dumpster; the smell hit him, and more bloody flies that had been laying their eggs amongst the warm festering rubbish flew out at him. He batted them away with a yelp and more spitting, and then moved to the back of the car.

She'd been so beautiful, even up until the end, just a few hours ago, when she'd cried and pleaded, her hair greasy, her clothes soiled. Now she was a limp thing. Her body was no longer needed, by her or him.

In one fluid movement, he hoisted her up and out of the boot and laid her lengthways on the black sacks, then slid the lid of the dumpster closed. He looked around; he was alone, more so now she was gone. He got back in the car and started the long drive home.

Later that morning, the neighbour opposite walked over to the print-works with a bulging black sack. There were no rubbish collections on the bank holiday, and her in-laws had been staying with their new baby. She slid back the lid of the first dumpster to drop it in, and a mass of flies seemed to explode out at her. She backed off, batting them away. And then she saw, lying on top of the black bags, the body of a young girl. She'd been savagely beaten: one of her eyes was swollen shut, there were gashes on her head, and her body was crawling with flies in the early morning heat.

Then the smell hit her. She dropped the black sack, and threw up over the hot tarmac.

CHAPTER 1

Monday, 9 January 2017

Detective Chief Inspector Erika Foster watched Detective James Peterson as he towelled flakes of melting snow from his short dreadlocks. He was tall and lean, with just the right mix of arrogance and charm. The curtains were drawn tight against the whirling snow, the television murmured comfortably in the background, and the small kitchen-cum-living room was bathed in the soft warm glow of two new lamps. After a long day at work, Erika had been resigned to a hot bath and an early night, but then Peterson had called from the fish and chip shop around the corner, asking if she was hungry. Before she could think up an excuse, she'd said yes. They had worked together previously on several successful murder investigations, when Erika had been Peterson's senior officer, but now they were in different units: Peterson was a member of the Murder Investigation Team, while Erika worked with the Projects Team – it was a role she had rapidly grown to hate.

Peterson went over to the radiator and draped the towel neatly, then turned to her with a grin.

'It's a blizzard out there,' he said, cupping his hands and blowing into them.

'Did you have a good Christmas?' she asked.

'It was alright, just my mum and dad. My cousin got engaged,' he said, taking off his leather jacket.

'Congratulations...' She couldn't remember if she'd heard about a cousin.

'How about you? You were in Slovakia?'

'Yeah, with my sister and her family. I shared a single bunk bed with my niece... You fancy a beer?'

'I'd love one,' he said.

He draped his jacket across the back of the sofa and sat. Erika opened the fridge door and peered in. A six-pack was wedged into the vegetable drawer, and the only food was a saucepan of days'-old soup on the top shelf. She went to check her reflection in the curved side of the stainless steel saucepan, but the shape of the metal distorted it, giving her a pinched face and a forehead bulging out like a freak show mirror. She should have lied politely that she'd already eaten.

A couple of months earlier, after drinks in the pub with colleagues, Erika and Peterson had ended up in bed together. Whilst neither of them had felt it was *just* a one-night stand, they had since kept things professional. They'd spent a couple more nights together before Christmas, and both times she had left his flat before breakfast. But now he was in her flat, they were sober, and the gilt-framed picture of her late husband, Mark, was on the bookshelf by the window.

She tried to push the anxiety and guilt from her mind, retrieved two beers and closed the fridge door. The red-and-white striped plastic bag containing the fish and chips sat on the countertop, and the smell was making her mouth water.

'Do you like yours in the paper?' she asked, popping the lids off the beers.

'It's the only way to have them,' said Peterson. He had one arm slung over the back of the sofa, and sat resting an ankle over the opposite knee. He looked confident and comfortable.

She knew it would kill the mood but they needed to have a talk; she needed to set some boundaries. She pulled out two plates and took them over with the bag and the beers, setting them down on the coffee table. They unwrapped their chip paper in silence, steam rising from the fish in crisp batter and the chips, squishy and golden. They ate for a moment.

'Look, Peterson, James…' Erika started.

Then his phone rang. He pulled it from his pocket.

'Sorry, I should take this.'

Erika nodded and gestured for him to carry on.

He answered his phone and listened with his brow furrowed. 'Really? Okay, no probs, what's the address?' He grabbed a pen from the table, and started to scribble on the corner of his chip paper. 'I'm close by. I can leave now and hold the fort until you can get there… Just go slow in this weather.' He finished the call, crammed in a mouthful of chips and stood up.

'What is it?' asked Erika.

'Couple of students have found the mutilated body of a young girl in a rubbish bin.'

'Where?'

'Tattersall Road, near New Cross… Damn those chips are good,' he said, stuffing more into his mouth. He picked up his leather jacket from its spot on the back of the sofa and checked he had his warrant card, wallet and car keys.

Erika felt another pang of regret that she was no longer on the Murder Investigation Team.

'Sorry, Erika. We'll have to do this another time. I was meant to have the evening free. What were you going to say earlier?'

'Fine. It was nothing. Who just called you?'

'DCI Hudson. She's stuck in the snow. Not stuck, but she's coming out from Central London and the roads are bad.'

'New Cross is close, I'll come with you,' she said, putting her plate down and grabbing her wallet and warrant card from the kitchen counter.

He followed her into the hall, pulling on his jacket. She checked her reflection in the tiny hall mirror, wiping chip grease from the corner of her mouth and running her hands through her short blonde hair. Her face was free of make-up, and despite her high cheekbones she noted it looked fuller after a week of Christmas food. Their eyes met in the mirror, and she saw his face had clouded over.

'Is that a problem?'

'No. We'll go in my car, though,' he said.

'No. I'll take my car.'

'Are you going to pull rank on me here?'

'What are you talking about? You take your own car, I'll take mine. We'll drive in convoy.'

'Erika. I came here for fish and chips…'

'*Just* fish and chips?' she asked.

'What does that mean?'

'Nothing. You got the call, which is work, and it's perfectly reasonable for me, as your senior officer, to attend the scene. More so if DCI Hudson is delayed…' Her voice tailed off; she knew she was pushing it.

'Your "senior officer". You won't let me forget that, will you?'

'I hope you don't forget that,' she snapped, pulling on her coat. She switched off the lights and they left the flat in an uncomfortable silence.

CHAPTER 2

Snow fell heavily, catching in the headlights of Erika's car as she left the line of traffic moving past New Cross train station and turned into Tattersall Road. A moment later, Peterson pulled in behind her. On the corner where the two roads met was a kitchen showroom set back with a large car park out front. The pavement was a churn of white, which reflected the flashing blue lights of three squad cars stationed out front. An unbroken line of terraced houses stretched away up a hill, and Erika could make out a few of the neighbours huddled in their glowing doorways, watching as police tape was unwound, cordoning off the car park of the kitchen showroom, which backed onto the first house in the terrace. Erika was pleased to see Detective Inspector Moss standing on the pavement in front of the police cordon, and talking to a uniformed police officer. She was a trusted colleague, and along with Peterson they had worked together on several murder investigations. Erika and Peterson found parking spots on the opposite side of the road, and then crossed over.

'Good to see you, boss,' said Moss, holding up the lapels of her coat against the whirling snow. She was a small, solidly built woman with short red hair and a mass of freckles covering her face. 'Are you here in an official capacity?'

Erika replied, 'Yes' just as Peterson said 'No'.

'Can you give us a moment,' said Moss, addressing the uniformed officer.

He nodded and moved off towards one of the squad cars.

'I was with Peterson when he got the call,' explained Erika.

'Always great to have you here, boss,' said Moss. 'I just assumed that DCI Hudson would be running this.'

'I'm here until she arrives,' said Erika, blinking against the onslaught of snow. Moss looked between them, and there was an awkward pause.

'So, can I see what we're dealing with?' asked Erika.

'Body of a young woman, badly beaten,' said Moss. 'The bad weather is also slowing down the CSIs and forensics. Uniform responded to the call; one of the students who lives in the end terrace over there went to the rubbish bins and found the body.'

'Do we have crime scene overalls available?' asked Erika.

Moss nodded. They moved to the police tape strung across the gate to the car park, and there was an awkward moment as Erika waited for Peterson to lift it for her. She shot him a look, he lifted it, and she moved past him and into the car park.

'Oh bloody hell, are they a couple now?' muttered Moss to herself. 'They say never work with children or animals, they never mention couples.'

She followed, and joined Erika and Peterson pulling on crime scene overalls. They then ducked under the police tape and went over to a large industrial rubbish bin chained to the brick wall of the kitchen showroom. The curved lid was tipped back. Moss directed the powerful beam of a torch inside.

'My God,' said Peterson, stepping back and putting a hand to his mouth.

Erika didn't flinch, but just stared.

Lying on her right side, on a pile of neatly stacked, broken-down cardboard boxes, was the body of a young woman. She had been badly beaten; her eyes were swollen shut and her long brown hair was matted with congealed blood. She was naked from the waist down, and her legs were criss-crossed with cuts and gashes. She wore a small T-shirt, but it was impossible to tell what colour it had once been, as it too was saturated with blood.

'And look,' said Moss softly. She directed the torch onto the top of the girl's head, where the skull had caved in.

'And it was students who found her?' said Erika.

'They were waiting outside when uniform arrived,' said Moss. 'You can see their front door opens out into the car park, so we couldn't let them back in when we taped off the crime scene.'

'Where are they?'

'Uniform put them in a car up the road.'

'Let's close things up until forensics get here,' said Erika, noting the snow which was forming a thin layer over the body and surrounding cardboard boxes.

Peterson placed his gloved hands on the dumpster, and slowly pulled the curved lid back, closing the body off from the elements.

They heard voices by the police cordon and the beep of a radio. They moved over to where DCI Hudson, a small woman with a bob of fine blonde hair, was standing with Superintendent Sparks, a tall thin man with a long, pale face pockmarked with acne scars. His greasy black hair was swept back off his forehead, and his suit was grubby.

'Erika. What are you doing here? The last I heard you were in a galaxy far far away,' he said.

'I'm in Bromley,' replied Erika.

'Same thing.'

DCI Hudson stifled a grin.

'Yes. All very funny,' said Erika. 'Just like the dead girl who's been beaten to death and left in the dumpster over there...'

Hudson and Sparks stopped smirking.

'Erika was just helping us out. The weather was holding things up, and she lives locally,' explained Moss.

'She was with me when I got the call. I also live locally,' started Peterson, but Erika shot him a look.

'I see,' said Sparks, noticing the look. He paused, as if he was
filing it away in his mind for later use against her, then moved to
the police tape, lifting it with a black gloved hand.

'Make sure you hand in your crime scene overalls, Erika.
Then wait for me outside. We need to have a little chat.'

Moss and Peterson went to say more, but Erika gave them a
small shake of her head and moved off towards the police cordon.

CHAPTER 3

Erika left the crime scene, and moved further up the street, pacing up and down in the pool of orange cast by one of the streetlights. The snow was whirling in thick flurries, and she hunkered down, turning up the collar of her jacket, her hands thrust deep into the pockets. She felt powerless, watching from the sidelines as a black van belonging to the CSIs parked on the pavement directly in front of the police cordon. Despite the freezing temperature, she didn't want to go back to her car. In the glove compartment was a packet of cigarettes she'd kept for emergencies. She'd given up some months ago, but in times of stress, still felt the gnawing of nicotine cravings. However, she refused to let Sparks be the reason for her caving in and lighting up. He emerged from the gates a few minutes later, and walked up to her.

'Erika, why are you here?' he said. Under the streetlight, she noticed his hair had streaks of grey, and he appeared gaunt.

'I told you, I was made aware that DCI Hudson was delayed.'

'Who made you aware?'

Erika hesitated, 'I was with Peterson when he got the call, but I'd like to stress it's not his fault. I didn't give him much choice in the matter.'

'You were *with* him?'

'Yes…'

'Enjoying a bit of strange, were you?' he said with a smirk. Despite the freezing air, Erika felt warmth flush her cheeks.

'That's none of your business.'

'And my crime scene is none of your business. I'm in charge of the Murder Investigation Teams. You don't work for me, and you're not welcome. So why don't you fuck off.'

Erika moved close and looked him in the eye. 'What did you just say?' His breath smelt stale and acidic.

'You heard me, Erika. Fuck off. You're not here to help, you're just meddling. I know you've put in for a transfer back to one of the Murder Investigation Teams. The irony. Considering you made such a stand, quitting when I was promoted over you.'

Erika stared back at him. She knew that he hated her, but in the past a thin veil of politeness had covered their dealings.

'Don't you dare speak to me like that again,' she said.

'Don't speak to me like that again, *sir.*'

'You know, Sparks, you might have been handed your superior rank by brown nosing, but you have to earn authority,' said Erika, holding his gaze. The snow was coming down heavier, in large fibrous chunks, which stuck to his suit jacket. She refused to blink or look away. A uniformed officer approached them, and Sparks was forced to break his gaze.

'What is it?' he snapped.

'Sir. The crime scene manager is here, and we've got the guy who runs the kitchen showroom coming down so we can run our lights off his grid.'

'I want you off my crime scene,' said Sparks. He strode back towards the police tape with the officer, their shoes leaving fresh prints in the snow.

Erika took a deep breath and composed herself, feeling tears prick her eyes.

'Stop it, he's just another arsehole at work,' she scolded. 'You could be the one lying in that dumpster.'

She wiped the tears from her face and started back to her car, passing a squad car with its interior lights on. The windows were starting to steam up, and inside she could just make out three young people: two girls in the back, and a young blond boy in the front. The boy was leaning through the seats, and they were deep in conversation. Erika slowed and came to a stop.

'Oh fuck it,' she said.

She turned and walked back up to the car. Checking there was no one else around, she knocked on the window and then opened the door, flashing her warrant card.

'Are you the students who found the body?' she asked. They looked up at her and nodded, their faces still in shock. They looked no older than eighteen. 'Have you spoken to an officer yet?' she added, leaning into the car.

'No, we've been here for ages; just been told to wait, but we're frozen,' said the young guy.

'My car's on the other side of the road. Let's have a chat with the heating on,' said Erika.

CHAPTER 4

Erika adjusted the dials in her car, until warm air came blasting out of the vents. The young boy sat next to her, in the passenger seat, rubbing at his bare arms. He was blond and thin with bad skin, and wore a T-shirt and a thin jacket with jeans. The two girls were in the back. The first sat behind Erika, and she was beautiful with caramel-coloured skin. She wore jeans, a red jumper, and a purple hijab fastened at the left side of her neck with a silver butterfly pin. Next to her, the second girl was short and plump, with a bob of brown hair. Her two front teeth were prominent, which gave her face a rabbit-like appearance, and she wore a grubby peach-coloured towelling dressing gown.

'Can I take your names?' asked Erika, pulling a notebook from her bag, and resting it on the steering wheel.

'I'm Josh McCaul,' said the boy.

She scrubbed at the paper, her pen not working.

'Can you see if there's another one in the glove compartment?' asked Erika.

He leaned forward to check and his T-shirt rode up at the back to show a tattoo of a cannabis leaf at the base of his spine. He raked through the old sweet packets and her emergency Marlboro lights, and handed her a biro. 'Can I have one of these?' he added, finding a half-full bag of mini Mars bars.

'Help yourself,' she said. 'Do you two want one?'

'No,' said the girl with the hijab, adding that her name was Aashirya Khan. The second girl also refused chocolate.

'I'm Rachel Dawkes, spelt without the "a"...'

'She means the Rachel is without the "a", not Dawkes. She's got a real thing about that,' said Josh, unwrapping his second mini Mars.

Rachel pursed her lips in disapproval and rearranged the folds of her dressing gown.

'Do you all rent the flat next to the kitchen showroom?' asked Erika.

'Yes, we're students at Goldsmiths University,' said Rachel. 'I'm reading English, so is Aashirya. Josh is on the Art course.'

'Did you hear or see anything suspicious in the last few days, anyone hanging around those dumpsters, or the kitchen showroom car park?'

Aashirya shifted in her seat, her arms crossed over her lap, her large eyes watching the CSIs who were now filing past their house into the car park. 'This is a rough area, there's always shouts and screams at night,' she said and started to cry.

Rachel leaned over to give her a hug. Josh chewed what was left of the chocolate and found it hard to swallow.

'What do you mean, shouts and screams?' asked Erika.

'There's four pubs, a big student population, and lots of these flats are housing association,' said Rachel primly. 'This is South London. There's crime on every corner.'

The car windows were now steaming up. Erika let that go and adjusted the heater.

'Who found the body?'

'It was Josh,' said Rachel. 'He sent me a message to come outside.'

'Sent you a message?'

'A text message,' said Josh as if she were being dim. Erika again was struck by the age gap. Her first instinct would have been to run inside and tell them, but Josh reached for his phone. 'Our bin was full, and the ones at the showroom can't have been used over Christmas, so I thought they would be empty.'

'We all came outside,' said Aashirya.

'What time was this?' asked Erika.

'Seven thirty-ish,' said Josh.

'What time does the kitchen showroom close?'

'It's been closed ever since the new year. We heard that the bloke who owns it has gone bankrupt,' replied Josh.

'So it's been very quiet over the last few days?'

They all nodded.

'Do you recognise the victim? Another student, or a local girl?' asked Erika.

They shook their heads, wincing at the memory of the dead girl.

'We've only lived here since September, we're first years,' said Josh.

'When can we go back to our flat?' asked Rachel.

'It's part of the crime scene and these things take time,' said Erika.

'Can you be more specific, officer?'

'I'm sorry, I can't.'

'It was probably a prostitute, the girl in the dumpster,' added Rachel primly, adjusting the lapels of her dressing gown. 'It's that kind of area.'

'Do you know any prostitutes in the area?' asked Erika.

'No!'

'So how do you know she was a prostitute?'

'Well, how else would a girl find herself... How else could that happen?'

'Rachel, being naive and judgemental won't get you far in life,' said Erika.

Rachel pressed her lips together and looked at the steamed-up window beside her.

'Is there anything else that you can tell me. Anything you saw, however small? Despite the usual weirdos, there was no one hanging around. No one who drew suspicion?' They shook their heads. 'What about the neighbours opposite? What are they like?' asked Erika, indicating the line of dark houses on the other side of the road.

'We don't really know them. A mix of students and there's a couple of old ladies,' said Josh.

'Where are we going to stay?' asked Aashirya in a small voice.

'A friend of mine has given me the keys to his place, so I can feed his cat. We could go there?' suggested Josh.

'Where is it?' asked Erika.

'Near Ladywell.'

'Officer, what happens now?' asked Rachel. 'Do we have to come to court or take part in a line-up?'

Erika felt sorry for them; they were only young, and just a few months ago had left home to come and live in one of the rougher areas of London.

'You might be called to court, but that would be at a much later date,' said Erika. 'For now, we can offer counselling. I can see about emergency accommodation, but it will take time. If you can give me the address, I can see about you getting a lift over to this friend's place? We will need to talk to you again, though, and get your official statements.'

Aashirya had herself more under control and was wiping her eyes with the back of her hand. Erika rummaged in her bag for a tissue.

'Do any of you need to phone your parents?'

'I've got my phone,' said Rachel, patting the pocket of her dressing gown.

'My mum works nights,' said Josh.

'My phone is still in the flat. I'd like to ring my father, please,' said Aashirya, taking a tissue from Erika.

'Use my phone, hun,' said Josh, passing his phone between the seats.

Aashirya dialled in a number and waited, the phone pressed to the material of her hijab. Josh wiped the condensation from the window. The pathologist's van had arrived, and they were wheeling a stretcher over the pavement and into the car park.

'She was dumped like a piece of rubbish,' he said. 'Who would do that?'

Erika stared through the window, and wanted badly to know the answer to that same question. Sparks appeared at the gate, dressed in crime scene overalls, and she knew the only thing she could do right now was leave.

CHAPTER 5

Erika woke up alone the next morning. She had hoped Peterson might call with more information from the crime scene, but when she switched on her phone there were no missed calls or messages.

It took longer than usual to drive to work; the gritters had been out overnight, but it was slow going on the grimy slush-covered roads. When she finally reached Bromley, the town centre was grey, and the morning light was struggling through a bank of low clouds. Snow continued to fall, melting as it hit the gritted roads, but it was cold enough to lie on the pavements. Bromley Police Station sat at the bottom of the high street, opposite the train station and a large Waitrose supermarket. Pale-faced commuters were filing into the station, past an impatient line at the small coffee shop.

She parked in the underground car park, and took the lift up to the ground floor. Several of the uniformed officers were coming off the night shift, and they said hello in greeting as she made her way past the staff locker rooms to the tiny kitchen. She made a cup of tea, and took it upstairs to the corner office she'd been assigned, sighing when she saw a pile of fresh files waiting on her desk. She was picking through them when there was a tap on her door. She looked up to see Detective Constable John McGorry, a handsome, dark-haired officer in his mid-twenties.

'Alright, boss?'

'Morning, John. What can I do for you?'

'Have you had a chance to look over my application?'

Late the previous year, John had been part of Erika's team during a historical missing person case, and after its success-ful conclusion, John had started the process of applying for the rank of detective sergeant.

'Sorry, John. I'll look at it today… It's been, well, Christmas and everything.'

'Thanks, boss,' he said with a grin.

Erika felt rotten. She'd had his application form since the week before Christmas. She sat down at her desk and logged into her mailbox to find the attachment, but was distracted by a new email:

ATTN: Detective Chief Inspector Foster,
I write in response to your application to transfer to the murder investigation team. Unfortunately, your application has not been successful at this time.
Yours sincerely,
Barry Mcgough.
MPS Human Resources Department

'Sparks…' she said, sitting back in her chair. She picked up the phone and dialled Peterson. He answered after several rings, sounding groggy. 'Bugger. I've woken you up.'

'Yeah,' he said, clearing his throat. 'We were there till two this morning.'

'What else did you find out?'

'Not much. Melanie Hudson had me and Moss doing a door-to-door. None of the neighbours on Tattersall Road saw anything.'

'Listen. Sorry if I railroaded you last night.'

'Why did you?'

'I hadn't told anyone, but I'd put in for a transfer to come back to one of the Murder Investigation Teams.'

'And work for Sparks?'

'No, to solve murders. I've been stuck behind a desk for the past couple of months, writing bloody reports. Anyway. It doesn't matter now. I've been turned down.'

'Sorry. Did they say why?'

'No.'

'Erika, when they judge this stuff your rank and pay grade goes against you.'

'I think being me goes against me. And I'm sure Sparks had a hand in the decision… If only they judged the application on the number of cases I've solved. The number of murderers I've put away.'

'Putting them away doesn't save money. Did you know that banging someone up in prison costs the same as it would to stay a night at the Ritz?'

'Is that what it comes down to?'

'For someone so smart, you can be pretty naive, Erika.'

'We can't think in those terms. Too many people think that money comes first…'

Peterson sighed on the end of the phone.

'Look. I've had three hours' sleep, Erika. I agree with you but I need some zees before I get into a debate,' he said.

'Okay. And sorry again about last night.'

''S'okay. Sit tight, something will come up.'

'I know. I'm just sick of being stuck here in the backwaters, trawling through endless paperwork for Ronald McDonald…'

Erika heard someone clearing their throat and looked up to see a man with a shock of red hair, standing in the doorway. It was Ronald McDonald himself: Superintendent Yale.

'Look, I have to go…' She hung up. 'Morning, boss, what can I do for you?' she asked, cringing.

'Erika, can I have a word?' he said. Yale was a large man, tall and stocky, with a bushy red beard to match his hair. His face was red and blotchy, his large blue eyes watery. Erika thought he always looked on the verge of a nervous reaction to something he'd eaten.

'Yes, sir. Is this about the knife crime statistics report?'

'No.' He closed the door and came in to sit down in front of her desk. 'I've had Superintendent Sparks on the phone...'

Yale had a habit of leaving a sentence hanging, waiting for you to put your head through the noose and incriminate yourself.

'How is he?' asked Erika breezily.

'He says last night you barged in on his crime scene.'

'I arrived with DI Peterson; I was with him when he was called to the scene, and the weather was slowing down the other officers, so I decided to lend a hand and I went with him...'

'Sparks says he had to order you to leave the crime scene.'

'Can "fuck off" ever be interpreted as an order, sir? I'm quoting him directly.'

'You then stayed at the scene, and took accounts from the three students who discovered the body of Lacey Greene.'

Erika raised her eyebrows. 'He has an ID on the victim?'

Yale bit his lip, realising that he'd given away more than he intended.

'For God's sake, Erika. You keep banging on about being promoted, but you behave like a teenager!'

'The three witnesses were left alone in an unheated police car. Tattersall Road is in a pretty rough area. It was late at night, and they weren't dressed for minus temperatures. One of the girls was in her dressing gown, and the other was wearing a hijab...' Erika let that hang in the air for a moment, then went on. 'These were vulnerable young women, sir, and we're having to deal with increased Islamophobia, especially around the more deprived areas...'

Yale raised a bushy eyebrow, and drummed his fingers on her desk for a moment. They were both aware she was going for the low option, but it was true.

'Sir, I took accounts from the three witnesses, arranged a safe place for them to stay, and I emailed a full report with all the information to Superintendent Sparks.'

'Erika, I know you're not happy here. I get it. I don't find working with you much fun either.'

'I applied for a transfer, but I've been turned down.'

Yale got up. 'Then we should make the best of things. I need to see the first draft of your report on knife crime statistics in the borough by the end of play today.'

'Of course, sir.'

He went to say something else, then nodded and left. Erika sat back and stared out of her window. The high street stretched away up to the crossing, where it became a pedestrian zone. There was a sprawling queue outside the pound shop. A young Asian man emerged, pulling up the shutter, and the crowd surged forward.

Erika was about to make another cup of tea when her phone rang.

'Is this Detective Erika Foster?' said a young male voice.

'Detective Chief Inspector, yes, speaking.'

'Hi. This is Josh McCaul, from last night…' His voice tailed off, and she heard the sound of a coffee machine in the background. 'Can I talk to you?'

'Josh, one of my colleagues will be getting in contact with you to take a formal statement.'

'Before I do it formally, I need to talk to you.'

'About what?'

'The murder victim,' he said in a small voice.

'You said you didn't know her?'

There was a long pause on the end of the line, then he said: 'I don't know her. But I think I know who killed her.'

CHAPTER 6

Erika agreed to meet Josh in the Brockley Jack, a traditional British pub on the busy Brockley Road, recently refurbished in a gastro-pub style. The bar was quiet at eleven in the morning, apart from two scruffy old men who each had a pint on the go, and another lined up.

Josh was behind the bar, wearing a long-sleeved black T-shirt, arranging clean crockery on top of a large silver coffee machine. He looked scared.

'Hello. Where do you want to talk?' asked Erika.

'Do you mind if we go in the beer garden? I need a ciggie,' he said.

A middle-aged woman with heavy make-up and a ruched red blouse appeared from a door behind him, and gave Erika a hard stare. 'I suppose you'll be wanting coffee?' she snapped.

'Black with no sugar,' said Erika.

'I'll bring them over. Put the space heaters on if you need them, Josh.'

The beer garden was small, with a high wall backing onto a row of houses. They sat under a small veranda on some decking. Josh got the space heater ignited with a click and a whoomph, and wheeled it closer. The warm air wafted down on Erika. The woman came out with their coffees and an ashtray.

'I'll be in the bar if you need me, Josh… Remember he called *you*,' she said, departing with a scowl.

'Is her bark worse than her bite?' asked Erika, taking a sip of her coffee.

'Sandra's cool; she's like another mother to me,' replied Josh, taking out a packet of cigarettes and lighting one. 'Where are you from? You've got an odd accent.'

'Slovakia, but I've lived in the UK for twenty-five years.'

Josh cocked his head and sized her up, gripping his glowing cigarette. 'You've got like a northern accent, with a bit of foreign underneath.'

Erika noted how pale and ill he looked in the weak January sun.

'Yes. I learnt English in Manchester, where I met my husband,' she said.

'How long have you been married?'

'I'm not. He died a few years back.'

'Sorry.'

Despite the cold, it was hot under the space heater. Josh went to push up his sleeves and then checked himself, but not before Erika saw needle marks on the inside of his arms.

'Josh, this isn't my case. You should have asked to speak to Superintendent Sparks.'

'The creepy guy who looks like a vampire with piles?'

Erika stifled a smile. 'That's him.'

Josh stubbed out his cigarette, lit another, and exhaled, biting his lip. 'I think I know something, about the dead girl. But telling you means I have to admit to something illegal.'

'Start by speaking hypothetically,' said Erika, placing a hand on his shoulder.

He shrank back a little. 'What if a person bought drugs from a dealer, but then saw that dealer at a crime scene?' he asked.

'What are we talking? Cannabis?'

He shook his head. 'Much worse.'

'Does this person have any previous convictions?'

'No… They don't, I don't,' he said softly, looking at the floor.

'Then I doubt the CPS would push for a prosecution. Do you need help?'

'I've got all the numbers; I just have to get around to calling…' Josh stamped out his third cigarette, furiously blinking back tears.

'Josh, you saw the girl in that dumpster. It was a brutal death.'

He nodded and wiped his eyes.

'Okay. There's this dealer, he hangs around the student union all the time. I went to take out the rubbish earlier than I said I did. The first time I went out, he was there, the dealer. So I went back inside.'

'What time?'

'Five, five-thirty.'

'Why did you go back inside when you saw him?'

'I owe him money… nothing major, but he's a nasty piece of work. I thought he'd come for me.'

'What exactly was he doing?'

'He was just, like, standing beside that dumpster.'

'Just standing?'

'He had his hand inside. Then he stepped back and was just staring.'

'Do you know his name?'

'Steven Pearson.'

'Address?'

'He's homeless as far as I know.'

'Josh, did you find the body, just as you told me, around seven thirty p.m.?'

'Yes, that part is true. I came back outside with the rubbish around seven thirty, when he was gone.'

'Would you be willing to put this on the record, give us a statement?'

'And if I say no?'

'If you say no, you'll have a drug problem *and* the murder of a young girl on your conscience.'

Josh looked at the ground and then nodded. 'Okay.'

When Erika was back in her car she made a call to John at Bromley, and got the number for DCI Hudson. Melanie's phone went straight to voicemail, so she left a brief message with details of Josh and what he had seen.

Erika looked out of the window at the car park. It had started to snow hard, and Sandra darted out of a fire exit with a bag of rubbish and slung it into the open dumpster.

Then, Erika made another call to find out who would be conducting Lacey Greene's post-mortem.

CHAPTER 7

Just after eleven the next morning, Erika arrived at the mortuary in Lewisham, where she was met by Forensic Pathologist Doug Kernon. He was a big jovial bear of a man in his early sixties, with short grey bristly hair, and a red florid face.

'Erika Foster, glad to finally meet you, I've heard a lot about you!' he boomed cheerily, shaking her hand and showing her through to his small office next to the morgue.

'Good or bad?'

'Both.' He grinned, pushing his glasses up on his nose. Erika had lied, saying she was involved with the Lacey Greene murder investigation. Her rank and reputation meant that this was accepted, but with her rank and reputation she acknowledged she should know better.

'You've just missed DCI Hudson. I presumed as SIO she would be briefing you?'

'She wanted to get my angle on things,' Erika lied. 'I hope you don't mind running through it again?'

'No. Not at all,' he said with a wave of his hand. His office was crammed with the usual shelves of medical tomes, and the quirks that senior members of the medical profession acquire. There was a lava lamp, and a treadmill under a small window, but the conveyor belt was lined with seed trays full of home-grown salad leaves. He seemed to have quite a fancy for the British actress Kate Beckinsale. Erika counted nine pictures of her in her various movie roles. On his desk were various open parcels of greaseproof paper containing meats and cheeses, and a loaf of artisan bread on a wooden board.

'Not peckish, are you?' he asked, following her gaze. 'I was about to tuck in and open a jar of my wife's piccalilli.'

'No, thank you. I have to be back at the office,' said Erika. She'd dealt with death for many years, but wasn't sure chorizo and stilton would sit well before viewing the body.

'Of course, let's go then.'

His demeanour changed when they moved from his cosy office and into the chilly morgue. There was a scrape of metal as he pulled out one of the mortuary drawers on the large back wall, which contained the black body bag.

Erika moved to a computer screen in the corner of the morgue, which had details of Doug's report and a driving licence photo of Lacey. She had been an attractive woman, of medium height with long glossy brown hair, a beautiful heart-shaped face. There was a youthful almost cherubic beauty about her, and this was all captured in an ID photo. Erika presumed she had been even more beautiful in real life.

From behind, Erika heard the slow oily sound of a zip being opened and the crackle as Doug flicked back the folds of the body bag. She took a deep breath and turned.

The blood had been washed from her body, but she was unrecognisable from her picture, with two huge swollen pouches for eyes. Lacey had been lying on her side in the dumpster, and now she was on her back, Erika could see the left cheek bone of that heart-shaped face was broken. Scores of deep cuts covered her chest, upper arms, and thighs.

Doug gave her a moment to take it in, then started to explain his findings. 'These cuts are consistent with an extremely sharp object. They have an even depth and line, which makes me think she was slashed repeatedly with a small sharp blade. There is blunt force trauma on the back of the skull, the left ocular bone – that's the eye socket – and the left cheekbone was shattered. You can see that her ears were pierced, and an earring was ripped out of her left ear.' He indicated a torn earlobe.

'Was she sexually assaulted?'

'There's no evidence of semen, or any latex residue,' he said. 'But she has internal injuries on the walls of her vagina. The cuts are small but again they are consistent with a small sharp blade being inserted... Perhaps a Stanley knife or scalpel.'

'To torture,' finished Erika.

'I believe so, yes. Also, see the wrists. There is bruising consistent with her wrists being bound. I think in this instance her wrists were tied with a thin chain: see the linking in the bruising. She has identical bruising on her neck.'

'She was tied up... Did you manage to take anything from under her nails?'

'Note the fingers,' he added, gently lifting one of the hands.

Erika's stomach lurched. The fingernails had been pulled out.

'When I saw her at the scene, her fingers were curled against her cheek. I hadn't noticed this... Maybe she scratched him, and he didn't want us to get his DNA,' said Erika.

Doug nodded. 'Her right arm is broken in two places, and you can see the toes on the right foot have been crushed,' he said.

'Cause of death?'

'Despite all of this, the actual cause of death was catastrophic blood loss from an incision in the femoral artery in her left thigh.' He moved to the side of the table, and gently parted her legs to show a small incision, high on her inner thigh near the groin.

Erika noticed that her pubic hair was shaven, with a tiny amount of stubble.

'Was her pubic hair shaved during the post-mortem?' she asked.

'No.'

Erika didn't want to jump to conclusions, but was this a sign of promiscuity? She looked back to Doug.

'I wouldn't use it as a moral compass on the poor girl,' he said, reading her thoughts. 'Was it a bad choice on her part? Or were events thrust upon her, out of her control? That's up to you to find out.'

'She was reported missing last week, and her body was found several days later,' started Erika.

'Yes. I believe the wounds were inflicted over a period of several days; some had already started to heal. The incision to the femoral artery would have been fatal, and I would expect her to have bled out within minutes.'

'So you think she could have been held somewhere and tortured?'

'All I can say is that the injuries were inflicted over a period of two to three days...'

'I'm impressed you were able to ID her so quickly,' said Erika.

'When the victim is found with her bag, wallet and ID, it's fairly easy... but you should know this?' he said, narrowing his eyes.

'Yes. Of course.'

He looked as if he wasn't buying it, but continued. 'The incision on the inner thigh, the femoral artery, is precise. He knew where he was going with the knife...'

'You think it's a "he"?'

'Are you going all politically correct on me, Erika?'

'No. I've seen the havoc and violence women can inflict just as much as men...'

He beckoned her over to a large anatomy poster fixed to the tiled wall. The body, of undetermined sex, lay with arms splayed outwards and it showed the position of all the major organs and arteries.

'You see here, the inner thigh at the femoral artery,' he said, indicating with a biro. 'The artery is buried in folds of fatty tissue. The femoral artery is used as an entry point for heart procedures: for example, when a stent is inserted to widen a heart valve. It's non-invasive; instead of opening up the chest cavity you can go through the groin.'

'You think the killer had medical knowledge?'

'Again, that's for you and your SIO to work out.'

'Do you have a time of death?'

'Looking at the rate of rigor mortis, I'd say she has been dead for 48 hours or more.'

Four days are unaccounted for since she went missing, thought Erika. *Four days of fear, agony and pain.*

She turned away from the anatomy diagram and went back to the table to look at Lacey, and the incision in her upper thigh. 'Could it be a lucky guess on the part of whoever did this? Finding this femoral artery and making the incision?' she asked.

'Yes, but it would be a fluke to find it, and then make the correct incision first time. If she'd been unconscious, it would have been easier to locate, but you can see that she put up a fight.'

Erika looked down at Lacey's beaten and broken body. The long neat line of stitches from her navel to chest, completed after the autopsy, were at odds with the random violence inflicted on her. Erika wished that the other cuts had been sewn up too. It just seemed to expose her even more.

'It would be really good if you could catch this one,' said Doug, his face set in grim sadness.

Erika nodded. 'I will. I always do.'

CHAPTER 8

Erika drove back to the police station in Bromley, and spent the rest of the afternoon staring gloomily at a spreadsheet on her computer. She couldn't focus on the numbers, which kept blurring in front of her eyes. All she could see was the battered body of Lacey, lying in the morgue.

Just before five she was about to go and grab a coffee, when she made a decision and picked up her phone. This time, Melanie Hudson answered.

'Did you get my message?' Erika asked. 'Josh McCaul, the lad who lives next to the kitchen showroom, states he saw a man called Steven Pearson acting suspiciously in the hours leading up to when he discovered Lacey Greene's body...'

'I got your message,' she said irritably. 'We have Steven Pearson in custody.'

'Already?'

'Yes. We brought him in a couple of hours ago. We did another door-to-door, and got a positive ID on him from a neighbour. Steven Pearson's well known to the police in the area: GBH, ABH, attempted rape. He had Lacey Greene's wallet on him, with her cash and bank cards, and he had a surgical scalpel. His arms and face are also covered in scratches...'

'Did he have her mobile phone?'

'No... Look, Erika, I appreciate you passing info on to me, but Superintendent Sparks gave you a direct order to stay away from this investigation.'

'He did, but—'

'I just want to do my job, Erika. I have Lacey Greene's killer in custody, and it looks like this case is moving towards a successful conclusion. Stay out of this, or I'll make things difficult for you.'

There was a click and she hung up. Erika slammed down her phone, bristling. The snow whirled thickly against the window, blanketing the high street. It usually lifted her spirits, the cleansing power of snow, but she felt angry and isolated in her small office in Bromley. She turned back to her spreadsheet and attempted to concentrate.

Lacey Greene was abducted, held somewhere for four days, and then tortured before her femoral artery, an artery hard to find, was cut with surgical precision.

Would a homeless drug addict have the brains or the resources to execute all of this? And why would he then hang around the crime scene, allowing himself to be seen by two witnesses?

CHAPTER 9

Erika couldn't sleep that night. After lying in the darkness for hours, she got up and went to her window. It gave her a clear view over the small car park outside her block of flats. Snow continued to fall, and had reduced the cars to humps of white. In the corner, against a high brick wall, was a line of three dumpsters for the building. It was quiet; the only sound was a faint tapping as snow fell against her window. She couldn't get the image of Lacey Greene's battered body out of her head. Lacey was only twenty-two, she had her whole life ahead of her.

From past investigations, Erika knew how much fate played its part in murder cases. If the victim had left the bar ten minutes later, or remembered to lock the car door, or taken a slightly different route, they would still be alive.

She pulled herself away from the window and took a shower, standing under the hot water for a long time. She wondered how many times her twenty-two-year-old self had narrowly avoided death. How many times might she have passed a predator waiting in the shadows, who reached out to grab her, but only just missed.

When she left her flat at six it was still dark. The ground was undisturbed; hers were the first footprints in the snow, which glowed orange under the streetlights. She had emptied the small bin in her kitchen before she left, and she crossed the car park to the dumpsters, the snow creaking underfoot, seeming loud in the morning silence. She stopped at the black dumpster with the curved blue lid. There was no noise from the main road behind her building; the snow seemed to close in around her ears, muffling the world. She stood for a long few minutes, between two parked cars, and became convinced that there was a body inside the black dumpster. When she closed her eyes, she saw Lacey Greene, filthy with dirt and crusted blood, her face misshapen, a thin layer of snow covering her body with a ghostly sheen.

''S'cuse me,' came a voice behind her, and she nearly cried out in shock.

One of her neighbours, a middle-aged man, leaned across, pushed back the snow-covered lid of the dumpster, and dropped in a bulging black sack. It hit the bottom with a hollow clunk.

'Morning,' she replied, her heart thumping.

He frowned and trudged off to his car.

Erika turned back to the dumpster and peered into the gloom. She could just make out that it was empty; his was the first bag nestling on the bottom. She placed hers inside gently, and pulled the lid closed. She moved along, sliding back the lids of the other two dumpsters: the paper and plastic, and the one for glass. They were all empty.

Erika turned and trudged over to her car. The neighbour had almost finished scraping the snow off a small van, but he was looking at her strangely.

When she arrived at Bromley Police Station, it was quiet. She made tea and took it up to her office. Breakfast was half a packet of biscuits found at the bottom of her drawer. Dipped in the hot tea they cheered her a little, and as she munched she fired up her computer. She found Lacey Greene's Facebook profile, but it was set to be limited unless they were friends. She hovered the cursor over the friend icon, and felt an overwhelming sadness that Lacey wouldn't be accepting any new requests. She looked up and saw it was getting light, the empty high street below taking on an eerie shade of blue. A deep freeze, that's what the weather reports on the radio had called it.

It was frustrating that she was locked out of the Lacey Greene murder case; she was unable to access the case details on Holmes, the police database. Yesterday she had been able to access Steven Pearson's criminal record on CRIS, the Crime Record Information System. She opened it again on her screen. Pearson's record went back to 1980, and included twenty-five arrests for theft, credit card fraud, rape, actual bodily harm, and attempted murder. He'd served three stretches in prison, most recently, from 2003, spending ten years in HMP Blundeston for rape and attempted murder.

Erika jumped when she heard a whistle. She turned from the screen. John was behind her with a stack of paperwork.

'He looks like a right charmer,' he said.

They looked at the photo on the screen. Steven Pearson had a sharp little face with bad skin and was almost bald. Wisps of brown hair clung onto the sides of his head. There were large bags under his beady eyes, and he looked older than his fifty or so years.

'He's just been arrested for the Lacey Greene murder in New Cross,' said Erika.

'That was lucky; they caught him fast.'

Erika's initial thought came back to her: *would a homeless drug addict have the brains or the resources to plan out a kidnap and murder?*

'What can I do for you, John?'

'Superintendent Yale's been through the next draft of your report, and he's made notes,' he said, handing her a stack of printouts. The first page was covered in Yale's red scrawl. 'He'd also like to see you, after lunch.'

Erika put them on her desk and turned back to her screen. 'John. Do you have separate bins for recycling at home?'

'Oh lordy,' he said, rolling his eyes. 'My girlfriend is the biggest recycling freak: paper, metal, plastic; if it's not in the right bin, I'm in trouble... If I was going to dump a body, my girlfriend would be more concerned that I put it in the right bin.'

Erika shot him a look.

'Sorry, boss, bad taste.'

'There were three dumpsters at the scene. Lacey Greene was found in a dumpster for general waste. Why that one?'

'General waste ends up in landfill, so it would have taken much longer to find and identify her, if at all. The landfill is huge, over at Rainham. All the recycling waste ends up in a high-tech sorting facility in East London. My girlfriend made a point of finding this all out.'

'Something doesn't add up for me. Some of the cuts on Lacey's body had started to heal, which means she could have been held and tortured for four days before being killed. Every crime Steven Pearson has committed was the result of a violent outburst, or drink and drugs. He could have killed Lacey, but looking at his history, wouldn't he just have done it there and then?'

'Even if he didn't do it, it would be good to have someone like him off the streets.'

'That's a sloppy way of thinking, John.'

'You also say that we shouldn't underestimate people. Just because he hasn't done it before doesn't mean he isn't capable.'

Erika nodded and looked back at his record. 'I dunno. It's not even my bloody case.'

'Boss, I don't mean to hassle you, but did you get the chance to look at my application?'

'Sorry, John. It's on my list for today. I promise.'

John nodded, looking doubtful, and left her office.

Erika looked through her bag and pulled out the notes she'd made after her visit with Doug Kernon at the morgue. She brought up the police crime database and did a general search on victims with a femoral artery incision, including details of the crime scene and the victim's age and sex.

The results which came up stopped Erika in her tracks.

CHAPTER 10

Forensic Pathologist Isaac Strong lived in a smart terraced house on a quiet street in Blackheath, South London. It was dark, and snow was falling softly when Erika knocked on the door. She stood tapping her feet impatiently, and a moment later heard a creak of floorboards before it opened. Isaac was a tall, handsome man with close-cropped dark hair and a high forehead. His eyebrows were thin and arched, and he was looking tanned and relaxed.

'I've got the file here,' said Erika, bustling past him and into the warmth of the elegant hallway. 'I ended up having to drive over to the nick in Croydon where they kept the original records. And you know what the one-way system is like and the traffic from that bloody IKEA...' She shrugged off her coat and hung it over the end of the polished bannister. Isaac was staring at her with wry amusement. 'What?'

'Hello, Isaac. That would be a nice start, and then you could ask if I had a good Christmas?'

'Sorry,' she said, catching her breath and shrugging off her shoes. 'Hello. Did you have a nice Christmas?' She leaned over and gave him a hug. His body was thin and she could feel his ribs.

'Not really. Remind me never again to book a holiday in such a... remote place.'

They went through to the kitchen, and Erika sat down at a small dining table. Isaac moved to a dark blue Aga and, using a tea towel, crouched down and opened one of the doors.

'Where was it you went again? Thailand?'

He stood back as steam rushed out from the door. 'No. The Maldives. Six little huts perched on a finger of sand surrounded by miles of endless ocean. I ran out of books.'

'Was there anyone interesting to talk to, or…?'

He shook his head. 'All couples. Five Russian businessmen with their wives. The wives had had so much plastic surgery that when they went sunbathing, I thought they'd have to prick themselves with a fork.'

Erika laughed. He closed the Aga and went to a cupboard, taking out a couple of wine glasses.

'Red or white wine?'

'Red, please,' said Erika, placing the file on the kitchen table.

'How was your Christmas?' he asked.

'Fine. It was great to see my sister and the kids. Her husband is still mixed up in all kinds of dodgy dealings, and she feels trapped… But I don't think Lenka will ever leave him.'

'What does he think of having a police officer for a sister-in-law?'

'We actually get on quite well. I'm just an ordinary citizen back home, and he told me I make the best *kapustnica*.'

'What's that?'

'A meat and cabbage soup we have at Christmas. Soup is a big deal in Slovakia.'

'You should make it for me some time.' He grinned, placing a glass of red wine in front of her. She took a sip, feeling it warm through to her cold bones. 'What about James?'

She shook her head. 'I think that should remain a fling. It's too complicated to try and have a relationship with him…' She placed her hand on the grey file next to her wine glass. 'Anyway, as I said on the phone…'

'Erika. When did you last eat?'

'Breakfast.'

'Which was?'

'Biscuits…'

He tutted and shook his head. 'An army marches on its stomach. You seem to think you're a one-woman army, so you should at least eat properly. We'll have dinner, and then we'll talk about this case.'

'But Isaac, this case…'

'Can wait. I'm bloody starving, and by the looks of it, so are you. We eat, and then you have my attention.'

He held his hand out for the file, and in turn handed her a warm plate.

'Okay, but you know I'm a quick eater,' she smiled.

After a delicious meal of cottage pie and steamed greens, Isaac cleared the plates and Erika regained custody of the file. They settled down at the table and she brought him up to speed on the case.

'I ran the details of Lacey Greene's murder through the system, looking for similarities,' she said. 'And this came back: twenty-ninth of August last year, the body of twenty-year-old Janelle Robinson was found in Chichester Road in Croydon.' Erika took out a crime scene photo and slid it across the table to Isaac. The girl in the photo lay on her side in a dumpster. Like Lacey, she had long brown hair, she was naked from the waist down, and her face was battered so badly that her eyes were swollen shut.

'Hang on, I recognise this case,' said Isaac.

'You should. You did the post-mortem.'

He stared at her then pulled the file across the table and started to sift through the papers. 'Yes. I remember. Blunt force trauma to the back of the head, cheek and orbital bone, her vagina had been mutilated, and the femoral artery had been sliced through,' he said. 'Although, butchered is more the term I'd use. Where the artery meets the groin it looked as if it had been hacked at crudely...'

'But the police report questions if this was a sex game gone wrong,' said Erika.

'I didn't write that. Did I?'

'No, the SIO at the time did. A DCI Benton; he retired three weeks later.'

Isaac looked up at her again with his thin eyebrows raised. He held up a school photo of Janelle Robinson, taken when she was around sixteen. She was a rosy-faced young girl with small piercing blue eyes and long brown hair. She smiled into the camera and wore the uniform of a blue blouse with the embroidered crest of her school, the Salt Academy. The stitching was surrounded by a circle of thistles.

'Didn't Janelle's case come up when the Lacey Greene case was created on the system?' he asked.

Erika shook her head. 'No. Janelle Robinson was never reported missing.'

'Why?'

'No one missed her. She had no family. Was brought up in a children's home near Birmingham, and moved to London when she left school. For the past year, she'd been living and working in a youth hostel in central London. The manager was tracked down and interviewed a week after her body was found. She said it wasn't unusual for Janelle to go AWOL for a few days. It's also wrongly stated in the police report that Janelle's body was found in a car park, but the crime scene photos show that she was found, like Lacey, inside a dumpster in the car park.'

Isaac shook his head as they stared at the photos spread out over the table.

Erika went on: 'The remaining clothes Janelle was wearing, a low-cut top and a see-through black lace bra are described as "provocative" in Benton's report, so he leans on the theory that she may have been a prostitute who met a nasty end…'

'As opposed to Lacey Greene who was a nice middle-class university graduate who went missing,' finished Isaac.

They looked back through the crime scene photos of Janelle. The black lace bra, and a flimsy top with spaghetti straps she wore were both filthy and soaked with blood, and she was naked below the waist. Like Lacey, her legs were criss-crossed with cuts, and streaked with blood.

'Were there any witnesses in Chichester Road?' asked Isaac.

'No. But there are striking similarities to the Lacey Greene crime scene. This time the dumpster was in the car park of an old print-works at the end of a residential street. The car park is shielded by trees. A neighbour found her body when she went to put a bag of household rubbish in the dumpster.'

'Erika. Is the SIO on the case aware of this?'

'I hope so. I've left Melanie Hudson three messages: two this morning, one this afternoon… I also called the nick and told them I left messages. She hasn't got back to me.'

'You know how crazy things can get…'

'Isaac, if this was my investigation I'd leap on this. It would go to the top of the queue,' she said, jabbing her finger at the crime scene photos.

Isaac flicked back through the report. 'The flies had got to her, I remember. There were larvae in her wounds.'

'There's another thing. Your report on the post-mortem is incomplete.'

'Incomplete?'

'You can see the file is a mess. I've tried to get in contact with DCI Benton, but he's now on an extended holiday in the Australian outback.'

Isaac studied the printed pages. 'Yes, there seems to be a page missing. Do you think something is being covered up?'

'No. I've had a look at Benton. He's had a long distinguished career. It looks like in this instance he was sloppy.'

'Presumably concentrating more on his imminent retirement,' said Isaac.

'I just need to know what the missing section of your report contains. Specifically, if Janelle's wounds had started to heal, and if you found bruising to her wrists and neck consistent with her being chained up?'

'Hang on. I can check. I backup all of my reports,' said Isaac, getting up. He went upstairs and returned a few moments later with a printout. 'Yes, the wounds had started to heal, and I identified bruising consistent with her wrists and neck being bound with a small-link chain.'

Erika took the printout from him and read it. 'How long can you work on this from the sidelines?'

'Not much longer,' she said.

'You're going to have to pass all of this on, and let it go, Erika.'

'I can't.'

'But Sparks is running the Murder Investigation Team, and DCI Hudson reports to him. What makes you think he'd hand it over to you?'

Erika hesitated. 'Isaac, I've been thinking. Perhaps I should apologise to Sparks.'

'Are you mad?'

'No. What if I went to see him and laid it all on the table? I apologise and I ask if we can wipe the slate clean. I'll say I'm prepared to eat humble pie and work with him.'

Isaac's eyebrows shot up. 'Humble pie isn't a dish I've ever seen you order, and after all that's happened, you're going to apologise to him? That's not the kind of thing you do, Erika.'

She sighed. 'Maybe it should be. I'm so stubborn and blunt with so many people. Maybe it's time to change. This case has got under my skin. I *need* to work on it. My pride and my stubborn attitude has resulted in me pushing paperwork, stuck in a desk job.'

'You really think you can wipe the slate clean with Sparks? You had him thrown off the Andrea Douglas-Brown murder case. And you didn't pull any punches.'

'I have to at least *try*. What matters to me is finding who did this to these two young women. These murders were sadistic and well planned... And I don't think it was Steven Pearson. Which means not only do they have the wrong man, but the bastard who did this is still out there, waiting until the dust settles so he can do it again.'

CHAPTER 11

It was early evening when Darryl Bradley left the train. He was often the only person to alight at the small station on the outskirts of London, the last stop on the daily commute. He walked out of the station and went to his car, parked in its usual spot by a wire fence, backing onto snow-covered trees and fields.

It was cold inside the car as he set off home, keeping to the speed limit as he drove through a small village, the shops and houses shuttered up for the night. At the end of the village was a set of crossroads and the traffic lights were red. He came to a stop and glanced over at the Golden Lion pub, which sat on a grassy bank to his right. The windows were steamed up, and glowing softly. A minicab pulled into the car park, and two attractive young girls got out. One had dark hair and the other was blonde. They were dressed for a night out, in tight jeans and smart little jackets.

A car came roaring up to the lights, swerved around him, and drew level, on the wrong side of the road. Darryl saw it was Morris Cartwright driving. He was a thin man in his late twenties, with lank greasy hair and a grimy virility. He was employed by Darryl's father on their farm. Morris's windows were open, and he made a sign for Darryl to wind his down, which, reluctantly, he did.

'Alright, office boy?' he grinned. His gums showed pink and wet above a line of yellowing teeth. Morris was well known in the surrounding villages. He had a dodgy past, but never seemed to have any trouble finding a woman – not that he was known for his high standards.

'Evening,' said Darryl, looking back pleadingly at the traffic lights, which remained red.

Morris tipped his head towards the pub car park, and the two young girls. The dark-haired one was bending into the mini cab to pay the driver. Her short jacket had ridden up, revealing taut honey-coloured skin and a black Chinese symbol tattoo at the base of her spine. Her blonde friend was waiting patiently to one side, and she noticed Morris staring.

'You want my fucking autograph?' she snapped.

'Nah. I was just admiring your friend's tattoo. What does it say?' he asked as the mini cab pulled away. The dark-haired girl turned her attention to Morris, and gave him the once over, clocking him as a loser.

'It's the Chinese word for peace,' she said.

'That's nice. I like having something to read when I'm in the shitter!' said Morris, thrusting his hips up and down at the steering wheel and sticking out his tongue. The lights turned green, and he roared away with a crazy laugh and screech of tyres.

Darryl was left staring at the two girls.

'What are you looking at? Fucking loser,' snapped the dark-haired one, and stalked off to the pub entrance. The blonde raised her middle finger at him and followed.

Darryl's face was burning as a horn sounded from behind, making him jump. A white van pulled out and roared past, muffled shouts echoing as the tail lights vanished around a corner into the trees.

Then the traffic lights turned back to red.

The road stretched away dark in both directions, but Darryl chose to wait. He tilted the rear-view mirror and regarded his face which was pale, pudgy, a little piggy-eyed, and topped with mousy hair. It didn't feel like it belonged to him. The real him; the exciting virile young man was deep inside this ordinary loser. He thought of the dark-haired girl again: she had a harsh beauty, but her figure was hot.

Darryl had asked his father once why he employed Morris. This had been a few years back, when Darryl had also been working on the farm. Morris was constantly in trouble with the police, and had just been bailed after forcing himself on several of the young Polish women picking strawberries on the top field.

'He's a good lad really, and a hard worker. And a bloody good milker,' his father had replied bluntly. 'You could take a leaf out of his book.'

'But he tried to rape those girls!'

'It wasn't like that, Darryl. He's just being a lad! And young lads make mistakes.'

It hurt how his father seemed to admire Morris for his strength and masculinity. And how he regarded him in comparison as a disappointment.

Darryl saw that the road and car park were now empty. The lights went green, and he put the car in gear and pulled away. The last part of his journey was along dark, winding country lanes. The sky was clear for the first time in days, and the moon striking the snow on the surrounding fields was dazzling. He flicked off his headlights and slowed, enjoying the view. He passed two houses, the windows dark, and then banked down a steep hill which curved to the left. He slowed when he reached a large set of iron gates. They opened automatically, swinging inwards as snow started to fall again. He drove down the gravel driveway, past an ornamental pond, and the large farmhouse, its windows glowing invitingly, and he pulled in under the plastic roof of the carport.

He froze when he saw Morris's car parked behind his mother's Jaguar, and his father's large mud-spattered 4 × 4. Darryl locked his car and went to the back door. As he opened it, there was a volley of barks. He went through to the boot room and a huge white dog with pale black spots came bounding up.

'Hey, Grendel,' he said as the dog began to lick at his hand. She was a Dalmatian crossed with a Staffordshire Terrier, which gave her height and power as well as a wide face and jaw. Her watery blue eyes had a blankness, like they were made of glass.

A toilet flushed behind an adjoining door, and his mother emerged. She was a short round woman with a bob of hair dyed a little too dark for her advancing years. Her eyes were bloodshot.

'Good day at work?' she chirruped as Darryl took off his shoes and placed them by the wall. They were neat and polished next to the row of muddy boots.

'Why is Morris here?' he said.

'Farm business,' she said with a shrug, skirting warily around Grendel and moving into the large messy kitchen. Raucous laughter came from behind the closed door leading off the kitchen to the farm office.

'You want your tea?' she asked, opening the cutlery drawer.

'Yeah, I'm starving,' he said, as Grendel went to her bowl and began to drink, the ID disc on her collar clinking against the metal.

The door from the office opened and Darryl's father, John, emerged with Morris. They were both laughing.

'Here, Mary, give Morris the rest of that pie,' said John, giving Darryl no more than a glance. He was a tall, broad man with a weather-beaten face and a full head of pure white hair. Darryl looked to his mother but she was already taking the plate of steaming shepherd's pie from the Aga. 'Morris could do with a good feed, he's been working up on Colin Harper's land all day,' added John.

Morris gave him a dirty gummy grin and hitched up his jeans over his skinny hips. 'And Mrs Harper don't feed us like you do.'

'Ah well, she has other qualities,' said John with a wink, and they both laughed again.

'That's my dinner,' said Darryl in a small voice.

'You've been sat on your fat little arse all day. Morris works the land on four farms,' said John, fixing him with cold blue eyes.

'I'll put this on the table for you, Morris,' said Mary. Darryl looked to his mother, but she avoided his gaze, and carried the steaming plate through the door to the dining room.

'Aww. Look at that chubby little face,' said Morris, moving to Darryl and gripping his cheeks in his hand.

'Like his mother,' muttered John, following Mary through to the dining room.

Morris kept his grip on Darryl's face. 'Tweek,' he grinned. 'Tweeek!' Darryl panicked and tried to loosen Morris's hand, but his grip was strong. 'My brother used to do this to me, we called it a Tweek. You grip the cheeks, and look, your little pink tongue pops out. There it is!'

'Come on, Morris, it's getting cold!' shouted John from the dining room.

'On my way, John,' he shouted. He turned back to Darryl, where his glistening tongue poked out between his teeth. 'Then he'd make me taste his finger...' he added touching the tip of his grimy index finger on Darryl's tongue. He leaned in, and Darryl could smell his rancid breath as he whispered, 'Can you taste that? It's been up my arse—'

Grendel turned from where she had been drinking, and lunged at Morris, sinking her teeth into his left calf. Morris yelled and let go. Darryl fell against the counter, spitting into the sink and rubbing at his mouth. John came back into the kitchen at the sound of Morris's shouts.

'Darryl! Get that bloody dog off him, now!' he yelled. But Grendel held on fast, her blank eyes looking up at Morris. 'Darryl, call her off!'

'Grendel, down girl, down,' said Darryl. She let go of his leg and started to bark. Morris yelled and clutched at his trouser leg. Blood was soaking through the material.

'Take that fucking animal out, and Mary, get yourself in here and find Morris some antiseptic, quickly!' said John.

Darryl dragged the barking Grendel out to the boot room, and the moment he closed the door she calmed down. He heard through the door his father shouting at his mother. He went to the coats hanging on the wall, and took a little dog treat from one of the pockets and gave it to Grendel. She swallowed it down whole and barked for another.

'Shush, shush. You're a good girl, Grendel,' he said, giving her another treat. He stroked her large white head and she looked up with her blank eyes, licking his hand with her rough tongue.

'You watch out for Morris. He's a bad man. You be careful.'

CHAPTER 12

Erika left Isaac's house just before nine o'clock. The air was clear but very cold and she sat inside her car for a few minutes, waiting for the heater to kick in. She had been intending to go home, had promised Isaac that she would go straight home and get a good night's sleep, but the idea of speaking to Sparks came back to her. She'd heard him talking, once, about a new place he and his wife had bought in Greenwich, and Greenwich was close to Blackheath.

She looked back to Isaac's house and saw him watching her from his window, making sure she got home safely. She started her engine and gave him a wave as she drove off. Once around the corner, she pulled over and made a call to control at Bromley Police Station. When she came off the phone, she eyed the clock on the dashboard.

'Nothing to lose,' she said as she started the engine and pulled away again.

Superintendent Sparks lived in a shabby house in an up-and-coming area. She parked at the end of his road and walked the hundred yards to his house. As she approached the front gate, she could see the front room was empty. A light was on, just a bare bulb hanging from the ceiling. There was a ladder resting against one wall, where a block of light blue had been painted over the beige wall, and a tray of paint with a roller sat at the base of the ladder. Erika walked up the small front path, past the glare spilling out from the bay window and into the shadows by the front door. The hall light was off, and as she raised her hand to ring the bell, she heard shouting from inside.

'He's long gone... He wasn't going to stay around, was he?' cried a female voice.

'So you did it. You admit it?' came a male voice. Sparks.

'Yes! I DID IT, and it was GREAT!'

'You are such a cliché,' he shouted.

'I'm a WHAT?'

'A CLICHÉ! A painter and decorator!'

'So what? He made me feel alive! Having a fancy degree in criminology doesn't mean you know how to fuck! He fucked me like a proper man!' The woman's voice was cracking with hysteria.

Erika winced, but she was transfixed. The voices dropped to a murmur and she strained to hear.

'How much have you had?' said Sparks.

'How much *sex* have I had?' she shouted. 'LOADS! In our bed. IN YOUR BED!'

'Why is this bottle empty?'

'What? I'm not suicidal. Far from it!'

'You only got this new prescription last week,' said Sparks. His voice sounded broken.

'I'm not sorry. Do you HEAR ME! I'M NOT SORRY! I DON'T LOVE YOU ANY MORE, ANDY.'

There was silence. It was the first time that Erika had heard Sparks's first name. She knew she had to go, but then there was a huge crash and a tinkling of glass. The front door opened.

'Crazy bitch!' Sparks shouted over his shoulder. He turned and stopped, staring at Erika. He wore jeans and a jumper, and a black leather jacket. The left shoulder was splashed with what looked like milk. A small dark-haired woman lurched up the hall behind him. Her eyes were unfocused and her hair in disarray. She held a bag of flour and threw it at him, but it missed and exploded against the wall.

'Who the hell is that scrawny bitch?' she said, pointing at Erika, who was backing away to the front gate. 'Yeah, go on, you screw HER!'

The woman rushed at Sparks and gave him a shove outside, and the door was slammed shut behind him. There was a scrabbling as the locks were turned and the chain put on.

Sparks stalked past Erika, and out onto the street.

'Are you okay?' she asked, following him, the sheen of milk on the back of his jacket glistening under the orange from the streetlights and dripping off the hem.

'What the hell are you doing at my house?' he said, still walking.

'I came about the case, the case you've been working on.'

'And you think this is a good time?'

'No, I don't. I didn't know you were having…'

He stopped dead, and turned. Erika almost crashed into him.

'This must be funny for you, Erika. Is it? Having a good laugh?'

'No. And for what it's worth, I'm sorry.' She rummaged in her bag and pulled out some face wipes, indicating the milk as she handed them to him.

He took them and tried to wipe at his shoulder with his opposite hand, but he couldn't reach. Erika took another out of the packet, and was surprised when he let her wipe the milk away.

'She's had problems for years… That was the alcohol. Not her,' he said. Under the streetlights he looked like a ghoul. His eyes were etched with deep circles and his cheeks hollow. Erika kept on scrubbing at the base of his leather jacket. 'Do you understand? She's ill.'

His jacket was now clean. Erika bunched up the wet wipes and nodded. 'I understand.'

Headlights appeared round the corner and a car moved slowly past. Sparks turned away from its glare. When it had passed, he turned back to her.

'Why did you come to my house?'

'It's about the Lacey Greene murder case.'

'What?'

'The girl who was found in the dumpster, near New Cross.'

'Melanie has arrested someone for that, a dosser off the street. Found with her wallet; we have two witnesses…'

'Yes, but I've found another case, where there are similarities, well not just similarities. The method of killing is exactly the same…' She rummaged in her bag and pulled out the file. 'I'm serious. Look, can we do this somewhere else?' He looked at her for a long moment.

'Please. I just want to give you the information so the case can be solved.'

'There's a pub at the end of the road. You're buying,' he said. He turned and walked off.

Erika followed, convinced he needed an excuse to have a drink more than he wanted to talk to her.

CHAPTER 13

The pub was small and cosy, with tatty furniture, and horse brasses on the dark walls. They found a quiet corner, away from a darts match and the big screen showing sports. Erika bought them each a pint of lager, and she was surprised when Sparks listened to what she had to say.

When she'd finished, he sifted through the report in front of him on the polished table, taking care to mask the crime scene photos when a large bloke from the darts team lumbered past to the toilets.

'The first thing we need to do is go back and confirm where Steven Pearson was when Janelle Robinson went missing,' said Erika. 'We need to rule him out, but as I said, I don't think he was capable of a planned abduction. I'd like to see all of Lacey's phone records, social media—'

'Hang on, hang on. Melanie has been assigned as SIO on this. I won't replace her. She's worked hard, and she's a bloody good copper. I agreed to have a drink and listen,' he said, indicating the last few inches of his pint.

'Okay. I'd like to assist. Be involved as an advisor. You know I have experience with cases like these.'

Sparks sat back and ran his fingers through his hair. 'Don't you have any pride?' he asked.

'I've ballsed up a lot, and I'm stuck in the backwaters. I care only about rank when it means I can get things done.' She downed the second half of her lager in one.

Sparks grinned. It was an odd sight. He had small crooked teeth which gave his face a flash of childish mischief.

'Bollocks!' he said, not unkindly. 'You could have killed me when I was promoted over you.'

'Yeah. I could have.'

Sparks downed the rest of his pint, then sat back crossing his hands over his stomach. 'I'm not sure it's worth it...'

'I'll make sure it's worth it. I will work with Melanie. I'll keep my head down...'

He shook his head. 'I'm talking about the rank. Superintendent. I'm not sure it's worth it. I'm supervising eighteen cases right now. Top brass is cutting everything to the bone, and everything we do is public property.'

'But we're public servants...'

'Servants? Don't give me that shit!' he said, slamming his hand down on the table. 'You know the score. We have to get things done, and it's not all rosy. We have to lean on people. We have to, or the job won't get done, but now every scumbag out there has a mobile phone with a camera. Stuff gets posted online and then every armchair critic weighs in. Last month, one of my officers was attacked by a guy during a stop and search. This young guy had a kilo of heroin in his glove compartment. He hits my officer with a crowbar, breaking his arm, then goes to drive away, forgetting my officer with the broken arm has his keys. Realising he's trapped, the young guy starts filming my officer as he saws open the front window with a cutting tool, and drags him out. The video of just that part gets uploaded to You-Tube, and I've got top brass on my arse saying people online are posting messages to complain about police brutality! My officer is a good lad, always follows things to the letter, but his true account of what happened isn't as important as the grainy mobile phone footage on YouTube! Do you know what the Assistant Commissioner said?'

Sparks was animated now, his fists clenched.

'I can guess it wasn't helpful?' said Erika.

'You're fucking right it wasn't helpful. "The video has been liked and commented on by fifty thousand people, and shared thousands of times on Twitter,"' he said, mimicking the Assistant Commissioner's voice in falsetto. 'What kind of a world do we live in where ordinary Joes, at home and one stop away from whacking off to porn, or shopping for shoes, are forming public opinion? Worse still, directing the opinion of our superiors! Distorting reality!'

Sparks sat back; he was shaking with anger. His face was still white, but two small circles of scarlet adorned each cheek. He coughed and winced, downing a last dribble of lager and wincing again.

Erika got up and bought another round. When she came back he was having another coughing fit.

'Thanks,' he said, taking a gulp of lager.

'I want to say sorry,' said Erika. He sat back and looked at her. 'I'm sorry, for everything that went down between us. I should have behaved better when I first came to London and took over the Andrea Douglas-Brown case. It was yours. I was a bitch.'

'You were a bitch. I was a bastard.' He grinned ruefully. 'That's how the world turns.'

'I just want to catch this one, Andy. I have pride. Pride in bringing people to justice. It's not about me. I'll work in your team. We can have a trial period; I'll work subordinate to Melanie on the enquiry, despite us being the same rank. I can't stay working in the Projects Team, pushing paper.'

Sparks took another pull on his pint and watched two large guys engrossed in their darts match.

'If I'm honest, I feel like I've fought my way to a prize that's not worth it.'

'The money's good,' said Erika.

'And I'm about to see it all vanish. Divorce. Followed by custody battles…' He downed the last of his pint.

'Sorry.'

'Not your fault. Look, I'll sort something out with Melanie, Okay?'

Erika nodded. 'Okay.'

'Now, I have to go home,' he said.

When they came out onto the street, it had started to snow again. Sparks pulled up his collar against the wind.

'Come to the morning briefing tomorrow,' he said. 'Although the ball is in your court. It's up to her if she wants to work with you.'

'I can make it work.'

A car drove slowly past, its mudguards thick with dirty snow. Sparks turned his head away, and didn't turn back until it was far down the street.

'What is it?' asked Erika.

'Did you see that car before?'

'No.'

'Earlier, just before we went to the pub?'

'I don't think so. Why?'

He squinted at the spot where the car had turned off the street. 'I feel like… I've seen it three times now over the past few days.'

'You think you're being followed?'

He was even more pale and haggard than before they went into the pub. His eyes scanned the empty street. He saw she was watching him closely and changed the subject.

'Can your nick spare you? I haven't got time to go smoothing shit over with your superintendent.'

'I don't think my superintendent really cares either way,' she said.

He nodded. 'Okay. West End Central tomorrow, nine a.m.'

'Thanks, Andy.'

'Steady on. I don't want us to end up actually liking each other.' He gave her a nod and walked away, towards his unhappy home. Erika watched him, feeling a mixture of anger and relief. She hadn't got an apology in return from him, but she was pleased they were moving forward, and that she had a crack at working on the case.

CHAPTER 14

The next morning, Erika took the train to Charing Cross and emerged with a throng of commuters into the cold air. The crowds thinned as she walked through Trafalgar Square, which had been cleared of snow, save for the giant bronze lions that wore little white toupees. By the time she reached Leicester Square, and then Chinatown, there was just a smattering of early bird tourists, blinking in the dull grey morning. She found West End Central Police Station. It was a post-war concrete square, tucked away in a side road at the edge of Soho amongst a street of offices under renovation. She showed her warrant card at the front desk, and then took a lift up to the fifth floor which came out opposite a set of doors marked: MURDER INVESTIGATION TEAM.

She took a deep breath and paused at the doors. Was she really going to do this? She had said last night that she didn't care about rank, but was she putting too much on the line to work with Sparks on this case? The question had kept her awake for most of the night, but she kept coming back to Lacey Greene and Janelle Robinson, their bodies dumped like rubbish… And Janelle's circumstances had affected her deeply. Here was a girl born with nothing, who went through life with nothing, and then in death was thought of as nothing. *Another runaway turns up dead, terrible, awful, but shit happens, case closed.*

It was a similar attitude which had rankled her when she first came to the UK on an au pair's visa. She was paid a pittance, and the prevailing attitude was that Eastern Europeans weren't worth quite as much as people from the West. 'We're disposable people,' a Polish girl had told her on the long coach ride across Europe. This was why, in later years, Erika had striven to rise through the ranks in the police force, to show she was an asset. That she wasn't disposable.

She was still unsure of her decision, but she pushed open the door and went inside. It was a vast open-plan office, and several groups of desks were partitioned off with glass. She moved past teams working: in one an officer was briefing his team about a case; pictures on a board behind him showed a row of burnt bodies laid out, and close images on each, features melted in a crisp mask of pain.

Erika approached a young uniformed officer by a photocopier.

'I'm looking for Superintendent Sparks?'

'Right down the end,' she replied.

Erika thanked her and moved off, past commanding views of snow-covered rooftops and the sky hanging low over the buildings like a sheet of slate. When she reached the end of the office, Sparks was standing against a series of large whiteboards, surrounded by a team of ten officers. Piles of case files were stacked ominously beside him. Erika recognised the case he was briefing: a triple murder in a North London pub. He looked terrible, exhausted and washed out, and was leaning on the corner of a table, using his free hand to emphasise his point. He saw her at the back and gave her a curt nod, but carried on speaking.

'As I say, the family is going to close ranks pretty fast, and they've got one hell of a history. I need their movements crosschecked before we split them up for questioning.'

As he moved off towards a row of glass doors at the end, chatter rose in the team. Erika hurried over to catch him up.

'I got in contact with Melanie last night,' he said. 'I gave her everything we talked about. She's now following up the death of... of...'

'Janelle Robinson,' finished Erika.

'Yeah. She's gone over to Croydon to look at where her body was discovered, and talk to the neighbours.'

'Will you be briefing her team about my involvement in the case?'

'Yeah. This afternoon. The info you gave had to be checked up on, so we rescheduled. Come back at four.'

He reached a frosted glass door, moved through and went to close it. She held out her hand, stopping him. 'Andy, I meant what I said last night. I will work with you, but please, no games.'

He stopped to stare at her. His eyes were bloodshot.

'And you heard me when I said that I'm deluged. You know the score, things change. It was a priority that Melanie and her team followed up on what you brought to me. Steven Pearson can only be held for another twenty-four hours before we have to charge him or let him go.'

'And she couldn't have picked up the phone before I came into London?' snapped Erika.

'What do you want me to do?'

'Get me involved now. I don't want to sit around all day.'

He stared at her again through those bloodshot eyes, and then indicated to her to come into his office.

'Thank you,' said Erika. She went through to his office and closed the door.

Sparks moved to a set of shelves behind the desk which was packed with files. He rubbed at his left arm, and scrabbled around for a packet of painkillers. His skin seemed to drain of what little colour he had left, and a sheen of sweat appeared. Sparks popped a couple of tablets from the foil and swallowed them down without water, wincing. He went to the phone on his desk, but then hesitated, gritting his teeth in pain.

'Are you okay?' asked Erika, moving to the seat opposite his desk.

'Jesus! Do I look bloody okay?' He paused over the phone keypad, taking deep breaths. 'What's her number again?'

He started to move around the desk, but staggered. He grabbed for the edge, but his arm gave way and he crashed face down onto the carpet.

'Shit!' cried Erika, rushing around to him. She turned him over and he was making ragged gasping noises, sweat pouring from his grey face. He clutched at his left arm, and clawed at his shirt collar.

'My chest... I can't... breathe. My arm, the pains,' he wheezed. His bloodshot eyes bulged hideously.

Erika quickly unfastened his shirt collar and loosened his tie. She gently pulled him up to a sitting position, propping him up against the edge of the desk.

'I need you to keep calm, and breathe,' she said.

He clutched at his left arm, pouring with sweat and shivering. She took off her long leather jacket and draped it over him. He started to groan and wheeze, flecks of spit building in the corners of his mouth.

'Please, help me,' he gasped.

Erika moved around the desk and picked up his phone, finding it strangely ironical that she was calling the emergency services from one of the largest police stations in Central London.

'It's a police officer,' she said when she got through. 'I think he's having a heart attack.' She gave all the details and then slammed the phone down, rushing back to Sparks. He was now a deathly grey, and frothing at the mouth. 'Aspirin, Andy, do you have aspirin?'

He coughed and a fine spray of foam filled the air. She moved to the shelf where he kept the painkillers, but they were all paracetamol. She then started to rifle through the drawers of his desk. Sparks was now trying to stand; he got half up, but his legs flailed uselessly and he slid down again, hitting the back of his head on the corner of the desk.

'Please, stay still, the ambulance is coming,' said Erika, moving to crouch beside him. She draped the jacket over him again, and then ran to his office door and yanked it open, shouting: 'I need help in here! He's having a heart attack.'

Faces turned to see what was going on, merely curious.

'Superintendent Sparks has collapsed. He's having a heart attack. I need help!' she shouted.

Suddenly people leapt to life, and two male officers dashed over, followed by one of the officers Sparks had addressed just minutes earlier.

Erika went back into the office, and felt her blood roar in her ears as she turned and saw Sparks had toppled over and lay on the carpet on his side. She moved to him, and gently turned him over onto his back. His lips were now starting to turn blue. He looked up at her with fear in his eyes.

'My wife... Tell her... I love her... The money from our account... They'll freeze it...' he croaked.

'Andy, you are going to be okay, do you hear me?' she said.

The office was now filling up with officers who were milling around uselessly, watching. His hand came up and grabbed for hers, but it fell back down and hit the carpet.

'No!' said Erika, as what little colour Sparks had in his face began to rapidly drain away. 'One of you! Find out where that ambulance is!'

She unfastened the next couple of buttons on Sparks's shirt, exposing his chest. She tipped his head back, and began to perform CPR, working on chest compressions and then dipping down to breathe into Sparks's mouth.

'He said he's been feeling ill for a while…' said a voice behind Erika as she counted fifteen chest compressions.

'I've known him for over a year, and he always looks ill,' said another.

Erika leaned down and blew into his mouth again. Sparks's chest rose, but his face stayed slack and white. The room was strangely silent as the officers watched her.

'Come on, you're a fighter… Fight! Don't stop now!' she said.

His eyes remained closed, and his head lolled slightly on the carpet as she counted chest compressions, *thirteen, fourteen, fifteen.*

From the corner of her eye, she saw a picture on the desk; Andy Sparks with his wife. They were both crouched down on a sunny patch of grass with a small girl, grinning a gummy grin as she sat on a little pink toy scooter. She continued to work on his chest, alternating between artificial respiration. Sweat poured off her face from the exertion. It seemed to go on and on, the silent room watching her.

Finally, two paramedics in yellow jackets, carrying a first aid kit, entered the office, and took over, but it was too late.

They pronounced Superintendent Andy Sparks dead at 9:47 a.m. The irony wasn't lost on Erika that this was Friday the thirteenth.

CHAPTER 15

Erika watched as Sparks was wheeled out of his office in a shiny black body bag. Her legs started to tremble with shock, and she had to sit when she gave her statement to the uniformed police who'd arrived on the scene. It was a strange situation, police interviewing police, and the confusion as to how to deal with the tragedy. Andy Sparks was only forty-one years old. He'd been her bitter enemy until the previous evening, and now he was dead.

She was unsure of what to do, and how to feel, when she emerged from the main entrance of West End Central. A freezing wind was blowing, and a large expanse of green mesh covering a scaffold opposite hummed and keened. She didn't know any of the police officers at the nick. There was no one to talk to. She crossed her hands over her chest, feeling the icy wind pierce her thin jumper. Sparks had been wrapped in her jacket when he was loaded up into the body bag, and it didn't seem appropriate to ask for it back. She pulled out her phone and called Peterson. He told her to get in a cab and come over.

When he ushered her into his warm flat, an hour later, she was shaking with cold, her teeth chattering almost comically. They stood in his living room, and he held her for a long time, just the sound of the water filling up the huge tub in the bathroom.

'Jeez, Sparks dead… I assumed he was in it for the long run,' said Peterson.

'He's got a small daughter, and a wife who needs him, and the last person he spoke to was *me*.'

'You said you tried to save his life.'

'I did. But I can't imagine dying and the only person there to hold your hand is your worst enemy.'

Erika wiped her eyes with the back of her hand. She'd stopped shivering.

'You're a good person, Erika. You are on the side of good,' said Peterson, pulling back and looking in her eyes.

She was overwhelmed with tears again. 'James. I've watched so many people die young, my husband, my colleagues, and… why them and not me?'

'You shouldn't feel guilty.'

'I do.'

'Look. The hot bath is ready, I'll get us a drink,' said Peterson.

She soaked in the hot water for a long time, cradling a large tumbler of whisky, and Peterson sat with her, perched on the lid of the toilet. Erika told him what had happened the previous evening.

'Why do you think he changed his mind about working with you?' he asked.

Erika shrugged. 'Maybe I saw another side to him. I overheard the argument with him and his wife, and he still defended her to me… I made a snap decision about him, and it never changed. Maybe he was just…'

'Erika. He was an arsehole.'

'Yes. At work he was…'

'But we had to work with him. We didn't see this other side, so to us it didn't exist.'

'But it did.'

'Okay it did, but if you'd started to work on this case with him, do you think he would have kept his word? And what would it have done for your reputation?'

'I don't care about my reputation.'

'That's a really stupid thing to say.'

Erika smiled weakly. 'Yeah, you're right.'

'What's going to happen with the case?'

'I don't know. They have to release Steven Pearson by tomorrow lunchtime. Melanie Hudson now has everything: the files on Janelle Robinson. And, of course, her incentive to work with me is now gone.'

'Because Sparks ordered her to,' finished Peterson. They were silent for a moment. She shivered, and he turned on the hot tap. 'Erika, I know I'll never replace Mark. And that's cool. You take all the time you need.'

He leaned across her and turned off the water. She looked at his proud handsome face, his dark hair now clipper cut short. She leant up and placed her hand on his cheek.

'I can't replace someone who's gone… Mark is gone, James. I have to live my life. He always said that if he died he would want me to…' She hesitated.

'He'd want you to live?'

She nodded. 'But that's the hardest thing. Just living. Knowing how to live on my own and then with someone else.'

Peterson took her hand, leaned over and planted a kiss on her wet hair.

It was dark outside when Erika emerged from the bath and sat on the sofa in a large squishy bathrobe. Peterson switched on the early evening news. The lead story on *BBC London* was that Steven Pearson, who'd been arrested in conjunction with the abduction and murder of Lacey Greene, had been released due to lack of evidence.

'So they're taking the info you gave them seriously?' said Peterson, topping up her drink.

'They have to,' said Erika, watching as a news reporter spoke from outside the revolving sign of the New Scotland Yard building.

'And they're keeping Janelle Robinson's murder quiet.'

'Her abduction *and* murder. She was a missing person, James. Just because the poor girl had no one to miss her doesn't mean she wasn't missing.'

'I know… You can chill out, I'm not against you,' he said.

'Sorry. It's so frustrating. Melanie Hudson was ready to charge Pearson and close the case, and now she gets to pursue things, and she'll probably make an arse of it all.'

Erika's phone began to ring in her bag, and Peterson passed it to her. When she pulled it out, she saw a number she didn't recognise and she answered. Peterson watched her talk, swirling whisky in his tumbler. The news bulletin in the background moved onto a different story, about life for residents of the Olympic Village in East London.

'Who was that?' he asked when she finished the call.

Erika tapped the phone against her teeth. 'Camilla Brace-Cosworthy, the Assistant Commissioner. She wants me to come in for a chat on Monday morning.'

'A chat? Interesting choice of words.'

'That's what she said. A chat. Apparently there are some loose ends to tie up about Sparks's death.'

'Loose ends? It was suspicious?' asked Peterson.

'She didn't elaborate… She's just left me to stew over the weekend. She wants to see me in her office at New Scotland Yard.'

Erika thought back to when Sparks had believed he was being followed, and she wondered exactly what he had got himself involved in.

CHAPTER 16

Darryl woke early on Saturday morning. The snow was tapping against the dark windows, and he heard through his bedroom wall the groan of bedsprings as his father got out of bed, and said a few short sharp words to his mother. Darryl couldn't make them out, but the barking tone he recognised. The doors in the farmhouse all had latches instead of handles, and when his father left to do his rounds, he heard it lift and fall before he stomped down the hall, the floorboards creaking.

When the footsteps had faded, Darryl heard the ominous sound of his mother rolling over in bed, and the squeak of the small door in the base of her bedside table. This was when she took her first drink of the day, usually vodka, although like most alcoholics she wasn't picky. His mother's drinking was something he'd grown up with. It had intensified since the death of Joe, his younger brother, eleven years before.

Darryl turned over in bed, heard the cupboard squeak again, and decided to get up. He still occupied the same bedroom from his childhood, with high ceilings, wooden floors, and dark heavy furniture which seemed sinister against the Winnie the Pooh wallpaper. It was still dark when he padded downstairs in his slippers, and the kitchen was deliciously warm. Grendel lay in the shadows in front of the Aga, soaking up its heat. When he switched on the light, she blinked and got up, sniffing at his feet.

As long as you kept your wits about you, Grendel was good, but you couldn't make any sudden movements. This was when she would panic and attack. Last summer she'd attacked a young excitable Polish girl working on the strawberry fields. She'd needed seven stitches and had nearly lost an eye.

'Thank God Grendel went for the Polak, and not one of the locals,' his father had joked after returning from the hospital. The girl had been working illegally, so pressing charges hadn't been an option. John let him keep Grendel because she was a good guard dog. Just like he kept Morris because he was a good milker. Darryl mused that Morris and Grendel were probably both the result of too much inbreeding.

Darryl ate a bowl of cereal and fed Grendel, then they left the house. It was just starting to get light as he emerged from under the carport, Grendel bouncing along beside him on the compacted snow. He passed the huge straw barn, its corrugated roof thick with snow, and the other outbuildings. The air was crisp and cold, and underneath the freshness was the ever-present farm smell of manure mixed with rotting straw.

The milking sheds were brightly lit and busy with the sounds of mooing, hooves stomping, and the rhythmic suck of the milking machines. Two of the farm workers gave him indifferent stares as he passed, and Grendel raised her pale pink nose at the smell and the sound of the cattle. They passed John coming out of the shed housing giant silver tanks for the milk. He nodded curtly at Darryl, and his eyes passed over the pristine winter jacket he wore, and he shook his head. It had been a gift to himself, and Darryl resisted the urge to muddy it up a bit.

At the bottom of the yard, the farm buildings ended at a wide gate looking out over fields. Once they were through, he let Grendel off the lead. She ran ahead along the track, delighting in disturbing a flock of birds huddled in the snow. She barked as they rose up into the sky, cawing.

Half a mile down the track they passed a long low building with a circular tower, topped off with a roof like a bent funnel.

The dawn was just beginning to break, and it made a sinister black outline against the blue sky. It was the old Oast House. It had been built in the 1800s for drying hops, when this was the farm's main crop. It had been abandoned for as long as Darryl could remember, and growing up it was a great place to play. He and Joe had spent many summer evenings climbing up the inside, through the three slatted wood levels where hops had been laid out to dry. The base of the tower had housed a furnace, and above it were beams where you could perch and peer through the spouted chimney and see across the countryside for miles. In the winter months, it was eerie, and took on a desolate air. On a winter's night, when conditions were right, you could hear the wind groaning through the ventilation system from the farmhouse.

It was also where his brother Joe had hanged himself, aged fifteen.

Darryl slowed and came to a stop outside the large brick building. A gust of wind disturbed the dry powdery snow, and gave a high pitched whine as it blew over the spout of the tower.

'Joe,' whispered Darryl. He moved off, passed the large brick building, and then picked up pace, walking another mile or so across snow-covered fields and past a bank of bare trees. As the horizon turned from light blue to pink a vast frozen lake came into view. Darryl called for Grendel, who came loping back, tongue lolling to one side. It started to snow again, fast twirling flakes, and an ice crystal landed on one of her black eyes and made her blink. He scratched her ears, and gave her a dog treat. She trotted obediently alongside him as they picked their way down the track to the edge of the lake. A concrete barrier lined the water where it met the footpath. The ice was thick, and dusted with snow. The footprints of geese and small birds dotted the surface. Grendel leapt up onto the concrete barrier, and landed on the ice with sure paws, looking back as if to say the coast was clear. Darryl tentatively followed, stepping out slowly, listening for the tell-tale squeaking sound of weakness, but the ice was like concrete. He walked out to where Grendel was barking and circling a giant tree trunk which emerged through the ice.

'It's okay, girl,' said Darryl, reaching out carefully. Grendel froze with her teeth bared and shot him a wild-eyed look, but he slowly moved his hand closer, until she let him rest it on her soft furry head. 'It's just a tree. It was floating the other day, remember?'

She let him pat her, then cocked her head, rolled over onto the ice and let him tickle her belly. He sat on the frozen trunk and ate a chocolate bar, watching Grendel race after birds at the edge of the ice, and checking his emails and social media on his phone.

It was light when he and Grendel arrived back at the farmhouse, and as they turned the corner by the carport, Morris was sitting on the open boot of his car. He had on one wellington boot, and was just pulling on the second over a bare foot with long yellow toenails. Darryl tightened his grip on Grendel's lead.

'You keep that bloody dog on its lead,' said Morris, flinching as Darryl squeezed past with Grendel, who was growling.

Darryl glanced inside the open boot and saw a coiled length of thin chain, and a leather hood with eyeholes.

Morris turned and swiftly slammed it shut.

'Got a problem?' he said.

'No,' said Darryl, moving quickly to the steps up to the back door.

'Me and... er... the girlfriend, she likes it kinky,' said Morris, tipping his head at the closed boot.

Darryl shrugged. 'None of my business.'

'No. It's not... And it's up to us what we do in the bedroom...'

Morris was shaking, almost a little afraid.

'I didn't see anything,' said Darryl. He was now at the back door and he reached for the handle. Morris moved to the bottom of the steps, and Grendel's growls went up a notch.

'Good, you stick to that. Just remember your fucking mutt won't always be there to protect you.' He stared at Darryl for a long moment, then locked his car with the key fob, and limped off to the yard.

Darryl watched him, unease creeping into his stomach. Then he unclipped Grendel's lead, and took her back into the warmth of the house.

CHAPTER 17

When Erika arrived at the New Scotland Yard building on Monday morning, she was shown straight in to the Assistant Commissioner's office. Instead of indicating the chair in front of her desk, Camilla Brace-Cosworthy led Erika to a couple of armchairs by the large floor-to-ceiling window overlooking the Thames. Her assistant brought in a tray with a pot of coffee and biscuits as Erika sat down with her back to the glass. She thought how exhausted Camilla appeared; her blonde shoulder-length hair was as sleek as ever, but her pale face was haggard and devoid of make-up. The assistant, a smart young man with striking green eyes, gave her a nod and a smile, and left.

I've been summoned, but for coffee and biscuits; this could be interesting, thought Erika.

'Shall I be mother?' said Camilla, lifting the coffee pot. She was well spoken, with a fruity upper-class accent. It made Erika feel conscious that she flattened her vowels. 'Childhood eczema flared up again for no rhyme or reason,' she added, noting how Erika had studied her face. 'I've had to retire the warpaint for a few days… Cream?'

'No, thank you.' They sat back and sipped at their coffee. Erika eyed the biscuits on the little three-tiered china stand; expensive-looking ginger thins half dipped in dark chocolate. She was starving, but felt that if she took one she'd somehow be buying into the bullshit that this was just a chat over coffee.

'How are you, Erika?'

'Fine, thank you, ma'am.'

'Are you? One of your colleagues just died. You tried to revive him, and failed...' She tilted her head in sympathy.

'It was a terrible tragedy, ma'am, but my training kicked in. And I didn't really know Superintendent Sparks. Nor did I fail. He had a colossal heart attack.'

'Yes, of course... But you worked together on more than one case. When you were first assigned to Lewisham Row, you replaced him on the Andrea Douglas-Brown murder enquiry.'

The Andrea Douglas-Brown murder had been the highest profile case in Erika's career; Andrea's body was found under the ice in the boating lake of a South London park.

'I had Sparks removed from that case.'

'Why?'

'It's all on record, ma'am.'

'Yes. You thought he was sloppy in his investigative style, and that he helped suppress evidence,' said Camilla, sipping her coffee.

'No. Andrea Douglas-Brown's father was a high-profile member of the Establishment. And I thought Sparks had allowed himself to be star-struck by Simon Douglas-Brown. Sparks allowed him to influence our enquiries.'

'Had you been in contact with him recently?'

'Simon Douglas-Brown? No. He's in prison.'

'I'm talking about Superintendent Sparks, and in particular the meeting you had with him in Greenwich at the Crown pub the night before he died...'

Erika didn't let her surprise show.

'It seems odd you met him socially, Erika, if there was so much animosity between you?'

'I'd been talking to him about joining one of his investigations. I'd doorstepped him to be honest, ma'am. He did say he thought he was being followed. I assumed he was being paranoid, but obviously not.' Camilla tilted her head and kept her gaze even. 'Ma'am. Is this a formal interview? The coffee and posh biscuits make me think not, but why am I here?'

'Erika, I can confirm Superintendent Sparks was under covert investigation.'

'By who?'

'By whom? I can't go into that. What I can tell you is that I have reason to believe we weren't the only people paying his wages.'

'Can I ask who else you think was paying his wages?'

'No. You can't.'

'Me and Sparks were enemies. I don't know the first thing about his work relationships, or his personal life. Well, I know him and his wife were having problems.'

'What kind of problems?'

Erika briefly outlined what she had overheard when she went to Sparks's home. When she had finished, Camilla rose, went over to the window and looked out at the view over the Thames. There was a long silence.

'Erika, when you worked on the Andrea Douglas-Brown case, were you party to any meetings with Superintendent Sparks and Sir Simon Douglas-Brown?'

'You mean Simon Douglas-Brown. He was stripped of his title. Let's not forget that.'

'Answer the question, please.'

'From the beginning of the investigation, I was closed out of meetings with the family. Simon wanted to retain Sparks as SIO. His wife wasn't keen on me either.'

'Why not?'

'Like me she's Slovak. I think I reminded her of where she came from.'

'And where is that?'

'The wrong side of the tracks... A working-class family. Look, I'm the last person who can give you any information about potential corruption in the force. I focus on policing, not politics.'

Camilla turned from the window and laughed.

'So you infer that you are squeaky clean?'

'I'm squeakier than most, ma'am. I'm not afraid to speak my mind. It's the reason I was passed over for promotion by your predecessor.'

She came back from the window and sat down.

'Erika, are you aware of the Gadd family?'

'Yes. They're well known to the police in South London. They've been allowed to operate their import/export business a little too freely, in return for keeping order in the area.'

'How are you aware of that?'

'It's an open secret. Not really a secret, more unofficial policy. Was Sparks on their payroll?'

'We believe so. I'm also looking into the cases Superintendent Sparks was working on, and his dealings with Simon Douglas-Brown may come under the microscope, and, of course, if this happens, the press will be all over it.'

'Simon Douglas-Brown is high-profile news fodder.'

'Yes. The cult of celebrity.'

'Why are you investigating all this now? The Gadd family have been working unofficially with the Met for years. They've stopped a lot of drugs flooding into the capital.'

Camilla regarded Erika, her eyes now colder and devoid of mirth.

'You're close to Commander Marsh, correct?'

Erika felt her stomach lurch. Marsh had been Chief Superintendent at Lewisham when she and Sparks worked together.

'Me and my late husband trained with Paul Marsh at Hendon, but as much as we are friends, we have clashed in the past on the direction of my investigations…'

'You rented a flat from him; you were at his wedding, and the christening of his twins…'

'He was also involved in the decision to promote Andy Sparks to superintendent over me.'

'You deny you're close?' snapped Camilla.

Erika wondered if she had anything, or if she was just digging for dirt. She was obviously on some crusade. Was it to root out corruption? Was it a personal vendetta? Was it easier now to smear a dead officer? Either way Erika was finding this meeting a tedious waste of time. Time she could use being a police officer. Suddenly, a bulb flickered on in the back of her mind.

'I'm saying we're friends, yes. But I remain professional and impartial. There are advantages to being the outsider. You have less to lose. I'd be willing to give evidence, of the limited information I have. Of course, I'd be willing keep my mouth shut when it comes to the press, you know how they love to get public opinion whipped up. People love to get enraged and take to social media, and I can see the headlines: the Met suddenly discovers its morals after twenty-five years cosying up to the Gadd crime family.'

Camilla tapped her fingers on the arm of her chair.

'And what do you want in return, Erika? For toeing the line.'

'I'd like to be considered for the vacant post of Superintendent. More than considered. And I'd like to be made SIO of a murder case. Lacey Greene...'

'I asked you to come here to talk to me, Erika.'

'With respect, ma'am, you called me in to dig up dirt on my colleagues. One of whom died when I was trying to revive him. If you're having to pump me for information about police corruption, you must be pretty desperate. If I were you I'd concentrate on your predecessor.' Erika's heart was pumping so loudly that she was convinced Camilla would hear.

She stared at Erika for a long moment, sizing her up. Devoid of make-up, it was the first time Erika had noticed how blue her eyes were. It was a sharp cold blue, as if they were chips of glass.

CHAPTER 18

Erika left the New Scotland Yard building and walked to a coffee shop on Victoria Street, where she ordered a large latte and took a seat in the corner. She took out her phone and called Marsh, but he wasn't picking up, so she left a message explaining that she'd been called in to a meeting with the Assistant Commissioner, and to call her back asap.

When she came off the phone she had a new email asking her to report to West End Central Police Station tomorrow morning, where she would be taking over the Lacey Greene murder case.

'You're a fast worker, Camilla,' said Erika. And then her phone chimed again. This time it was an email from Superintendent Yale asking where the hell she was. In the whirlwind of the past few days, she had neglected to keep him up to speed.

Erika downed the rest of her coffee and sped over to Victoria station.

An hour later she arrived in Bromley. She was on her way up to Yale's office when she passed the kitchenette and saw him making a cup of tea.

'Sir, I got your email, sorry I haven't been here,' she said. He carried on dunking the teabag in his cup, then fished it out. 'Did you hear about Superintendent Sparks?'

'Yes. You were with him when he died?'

'I was…'

'And then you met with Camilla, to discuss promotion.'

Erika didn't like his accusatory tone. He opened the small fridge and took out a carton of milk. It was the first time Erika had realised just how small the kitchenette was. The tiny fridge, a tiny travel kettle which one of the uniformed officers had donated when the big one broke. Yale was a huge man and this kitchen made him look like a bear at a doll's tea party. He stirred his tea, his huge sausage-like fingers daintily holding the spoon.

'I had to try and save an officer, sir. I hope you would do the same if you were put in that position,' said Erika.

He picked up his cup and left the kitchen. She followed him out into the corridor.

'Sir, I have things I need to discuss with you. I've been reassigned. I'll need to brief whoever replaces me—'

'Erika, you've never enjoyed working here. You've constantly gone over my head and defied orders. You struck a deal to work on one of the MIT teams without even talking to me. I think you should just go.' He walked off to the double doors, and Erika opened her mouth to protest, then for once, she closed it.

She went upstairs and looked around the small office she'd reluctantly inhabited. There were no personal touches or belongings other than her phone charger, which she unplugged, and a lone shortcake biscuit still balanced on the edge of her keyboard. She bit into it but it had gone soft, so she spat it out and dropped the rest in the bin.

There was a knock at the door; John poked his head around.

'Sorry, boss. I'm just chasing up if you've managed to read through...'

'No.'

'Oh. Okay. I heard about Superintendent Sparks. Sorry.'

'Thank you.'

'Life is too short, isn't it? The thought of dropping dead at the office. I want to go out on a high, extreme sports, having a laugh, in bed with my girlfriend... I don't mean to speak out of line here, but I've asked you so many times to read through my application, and you've been fobbing me off. If you don't want to read it then fine, just don't lie to me.'

He stood in the doorway and Erika could see he was trying to remain composed, but his hands were shaking.

'I've been transferred to the Murder Investigation Team working out of West End Central.'

'Oh,' he said, trying to hide his disappointment.

'I'd like you to come with me to work on the case; it's the Lacey Greene murder. This could give you the chance to show you are promotion material. I valued you working on the Jessica Collins case last year, and I could use your instinct, and another friendly face.' John looked surprised. 'I can give you time to think about it.'

'No. I'd love to. I mean it would be good, great. What about Yale?'

'I've got approval to assemble my team. It shouldn't be a problem, but if it is let me know. I'll need you to report to West End Central at nine tomorrow morning.'

'Thank you, boss,' he said and surprised her by swooping in for a hug.

'Okay, easy tiger,' she said, but inside she was pleased to have someone who believed in her, even if it was someone with the overconfidence of youth.

It was snowing again when she stepped out of the main entrance of Bromley Police Station. Her goodbyes had been few, and she was pleased to close the door on a difficult period in her career. She crossed the road to catch the train, and didn't look back.

CHAPTER 19

The next morning, Erika found herself back at Sparks's old office in West End Central Police Station. The door was ajar so she knocked and went through. Melanie Hudson was at his desk, deep in conversation on the phone, and motioned for her to come in. Erika walked into the office, doing a little detour around the patch of carpet where Sparks had collapsed. Little had changed in four days. There was the same view of the grey sky and the snow-covered rooftops. Melanie was now 'Acting Superintendent', and had accordingly written this on a piece of paper and taped it over Sparks's nameplate on the desk. There was no malice in this act, and Erika might have done the same, but it highlighted the clinical nature of the force.

'Right, Erika, I'm hoping you can just get on with things,' said Melanie, putting the phone down and rubbing her temples. 'Sparks has left me with a ton of messy cases, paperwork missing, promises made for resources that he shouldn't…' Her voice tailed off. 'Sorry, it must be tough coming back in here. Did you get eyeballed?'

'No.' Several officers had averted their gaze when she'd walked through to the office. She didn't blame them, she'd probably have done the same.

'Good. I've organised a whip-round for Sparks: look out for a yellow bucket. We're gonna get a posh bunch of flowers and, er, the rest we'll give to charity.'

'Do we know when the funeral is?' Erika asked. Melanie shook her head. 'What's the charity?'

'Something to do with special needs, I think. It's taped on the bucket. You got my notes and the case files on Lacey Greene and Janelle Robinson?'

'Yes, and I'm up to speed—'

Melanie's phone rang and she picked it up. 'Can you hold on…' She put her hand over the phone. 'Erika, I'd advise a bit more digging before we link the two murders.'

'The evidence is there. I don't want to go public yet, but we need to start asking questions.'

'Ask questions, by all means, but do it with a bit of nous… I've got you set up at the other end, and I'm happy with everyone you've requested for your team.'

'They'll work well with everyone here and…'

'Shut the door on your way out,' said Melanie and then went back to her phone call.

At least she didn't ask me to call her ma'am, thought Erika as she left the office. She was pleased Melanie was getting on with it, and there was no hostility coming from her. She wondered if she was Acting Superintendent with a view to her taking on the role full-time, but she pushed this to the back of her mind.

The various teams in the open-plan office were busy, and there was a loud background noise of chatter and phones ringing. When she walked back down the office, she saw the area she'd been assigned; a small cramped section with desks, book-ended with two frosted glass panels. The low ceiling added to the feeling of claustrophobia.

Moss and Peterson were the first to arrive a few minutes later.

'Alright, boss?' said Moss, sloughing off her huge winter coat. 'So this is our new digs?'

'It's a bit smaller than I thought,' said Erika.

'It's Soho. It's all about square footage,' said Peterson.

'Thanks both of you for joining the team.'

Moss and Peterson exchanged glances.

'What?'

'We just wanted to check you're okay,' said Moss. She lowered her voice. 'No one wished Sparks dead more than me, but there's wishing, and it actually happening...' There was an awkward silence and Peterson shook his head. 'What? I'm just being honest.'

'I appreciate you asking, and I'm fine. I just want to get on with things,' said Erika.

Moss nodded and went to hang her coat up in the corner.

'And are we cool?' asked Peterson, moving closer.

'Course.'

'You haven't called,' he said, searching her face.

'Did I say I'd call?'

'No. But I thought you'd call personally about me joining the team.'

'I was being professional,' said Erika, looking round the cramped office and feeling awkward.

'Like it or not, Erika, we have something. I don't know what that is but it goes beyond our professional relationship.'

Erika could see Moss was busying herself with her bag in the corner, deliberately giving them space.

'We do, James. But a lot has happened, and I need to concentrate on this case. Okay?'

He didn't get the opportunity to say any more as John appeared at the glass partition slightly out of breath and rugged up in a coat, hat and gloves.

'Morning, boss,' he said, and seeing Moss and Peterson his face broke into a big smile. 'Nice one, really pleased to be working with you again.' He and Peterson shook hands, and he went in for a hug with Moss.

'Okay, I make it ten to nine. I need to go and make a phone call. We should have another five officers joining us for the briefing,' said Erika and left the office.

Moss looked at Peterson as he folded his coat and sat at one of the desks.

'It's going to be fine. She wouldn't have asked you to join the team if she didn't want you here.'

'I want to make sure I'm here for the right reasons,' he said.

'You are. She sees beyond whatever is going on between you personally, and sees what I see. A brilliant officer.' Moss perched on the edge of his desk, and it gave a lurch to one side, and the computer monitor began to slide off. 'Whoops, fat arse alert!' She laughed, leaping up and grabbing the monitor just before it hit the carpet. 'It's very wobbly, not at all sturdy.'

'Are we still talking about your backside?' Peterson grinned.

Moss grabbed a folder off the desk and whacked him over the head.

At nine a.m. Erika's team were assembled, and she stood up to address them. Along with Peterson, Moss and John, she had requested Sergeant Crane, a sandy-haired officer with a cheeky grin she had worked with on the Andrea Douglas-Brown case in Lewisham. There were two other detective constables, DC Andy Carr and DC Jennifer House, both young and smartly dressed, and eager to impress, and her team was backed up by three Civilian Support workers: young women in their mid-twenties with equal enthusiasm. As Erika opened her mouth to speak, she realised that Andy, Jennifer and the three support staff would have been four or five years old when she graduated from Hendon. Melanie Hudson was ten years her junior, and might shortly be her senior officer. She shook these thoughts away and turned to the whiteboards, to where the crime scene photos of Lacey Greene and Janelle Robinson were pinned up.

'Good morning everyone. Thank you for being punctual.' There were murmurs of appreciation. 'For those of you who need to get up-to-speed on this case, Sergeant Crane will be passing out the case notes so far.' She tapped the two photos of the dead girls, their battered bodies lying in the dumpsters. 'Twenty-year-old Janelle Robinson, and twenty-two-year-old Lacey Greene. Janelle's body was found on Monday the twenty-ninth of August in a dumpster adjacent to a small print-works on Chichester Road in Croydon, South London. Lacey Greene was found on Monday the ninth of January in a dumpster adjacent to a kitchen showroom in Tattersall Road in New Cross... As far as we can tell, the victims have no connection to these properties, but their deaths show consistencies. There is evidence that both were tortured over a period of three to five days, and sexually assaulted with a scalpel. Both victims' femoral arteries were severed, which would have resulted in rapid, fatal blood loss. There is no evidence of fatal blood loss at either scene. Severing the femoral artery would have resulted in six or seven pints of blood being rapidly expelled.'

Erika took two passport photos of Janelle and Lacey, both young and fresh-faced, staring into the camera.

'Lacey Greene was reported missing on Thursday the fifth of January; she was living at home in North London, and hadn't returned after a night out on the fourth of January. She had been due to meet someone for a blind date at eight p.m. in the Blue Boar pub in Widmore Road, Southgate. CCTV footage has been requested, but this is taking time.'

Crane was now squeezing in between the desks and passing around printouts summarising the cases.

'Janelle Robinson's circumstances are unclear. She wasn't reported missing back in August, so we have more of a blank on her last movements. She was living and working in a youth hostel near the Barbican Estate within the square mile, and from the original case notes, it wasn't unusual for her to spend time away…'

'What does that mean, "time away"?' asked Peterson.

'I suppose it's a nice way of saying that she used to go off, go AWOL, particularly if she had met a new boyfriend. I've been asked to exercise caution with linking these two murders, but the circumstances of their deaths have striking similarities.'

There was silence for a moment as the team flicked through the briefing document.

'Steven Pearson was arrested in conjunction with Lacey Greene's murder, but he was released a few days ago due to insufficient evidence. Steven is a homeless drug addict who has been living rough and in and out of homeless shelters for the past three months. I don't believe he had the resources or nous to plan an abduction. He was finishing off a long stretch at Pentonville when Janelle's body was found, and he wasn't released from prison until the fifteenth of September. He couldn't have killed Janelle, and I'm convinced that it was the same person who killed Lacey and Janelle… We need to start from the beginning. I want a detailed profile of both girls, everything we can find out. I want details on the locations where their bodies were found; I want CCTV to build up both of the girls' final movements. And I want their phones, their computers, any online history. Lacey's laptop is with Digital Forensics, and her last known phone signal has been triangulated to close to where she was abducted, but there is still no phone… Andy and Jennifer, I want you to get to work on this with Crane. Peterson, I want you and John to pay a visit to the youth hostel in the Barbican; we should start there with building up details of Janelle. Moss, you're with me. We're going to see Lacey Greene's parents. We'll reconvene here at four p.m.'

CHAPTER 20

An hour later, a squad car was waiting for Erika and Moss when they emerged from Southgate tube station in North London. The circular concrete and glass structure seemed to float above the busy intersection, and the light filtering through was strangely beautiful in the weak January sun. Lacey Greene's family lived a couple of miles from the station, in a large detached house on a quiet, tree-lined street.

Erika rang the bell, and there was a scrabbling sound as the locks were turned and the door was opened.

Charlotte Greene, Lacey's mother, was in her early fifties, and bore a striking similarity to her daughter. But her long dark hair was shot through with grey, and her eyes were bleary. Detective Constable Melissa Bates, the Family Liaison Officer, appeared behind her in the hallway.

'Hello, Mrs Greene. May we come in, please?' asked Erika as she and Moss showed their warrant cards.

Charlotte nodded absently. They followed her through to a beautifully furnished living room with bay windows overlooking the front and back garden. Beside a large brick fireplace was a large Christmas tree, still decorated but bald and brown, its needles in a thick circle on the carpet. A man kneeled in front of the dying embers of a glowing fire coaxing a pile of fresh wood with a poker. He was thickset, with dark hair thinning on top. When he stood up and turned they saw he wore glasses and had a beard.

'Hello, Mr Greene,' said Erika.

He wiped his hands and shook with Moss and Erika.

'Call me Don,' he said. He had the same blank-eyed stare as his wife.

They all sat, and Erika explained that she would be taking over the investigation from DCI Hudson.

'Why did Melanie have to leave? We liked her. She'd caught *that man*,' said Charlotte, looking from Erika to Moss.

'I'm afraid police investigations go through staff changes much as in other workplaces,' said Erika. She realised it sounded like bullshit as soon as it came out of her mouth.

'Why did you let him go?' said Don, his arm gripping his wife around her shoulders.

'We don't believe Steven Pearson was responsible for your daughter's death.'

'How can you be sure of that!? You've been on the case for, what? Five minutes?'

'We believe your daughter's death and the death of another young woman are linked,' explained Erika.

'What do you mean, "another young woman"? Who?' asked Don, looking from one to the other and pushing his glasses up his nose with his free hand.

Erika briefly outlined the details of Janelle's death, but omitted telling him her name and the location where her body had been found. 'I'm telling you this in confidence. We haven't released this information, and we won't for the time being, but I wanted to explain our reasons for releasing Steven Pearson.'

Don sat forward, unhooking his arm from Charlotte.

'So what you're saying is that you've known about this bastard since August, yet you've done nothing?'

'Mr Greene,' started Moss, 'the other young woman was a runaway; she didn't have family and, sadly, no one reported her missing. Her body remained unidentified for quite some time…'

She omitted to say that the previous investigation had screwed things up and misreported key information.

'We're doing everything we can, Mr Greene. I know that sounds like a cliché, but we want to talk to you, to help us build a picture of events leading up to Lacey's disappearance,' added Erika.

'We told Melanie all of this, and now you're making us go through it all again!' started Charlotte.

Don put up a hand to placate her.

'Wednesday the fourth of January. Lacey left at seven p.m. to meet a bloke; a blind date, she told us. She'd been talking to him online for a couple of weeks. She told us his name was Nico,' he explained.

'She met this Nico online?' asked Erika.

'Yes, online dating, a website...' started Don.

'Don. It was a dating app. An *app* is not a *website*,' snapped Charlotte.

'App, website, what does it matter?'

'What do you mean, "what does it matter"? They need to know the correct details! Match.com, it's called, the app.'

'Had she met anyone before this through this app or any other social network?' asked Erika.

Charlotte shook her head. 'No. Never.'

'This Nico. Do you know how old he was? Where he lived? Do you have a surname or address?' asked Moss.

'No, and you should know this, we told Melanie all of this,' said Charlotte. 'I was against Lacey going, but this bloke seemed, well, she said she'd spoken to him on the phone. He had a Facebook profile.'

'I was against her going too—' started Don.

'You were too busy watching telly to care!'

'She's... She was twenty-two!' cried Don, tears in his eyes. He lifted his glasses again to wipe them away.

'*I* didn't want her to go,' said Charlotte with pointed venom. 'But she said it was only around the corner, the Blue Boar pub, and they'd be meeting in public... At first I thought she was late back, which wasn't unusual. But then it was two, three, four in the morning and she still hadn't come home... I watched from that window. I always do it when she's due home, and I'd see her. This time, I didn't. We tried her mobile, but it was off... and...' She crumpled against her husband again.

Don put his arm around her and took over, struggling with his emotions.

'That's when it dawned on us that we'd have to phone the police,' he said. 'She'd just graduated last summer, from Northumberland Uni. She got a first. She had loads of friends there, had a whale of a time. It was the shock of coming back here, to the real world, that she found hard. Hotel Mum and Dad we called it. She paid us a little bit for housekeeping, and she was in her old room, but she was restless, waiting to start her life. This shouldn't have happened. You think this kind of thing only happens to other people.'

Erika and Moss nodded, giving them a moment to compose themselves.

'Was Lacey working?' asked Moss.

'Temping through an agency in offices. Different one each week. You know, admin and the like,' said Don.

'There was no one new in her life, no new friends she talked about?' asked Erika.

'She didn't have any friends here,' said Charlotte. 'She was bullied badly in high school, and was glad to see the back of Southgate. University was the making of her, she blossomed. She kept in contact with all of her university friends online. They were due to meet up next month.' She looked up at Erika with swollen eyes. 'They're all coming down for the funeral; they've been calling, asking when it is... They want us to make her Facebook a Memorialised Account... I can't bear it.' She broke down again and hid her face against Don's chest.

'Was there an ex-boyfriend from school, before she went to university?' asked Erika.

'No. *I told you* she wasn't happy here. There was a lad at uni, he was nice, came to stay once, but it fizzled out. She concentrated on her studies. She got a first; she had everything in front of her... everything,' said Charlotte. She bit her lip. 'Do you think she suffered?'

'Did you view Lacey's body?' asked Erika.

They nodded.

'Then you saw what happened. I have a brilliant team of officers. I give you my word that I will find out who did this. They won't get away with it.'

Charlotte continued to sob, and Don pulled her closer, tears magnified behind his glasses. They looked to the Family Liaison Officer who had remained quiet; she gave Moss and Erika a subtle nod.

'Would you mind if we took a look at Lacey's bedroom?' asked Moss.

'Please, don't mess anything up. Lacey had tidied up before she left, so keep it as she left it,' said Charlotte.

'Of course,' said Erika, and she and Moss left the room just as flames sprang to life in the fireplace.

CHAPTER 21

Lacey's bedroom was at the back of the house, overlooking a smart garden with wooden decking. A wooden table and chairs were stacked against the wall of the house, and the silver feet of a large gas barbecue poked out from underneath a beige plastic cover. Towards the back of the garden, there was a swimming pool with a curved retractable roof, and beyond, a tall stone wall separated it from a strip of woodland. Through the trees a train clacking past broke the silence.

'They're posh, aren't they?' said Moss. 'Look at that wardrobe. That didn't come in here in bits. Nor did the bed, or the desk there under the window.'

The bedroom was frozen in time, from when Lacey was fifteen or sixteen. There was a row of cuddly toys on the bed, and on the wall were posters of Lily Allen and Duffy. The desk was covered in make-up, some bottles of perfume, and a big mirror was propped up against the wall.

'I really want to know what's on her laptop,' said Erika, indicating a square in the dust on the desk. 'We need to keep chasing the Cyber Team.'

'If she was using a dating app, it would be on her phone,' said Moss.

Erika went to the mirrored wardrobe and slid it open. There was a huge number of clothes packed in on the rails, and it was a mixture of casual and skimpy clothes, all high quality, and some designer labels. Moss went to one of the bookshelves, took down a heavy brown photo album and started to flick through.

Erika looked out of the window again. Charlotte had emerged in a long black Puffa jacket and was throwing bits of old bread onto the snow. A flock of birds came swooping down to feed.

'Boss, look at this…'

Erika went to Moss who was perched on the bed. The photo album was open on a page of polaroids. In all of them Lacey was pictured with the same pouty young girl with long mousy hair. One was taken on a summer's day in the garden by the pool, where they wore bikinis; in another they posed in front of the statue of Eros in Piccadilly Circus. The third was taken underwater – they were grinning with their eyes wide open, hair spread out like halos, and bubbles escaping from their noses.

'Do they look like they're more than friends?' asked Moss. She turned the page with a creak of cardboard, and there were more polaroids of the girls, singing into a mirror with hairbrushes, and lying together on a bed; the mousey-haired girl was nuzzling Lacey's shoulder.

'The polaroids are thicker here, don't you think?' asked Erika, running her fingers over the cellophane-covered square edges.

Moss carefully peeled back the clear cellophane, and lifted out the polaroid which felt thicker. Underneath it was a polaroid of both girls naked. They were pictured side on, pressed against one another with their heads turned to the camera, and under it was another where they faced the camera completely naked, arms slung over shoulders.

'This was taken in front of the wardrobe in this room,' said Moss. 'Why didn't Charlotte and Don mention this when you asked about relationships? It looks like this was more than just a friendship.'

Erika looked back at the photo of the two girls pressed against each other.

'We need to know who this girl is, and if Lacey was still in contact with her. She might know something.'

CHAPTER 22

'I can see why they call this Brutalist architecture,' said John, looking up at Peterson from under his woolly hat. They had emerged from the tube station onto the Barbican Housing Estate, which was devoid of colour, the grey sky matching the concrete tower blocks. Blake's Tower rose up directly in front of them: a seventeen-storey block that housed the YMCA youth hostel, a gym and a small cafeteria.

They went through the doors of the Youth Hostel, relishing the warmth. Inside it was quiet and starkly lit, with a long polished Formica front desk and bare concrete walls. A woman in her twenties sat at the desk. She had long scrappy red hair and thick black glasses which reflected the glow of her computer. There was a smell of old gym shoes mixed in with cleaning fluid and floor wax, and behind her were rows and rows of small lockers, many ajar with keys hanging from the locks.

'Hi, are you Sada Pence?' asked Peterson.

'It's pronounced *Shaday*,' said the girl, disinterested, her eyes not leaving the computer screen.

Peterson and John pulled out their warrant cards and introduced themselves, explaining that they wanted to talk to her about the murder of Janelle Robinson.

'I spoke to the police already,' she said, continuing to type. She had a slight northern accent.

'We'd like to talk to you again,' said Peterson.

'So talk,' she said, the spindly office chair squeaking as she sat back and crossed her arms.

'How long did Janelle Robinson live here?'

Sada shrugged. 'Nine, maybe ten months.'

'So she moved in here… late in 2015?'

'Sounds about right: November time. She started off paying, then she ran out of money close to Christmas, and asked if she could work in exchange for accommodation.'

'Is that normal?' asked John.

'Depends what your notion of normal is? You look like guys who can afford to live in London.'

'I live near Bromley,' said John.

'Just answer the question, please,' said Peterson.

'It wasn't up to me. The guy who manages the place makes the decision. He liked her and took pity…' She leaned forward, her eyes wide and magnified behind her glasses. 'There was a rumour that she blew him, but I dunno.'

'Was Janelle working here up until she vanished?'

'No, she just did the Christmas and then went back to paying her way.'

'How did she do that?' asked John.

'When the weather got better she ran a coffee bike.'

'A coffee bike?'

'You know, one of those little coffee machines in the back of a bike. She biked around and sold coffees. She did well.'

'Do you know where she sold coffee?'

'All over. Covent Garden, London Bridge, Embankment. She didn't have a permit though, so she was moving around a lot.'

'Where did she get the bike from?' asked John.

The girl smiled. She had a grey front tooth. 'I didn't ask. Ask no questions and you get no lies. It was a nice one, chrome and classy. It was her dream to run her own coffee place.'

'You think she stole it?'

The girl grinned again and shrugged. 'The manager let her keep it here in the bike store when things were quiet.'

'Did you ever meet any of her friends or family?'

She shook her head. 'Family, no. Janelle's mum died when she was little. She didn't know her dad. She was brought up in a children's home, but ran away just before her sixteenth birthday.'

'Why did she run away?'

'A couple of the men who worked there had wandering hands,' she said, pursing her mouth at John's question.

'Did she mention any of the men she dated?' asked Peterson.

'Sometimes, in passing. But there were lots of men. She liked men, and sex. She was always dating someone new.'

Peterson received a text message, and pulled his phone out, seeing it was from Erika.

'Did she ever mention a man with the name Nico?'

Sada shook her head.

'When was the last time you saw her?'

'We had a row. It was the twenty-third, or the twenty-fourth of August. We had a big group of cyclists from Holland staying, and I'd told her she couldn't keep the coffee bike here because the bike store would be full. She left that morning, telling me to fuck off and she took the bike with her. It was the last time I saw her.' A tear formed in the corner of her eye, and she wiped it away. 'I can still see her, pushing it across the forecourt outside. It was a nice sunny day too.'

'So this was the twenty-fourth of August. Can you remember what time?'

'I dunno; nine in the morning.'

'She didn't say she was going?' asked John.

'I told you, we had a row.'

'What did you do when she didn't come back? What about her belongings?'

'She didn't have much stuff, and she usually took it with her. As I say, I thought she fucked off cos she was annoyed with me.'

She took out a tissue and blew her nose. 'You lot are on the back foot, aren't you? The only reason you finally tracked me down was cos Janelle been to give blood at one of those vans they set up in library car parks. She'd put my name and this place on the next of kin form… When I went to see her body in the mortuary, it was like she'd been bled out. Bloodless, like wax. Even the cuts and scratches on her body were faded. I organised a whip-round to pay for her funeral.'

'Thank you,' said Peterson. 'Just a couple more things. Was she on social media?'

'I think so.'

'Are you on social media?' asked John.

'No.'

'Really? Not even Facebook?'

The girl shook her head. 'I think Facebook is a surveillance tool… A friend of mine has an iPhone, and he's on social media. He says that when he talks about stuff with his mates, you know, like a type of flat-screen telly or a kind of beer they like, he starts to see adverts popping up for them on his phone. And this is stuff he hasn't searched for on Google or nothing. So I'm off the grid.' A look passed between John and Peterson. 'Well, apart from when I'm at work,' she said, indicating the computer on the desk in front of her.

'Can we get a list of all the people who were staying here in the month up until Janelle went missing?' asked Peterson.

'What? That'll take ages…'

'I want it fast, or we'll have to organise a warrant and that could be disruptive for your boss,' said Peterson, sliding his card across the desk.

She took it and nodded.

An hour later, John and Peterson emerged into the cold air.

'What's the link? There's nothing to link Lacey and Janelle,' asked John.

'They were both pretty girls,' said Peterson. 'Both worked in jobs which took them around London. Lacey was a temp; Janelle had her coffee bike. He could have been anywhere; he could have seen the girls anywhere…'

'In a city of nine million people,' added John. It started to snow again and a freezing gust of wind blew across the stark concrete. 'Come on, let's get a coffee and get out of here.'

CHAPTER 23

There had a been a tense scene when Erika and Moss had come back down to the living room and asked Charlotte and Don about the girl pictured with Lacey in the photo album. And then much to their surprise, Charlotte had rushed out of the living room, locking herself in the bathroom. It had been left to Don to confirm that the girl's name was Geraldine Corn.

'We both knew Lacey and Geraldine were close,' he said. 'They got to know each other at high school; Lacey hated it there, and Geraldine seemed to be her only friend… For a time, she was here a lot after school; she stayed for supper and… slept over.'

'When did you find out they were more than just friends?' asked Moss.

Don took off his glasses and rubbed his face. 'Charlotte walked in on them, one evening… They were in bed together.'

'What happened?'

'She went bonkers. Banned Geraldine from coming over again. Charlotte said that it would have been the same if we found Lacey with a boy, but the fact it was a girl, it really bothered her.'

'Did she carry on seeing Geraldine?' asked Erika.

'I think so. She wasn't allowed to have her here, but they were together at school; I'm sure at the weekends too. Charlotte didn't want to know, and it was just brushed under the carpet, as long as Geraldine didn't come here. I'd told Charlotte it was a phase, and I was right. When Lacey went off to University she drifted apart from Geraldine, and she had a boyfriend at university, nice lad he was, but it fizzled out.'

'And you're sure it was a man she was meeting for this blind date?' asked Moss.

He looked up at them and put his glasses back on.

'Well, yes. That's what she said. Do you think different?'

'We don't know. We're still waiting on Lacey's phone and computer records. Thank you, Mr Greene,' said Erika. 'The only reason we ask about this is so we can talk to Geraldine. I'm disappointed that you didn't come forward with this. We asked you specifically to tell us about the people Lacey knew,' said Erika.

'This was years ago!'

'We need to know. When you lie, you stop us being able to do our job. Please, no secrets. I promised you I would find who did this, but I need you to be honest and open with us.'

Don nodded, put his head in his hands and started to weep. Erika briefly laid a hand on his back, and they quietly left.

'You shouldn't make those promises, boss,' said Moss, when they emerged from the house and got into the waiting squad car.

'Promises?'

'Promising them you'll find Lacey's killer.'

'I do it to hold myself to account,' said Erika. 'And I've never broken a promise.'

'But those promises have almost broken you…'

Erika looked at Moss for a moment and then her phone rang. It was Peterson. She listened as he relayed the information they'd learned from Sada at the youth hostel in the Barbican. When she came off the phone she told Moss.

'We should get in touch with the transport police – sounds like Janelle "acquired" this coffee bike; maybe one was reported stolen. This also puts Janelle at any number of locations across London before she went missing,' Erika finished.

'I've got details for Geraldine Corn,' said Moss, consulting her phone. 'She works at the local pharmacy, it's about a mile away.'

'Good. Let's see if she can give us anything,' said Erika.

CHAPTER 24

They found the small run-down pharmacy on the end of a parade of local shops. A bell jangled when they opened the door, and inside was a quiet, studious atmosphere. The shelves were crammed and there was a smell of antiseptic and dust. They recognised Geraldine behind a scratched wooden counter, serving an elderly lady who had a white compression bandage taped over one eye. She was now a serious-looking young woman, compared to her teenage self in the photo album. Her white uniform was starched and spotless; her skin was very pale and flawless, and her long mousy hair was tied back at the nape of her neck.

Through a hatch behind her came a rattle of pills tipping onto a metal scale, and a fleeting glimpse of a small Indian man.

Erika and Moss waited until the lady had left, then went to the counter and introduced themselves, showing their warrant cards.

'About time,' said Geraldine.

'You're expecting us?' asked Moss.

'I had to find out from the local news. I was her best friend…' She said it with anger, as if her status of best friend had been denied.

There was a buzz as the door opened and an elderly man came inside.

'Hold on a moment,' said Geraldine, going to serve him.

'No. You hold on. We'd like to talk to you. Now,' said Erika.

Geraldine looked back to the man through the hatch, and he nodded.

She led them through the packed shelves to a small door which opened out into an equally cramped stockroom with a table and chairs and a small sink with a kettle.

'We're sorry about Lacey,' said Erika when they were settled at the table. 'You two were close.'

Geraldine shifted in her chair and shrugged.

'Two minutes ago, you told us you were best friends?' added Moss.

'We were. Off and on. It was complicated.'

'We know you had a relationship. We found the polaroid photos hidden in a photo album,' said Moss.

'Hidden... Sums up everything really. When Lacey went away to university, it was like she dropped me.'

'You didn't want to go to university?'

'My parents couldn't afford the tuition... But this is a good job, secure. People are always ill, aren't they?' Her voice tailed off wistfully.

'What did you know about Lacey's friendships and relationships?' asked Erika.

'There was me. Three or four guys at Northumberland uni. She got around a bit,' said Geraldine disapprovingly. 'She was a very pretty girl; that's what pretty girls do.'

'When did your relationship end?' asked Moss.

'It never really ended. Whenever she was home in the holidays, she'd get miserable and call me, and we'd meet.'

'Where?'

'At my house. My mum's cool with things. I think Lacey liked that she could relax. Charlotte is highly strung, and Don is properly downtrodden.'

'All we saw were two devastated parents,' said Erika.

'They airbrushed me out of Lacey's life,' said Geraldine, crossing her arms.

'Did you see Lacey in the months leading up to when she went missing?'

'Yeah. We'd picked up again, September last year.'

'How do you mean "picked up"?'

'Friends… friends with benefits, sometimes. But it wasn't the same. She was focused on other things. I was just, just a pastime for her.'

'What other things was Lacey focused on?' asked Moss.

'She was applying for jobs; she wanted to work for the Arts Council or for an African charity. Typical rich girl bollocks. And she'd joined a dating app in the hope of finding Mr Right.' Geraldine winced, as if the words had tasted bitter.

'You can't join an app,' said Moss. 'You can download an app, or join a dating site.'

'I'm not on social media. I'm just answering your questions.'

'Do you think that's why you lost touch? It can happen, if you're not on social media and your friends are. So much interaction goes on through them,' said Erika.

'I know how they work,' snapped Geraldine.

'Do you think Lacey was a lesbian?' asked Moss.

'You are, obviously. What do you think?' Geraldine shot back.

'I'm asking you,' said Moss evenly.

Geraldine shrugged. 'I sometimes think she was put on this earth just to make me feel every emotion.'

'You loved her?'

'Loved her, hated her… But I wish I'd loved her more, now she's gone… Wish I'd told her not to meet that bloke.'

Geraldine took a little packet of tissues from the pocket of her overall and took one out, blotting her eyes.

'Which bloke?' asked Erika, exchanging a look with Moss.

'The last time I saw Lacey, she was asking my advice about meeting this bloke. I felt she was asking to hurt me. So I told her to go ahead.' She wiped tears from her eyes.

Erika and Moss exchanged another look.

'When was this?' asked Erika.

'Between Christmas and New Year. She'd been chatting to him online for a few weeks. He wanted them to meet. She thought he was so handsome; he just looked a bit oily to me.'

'What do you mean? You saw his picture?' asked Erika.

'Yes, she showed me it on her phone.'

'What do you mean by "oily"?'

'Swarthy. He had black hair, slicked back black hair, and a thin face with dark features. In lots of the pictures he was stripped from the waist down.' She rolled her eyes. 'I think that she wanted me to be jealous, so she must have still cared.'

'When exactly was this?' asked Erika.

'The Friday before New Year, the thirtieth. We met for coffee. She told me she was going to meet this Nico on Wednesday.'

'His name was Nico,' said Erika.

Geraldine scrubbed at her eyes with the balled-up tissue. 'I've tried to tell this to the police.'

'How?' asked Moss.

'I dialled 999, who told me to ring 101, which I did and I left a message. That was two weeks ago,' said Geraldine. 'Two weeks!'

'What about Lacey's parents, did you mention any of this to them?' asked Erika.

'I called them, but Charlotte put the phone down on me.'

Erika looked at Moss; they would have to follow this up. 'Geraldine, if we can get an e-fit artist, do you think you could help us put together a likeness of the picture you saw on Lacey's phone of this Nico?'

'Yes, of course... How did she die?'

'We can't give details, I'm sorry,' said Erika.

'It was violent, though, wasn't it? The way she died?'

Erika nodded. Geraldine broke down again, and this time Moss moved to comfort her.

CHAPTER 25

A few hours later, Geraldine was working with an e-fit artist in the small stockroom at the back of the pharmacy. Erika was standing outside on the cold street, talking to Peterson on the phone. The sky was beginning to turn a deeper shade of grey, and the lights had come on in the window of the run-down dry cleaner next to the pharmacy.

'Moss is on the way back to you at the nick; she's trying to get things moving on Lacey's laptop and phone.'

'Do you think you're doing any good hanging there?' asked Peterson. He too was back at West End Central, and Erika could hear Crane's voice in the background.

'It's two weeks since Lacey went missing,' said Erika. 'And I only heard today that her closest friend was trying to get in contact, and she's the only person who saw a photo of the guy Lacey went to meet. If we'd had an e-fit two weeks ago, just think…'

'There's not much point in talking about shoulda coulda woulda.'

'I was lucky that an artist was able to get over so fast. As soon as I have something I'll get it emailed straight over. How are things going with the CCTV?'

'There's an ATM opposite the Blue Boar pub where Lacey was due to meet this Nico guy. Crane's trying to track down if it has any footage. We're working on the assumption that Lacey was abducted in or around the pub, so there could be other points where CCTV might have picked something up. We're working on tracing the different routes away from the pub.'

'Good. What about coffee bikes?'

'I've been in touch with British Transport Police to see if one's been picked up or reported stolen,' said Peterson. Erika heard a knocking and looked up. The e-fit artist, a young dark-haired guy in his early thirties, was at the pharmacy window, beckoning her in.

'Sorry, I have to go,' she said.

Erika came back into the pharmacy, relishing the warmth. The manager watched her pass from his little hatch, a little bewildered by his pharmacy being commandeered for a police enquiry. Geraldine was sitting in the stockroom at a table behind the e-fit artist's laptop. She looked exhausted, but gave Erika a weak smile.

'Okay, so this is who we have,' said the e-fit artist, twisting the laptop to face Erika.

The face on the screen was of a man in his late twenties or early thirties. It was long and thin, with a wide nose, pronounced cheekbones, and brown eyes. His skin was smooth with very little stubble, and his black hair was long and brushed back from his forehead with a pronounced widow's peak. It was eerie, a little blurred and unreal.

'And you're sure this is him?' asked Erika.

'Yes,' said Geraldine, twisting her hands in her lap. 'Do these things usually work? Will it help catch him?'

The e-fit artist shot her a look.

'Yes, they do help,' said Erika. 'Thank you for doing this, Geraldine.'

* * *

When Erika came back out to the waiting squad car, the wind was blowing hard, and it felt like it was slicing through her skin. She called Peterson again.

'I've just sent the image over,' she said. 'The second you have it, I want it shared with as many boroughs as possible, and I want it out to the media too. Let's get this bastard.'

CHAPTER 26

It had been a nightmare commute for Darryl back from London. There had been no seats when he boarded the train at Waterloo East, so he'd had to stand crushed against the door, amongst people coughing and sneezing for the best part of an hour. It had started to snow when he left the train station in his car, and this slowed his progress home even more.

It was seven thirty when he reached the brow of the hill leading down to the farm, and he saw a pair of car headlights about to pull out of the gates. He slowed on the approach, thinking they would pull past him, but they were stationary, and when he neared, he saw one of the large iron gates had jammed. He stopped the car and got out. The snow was coming down thick, and he dashed over to a figure in dark blue, wrestling to get the gate open. It was only when Darryl got closer, and looked past the glare of the headlights, that he saw it was a police car waiting to leave the driveway, and it was a uniformed officer pulling at the gate.

'Evening, you want help?' asked Darryl, holding up his hand against the snow and glare of the squad car. The police officer looked up at him.

'Who are you?'

'This is my parents' farm.'

'I think it's the mechanism jammed,' said the police officer. He was young with a boyish face and a dark goatee.

'It does this sometimes. I keep telling my dad to get it fixed,' said Darryl. 'If we grab just under the middle section, we should be able to lift and release it.'

Darryl stood to one side of the gate, and directed the police officer to stand at the other side, and they lifted it up a few inches off its hinge. The mechanism began to whir and they had to step back quickly as it swung inwards.

'Thanks,' said the police officer, seeing his mucky hands and wiping them on his trousers. 'You should tell your dad to get this fixed. Not much help in an emergency. They weigh a ton.'

'Yes. I will. Is everything okay?' asked Darryl, looking back at the squad car. He could see another officer in the passenger seat, and the outline of a figure sitting in the back.

'We've had to arrest one of the men who works for your father...'

'Who?'

'Morris Cartwright.'

Darryl's heart began to thump. 'Something serious?'

The police officer raised his eyebrows. 'You could say that. I can't go into detail, but your dad will probably tell you. Thanks again.'

He sprinted back to the car, dodging one of the ice-filled potholes in the gravel.

Darryl stood to one side as the car pulled past. He could see Morris in the back, his hands cuffed together on his lap. His long thin face stared back at Darryl, black eyes devoid of emotion.

Darryl waited until the squad car was halfway up the hill, then went back to his car and drove through the gates. His heart was still thumping as he passed the farm house, seeing the lights on in the front room. He parked under the carport behind Morris's car. He got out and went over to it, and tried to open the boot. It was locked. He walked round to the front of the car and placed his hand on the hood. It was cold.

Grendel met him at the back door with a volley of barks and licks, and he hung up his coat in the boot room. He could hear his mother and father beyond the kitchen, talking in hushed voices. He went through and found them in the farm office.

John was sitting at the messy desk, which was dominated by a huge old desktop computer. Mary was standing by his side, her hand leaning on the desk. They both looked concerned. The walls were packed with floor-to-ceiling shelves stuffed with paperwork. There was an aerial map on the back wall, slightly faded, and it showed the land as it had been twelve years earlier. The trees surrounding the swimming pool had just been planted, and were yet to turn into towering giants.

'I just saw the police. What's Morris done?' asked Darryl.

John shook his head.

'Bloody fool. He's been nicking fertiliser off us, and trying to flog it to the neighbouring farms...' Mary placed a hand on John's shoulder, but he shook it off. 'Problem is that when anyone tries to sell the combination of chemical fertiliser Morris got hold of, it rings alarm bells... and farmers are told to contact the police. Terrorists can make bombs with the chemicals.'

'They think Morris is a threat to national security,' said Darryl, unable to mask a smile.

'It's not funny, Darryl!' shrilled his mother.

'Come on, it is. The police think Morris is a terrorist? He couldn't blow up a balloon without screwing it up,' said Darryl, trying not to laugh.

'He was only ever going to make a couple of hundred at most. He should have come to me. Now I've lost a good milker,' said John.

'Now come on, John, it might only be for a while,' said Mary, placing a hand on his shoulder.

'Go on, get supper on the table. Darryl's home,' he snapped, shaking her off. She nodded obediently and moved off to the kitchen.

'What happens now?' asked Darryl.

'Morris has a record, and they like to come down hard on stuff like this. He could go down.'

Darryl had a sudden image of skinny little Morris in a prison cell, begging and squealing as he was held down and raped by three big blokes. A snorting laugh escaped him, and John shot him a look.

'Sorry, Dad... I'll just go and wash my hands for dinner,' he said.

Darryl went through the kitchen and up to his bedroom, where he turned on the light and shut the door, and burst out laughing. It went on for a few minutes, until he wiped his eyes and got himself under control.

He went to the window by his desk and drew the curtains. He jiggled the mouse to wake up his computer and sat down, typing in his password. His home screen appeared with a huge image of Grendel. He fired up the VPN, which masked his internet location, then logged into the new profile he had created on Facebook. A small chime indicated he had a new message, and he was pleased to see it was from the girl he'd been flirting with. She said how much she liked his photo, how cute he looked.

Darryl had decided after Lacey and Janelle that he would stop using the profile he had created with the name Nico. Twice had been risky enough, and he didn't want to risk a hat-trick. He wasn't sure if the police were on to it; so far they seemed to be clueless, and besides, he realised now that the picture looked a little like Morris. Not enough for people to make the link, but he'd had a scare earlier when he'd seen Morris in the back of the police car.

Poor stupid Morris. He thought back to the mental image of Morris in the prison cell, and this time added another two blokes queuing up to bugger his skinny writhing little arse.

Darryl sat back in his chair, and started to write a reply to the girl's message. Her name was Ella, and he needed to lay some groundwork before he asked her to meet him.

CHAPTER 27

Erika woke on the sofa, disorientated. Instinctively she sat up and made for the bathroom to have her morning shower, then saw the television was showing the *BBC News* channel, and it was 2.16 a.m. She went to the kitchen and drank a glass of water, then checked her phone. Since she'd called Commander Marsh earlier in the evening, leaving him a message, he still hadn't answered. It was unusual for him not to get back to her.

She went back to the sofa, and picked up her laptop from the coffee table. The e-fit picture of Nico had been uploaded to the Met website for the Lewisham and Croydon boroughs, asking for any information from the public. It had also been tweeted out by their Twitter accounts. She checked to see if there had been any responses, or retweets. There was one, on the Lewisham account, from a young woman who'd tweeted in reply:

@MPSCroydonTC I wouldn't kick him out of bed!!

'Bloody hell,' muttered Erika.

She clicked on the e-fit image again so it filled the screen. It was a chilling face. Determined. Ruthless. A bit of rough. His face had mixed heritage, British or French with a little South America perhaps. Would he blend into all the other e-fits? All faces were unique, but e-fits seemed to all have a slightly blank and sinister expression. She often wondered if having a smiling face alongside the neutral expression would work, particularly with sex attackers.

After all, they often started out attempting to charm their victims. It was only when that failed that the mask slipped.

She stared at him for a moment longer then slammed her laptop shut and shuffled off to the bedroom to get some sleep.

Later that morning, her team regrouped at West End Central. Crane had managed to track down some CCTV footage from the ATM opposite the Blue Boar pub in Southgate. The lights in their section were off, and they were watching back the grainy black-and-white footage projected onto a section of the whiteboard.

'The problem we have is that the built-in camera in the ATM is positioned at a high angle looking down,' said Crane. 'The people on the other side of the road, where the pub is, can only be seen fully in their approach, before the top half of their bodies is out of shot.' They watched as a man with a dog walked past, the top of his body vanishing when he reached the pub, so that his black Labrador trotted along beside a pair of moving legs.

'So, in other words, it's useless,' said Erika.

'Not completely useless,' said Crane. 'We've got the time-stamped footage from Wednesday the fourth of January. Lacey Greene was due to meet this Nico at 8 p.m...' He fast forwarded the footage through the afternoon and then slowed it down. The timestamp sped through 6 p.m. 'Okay, we're running through the footage at twelve times the speed from 7 p.m. onwards. There's no one around. Only a smattering of cars passing. It's just coming off rush hour. However, this car goes past three times in the space of five minutes...' He paused on a small car moving from right to left. 'See. First time is 7.55 p.m.' He sped the footage again. 'Then a minute later, look, it comes back into shot in the other direction... Here it comes again; it goes past a third time at 7.58 p.m., goes out of shot past the pub...'

On the screen a blurred image of a young woman walked along the road, towards the pub, her dark hair catching in the breeze. Crane paused the image. She wore dark knee-high boots and a dark jacket.

'And here we have Lacey Greene.'

It took Erika's breath away for a moment to see Lacey alive and well. Here in the incident room they all knew what was going to happen, but the girl on screen was clueless what awaited her. Most probably she was excited at the prospect of a date. Crane pressed play and Lacey started to walk, but as she reached the pub, the top half of her was cut out of shot.

'Are we sure that's Lacey?' asked Erika.

'It's the only young woman matching her height and appearance who passed the pub all evening,' said Crane.

On screen Lacey's legs had moved out of shot.

'We can't see the bloody entrance to the pub, so we don't know if she went in?' asked Erika.

'She didn't,' said Jennifer. 'I spoke to a lad who was working on the bar on Wednesday the fourth of January. He said it was very quiet, being just after New Year, and only a handful of regulars came in all night. Lacey wasn't one of them. Another girl he was working with backs this up.'

'So she vanishes out of shot, just past or by the pub, at 7.59 p.m.,' said Erika. 'What about that car? The bloody footage is blurry as hell, and it's black and white. Can we get a number plate?'

'No. I've already asked the boys at Digital Forensics. They can enhance an image but it needs to be clear in the first place. All we'll get is a mush of pixels. We also can't tell what colour the car is,' said Crane.

'What about the model?' Erika looked around the incident room.

'It looks like a Fiat or a Renault,' said John.

'Or one of those Ford Kas, perhaps a Citroën,' added Crane.

'We need to do better than that,' snapped Erika. 'How far along are you getting CCTV footage from the surrounding area that follows the car?'

'We got this footage late last night,' said Crane. 'There's no other CCTV cameras until you hit the area around Southgate tube; of course, I've requested and we're keeping our eyes peeled.'

'What about Lacey's phone?'

'We've had mast data back,' said Moss. She flicked the lights back on and went to her desk and picked up a printout. 'There are three mobile phone masts in the area of the Blue Boar pub, and we triangulated the last signal from Lacey's phone, which was at 8.21 p.m. on the fourth of January. After that there's nothing.'

'How far apart are these masts?' asked Erika.

'All within a mile of the pub.'

'Okay. I want another door-to door in the area. I want to know if anyone saw anything. There's houses, shops.'

'There's a big car park at the side of the Blue Boar. It backs onto a bus depot and it's badly lit,' said Crane, fiddling with his laptop and projecting another image on the whiteboards. This time it was a Google Street View image of the car park next to the pub. It had been taken on a summer's day. The road was busy and the surrounding trees green.

'He could have grabbed her there,' said Peterson. 'It was dark.'

'And switched her phone off so her movements couldn't be tracked,' said Erika. She looked at the Google Street View image as Crane shifted the view along Widmore Road. A bus was passing in one photo. 'Buses have CCTV. Find out what buses go on that route, and pull bus footage from TfL. It's a long shot, but one of those cameras might have got something. What about Lacey's laptop?'

'It's a priority case, but I've been told another twenty-four hours,' said Jennifer.

'I'll have a word with them...' Erika could see the team looked disheartened. 'We have to keep asking questions, however stupid they may be: answers solve the case. This devil, whoever he may be, is in the detail. I'm going to talk to the Acting Superintendent to see if we can get some increased manpower for the door-to-door. And if we can get this e-fit image out to the public. It's on the borough websites but it's not enough. I'd also like to release the CCTV footage of Lacey, and appeal for any witnesses to her and the car... What about Janelle Robinson, any CCTV where her body was found in Croydon?'

'Sorry, boss. It's a CCTV black spot. Residential, no shops, and no buses pass down the street.'

'Okay. Let's keep on it. We'll close in on this guy, I'm sure of it.'

CHAPTER 28

It was lunchtime in the large communal office where Darryl worked, which meant that between 11.30 a.m. and 2 p.m. the lifeless atmosphere took on a little excitement as packed lunches were opened and admired, and the best places to eat were discussed.

The anticipation of food and what was on television were the main topics of conversation during the day. The work was often an afterthought.

Darryl worked on a data entry team with three others: Terri, an anaemic blonde woman in her late thirties who was permanently cold; Derek, a dull, balding man in his late fifties, and Bryony, their Team Leader. She was a large woman in her mid-thirties, who, come rain or shine, wore black leggings and thick patterned acrylic jumpers. Her love of synthetic fabrics wasn't matched in her personal hygiene. A beefy tang of body odour permanently hung over their section, a grid of cubicles in the centre of the office.

Darryl had worked with this firm for almost three years, and mostly kept to himself. He'd started as a temp, and laziness and the ease of regular money had meant the time had flown by. He hadn't been to university, and after several disastrous attempts at working for his father on the farm, this job was an escape and an act of defiance. Since his brother, Joe, had died, Darryl was the only heir to the farm, and he was determined never to be a farmer.

Darryl had spent the morning inputting the results of a customer survey and, seeing it was seven minutes to one, he minimised the screen. He always took lunch at one, neatly halving the working day. Across the low partition, Bryony was sitting at her desk, chewing rhythmically like a cow, with a Big Mac in one hand, and a steaming cup of coffee in the other. She was reading something on her computer.

A tall, attractive girl came up to the cubicle next to her and took off her coat, shaking out her long dark hair. She placed a paper bag from a local deli on her desk. Her name was Katrina, and she was the new temp who'd started the week before.

'Is this about that poor girl who they found in the rubbish bin?' asked Katrina, indicating the screen.

Bryony swallowed. 'Yes. They've released an artist's impression of the bloke they're looking for,' she said and pushed the last of the burger into her mouth.

'Where do you see this?' asked Darryl, trying to keep his voice even.

Bryony flapped around, her mouth full.

'On the BBC homepage, halfway down,' said Katrina.

Darryl logged onto the website. It was a shock to see the e-fit, and details of the case. It had seemed like for so long the police hadn't cared. Now he saw it on the screen it made him scared, scared and a little thrilled. *Who led them to Nico?* he thought. He'd been careful, using a VPN to mask his footprints online. There was nothing they could trace back to him. Had they found Lacey's phone? Or got into her laptop? He took a deep breath. It was OK. If that was all they'd done, then he was OK. He scanned the rest of the article.

'They did arrest a man, but they let him go...' Bryony was saying, brushing crumbs from her jumper. 'I live quite close to New Cross.'

'You do? Where?' said Katrina, tilting her head in mock sympathy.

'Well, a few miles. I'm just down the road, near Bermondsey.'

'Don't worry, I don't think he'll come after you,' Katrina replied, patting her shoulder. Bryony gave her a look of pathetic gratitude.

As far as Darryl could see from the article, a friend of Lacey's had helped the police with the e-fit. It would figure that Lacey had shown her Nico's profile.

'Where do you live, Katrina?' asked Bryony.

'West London,' she said, sitting and taking out a boxed salad and a bottle of water.

'You're making me look bad,' said Bryony, glancing at her grease-spotted McDonald's bag.

'Don't be silly. I pig out all the time,' said Katrina with a flick of her immaculate hair.

What a liar, thought Darryl.

'I've heard West London is really nice?' said Bryony.

Katrina nodded.

'You must take the District line to work then?' said Darryl. Katrina looked across the partition, as if noticing him for the first time.

'Erm. *Sometimes,*' she said, tucking a long glossy strand of hair behind her ear and opening her salad. He kept eye contact with her and smiled.

'Darryl, I make it one o'clock. Aren't you on lunch now?' said Bryony, tapping her watch.

'Ah yes, McDonald's or salad… McDonald's or salad?' he said. 'You are what you eat.'

He flicked off his computer, and stood up, pulling on his jacket. He had a photo of Grendel tacked to the bottom of the monitor. He straightened it, and picked up his wallet and phone, studying Katrina from the corner of his eye. He knew exactly where she lived: in a small flat just off Chiswick High Road. She had a Facebook profile which she hadn't bothered to secure; she also used Instagram and Foursquare. He knew she was single, and she'd been on two disastrous dates in the past month, the first to see a movie with a bloke 'with hands like an octopus', the second with a rich city worker, to a bar at Canary Wharf. She'd drunk Long Island Iced Teas, one at 7.30 p.m., and the second at 7.53 p.m. – if the timings on her Instagram photos were accurate – and she'd posted that she was debating a third drink, but she didn't want the bloke she was with to think she was easy. However, judging by the hundreds of photos Darryl had copied from her Facebook page to the hard drive on his computer at home, Katrina *was* easy.

He'd spent a couple of hours the previous evening masturbating over pictures of her dressed in a schoolgirl outfit for Halloween, and a bikini shot taken on a beach in Ibiza.

Katrina caught him looking at her and smiled awkwardly. He grinned back at her and left.

'It's 1.02 p.m. Don't forget to put that in your time sheet,' called Bryony after him.

Darryl stepped out of the office and joined the lunchtime crowds near Borough Market. Wearing a decent suit and black jacket he blended in with scores of office workers on the lunch run. He wasn't interested in Katrina. Well, he was, but as a colleague she was too close. It could be traced back to him.

He had his sights set on Ella. He'd found her a few months back, working in the Bay Organic Café further down the road from Borough Market. The first time he'd seen her, he'd genuinely gone in to buy lunch. She was beautiful, in an earthy way, with long dark hair, olive skin and a gorgeous figure.

He'd started going there regularly for lunch, to see how often she worked. He'd had a breakthrough on his sixth visit, when he'd gone to pay for his salad. It was a quiet day and Ella had been working on the checkout and engrossed in her phone.

She'd given him a broad smile, and placed her phone face up on the counter whilst she put his lunch through. Her Facebook profile was open, and with one glance he knew her name was Ella Wilkinson.

He'd paid in cash, and she'd smiled at him again, but it was the kind of smile you gave a little brother and he'd hated her for that. Later that evening, back at the farm, he'd shut himself in his bedroom and found Ella on Facebook, dragging her profile picture onto his desktop. Then he'd opened Social Catfish's Reverse Image Search. It was a remarkable piece of software, and within a few minutes he had her email address, a list of all the social networks she belonged to, and where she lived.

She was a part-time art student at St Martins, and she lived in North London. She also had a profile on Match.com, which made him think that things couldn't be better.

He spent the next couple of months building up a brand new Facebook profile, adding friends, posts, and a legitimate history. He also created a profile on Match.com, aligning his likes to hers. It had been a difficult choice: how to choose someone's identity to steal, and after much research he had realised that profiles of dead people were the way forward. This new profile was for Harry Gordon, a handsome blond who had just returned from travelling. In reality, the photo was of a person named Jason Wynne, from South Africa, who had died a year ago, while base jumping.

After several weeks spent building up the fake Harry Gordon profile, he started to work his way into Ella Wilkinson's world. She had 650 Facebook friends, so he went through them all to find which of them he could friend without looking suspicious. Two of them friended him back, giving him and Ella mutual friends.

Just after Christmas, Darryl, as Harry Gordon, sent Ella a message on Match.com. She took the bait, and then he started to reel her in, slowly, at first, chatting to her within the Match.

com messenger system, never trying too hard, and leaving gaps between responses. He knew he had her when she friended Harry Gordon on Facebook. The flirting had intensified, and now he just had to make the final crucial step. Harry Gordon needed to talk to Ella on the phone.

Darryl reached the Bay Organic Café, and saw it was crowded in the lunchtime rush. Ella was on the checkout and had a huge queue of people waiting. He watched her for a moment and then carried on walking, thinking, today, he'll get a sandwich from Sainsbury's. Yes, cheese and salad would be nice. He didn't mind that the café was busy. He'd be talking to Ella later, and then he'd have her all to himself.

CHAPTER 29

On Thursday morning, Erika and her team were back in the incident room. Crane had just wearily informed her that despite an exhaustive search through hours of CCTV, from several locations, they hadn't been able to track the movements of the car after it had left the Blue Boar pub.

'For Christ's sake!' said Erika. 'He's a lucky bastard. Twice I've been given points on my licence when CCTV cameras managed to produce pin precision images of me straying into a bus lane.'

'Tell me about it,' said Peterson. 'My mum got caught in a bus lane with her hand in a tube of Pringles. She got three points and a hundred and twenty pound fine. *And* the camera picked up that they were salt and vinegar flavour.'

Despite this, Erika smiled. 'That's not true?'

'It is! If you ever meet my mother, you'll believe it,' he said, sitting back in his chair and rubbing his tired eyes. There was an awkward pause.

'Thank you for putting in the time, Crane, but we still have nothing on the killer's car,' said Erika. 'Can anyone give me some good news?'

John got up and went to the whiteboard carrying some print-outs. 'We've had a response to the e-fit from a Geovanni Manrique, an Ecuadorian national living in Ealing...' He pinned up a photo of a young man, almost identical to the e-fit. In the photo he was grinning against a backdrop of a beach. 'This is Sonny Sarmiento. Nineteen years old, an extreme sports fanatic from Ambato, a city in central Ecuador. Sonny was killed in a climbing accident two years ago. Geovanni is a friend of the family, and often goes back home. He recognised the e-fit.

'We've also had word back from the Cyber Team. They've been through Lacey Greene's laptop and her Facebook history.' He pinned up a screenshot of the same photo taken from a Facebook profile: the name underneath it was 'Nico Brownley'. 'As you can see, our killer has been using Sonny Sarmiento's profile picture. He also lifted off another sixteen photos, mainly of Sonny with friends on a trip to London. The Nico Brownley profile was created last summer. It looks like a lot of time was spent building up friends and a history to give the profile legitimacy.'

'Can they access the Nico Brownley profile?'

'No. It's been deactivated. The IP address used was a VPN – a virtual private network – which makes it impossible to track where the profile was set up.'

The room was silent. A phone started to ring and Moss picked it up.

'What about Lacey's mobile phone records?' asked Erika.

'We should be getting those after lunch,' said John.

'Okay, this is a start. I want you to look through Lacey's Facebook history and chat logs for anything that might lead us closer to whoever set up this fake profile of Nico Brownley. Find who else he had friended, get in contact with them.'

'Boss,' said Moss coming off the phone, 'that was British Transport Police. They've found a coffee bike abandoned near London Bridge. Looks unusual, so they're thinking it might be the one which belonged to Janelle.'

CHAPTER 30

An hour later, Erika and Moss arrived at London Bridge station. Alan Leonard, one of the project managers working on the redevelopment at London Bridge, met them on the paved concourse outside the station. He was a fresh-faced young man, rugged up for the cold with a hard hat hanging from his utility belt. It was now mid-morning and the concourse was fairly empty; only a few commuters were crossing in and out.

Erika introduced herself. 'And what the does the redevelopment include?'

'A new train station, development of the arches underneath, and of course, the Shard,' said Alan.

They tipped their heads back. Above them towered the huge glass skyscraper, one of its giant wrought-iron legs sitting flat-footed on the edge of the concourse.

'Ninety-five storeys,' he shouted above a deep buzz of drilling which had started up. They couldn't make out where it was coming from; it seemed to originate from both around and underneath them. 'It's 309.6 metres, 1,016 feet high,' he finished.

'And most of it's still empty. And will remain so, bought up by foreign investors?' shouted Moss.

'Always nice to meet a socialist in the flesh,' he said.

'I'm Detective Inspector Kate Moss,' she said, offering her hand. 'And yes, my mother really called me that, and no I don't ever get mistaken for her...'

He grinned. 'Well, I'm still going to tell my mates I met Kate Moss… Would you ladies like to go up to the top?'

Erika felt he was about to give them a guided tour, so she steered the conversation back to why they were there.

'Thank you, but we need to see this coffee bike.'

'Let's walk and talk,' he said, leading them across the concourse and around the front of the station into Tooley Street. 'Most of the businesses have vacated. The major structural work is now mostly being done underground… This is one of Europe's biggest civil engineering projects.'

They passed under the low railway bridge next to Borough Market and then they had a clear view of Southwark Bridge, the traffic pouring across and around the lights. Southwark Cathedral towered up beside the bridge, seemingly squashed in as an afterthought.

'We work under very strict conditions,' he said. 'When we demolish, clear or excavate, we have to catalogue everything we find, and dispose of it properly. Your coffee bike had been sitting there for the past few months…'

'Where was it?' asked Erika as they took a sloped diversion across where the road and pavement had been dug up, exposing a huge hole and an ancient network of rusting pipes.

'The London Dungeon, the old site. It's now moved to the South Bank,' he said.

They continued along Tooley Street, weaving along ramps above the excavated pavement. The empty road was also closed off and filled with earth movers, electrical cables, and builders shouting above the noise. They passed one of the entrances to London Bridge station, and then reached a large boarded-up door, where above two stone columns could faintly still be read the words:

Enter at your peril.

'This was the main entrance to the dungeon, but the only access is further down,' shouted Alan.

They carried on walking, past a bar, and a bike shop, both abandoned and boarded up. They reached a junction road emerging from a tunnel, and the works finished. Alan opened the barrier for them, and they stepped onto the pavement.

'It's halfway down,' he said.

They started down the tunnel, which was damp and bare, clad in stained concrete, with a line of swinging lights. Only one person passed them: a man togged in winter gear on a mountain bike.

Alan came to a stop by a rusty fire exit, and took a key from his utility belt. He opened it with a scrape and they went through into the dim gloom. Inside was a bizarre sight: a Victorian cobbled street ran the length of the space, about twelve metres in length, and there was a wrought-iron street lamp against a kerb. The lamp was on, and it cast a weak flickering light over the space. Next to the lamp was parked a coffee bike. A gleaming silver contraption with a wooden box mounted on the back. In front of it, in the centre of the cobbles, was a bundle of what looked like rubbish.

'Hard hats, please,' said Alan, handing them each one from a pile in the corner.

A large wooden door to the left was bolted shut. The temperature was freezing. He passed them each a torch too.

'Jesus Christ!' said Moss as the light from her torch played over the pile of what they had thought was rubbish.

It was the body of a woman, bundled up in filthy clothes, and her face was still in anguish. Moss instinctively reached for her radio to call for backup, but Erika put a hand on her shoulder, training her own torch onto the woman.

'Moss. It's not real. Look. It's a wax figure.'

They moved closer.

'She's so realistic,' said Moss, peering down at the woman's anguished face and noting the detail: the stained teeth protruding from her mouth; the hair poking out from under a greying bonnet.

'This was the Jack the Ripper section of the London Dungeon tour,' said Alan. 'An actor dressed as a policeman would usher the tour group inside, tell them all about the Ripper's first victim. That's the body of Mary Nichols, found in Buck's Row, Whitechapel.'

Erika shone her torch onto the wall and they saw a road sign painted in black. Despite knowing this was all an illusion, Erika felt her heart beginning to pound.

'She's not real, but she is. She was a real person,' said Moss. 'As real as Lacey Greene and Janelle Robertson.'

'Why is this all still here?' asked Erika.

'The site is being redeveloped, so the London Dungeon moved to the South Bank. This interior is due to be ripped out next week.'

Erika was feeling chilled; she forced herself to focus on the bike, leaning on its stand next to the lamp post.

Alan went on: 'I'm in contact with the British Transport Police every day, because the tube and train stations have to remain open during all of this construction. I heard they were looking for a coffee bike and remembered this.'

Erika and Moss pulled on their latex gloves, and moved to look at the coffee bike. Alan trained his torch onto it. The wooden box at the back was padlocked.

'Have you got a bolt cutter?' asked Erika.

Alan went to the corner and found a pair. Erika took them and clipped open the padlock. Moss unhooked it, and they carefully opened the wooden box at the back. The top of the box tipped back onto the bike seat, and the two sides came apart in flaps and hung down over the back wheel. Printed on the inside was the price list. Inside the box was a small shelf with a metal coffee machine, a tiny fridge, paper cups, condiments and a small cash box.

'Jeez,' said Moss, opening the fridge and quickly closing it. 'That milk has been in there a long time.'

The nasty smell of sour milk wafted over, and Erika felt her stomach lurch. She gulped and ran her hands along the sides of the coffee machine, and came into contact with something. She gently teased out an iPhone.

'Janelle's?' said Moss, her eyes lighting up.

There was a compartment under the coffee machine where clothes were neatly stashed. A pair of jeans, some tops, bras and pants. There was also a small washbag.

'Can we see a key for this cash box?' asked Moss, lifting it up. 'Jeez, this has to be Janelle's.'

Alan watched from his spot by the fire exit.

'And who has access here?' asked Erika.

'There's a security team who patrol every twenty-four hours, but this is a very strange site. There's all sorts of props still left over from when it was a working attraction. They just assumed that the bike was part of the tour, along with the body and the cobbled street.'

'They thought that during Jack the Ripper's era you could get a takeaway macchiato?' asked Moss.

Alan nodded wearily. 'We have a lot of foreign workers.'

'Can you find out when the bike appeared here?' asked Erika.

'I don't know. The staff turnover is huge; we use multiple agencies. I'll try.'

'Thank you.'

Erika looked around at the gloomy space and back to the wax body of Mary Nichols lying at the base of the stairs.

'Let's get this closed off. I want the whole area printed, and the bike going over with a fine-tooth comb.'

CHAPTER 31

Erika was back at West End Central, and had gone to see Melanie in her office. It was now dark outside.

'The coffee bike belongs to Janelle Robinson,' said Erika. 'It's been positively ID'd by a friend who worked at the Barbican YMCA where Janelle was living. We also found Janelle's mobile phone with the bike, and her clothes and toiletries.'

Melanie sat back in her chair. She looked tired.

'Hang on, hang on,' she said, putting up a hand. 'Why was she hocking her clothes and toiletries in a coffee bike?'

'Well, according to the friend...'

'Whose name is?'

'Sada Pencci she tells us Janelle had a real thing about not leaving her belongings anywhere. It started when she was in the children's home.'

'Okay. Have you managed to get anything off Janelle's phone?'

'It's being rushed through with the technical team... I've also just had word that we've found Lacey Greene's mobile phone.'

'Where?'

'On a piece of scrubland five hundred yards down from the Blue Boar pub. Looks like it was thrown there. It was switched off. We're running it for prints.'

'You still think these cases are linked?' asked Melanie.

'Of course,' said Erika. She was exhausted, both from the past few days and from Melanie's belief that they still had to prove a link.

'Do you have anything to back this theory up?'

'We're now working on the theory that Janelle was abducted near the Tooley Street tunnel,' explained Erika.

'But you have nothing concrete to suggest this? No CCTV images, no eyewitnesses?'

'Not yet.'

'This coffee bike could have been stolen; she could have left it in the tunnel.'

'It was her main source of income.'

'Yes, but unless we have concrete evidence that she was abducted…'

'She *was* abducted, Melanie. Janelle and Lacey died in exactly the same way. Their wounds indicate they were tortured for several days. They'd lost weight, and they both died from catastrophic blood loss from severing of the femoral artery… I need more officers on this. If I'd had more uniformed officers, Lacey Greene's phone might have been found days ago. The only reason it was found was because uniform arrested a couple of kids this afternoon doing drugs on that piece of wasteland. I've had to sweet talk two other boroughs to do door-to-doors in Croydon and Southgate.'

'Erika, you have six officers and four support staff working directly for you…'

'It's not enough.'

'Do you have any idea what this job is like?' said Melanie, unable to hide her anger. 'There are finite resources. You think I'm against you, I'm not. I fought for you to keep John McGorry.'

'John, why? What happened?'

'I had a call from Superintendent Yale, wanting him back. It's okay, he's not going anywhere, but you will have to work with what you've got.'

'What if this person abducts another young woman?'

'If he does, then of course, Erika, I will throw every resource your way,' she said, then went back to work at her computer. 'We're done here.'

Erika started to leave, then came back to the desk.

'Melanie, I've worked on so many cases like this. I'm not saying we have a serial killer, but there is a pattern. Two murders, just over four months apart. Now there may be others we don't know about...'

'And we both know how these cases work. He might vanish; he might not kill again for a year... Yes, perhaps he does it again, but I can't plan my budgets for might do and perhaps.'

'That's ridiculous. The whole counterterrorism unit works on that principle!'

'Well, Erika, we can't.'

Erika paced up and down in front of the window.

'I'd like approval to do a media appeal.'

'We've got the e-fit up on news outlets and Twitter.'

'Who goes on bloody Twitter to help the police solve crimes!?' shouted Erika.

'Remember who you're talking to. I'm your senior officer. I may be Acting Superintendent—'

'Sorry, can you please consider that we do a full media appeal.'

'For who?' asked Melanie.

'Janelle and Lacey. I'm not talking about a Crimewatch reconstruction, but a press conference. National news. If we haven't got the resources, let's get the public working for us. Put their disappearances in their minds, have them on the lookout.'

'Which means we open ourselves up to having another serial killer for the media to pounce on.'

'I don't want to mention serial killer, and I think there's enough other crap happening in the media right now. People are more concerned with who is President of the USA. Will another bogeyman faze them?' Melanie sat forward in her chair and laughed. Erika went on: 'I know you're taking a lot of shit from all quarters, but remember that part of being a police officer is preventing crime. Help me prevent this bastard from doing it again.'

'Okay, okay, I'll see what I can do.'

'Thank you.'

'By the way, Erika. Sparks's funeral is next Wednesday at 2 p.m. Thought you might like to know. St Michael's Church in Greenwich.'

'He was religious? I take it it's a burial?'

Melanie nodded. 'Yeah, he was Catholic. It's looking to be well attended; lots of people seem to be asking for time off. You going?'

'I'll think about it,' said Erika, averting her eyes from the patch of carpet in front of the desk. 'One more thing. You haven't heard from Commander Marsh?'

'No. I've been briefing Acting Commander Mason; he's been put in place for now.'

'What do you mean "put in place"?'

'Since Marsh has been suspended... You didn't know?'

'No. I've been trying to call him. Why has he been suspended?'

Melanie's phone rang. 'Sorry, I don't know. I have to take this. Can you close the door on your way out?'

Erika came back out into the office, where, despite the late hour, it was still busy. So Marsh had been suspended; why hadn't he told her? She pulled out her phone and tried him again, but the call went to voicemail.

CHAPTER 32

It was Saturday night. Things had accelerated with Ella Wilkinson after Darryl spoke to her on the phone. Ella had believed she was talking to Harry Gordon, and had said she would love for them to meet. He knew that her enthusiasm might be short-lived, and when she was enthusiastic, she would be easier to manipulate. He arranged to meet near where she lived, close to Angel in North London. It was a good location, packed with edgy bars and restaurants near a sprawl of residential streets. There were huge risks involved with being so central, but to Darryl it was all about perspective. He had manipulated the situation so that Ella believed she was the one in control; she'd friended him, she'd suggested they speak on the phone, and then she'd suggested that they meet... and meeting on her turf would make her even more relaxed.

At 7.40 p.m., Darryl turned into Weston Street, relieved to see it wasn't busy. It was a quiet road, a few streets back from Angel tube station, and there was a cool indie bar at the end – just the kind of cool place someone sexy like Harry Gordon would take a first date. The snow was just starting to melt and he could hear the sound of the slush under the wheels of the car. He'd checked online where the major CCTV cameras were placed, and he had managed to avoid most of them. He hadn't been able to avoid the Congestion Charge Zone cameras coming into London, but that only mattered if they were looking for him. Where he was due to meet Ella was clear of CCTV cameras for a few streets, and providing no one saw him grab her, he was home free.

He drove past the bar, which was on the corner of a main road and a quiet street of houses. Quite a few houses had their lights on, but this was a cold night, a cold Saturday night, and they had better things to do than peer out of their windows. He slowed when a taxi appeared in his rear-view mirror, and he pulled over to let it pass. The road was deserted again. He gripped the steering wheel with his leather-gloved hands, and took deep breaths.

He only had one chance to do this. He drove around the block a couple of times and then parked a hundred yards down from the bar, switching off his engine and lights. The bar was playing music, but it looked quiet. The smoked glass windows glowed red, and cast a hue over the snow-covered pavement. A bouncer was stationed outside in a huge coat and woolly hat, but he was absorbed in his phone.

The minutes ticked by, as Darryl sat in the dark. The car growing colder, his breath coming out in a stream of vapour, and then he saw her.

Ella Wilkinson appeared further down the street. She wore a long coat, boots and had a bag slung over her shoulder. Her long dark hair flowed behind her as she moved with purpose toward the bar. She wasn't wearing a scarf or a hat; clearly, she wanted her body to be seen, appreciated.

He reached down to the ignition, started the car and pulled out, passing the bar where Ella stood waiting on the corner. His heart skipped a little. *She came! She's really there to meet me!* he thought. Then he felt anger. She was there to meet Harry Gordon. He indicated and slowed, turning right into a side street, parking at the kerb. The entrance to the bar was now just around the corner, where soft red light was spilling out into the darkness and onto Ella waiting on the icy pavement. She shifted onto her other leg and checked her watch. Her striking beauty took his breath away, and he started to sweat despite the cold in the car.

Another taxi came rattling round the corner and trundled past. He used the delay to reach into the glove compartment and pull out a map. Underneath was a square leather sap with white stitching. He felt its weight in his hand. When the taxi passed he checked the road. He was parked in a pool of shadows just a few yards down from the corner. There were no lights on in the houses either side.

He took a deep breath. It wasn't too late… He could just go. His heart raced and he felt sick, but the adrenalin was pumping through him, and he looked back at Ella, waiting, for him. Keeping the sap under the map, he opened the door and got out.

CHAPTER 33

Ella Wilkinson checked her watch. It was quarter past eight. Her date, Harry, had said he'd be here at eight. She was freezing cold, waiting on the pavement outside the bar, and it was eerily quiet. Behind her a tall, dark-haired bouncer was shifting on his feet in the doorway, absorbed in a game on his phone. A low hum of chatter, and the click-clack of pool balls floated over. She glanced round, and the bouncer looked her up and down, taking in her low-cut black top and skinny jeans. She turned away again, buttoning up her coat, a sense of unease growing inside her.

When she'd left the house, her housemate, Maggie, had been lying in front of the TV wearing her tartan pyjamas, ready to watch *The Voice*.

'Ella, at least put on a scarf and a woolly hat. No man's worth getting pneumonia for,' she'd said, peering over her little round glasses.

'This is the first time he'll see me properly, not just from pictures online. I want to look even better in the flesh,' she'd replied, twirling her hand over her cleavage in the low-cut black top. 'First impressions are important.'

'His first impression will be that you're a sure thing,' Maggie replied. 'Text me when you get there, and text me if you stay out?'

'Course I will.'

'You promise?'

'I promise.'

Feeling the bouncer's gaze on her back, Ella opened her bag, and rummaged inside for her phone.

'Sorry, excuse me,' said a voice. She turned. A strange geeky-looking guy with brown hair was standing in the shadows, just around the corner of the building. He wore an ill-fitting black suit with a spotted bow tie. She ignored him and turned back to her phone.

'Sorry to bother you, hello? Can you help me?' he asked.

She turned back again as he moved closer into the pool of light cast by the streetlights. He was holding up a map and squinting. 'I'm trying to find the Hooligans theme pub? I'm singing there tonight for a birthday party.'

You look more like a bad comedian than a singer, she thought.

'Hooligans is further down there, towards Angel tube,' she said, pointing dismissively. Her hands were now numb. She turned back to her phone and opened her messages.

'Look, I'm so sorry to pester you, but I've got no clue about London; can you show me on the map?' he said. He had the map opened out on top of a car by the kerb, and was wrestling comically with the paper in the cold breeze. 'I'm supposed to be on stage any minute for a ninetieth birthday... I have to get there before the old girl kicks the bucket!' He looked up at her and grinned.

Despite everything, she grinned back.

'Go on. Make it quick, I'm freezing,' she said, slipping her phone back into her bag and moving over to him. 'Haven't you got GPS?'

'I should do... But I'm a bit of a technophobe,' he said, starting to fold up the map. 'I'm not from round here. If you can just show me quickly, I'm running a bit late.'

'Why are you putting the map away?' she said.

He folded it down to the last square, and placed it on the roof of the car.

'Harry's not coming to meet you,' he said.

'What?'

He was staring at her intently, his geeky amiable face now hard. Before she could say anything more, he raised his arm and she felt something hit her on the back of the head, and then everything went black.

CHAPTER 34

Darryl caught Ella before she slid down between the car and the kerb. Moving quickly, he dragged her limp body round to the boot, opened it and placed her neatly on the dark green bath towels he had laid out in preparation.

The bar around the corner remained quiet, but the road lit up behind with a car's headlights, and he quickly closed the boot. The car whooshed past, indicating right at the junction before pulling out. Darryl spied one of Ella's high heels in the kerb by the back wheel. He retrieved it and got in the car.

He'd been torn; he knew he'd had to move fast, to knock her out and get her in the car, but she'd looked so beautiful. He'd never seen her so close up, her green eyes were cat-like, and the smell of her perfume mixed in with the smell of her shampoo had wafted over. Mangoes. She had really gone to town for Harry.

He started the engine and pulled away, driving along a little way and then taking a left into a quiet cul-de-sac ending with a row of lock-up garages. He pulled into the shadows and got out. When he opened the boot, Ella lay on her side, moaning, her eyes fluttering. He punched her in the face, once, twice and had to stop himself giving her a third fist as her nose started to bleed. He took out a pale flannel which had his initials embroidered in red, and stuffed it into her mouth. Then he taped it over with silver masking tape, looping it around the back of her head twice. He bound her wrists tightly, and her legs, then finally he put a grain sack over her head and tied it loosely at the neck. He checked the pockets of her coat, and grabbed her bag still hooked over her arm. He took out her mobile and turned it off, then slipped it back into the bag. He covered her with a blanket and closed the boot, not forgetting to add the shoe which had fallen off.

He checked the cul-de-sac. Lights were on in the upstairs window in one house. He walked along the lock-up garages to the end, and then chucked her handbag down a tiny, rubbish-filled alleyway.

Darryl got back into the car, adjusted the rear-view mirror, did a U-turn, and started the long drive back to the farm.

CHAPTER 35

Fresh snow started to fall when Darryl reached the M25, and despite the late hour, traffic was heavy. He kept some distance from the car in front, but a small blue Honda kept on his tail, just as impatient as he was to get home. Every time the traffic surged forward he worried that the driver would misjudge his speed and road conditions and slam into the back of him.

It wasn't until he pulled off at the junction to the M20 that he relaxed. The road was empty, save for a gritter which rumbled past on the other carriageway. He drove past the front gates of the farm, and along the quiet road for a few minutes. He had the wipers on, but the snow was now coming down so thick that he almost drove past a gate in between two hedgerows. He turned too fast, and had to slam on the brakes. The car slowed, but nudged into the metal bars with a nasty crunch.

'Shit!' he shouted, getting out. He went around to the front of the car. The hood was slightly puckered and the paintwork scratched. 'Shit!' He opened the gate, drove the car through onto the edge of a snow-covered track, then closed it.

He had wanted to turn off the headlights on the half mile stretch of track, but visibility was dreadful and he didn't want to risk straying into a ditch. The half mile seemed to go on forever as the car creaked and lurched, the wheels sticking a couple of times and spinning on the snow. Eventually the Oast House appeared around a bank of bare trees. The round tower with the funnel-shaped chimney looked grey and alien lit up by the car headlights. He passed the trees and drew up to the tall round tower, killing the lights and the engine.

The wind roaring across the open fields shook the car, and when he climbed out he could hear the moaning sound as it blew across the spout-like chimney. Darryl waited until his eyes became accustomed to the dark and then went to the back seat of the car, taking out a metal steering wheel lock. Janelle Robinson had surprised him, kicking and scratching when he'd gone to get her out of the boot. Back in August, he'd been winging it when he'd abducted her, with no plan, and she'd fought him hard, almost getting away.

He went to the boot of the car, wiped away the snow and leaned down to listen. Nothing. He gripped the wheel lock, and pulled it open. Snow immediately began to cover the blanket over Ella. He peeled it away, and couldn't tell if her chest was moving. He pulled off the grain sack and saw she was very pale. He pressed the wheel lock into her ribs; there was a faint moan, *She was still alive.*

'I'm going to lift you out now,' he said, having to raise his voice above the wind and the moaning tower. 'If you're good you'll have shelter, and you can have some water.'

He leaned in, hooked one hand under her neck and the other under her legs, and heaved her out. She was taller and heavier than he'd expected. He shuffled through the snow to a large metal sliding door at the base of the circular tower. He put her down on the floor and took out a set of keys, finding the correct one, and opening a padlock. He slid the door open, and picked Ella up off the floor. It was cold inside, but not freezing. There was an electric light which he flicked on with his elbow, a bare bulb attached to the wall.

In the centre of the circular room was a small furnace chamber where the fire had once been lit. There was a small door into it, and its walls went straight up for six feet or so before spreading out like an inverted funnel to meet the ceiling. Darryl used his foot to open the door. Inside the furnace chamber it was a windowless square of red brick, three metres by three, and scorched by years of fires. Above it was a thick metal grate, leading to the inverted funnel of bricks, where the heat rose, drying the hops in a small chamber above. Above this chamber was a series of vents leading up to the conical-shaped funnel, or cowl.

Darryl had placed a large cage in the centre of the chamber, which had originally been used for transporting Grendel to the vet. He'd lined the bottom with blankets. He ducked down, and placed Ella inside the cage. He peeled the tape away from her mouth. He could just make out in the gloom that her nose was crusted with dried blood. She moaned.

Two lengths of chain and padlocks were hooked over one side of the cage. He wound one around her neck and looped it through the bars of the cage before padlocking it. In one corner of the cage was a large two litre bottle of water, which he placed beside her hands.

He came out of the cage and went to a table in the corner where there was a small orange plastic box. He opened it, and prepared a 10ml syringe of Ketalar. He moved back inside, and could see that her eyes were now open and darting around, confused. She tried to talk, but her mouth was dry. He opened the bottle of water and offered her some.

'Go on, it's water,' he said.

She took a sip and swallowed.

'Who are you?' she croaked. 'Where am I?'

'I'm just going to roll up this sleeve,' he said, pulling up the thick sleeve of her fur coat.

'Where am I?' she croaked. 'Please. Why are you doing this?'

He kneeled on her bound legs, and she squealed. With his free hand he pinned her against the bars of the cage and slid the needle into her bare arm, slowly pushing the drug into her vein.

He removed the needle and applied pressure with his thumb. She groaned and her eyes rolled back.

She went limp and he removed his thumb, sucking the small drop of her blood from its tip. Taking the second chain, he wound it around her wrists and padlocked it to the bars opposite. He taped up her mouth again, and tucked the blankets around her.

'There. You get some rest. You'll need your wits about you… You're on a date with Harry. Harry Gordon.' He smiled.

He came out of the furnace chamber and closed the door. Then, switching off the light, he left the Oast House, and slid the door shut with a soft clang. He fastened the padlock, and drove back down to the road.

It was warm when he entered the boot room, and Grendel came bounding up and licked his hand. His parents were in the living room watching television when he poked his head through the door. His father was bolt upright in his armchair by the window, and his mother lay on the sofa with a large gin and tonic. They were watching an episode of *Inspector Morse* on ITV4.

'Alright love,' said Mary, her eyes not leaving the screen. The fake flame fire rippled in the fireplace, throwing reddish light along the wall with the television. The picture cut out on the large flat-screen TV and went black. 'For God's sake,' she added.

'Now, let's see who this is,' said John, picking up the remote and leaning forward eagerly.

Mary got up unsteadily and shuffled over to the small bar at the back of the living room by the bay window. The CCTV cameras on the front gate and yard were motion activated, and the picture was beamed through to the living room TV.

'Would you fill this up, love?' said Mary, holding out the little ice bucket to Darryl.

On the screen a white van had stopped outside the front gates. It inched forward and the gates began to open. The CCTV angle changed to a close-up of the side of the van, where two lads inside were looking up the driveway, weighing up their options. Their features were a ghostly green and eyes two white circles in the night-vision camera.

'They'll be on their way if they know what's best for them,' said John.

On the television, the van sat there for a moment, then slowly reversed and drove away, as the gates swung shut. The screen flicked back to the episode of *Inspector Morse*.

'Gyppos,' said John. 'Up to no good.'

'Perhaps they're lost,' slurred Mary, settling back down into the sofa.

'You didn't see anything odd when you just drove back in?' asked John over his shoulder as Darryl left to fetch the ice.

'Nothing…'

'Did you have a nice drink at the pub?' asked Mary.

'Yeah. I met up with a couple of mates…'

He didn't bother to continue, they were both absorbed by *Inspector Morse*. Darryl watched them for a moment, bathed in the glow on the television, lost in the fictitious world of murder, unaware of the reality at the bottom of the yard.

CHAPTER 36

Erika's phone rang early on Sunday morning. She opened her eyes, disorientated, and saw Peterson's smooth dark muscular back beside her. She'd stayed over at his flat, and it took her a minute to remember her phone wasn't plugged in beside the bed, but in the kitchen. She padded through just as it stopped ringing. It was Crane, and she called him back.

'Boss?' he answered. 'I've got CCTV footage of Janelle Robinson. I think it's the night she vanished.'

'Where are you?'

'I'm at the nick, I've been up all night.'

'Okay, I'll grab you some breakfast, and I can be there asap.' She hung up.

Peterson appeared in the doorway, bleary-eyed, pulling on a dressing gown.

'Who was that?'

'Crane thinks he has footage of Janelle's abduction. I need to dash,' said Erika, moving to the sink and running the water. She filled up a glass and was taking a drink when she noticed the curtains were open. A couple of old ladies were standing at the bus stop on the road out front, peering in and tut-tutting. She looked down and saw she was only wearing her knickers. 'Bollocks!' she said, ducking down. Peterson went to the window and pulled the curtains shut. He started to laugh. 'It's not funny.'

'That's Mrs Harper. She lives in the flat next door,' he said. 'She's probably on her way to do the church flowers.'

'Great, so I can't show my face here again,' said Erika.

'You've shown her pretty much everything else!' he laughed. He went to her and took the glass from her hand and gave her a kiss. 'I'm glad you stayed over.'

'Me too,' she said. She pushed the ever-present spectre of guilt from her mind. Guilt that she had enjoyed herself. Guilt that for a few hours she hadn't thought about Mark. She looked up at Peterson and she could see he was reading her thoughts.

'Let's get going,' he said.

Erika and Peterson arrived at the incident room at West End Central an hour later, with hot coffee and pastries. Crane was looking dishevelled, with a day's stubble.

'Thanks, I'm starving,' he said, pulling out a chocolate croissant and taking a big bite. He took them to the laptop set up on his desk and opened a video file. 'There's a CCTV camera on the roof of a building on Bermondsey Street, which approaches the tunnel on the opposite side from Tooley Street. I found this from Wednesday the twenty-fourth of August.'

He clicked 'play': the road was empty for a moment, and then there was a back view of a girl with long brown hair, riding the coffee bike into the tunnel, where she was swallowed by the darkness. The timestamp on the video was 7.32 p.m. Moments later a red car followed her.

'Run it back a second,' said Erika.

Crane ran it back to where the car was approaching the tunnel. 'Stop. Look.'

'Shit. The plates are obscured,' said Peterson.

'Yeah. The car's filthy, splattered in mud,' said Crane.

'Bloody hell,' said Erika. 'And no one stopped him?'

'Hang on. Let's keep watching,' said Crane. He maximised another screen beside the car going into the tunnel. 'Here we have a CCTV camera on the other side of the tunnel. I'll run them both from 7.31 p.m...'

On the left-hand screen Janelle biked into the tunnel, followed by the car. They looked to the right-hand screen. Crane forwarded both timestamps, moving on both screens by seventeen minutes to 7:48 p.m. The red car emerged from the tunnel. Alone.

Erika stared at both screens, feeling a chill.

'How long after this have you run the two camera views?'

'Twenty-four hours, boss. No girl or bike emerges from either side of the tunnel,' said Crane.

'So the bastard had her in the back or in the boot of the car,' said Erika.

'Where does the car go?' asked Peterson.

'It avoids the Congestion Charge Zone camera. I'm going to see how far I can follow him through London. It's going to take a bit of time. It might be that he was stopped by police for having his numberplates obscured.'

'It was a Wednesday night,' said Erika.

'It would be on record... He'd have a fixed penalty fine,' said Crane.

'It's virtually impossible to avoid CCTV in Central London,' said Erika.

'But he's managed to get in and out twice without us having his registration number?' said Peterson.

'He's deliberately muddied his plates, hasn't he?' said Erika. 'Risky.'

'But he's abducting women. The level of risk involved must get his adrenalin pumping. And he's been lucky so far,' said Peterson.

'But luck runs outs eventually. And we have to be there waiting and ready when it does.' Erika watched again as Crane played the video of Janelle biking into the tunnel closely followed by the red car. They'd never know exactly what happened to Janelle in those seventeen minutes.

It was as if she vanished into thin air.

CHAPTER 37

Ella Wilkinson's housemate, Maggie, woke late on Sunday morning. She'd gone to bed early and slept until mid-morning. When she emerged from her room onto the landing, all was quiet. This wasn't unusual for a Sunday morning, but she didn't have any missed calls or texts on her phone, and Ella's bedroom door was open. Maggie passed the wooden bannister where their towels hung in a line, ready to be grabbed on the way to the shower. Ella's room was next to the bathroom. Maggie knocked and peered her head around. The bed was made, and still strewn with the outfits she'd been trying on the night before. Their other housemate, Doug, was on holiday with his girlfriend, and his door was open too. Maggie stood at the top of the stairs, feeling uneasy. She shook it away and went down to the kitchen.

As the morning and afternoon passed, she tried Ella's phone several times, and when she still wasn't picking up, her unease changed to panic. Ella was always glued to her phone. She would have texted to say she wouldn't be coming back.

At five p.m, just as the light was starting to fade, Maggie pulled on her thick winter jacket and walked over to the bar. The door was locked, but she peered through the window and saw a woman, wearing yellow marigolds, mopping the floor, and a young guy unloading bottles into the fridge. She knocked on the window. At first, they ignored her, but then as she was more insistent the woman finally came and opened up.

'What is it?' she snapped.

'Sorry to bother you. I live around the corner... My friend was here last night, and she hasn't come home...'

'How old is your friend?' she asked. She had a wrinkly smoker's face and a bristly bob of dark greying hair.

'She's twenty.'

The woman smirked. 'Well, she probably met some bloke. Now, I've got work to do.'

She went to shut the door. Maggie held out her hand.

'No. That's not good enough. Can I ask your barman? I have a photo of my friend.'

The woman eyed her suspiciously, then decided that a plump girl with a thick jacket and her tartan pyjamas sticking out of the bottom wasn't much of a threat. She opened the door.

It was a popular bar, but it looked sad in the fading light of day. The tables were stacked with chairs, and there was a strong smell of disinfectant.

'Sam, this girl wants to ask you something,' snapped the woman, picking up a plastic bucket and heading off through a door behind the bar.

Sam was handsome, with a nose ring and a shock of dyed blond hair. He smiled warmly.

'Who's your friend?' he asked. He had a soft Aussie accent.

'This is her, Ella Wilkinson,' said Maggie, holding up her phone, where Ella's picture was displayed on Facebook. She felt foolish talking to the hot barman in her coat and pyjamas. 'She was due to come here last night around eight. Was she here?'

He looked at the photo and shook his head.

'No. She's a pretty girl; I'd have remembered her.'

'You're positive she didn't come in here last night?'

'Yeah…' He saw her worried face. Her hair on end. 'The bouncer who was on last night has just rocked up. Let me give him a shout.'

Sam went to the door where the cleaner had left, and shouted for a man called Roman. Moments later a large beefy guy with a monobrow and a shaved head appeared, holding a steaming Pot Noodle.

'Vat?' he said with a thick Russian accent.

Sam explained the situation, and brought him over to Maggie. Roman took her phone in a large hairy hand and studied Ella's photo.

'Yes, she vas vaiting outside last night,' he said.

'She didn't come in?' asked Maggie.

He shook his head. 'No. She vas there and then she vasn't.'

'Where did she go?' asked Maggie.

'I don't bloody know. I vas working.' He stuffed a forkful of Pot Noodle into his mouth and walked off.

Sam smiled apologetically.

Maggie came back out of the bar. It was now getting dark. She looked up and down the street, and felt hopeless. She tried Ella's phone again but it went straight to voicemail. She saw that the road running next to the bar was a cul-de-sac. She set off down it and came up to the dead end, where there was a row of lock-up garages. They were all closed, and it was empty. She walked towards a row of evergreens by the last garage. She pulled the neck of her coat up against the wind.

'This is stupid. She's probably been having sex all day,' muttered Maggie. She turned to leave, then spied a flash of white and brown in the small passage between the last garage and the line of evergreens.

She pushed her way down, stepping over old bricks and rubbish and saw a handbag. Ella's handbag. It had a streak of blood on the front. When she opened it she found Ella's wallet, keys and phone.

She hugged it to her chest and started to cry.

CHAPTER 38

Darryl woke early on Monday morning and took Grendel for a walk. It was dark, and the wind blew softly over the fields, pushing the powder-dry snow into undulating drifts. When he reached the Oast House, he undid the padlock on the door and pulled it back. Grendel went in first, sniffing the frigid air and around the door in the furnace. The wind screamed across the top of the cowl.

He switched on the light, and opened the door to the furnace. Ella shifted in the cage and blinked, and began to wail in concert with the wind. She shivered, bound at the neck and wrists to the cage. One of her eyes was swollen shut. Grendel moved round the cage, sniffing at the back of her head. Ella tried to pull her head away from the bars, and Grendel gave a low rumbling growl.

'Please, please...' she started.

'It's alright. She can't hurt you,' said Darryl. Ella kept her eyes on him, shifting her head painfully when he crossed behind her to pat Grendel's head.

'Put your hands up,' he said.

'No, no, no, no more, please...'

'I'm not going to hurt you. Put your hands up. Now.'

She lifted up bloody hands with dirty fingernails, and jumped as he slid a small bottle of water through the bars.

'Take it, and drink,' he said. She took it between her bound hands. He watched as she checked it, and seeing it was still sealed she put it between her bare knees and winced as she opened it with a clink of the chains, then lifted her hands to her mouth and drank.

'Thank you,' she said breathlessly. Darryl moved back around the cage to face her. 'My parents have money,' she said. 'They'll pay.'

He crouched down on his haunches, and looked at her. Noticing how the light from outside the furnace chamber threw the squares of the bars over her face.

'I don't want money... Your friend is worried about you.'

'Friend?'

'One of the blonde skanks you work with at the café. With the trampy wrist tattoos.'

'Cerys? How do you know Cerys?' she said.

'I know Cerys, because *I know you*. You think I just grabbed you for the fun of it? You really don't remember me, do you?'

Her one good eye darted about, trying to conjure up where she'd seen him.

'I came into the café so many times, so many lunchtimes; you always had a smile for me, asked me how I was...'

'Oh, yes. Yes, I remember.'

'What's my name?'

'I, I...' She shook her head, and fresh tears appeared in her swollen eyes.

'Come on, Ella. You wrote it on my coffee cup, so many times...'

'I know it; I'm just tired and hungry...'

'LIAR!' he shouted, slamming his hand down on top of the cage. 'You fucking LIAR! You don't know me. You don't care.'

Grendel started to bark and circle the cage, agitated.

'I do care, I could get to know you and care, if you give me the chance. I could, I'm sure...'

Darryl got up and paced around the cage, mirroring Grendel. 'We talked about stuff, Ella. I told you that I lived on a farm, and that our milk was organic... I told you about my dog... You're just like them all.'

'No. I promise, I'm not!'

'You are. Another pretty bitch. A bitch who plays with men; you make us think you like us but you don't. You just want to play with us. Use us!' He was screaming at her now, his piggy eyes wide. Grendel joined in with a volley of barks. Darryl stopped and composed himself. He crouched back down beside the cage. Calm. He leaned into her. 'Ella. If you could have at least remembered my name, I would have let you go. But no. You're going to die, Ella.'

She spat at him, and it landed on his face.

'You're a creepy little freak. No woman would ever go near you!' she screamed.

He crossed behind her and he grabbed the chain, yanking it back so that her neck was pressed against the bars and she began to choke. She scrabbled with her hands, but the chain binding her wrists stopped them inches from her chest. Finally, when her face was turning blue, he let go, and she fell forward, coughing and gagging. He opened the door and Grendel trotted out.

'No one is looking for you; no one cares,' he said. Darryl left the furnace chamber and turned out the light.

He heaved the large sliding door closed, padlocked it and followed after Grendel, down towards the lake.

Darryl returned to the farm house at seven, had his breakfast then caught the eight a.m. train to London.

At lunchtime he went to the Bay Organic Café. It was busy with office workers picking at the salad bar. He dawdled over the baskets of bread, listening to Ella's colleague, Cerys, who was working behind the checkout, talking to a man who he presumed was the manager.

'It doesn't take much to pick up the phone, does it?' she was saying. She looked a little like Ella, although not quite as pretty. The manager was handsome with floppy dark hair, and he was struggling to change the till roll. He muttered something non-committal as Cerys went on: 'Ella's not committed. Students live in a fantasy land of parties and booze. I even heard her talk about drugs.'

She had her hand on one hip, and was twirling a strand of her long blonde hair as she spoke. *Her only priority is to get into the manager's trousers*, thought Darryl. He approached the checkout counter. The manager was now finished with the till roll.

'I was recommended Ella by a friend of her mum and dad,' he said. 'She's reliable. I don't understand why she hasn't called. I'm going to give them a buzz.'

Cerys turned to Darryl, but her eyes were on the manager as he retreated through a door at the back of the shop.

'Can I have a small cappuccino?' he said.

'What's the name?' she asked, picking up a paper cup and a black marker.

'Skank.'

She scribbled it down and then hesitated, looking up at him. 'Sorry, what's your name?'

'Surname is Skank, first name Cerys…' She looked confused, finally noticing him, the marker still poised above the cup. Darryl went on, 'My mistake, that's *your* name. Cerys Skank. Your manager is married, Cerys. With two small kids… Think about it.'

He left her with her mouth open, and went out onto Borough High Street. He knew what he'd just done was idiotic, but it was worth it to see the look on her face. All women were bitches, and you had to know how to treat them.

He thought of Ella back at the farm, and he knew tonight would be the night.

CHAPTER 39

Erika had been assigned a small room at the end of the communal office at West End Central. It barely fitted a desk, chair and a filing cabinet, and it had a thin window looking out over the rear of the building. She hadn't used it much, preferring to stay with the team in their glass-partitioned section, but this afternoon, with the press appeal looming, she needed some time and space to go through what she was going to say. She cared deeply about the victims, and like so many of the cases she had worked on over the years, it was not only the terrible circumstances of the victims' deaths which haunted her, it was the lives that had been snuffed out prematurely. Young women with so much life left to live: careers, babies, holidays, and all those joys now denied them.

There was a knock at the door and Peterson came in. He saw her face, and the desk strewn with paperwork.

'Hey, I've just had Colleen, the police media liaison, on the phone. There should be a good turnout from the press, so she wants to use the larger conference room at the Thistle Hotel in Marylebone.'

'Thanks,' she said. Peterson closed the door, moved behind her chair, and started to massage her neck.

'That's good, but not now,' she said, pushing his hands away.

'Erika. You're tense.'

'And you're at work. We're at work.' She ducked out from under his hands, and twisted the chair to face him.

His soft brown eyes narrowed. 'We're in your office, with the door closed.'

He twisted her chair back round, and started to work on her shoulders again.

'It's your bed... I'm not used to sleeping on such a soft bed,' she said, tipping her head back and enjoying the release on her tense shoulders.

'Erika, that's a really expensive memory foam mattress.'

There was a knock at the door and Moss entered, just as Erika said: 'Well, it's not hard enough for me...'

'Sorry, is this a bad time?' said Moss, looking between them. Peterson dropped his hands.

'No, we were... It's fine,' said Erika, sifting through the papers in front of her.

'And we were talking about my mattress, my mattress not being hard...' said Peterson, moving back around the desk.

'It's memory foam. The mattress. Very soft,' added Erika. There was an awkward pause.

'Thank God for that,' grinned Moss. 'Although I do have a friend who's tried Viagra, and he says it's changed his life... Another friend thinks laughter is the best medicine, but I suppose that's not very helpful when it's things going soft.'

'A soft mattress is very good for you,' said Peterson, a little defensively. Erika and Moss started to laugh. 'It is!'

'Come on, I'm only teasing,' said Moss, giving Peterson a nudge.

'Idiot.' He grinned. Erika was pleased they'd had the opportunity to laugh, even for a moment. It had broken the tension.

'Okay, okay, we're at work. Let's act like it,' she said.

'Of course, sorry,' said Moss. 'Right. I came in here to ask if Sada Pence from the YMCA, Janelle Robinson's friend, is taking part in the press appeal?'

'When I spoke to her, I got the impression she was the closest thing Janelle had to family,' said Peterson.

'Colleen has just found out that Sada has another job, working as a lap dancer at one of the seedier clubs in Soho,' said Moss.

'Shit,' said Erika. 'If we put her in front of the cameras, the press could dig around and use that as their angle…'

'Seedy double life of murder victim's best friend,' agreed Peterson.

'We've already got concerns about Lacey's past relationship with Geraldine Corn,' added Moss. 'You know how it works. If she was a lesbian, then it wouldn't matter as much, but the fact that she dated both men and women, well, that's just too much for the press who suddenly find themselves all moral and judgemental.'

'Okay. I can add something in, so I can appeal on behalf of Janelle,' said Erika. 'Tell Colleen that I can email something over to her in the next twenty minutes.'

'Yes, boss,' said Moss and she left the office.

Erika turned and stared out of the tiny window looking down to the small square of the concrete courtyard below.

'She had no one, Janelle. No one in life and no one in death,' said Erika. 'How does that happen? Some people's lives are so full of family and friends, and others walk through life alone.'

'You've got me,' said Peterson. 'You know that, don't you?'

'I wasn't talking about me…'

'I know.'

'Thanks, James… But I need to get on,' she said, her face still turned to the window.

Peterson left, closing the door. It was only then that Erika turned back and wiped away a tear.

CHAPTER 40

That afternoon, Erika went over to the Thistle Hotel where the media appeal was being set up in the large conference room. A line of huge windows looked out over the low grey sky and the traffic slowly churning around Marble Arch. She was taken through to see Lacey's parents, Charlotte and Don, who were waiting in a smaller adjacent room. They looked as if they'd shrunk in stature, sitting at a table with Colleen, a sturdy woman with short dark hair. Colleen was excellent at her job, but part of this meant that she disconnected from the situation, taking out the human element.

As Erika approached the table, they were looking at an iPad, where Colleen was swiping through the pictures of Lacey they'd chosen to use during the appeal. They were innocent, fun-loving shots: Lacey holding a tabby cat in the garden beside a bed of daffodils; Lacey's graduation photo where she beamed into the camera with a shiny face; and another of Lacey on the sofa, barefoot in a pale blue dressing gown.

'This one is lovely,' said Colleen, craning her head around to see it. 'I'd kill for thick shiny hair like that...' She saw Erika and said 'hello', then her phone rang and she excused herself.

Don and Charlotte watched Colleen as she left.

'That woman has a very unfortunate manner,' said Charlotte.

'Yes, I'll have a word with her,' said Erika. They could hear Colleen on the phone in the corridor outside, telling a journalist he should hurry up, as she'd saved him a 'front row' seat.

'Thank you for doing this, Mr and Mrs Greene,' said Erika, sitting in Colleen's vacated chair. 'I won't ask how you're holding up, I know this must be terribly difficult.'

'Is this just a show to everyone?' said Don. 'I can't help feeling we're just entertainment.'

'I can assure you nothing about this is entertaining,' said Erika. 'Colleen's manner might not be user-friendly, but she's doing all this to ensure as many news outlets as possible have the information of your daughter's death.'

They absorbed that for a moment.

'What about the other girl? Where are her family?' asked Charlotte. Erika briefly explained Janelle's circumstances. 'I know it sounds awful, but I was looking forward to meeting Janelle's mother. It feels like no one knows what I'm going through. I thought she might—'

'You said you'd catch the person who did this to our Lacey,' demanded Don. 'What's happening?'

'I won't lie to you. This person is good at covering his tracks; he seems to know London, and until now he's had luck on his side…'

'You're sure it's a "he"?' asked Charlotte.

'Yes. I've just heard back about DNA samples taken from Lacey and Janelle.'

'What kind of DNA?' asked Charlotte, her face a mask of horror.

'Hair. Two small hair samples. We ran these and were able to tell that this is a white male. But he's not on the DNA database… I've worked on scores of murder cases like this, and they always slip up. We have his DNA. We know he drives a Citroën C3, he's used it twice and he's obscured the number plate.'

'Why can't you get all the names of people who have these cars?' demanded Don.

'We can, but this is a common model. There are thousands of them in the UK.'

'He doesn't deserve to live in this world after what he did!' he said, slamming his hand down on the table.

'I can't bear the thought that he could be watching us on television. I'm not going to cry. I don't want to give him the satisfaction,' Charlotte spat. Don put his arm around her.

'I'm doing the talking, love.' Then he turned his attention to Erika. 'You think this will work?'

'In the past, public appeals have given us key breakthroughs in cases like this,' said Erika.

'"Cases like this". You mean serial killers, don't you?'

'I'm not saying that. Serial killers are very rare, and we don't want to jump to any conclusions. We want to keep to the facts of the case.'

'Don't bullshit me,' said Don, looking her square in the eye.

'I would never do that,' said Erika.

Colleen returned from speaking on the phone. 'Right, Mr and Mrs Greene, we've got about twelve minutes until we start. The press is almost all here, and we should have a full house.'

She bustled off, leaving Lacey's parents to digest the phrase 'full house'.

Erika's phone rang and she excused herself. She moved down a corridor, and found a corner tucked away from people streaming in and out. A technician walked past with half a doughnut in his mouth and a tall light on a stand.

'Alright, boss, can you talk?' asked John.

'Not for long. What is it?'

'There's been a missing person report come in. It flagged up because it sounds similar.'

'Familiar to our guy?'

'Yeah. Missing person is a twenty-year-old student called Ella Wilkinson. She was due to meet a bloke on a blind date in a bar near Angel in North London on Saturday night. She left the house alone just before 8 p.m. Never came home. Her housemate found her handbag on late Sunday afternoon, dumped around the corner from the bar. Ella had been chatting to this guy on-line. The bouncer at the club says he saw her, and shortly afterwards a red Citroën C3 pulled past and down the road beside the bar. He was distracted and a few minutes later she was gone.'

'Shit,' said Erika, her heart sinking. She checked her watch: it was now less than ten minutes until the press conference was due to begin. 'Has she gone missing before? Any history?'

'No. She's a student at St Martins, serious about her work, comes from a stable family. I've just emailed through her picture and the deets… Do you think you should mention this?'

'Mention?'

'In the press appeal, boss. Look at the photo: she looks just like Janelle Robinson and Lacey Greene. There's mention of a red car…'

'But no number plate?'

'No… Boss, she went missing three days ago. The official missing person report kicked in forty-eight hours ago. If we're working on the assumption that this guy keeps them somewhere for three to five days…'

Colleen appeared at the end of the corridor and beckoned to Erika.

'John, there's no time, we're about to go live…' Erika cupped her hand over the receiver as two big lads moved past noisily, lugging a large table.

'But what if this Ella girl is victim number three, boss? And she could still be alive…'

Erika felt torn. At the end of the corridor she could hear the loud chatter from the conference room, and Colleen was now greeting a middle-aged journalist accompanied by her greying cameraman.

'Fuck!' said Erika. 'Have the family been informed?'

'Officers are on their way to tell them officially, but apparently the housemate has already been talking to them.'

Erika felt her heart pounding: there was no time.

'John, the press conference has been structured around the existing victims. If we start talking about another girl being abducted, we have to be sure. Is Melanie in her office? What does she have to say?'

'I've left word with her, but she's away on a conference today.'

The journalists had now moved through to the conference room, and Colleen was approaching her saying, 'Erika, we need to put a bit of base on you, so you're not washed-out on camera…'

'John, find out as much as you can, and track down Melanie. I have to go.'

Erika hung up, took a deep breath and followed Colleen through to the conference room with a sickness in the pit of her stomach.

CHAPTER 41

The press appeal was done and dusted by 3 p.m. The *BBC News* channel had covered it live, but it would get its main coverage on the evening news programmes and the late editions of the London free newspapers.

Erika returned to West End Central feeling drained, and found the team scrabbling to assemble the information about the latest missing person, Ella Wilkinson. Crane came over, and she could see that Moss, Peterson, John and the rest of her officers were taking phone calls.

'Alright, boss, good job on the appeal,' he said.

'Did it generate any good leads?' asked Erika. The glass partition next to where they worked, which was officially, and rather ambitiously, called a 'suite', had been put aside, with four officers assigned to answer calls relating to the media appeal. They were all sitting in silence working on their computers.

'Nothing yet. I don't know if we will get anything until it runs again later with the helpline number.'

'Let me know if anything comes in,' she said.

She went to her office to make some calls, and to try and track down Melanie Hudson on her course in Birmingham, but she still wasn't answering her phone.

Just before five o'clock, Crane knocked on her door.

'I've got a man who's called the helpline wanting to talk to you. Says he's Ella Wilkinson's father.'

Erika put down her pen and followed him over to the suite of phones. Two male officers were sitting working and looked up when she came over. A blonde officer handed Erika a headset and she slipped it on.

'Is this Erika Foster?' demanded a clipped northern voice.

'Yes. May I ask who's calling?'

'Didn't that girl tell you? It's Michael Wilkinson. My daughter is Ella Wilkinson.'

'Hello, Mr Wilkinson. I'm sorry to hear your daughter is reported missing.'

Erika could see that word had spread, and Moss and Peterson along with John had crossed to her side of the glass partition to watch the call. She signalled to Moss, who grabbed a spare headset, pulled it on and plugged it into the phone.

'I watched your press appeal, DCI Foster. What I can't understand is why you didn't include Ella?'

'Mr Wilkinson, we're still trying to confirm if your daughter's disappearance is connected with—'

'Don't lie to me, woman!' he shouted. 'I'm a retired Detective Chief Superintendent!'

Erika looked at Moss, who pulled the computer keyboard towards her and started typing.

'I didn't know that, sir. I'm sorry…'

Moss indicated the computer screen, where she had pulled up a picture of Detective Chief Superintendent Michael Wilkinson, a thin greying man with soft brown eyes. He was wearing a dinner suit at an official function. Erika mouthed, '*Shit*.'

'I have spent the past few hours trying to raise *someone* in the Met who knows what they're talking about! I've been passed from pillar to post…' His voice cracked. 'It's a shambles! As a last resort I took to calling the fucking helpline on the news report.'

'I can call you back, sir, if—'

'Why would I want you to call me back? We're talking! Now tell me all you know.'

'Sir, we're not—'

'Spare me the bullshit. I've had a look at the casework on the two girls and I have the information about my daughter's disappearance. Tell me the truth. That's all I want, and I think I deserve it!'

Erika looked around and saw that the two officers had now ended their calls and were staring at her.

'Sir, can you just hold on for thirty seconds. I want to transfer you to my office where I can talk to you in private.'

Erika, Moss and Peterson moved quickly to her office and closed the door, where she resumed the call. She explained what she knew, and told him that she had been informed of his daughter's disappearance less than ten minutes before she had to talk to the media.

He calmed down slightly. 'I've had little contact from local police… Two officers came around to the house just as the press appeal went out on the news. It seems that Ella has been added to the long list of runaways and missing persons… I've had to get the doctor in for my wife… I've spent years working within the force and now I find myself on the other side of things. Powerless.'

Erika gave him her direct line and promised that she would have a Family Liaison Officer assigned to his house. When she came off the phone there was silence. Moss was sitting at her desk on the computer.

'Poor bastard,' said Peterson.

Erika nodded. 'He had every right to shout. I had nothing to give him, we know nothing. This man, whoever he is, must be laughing.' Erika perched on the edge of the desk and rubbed her eyes. 'I should have pushed to have Ella included in the press appeal, and fucked the consequences.'

'We still don't know for sure that she was taken by the same man,' said Moss. 'Crane is working again on pulling any CCTV, but it could take time.'

'I want us to go ahead and pull the names and addresses of everyone who owns a red Citroën C3 in London and the South East,' said Erika.

'That could run into the hundreds, if not thousands,' said Peterson.

'What else do we have? It's the only thing that's consistent in all the cases. Go ahead and get in contact with the DVLA.'

'Okay, I'll get on it,' said Peterson.

Erika grabbed her coat off the back of the chair and left her office. She took the stairs down to the bottom floor and came out of the front entrance. One of the women from CID was out on the pavement smoking a cigarette.

'Sorry to ask…' Erika started. The woman looked up wordlessly and offered her cigarettes. Erika took one from the packet, and leaned in whilst she lit it for her. 'Thank you,' she added, exhaling smoke into the cold air. The sky was murky and brown against the light of the city. In the next road they could hear the sound of drinkers moving between the pubs. 'This is my first cigarette in months.'

The woman finished hers and dropped it to the pavement, grinding it out in a flash of embers.

'If you're going to die you might as well enjoy yourself in the process,' she said, and she moved back up the steps and back inside.

The words clung to Erika as she finished smoking the cigarette. It satisfied her craving, but left her feeling revolting. She picked her phone out of her pocket and called Marsh. This time it said his number was no longer available. She scrolled through her phone looking for the number for Marsh's wife, Marcie, but she didn't have it. She thought about going over to his house, but it was late and she didn't have the energy to deal with it all.

'Where are you, Paul Marsh?' said Erika, staring at her phone and then slipping it back into her pocket.

CHAPTER 42

It was late afternoon, and Darryl looked across the communal office at the quiet studiousness of his colleagues. Like him, he knew that little was being achieved, but everyone was doing a good show of looking busy.

'You can start packing up your things,' said a voice behind him. He turned to see Bryony standing behind his chair, holding a pile of Manila folders.

'Okay, thanks. And thanks for letting me leave a bit early, Bryony,' he said.

'You've banked the overtime. Are you planning on doing anything nice?'

Her face was slack. It always held this slack look when she was waiting for an answer. He'd heard some of the guys from the other end of the office joking that this might also be her sex face. Darryl gulped back a laugh.

'Nothing much. A night of telly. We've just got Netflix,' he said. In truth he would be spending the evening with Ella.

Her last evening.

Her last breath.

'We?' asked Bryony, suddenly very interested.

'Me, my mum and dad. I still live at home.'

'So no girlfriend?'

The slack look had left her face, and she shifted her large bulk to the other leg.

'No girlfriend,' he said. She hung around for a moment longer, but he had turned away from her to shut down his computer.

Darryl made it home just before four thirty, and as he pulled in at the farm gates he noticed that it was only just getting dark. He was greeted by Grendel when he came into the boot room; he gave her a hug and crouched down so she could lick his face, then he went through to the kitchen. It was very hot, and his mother was red in the face after baking a batch of rock cakes.

'Alright, love, you want a cuppa?' she said, as he leaned over and gave her a peck on the cheek. He smelt gin on her breath, but just nodded. 'I'll bring it through with a couple of cakes.'

Darryl went to the living room. He switched on the fake flame fire and the television, and settled down in the red threadbare armchair. He was flicking through channels when Mary came through, a full teacup rattling in her hand.

'I'll want to watch *Eggheads* at six,' she said, setting it down beside him with a plate of warm rock cakes.

'Where are the kids' programmes?' he said.

'They moved them a few years back onto Children's BBC... You want to watch *Blue Peter*?'

'Course I don't want to watch bloody *Blue Peter*. I was just asking,' he snapped. He took the cup and saw that she'd slopped tea into the saucer.

'It doesn't seem like yesterday that you and Joe would come home and sit in here... Remember you used to fight over who got the armchair?'

'Not anymore,' said Darryl, slurping tea from the saucer.

Mary's eyes welled up, and she left the room.

She came back later, worse for wear and weaving unsteadily, and they watched the quiz show *Eggheads*.

Just as it was finishing, at six thirty, Darryl's father came into the living room. He stank of Old Spice and wore his best shirt and trousers; his white hair was neatly combed.

'Right then, I'm just off to see a man about a dog,' he said.

Darryl looked over at his mother whose glazed eyes stared at the credits rolling on the television screen. 'Say hi to the *dog*, give her a pat on the head from us,' he said.

His father narrowed his eyes, but left without a word. The dog in question was Deirdre Masters, a married woman who lived on a neighbouring farm. His father's affair with her had been going on for years. As a child, he had often wondered why his father stayed out all night when last orders were called at 10.45 p.m. Then one day, Joe had said he'd overheard Dad on the phone to Deirdre.

'Dad goes to hers, and they fuck all night,' Joe had said. 'Do you know about fucking?'

Darryl had said he didn't. And when Joe had explained, he'd had to rush to the toilet in the boot room to throw up.

His mother never let on that she knew about his father's Monday nights with Deirdre – she must have done because over the years people had talked – and when he'd left she would cook Darryl and Joe a telly supper consisting of fish fingers, chips and beans, which they would eat off trays in the living room.

This Monday was the same as in years gone by. But just as Darryl and Mary were settling down with their trays of food, the *Channel 4 News* came on, with a police appeal for witnesses to the murders of Lacey Greene and Janelle Robinson.

Darryl dropped his fork, spilling food over the carpet. He'd kept it all secret for so long that it was surreal to see a tall policewoman with short blonde hair sitting at a long table, flanked by Lacey Greene's parents. He saw her name was Detective Chief Inspector Erika Foster.

'The Met police would like to appeal for any witnesses into these brutal murders,' she was saying, as the Met Police logo flashed up on a screen behind her.

Darryl's heart began to hammer as he saw they had grainy CCTV footage of his car approaching Tooley Street when he'd abducted Janelle, and the Blue Boar pub when he'd taken Lacey. His ears started to roar with blood and his legs began to tremble. He couldn't keep his feet flat on the carpet. Vomit rose in his throat and he struggled with it, then gulped it back down. He reached out a shaking hand and took a drink of the orange juice on his tray.

The sound came back to his ears and he could hear his mother saying: 'They spend all our tax money on CCTV cameras to watch us, but they can't even read the number plate... It could be your car for all they know.' She looked at him for a moment and then heaved herself up off the sofa and moved to the bar.

'What?' he said.

Back on the screen, Lacey's mother was crying, and her father was reading out from a prepared statement, the bright lights caught in the lenses of his glasses.

'Lacey was a happy girl, with no enemies. She had her whole life ahead of her. There are two key dates where we want to appeal for witnesses. On Wednesday the fourth of January, Lacey was taken by the driver of a red Citroën outside the Blue Boar pub in Southgate, at around 8 p.m. Her body was found on Monday the ninth of January in Tattersall Road in New Cross. We believe she was...' At this point his voice faltered and he looked down. His wife squeezed his arm. He swallowed and went on: 'She was dumped in these rubbish bins in the early hours on the morning of Monday the ninth. If you have any information, please can you call the helpline number. Any information, however small, could help us find who did this.'

The CCTV images played again of his car driving up to the pub, and shortly after, Lacey walking along the street with her long dark hair flowing after her. Still images were also shown of the two locations where the bodies were dumped. An artist's e-fit then popped up on the screen. It was of Nico, the fake profile picture he'd used. It was a crude likeness. The forehead was wrong, it was too high and there were crease lines, and the nose was a little too wide.

The blonde police officer was now saying that their suspect had assumed the identity of a dead man called Sonny Sarmiento, a dead nineteen-year-old from Ecuador. 'We ask that the public are vigilant. We believe this man is targeting young women in the London area, using fake profiles on social media. He establishes trust through online friendships, before asking to meet,' she said.

Darryl's mind was racing... He looked over to his mother as she plucked ice cubes from the ice bucket with a little pair of tongs and dropped them into her glass with a clink. She was watching him. No, studying him.

'Horrible business,' he said.

'Yes, horrible,' she said, not taking her eyes off him.

He swallowed again and got a grip of himself. If the police knew his number plate or his name they would have been to the farm by now. They were clueless. They had just put a few of the pieces together. Mary stared at him for a moment longer, studying him intently, then she switched her attention to the television behind him. The appeal had now finished and the newsreader was reading out the number that people could call to give the police information.

'I think we should get one of those High D tellies,' she said, shuffling back over with her drink. 'I can't read that number.'

She sat heavily on the sofa, her breathing laboured. 'Eat up. I've made some jelly for afters.'

Darryl saw that she had that same alcoholic haze in her eyes, and the sharp curiosity had gone. He smiled.

'Dad won't give you the money for a high definition television?'

'I've been putting a little of the housekeeping he gives me to one side for quite some time,' she said, leaning over and patting him on his still trembling leg.

'I could check them out online,' he said, forcing a smile.

'Thanks, love, now eat up.'

He forced himself to make bland conversation and eat the rest of the bland food on his plate. As the television news moved on to the immigration crisis in Europe his heart began to slow. They hadn't mentioned Ella. If they had his number plate they would be knocking on the door, wouldn't they? *Wouldn't they?* He'd made sure that it had been obscured by the dirt. When he took Janelle, he had been lucky that the number plate was so filthy after summer storms and driving around the farm. The winter weather had been a gift. When he'd started looking, he was shocked at how many people let their number plates become so dirty that they were obscured.

He looked back at his mother and saw the gin was really kicking in. Her eyes were drooping; she was having trouble focusing.

'Here,' he said, getting up and taking her glass. 'Let me pour you another.'

Snow was falling thickly when he emerged from the back door an hour later. His mother was now dozing drunkenly on the sofa; his father was away with his lover. He would be left alone. Grendel barked in protest when she saw he was leaving without her, but he gave her a treat and closed the door behind him.

He walked down the yard, weaving along to avoid activating the lights and cameras, and when he reached the gate he vaulted it with ease.

The snow squeaked and crunched as he moved through the dark fields, until the outline of the Oast House loomed ahead. His eyes had adjusted to the dark, so he kept his torch off as he unlocked the padlock and slid the door open. It was pitch-black inside, but he could smell her. The soft smell of her freshly washed hair and perfume had been replaced with stale sweat, piss and shit. Very softly, he could hear her sobbing.

'Good, I'm glad to hear you've held on just a little longer,' he said.

He slid the door closed, and moments later Ella began to scream.

CHAPTER 43

The phones in the incident room started ringing shortly after the evening news reports. There were the usual calls from the whack jobs and the crazies – not words officially sanctioned for use by the Met – but unofficially, that's how they were known.

One of the calls that came through was flagged by Crane and, along with Moss and Peterson, he did some digging. They then took it to Erika.

'How can we be sure this isn't another crazy person who thinks they saw something?' asked Erika, looking across her desk at Moss, Peterson and Crane squashed into her tiny office.

'The witness is a Mrs Marina Long,' said Moss. 'She's married, with two young boys. They live in the village of Thornton Massey, which is just a few miles off the M20, close to Maidstone. Marina and her husband work as teachers at the local primary school. Their house backs onto farmland, and an old Oast House.'

'What's an Oast House?' asked Erika.

'They were used for drying hops,' said Peterson. 'There used to be hundreds of hop farms around Kent, and Oast Houses have a furnace and racks for drying them out so they can be brewed for beer.'

'Okay. What does this have to do with our appeal?' said Erika.

'Marina Long says that several times in the last few months, late at night, she's seen a small red car driving across the fields towards this Oast House,' said Crane.

'How could she tell the car was a red, if she saw it late at night?'

'Well, she says that often the next morning, it's still been there, parked outside. She also says she remembers seeing the car there on the twenty-fourth, when Janelle went missing, *and* she remembers seeing car lights moving across the field on the fourth of January,' said Crane. 'The night Lacey Greene went missing.'

'Do we know who owns the land?'

'The land belongs to Oakwood Farm. The farmer and his wife live there with their grown-up son,' said Peterson. 'And, get this. A red Citroën C3 is registered in the son's name.'

Erika was silent for a moment, rolling the information over in her brain. She looked at the clock; it was coming up to 8.15 p.m.

'We've been working on the theory that he abducts them, and holds them for a few days before killing them, so this out-building, this Oast House, would support this theory...' She sat back in her chair and ran her fingers through her hair. 'But this is far out of London. Why take them so far? Why risk all the surveillance and CCTV cameras coming in and out of London? Why not just grab local girls?'

The phone rang and she picked it up. It was Melanie Hudson. She covered the receiver and asked if Moss, Peterson and Crane could wait outside. When they'd gone, Erika quickly brought her up to speed with the appeal, and that she believed the daughter of a retired senior police officer was being held by the same killer.

'If it's like the last two victims, then he's had Ella Wilkinson for three days. We need to move fast,' said Erika.

CHAPTER 44

At 12.30 a.m. the next morning, a black van containing a team of Specialist Firearms Officers from Kent Police pulled into a lay-by close to the large iron gates of Oakwood Farm. The driver killed the headlights, and the engine idled. It was a lonely patch of country road with just a couple of other houses. To the left of the van, the empty fields stretched away, and a lone light glowed in the window of the farmhouse. Six Specialist Firearms Officers, headed by Sergeant Portman, crouched in the back of the van. They were used to waiting, and despite the cold, they sweated under their Kevlar vests and protective gear.

Less than forty miles away, Erika and her team were assembled around a computer monitor in the incident room at West End Central. Erika was impressed that Melanie had taken her seriously, and stepped up as Acting Superintendent. It had been no mean feat to pull together two teams of Specialist Firearms Officers from Kent Police with so much speed, and Erika realised just how much was on the line. The teams were being coordinated from the control room at Maidstone Police Station and everything was being relayed to them at West End Central, via a live audio feed. The rest of their office stretched away in darkness, the other teams having left for home hours ago.

'Okay, we're standing by,' said Sergeant Portman with the first team.

'Team two, are you reading me?' came a female voice. This was DI Kendal in the control room at Maidstone. The second team of Specialist Firearms Officers were approaching an access gate at the other end of the farmland, which, if the map was correct, was a quarter of a mile from the Oast House.

'Loud and clear. We're just on Barnes Lane, should be at the gate in a few minutes,' came the voice of Sergeant Spector, who was leading the second team.

Erika caught Moss's eye and saw she was uncharacteristically tense. The radio fell silent for a long minute. Just when they thought the audio connection was lost, they heard Sergeant Spector again,

'Okay, we've got the access gate open. Looks like there's no security lights down here.'

'Okay, proceed with caution, keep your lights off,' said DI Kendal in control. 'Team one, can you move into position?'

'Yes, standing by,' came Sergeant Portman's voice.

'The neighbour, Marina, has said that the gates open automatically on approach,' said DI Kendal. 'I want team two in position outside the Oast House before I give you the signal to activate the front gates.'

'Standing by...'

'Bloody hell. I can't bear this,' said Peterson back in the incident room. A bead of sweat trickled down his temple and he wiped it with his sleeve.

CHAPTER 45

The Oast House seemed to rise up as the van containing the second team drove slowly towards it across the frozen earth. Sergeant Spector crouched in the back with his team of three male and two female Specialist Firearms Officers. It was almost pitch-black, and boiling hot, their sticky bodies packed in together. Despite his years in the Specialist Firearms Unit there was always anticipation and fear. You needed it to stay sharp. His hands were sweaty under his gloves, but his grip on his Heckler & Koch G36 assault rifle was firm.

The van slowed and came to a stop.

'This is Spector. We're in position by the Oast House,' he said into his radio. He heard DI Kendal in control give team one the go-ahead.

'Gates and security lights have activated,' said Sergeant Portman. 'We're approaching the farmhouse.'

'Proceed with caution,' said DI Kendal. 'Team two, you are clear to proceed with caution.'

Spector then took over, and on his command the van door slid back. The cold air flooded inside and the team moved out with a practised fluidity, fanning out around the Oast House with its strange spout-like funnel. The snow and ice crunched underfoot. Spector stopped by a large metal door, and listened. There was no sound. Then the wind started to blow and there was a low groaning.

'I can hear screaming or moaning, please report, over,' said DI Kendal's voice in his earpiece.

Spector looked up at the tower against the black sky, and as the wind rose and fell so did the moaning.

'I think it's ventilation on the roof, over,' he said.

His team paused, guns held, feet splayed, ready and waiting to move. They listened to Sergeant Portman through their ear-pieces as he gave updates on team one's progress.

'We're coming to a stop at the farmhouse. Looks deserted...'

Another moment passed, and they heard the van door slide back. It was often difficult to listen to another team and keep your surroundings in focus. The wind was now blowing the snow across the surrounding fields and whipping it into their faces like powdered sugar. The vent in the spout-like roof moaned and metal creaked.

Spector looked around at his team, and then gave them the order to go. Using bolt cutters, one of the officers clipped open the padlock on the huge sliding door. They all activated the lights on their protective headgear as he pulled back the door.

'POLICE! GET DOWN!' shouted Spector, as their torches shone through the open doorway and over the inside of the Oast House.

Something flashed, and there was a face frozen and still.

'THIS IS THE POLICE. COME OUT WITH YOUR HANDS IN THE AIR!' shouted Spector.

But the person wasn't moving. Then he saw a flash of an arm holding a gun, the face came towards him, and he fired.

CHAPTER 46

At the back door of the farmhouse, team one were in position. Sergeant Portman had knocked on the wooden door, and there had been no response. Just as two of his officers were preparing to break down the door with a battering ram, a light came on above their heads.

'Hang on, cuddles, you come here,' said a male voice through the door. 'No. I don't know who the hell it is at this hour, but I don't want you running out in this snow!'

'THIS IS THE POLICE! STEP AWAY FROM THE DOOR!' shouted Portman.

'What? I'm trying to open the door!' came the voice.

The two officers with the battering ram stepped back and they aimed their rifles at the wooden door. They heard bolts being pulled back, then it opened, and they were confronted by a slim man in his early forties. He wore a thin silk robe covered in a pattern of red roses. His long blond hair hung limp down to his shoulders and he had a large hooked nose and a turn in one of his piercing green eyes. He was holding a tiny white kitten, which was mewling and doing its best to escape. He stepped back, but didn't seem too fazed by the six armed police.

'PUT YOUR HANDS IN THE AIR!' shouted Portman.

The blond man did so, holding the kitten above his head where it blinked and mewled in the torch light.

'I haven't got any weapons, officers! Nor has mother; she's asleep upstairs…' he said.

'Where is the third person who lives here?' shouted Portman.

'My father? He's dead! He died last month. Pneumonia…' said the man, this situation with the armed police starting to dawn on him. The kitten held above his head was starting to panic and scratch his arms. 'Please, can I put my hands down? She's going to cut me to ribbons.'

Back in the incident room at West End Central, Erika and her team had listened with mounting confusion to what was unfolding on Oakwood Farm with the two Specialist Firearms teams. When they'd heard the shot fired in the Oast House, DI Kendal at the control centre had started to shout out, demanding to know what was happening, and if any officers had been injured. After a few moments of chaos and confusion, they heard Sergeant Spector's voice.

'It's okay. No one's injured. I repeat. There are no officers injured. The inside of the building… It's full of mannequins… bloody shop mannequins…'

'Please can you clarify, why was a shot fired? Over,' came DI Kendal's voice.

'We believed the suspect was armed, but the suspect was a mannequin holding a plastic gun,' said Spector.

'Again, please can you clarify? Over,' came Kendal's voice.

'The Oast House, it's full of plastic shop mannequins in outfits, some of them are just torsos, and a few are propped up against the walls… And there's rails and rails of costumes. We've secured the building and there's no threat. No one here, over,' said Spector. He sounded shaken, and embarrassed.

Back in the incident room at West End Central a look passed between Erika, Moss and Peterson. John rolled his eyes and put his head in his hands.

'To be sure, we're going to search the rest of the outbuildings and take a look at the car,' came Spector's voice through the radio.

An hour passed, and then two. They all listened to the two teams moving throughout the farm buildings. There was no sign of Ella Wilkinson.

'Boss, look at this,' said Crane, handing Erika a printout from Yelp.

She took it from him and read:

'Mr Bojangles, The Premier Kent supplier of quality theatrical and historical costumes throughout Ireland & the UK, Oakwood Farm, Thornton Massey, Maidstone, Kent...'

'The company is registered to Darius O'Keefe. He also has a red Citroën registered in his name, but it's a different model to the one in our CCTV footage,' said Crane.

'Fuck,' said Erika, slamming her hand down on the desk.

It was two thirty in the morning when Erika and the team emerged from West End Central. Taxis had been arranged to take everyone home, and were parked in a line by the kerb. The early morning trains wouldn't start running for another three hours.

The atmosphere was muted as the members of her team said good night and climbed into the waiting cars.

'Night, boss, get some rest,' said Moss, giving Erika's arm a squeeze.

She hung back as the cars started to pull away, and noticed Peterson beside her.

'What's this?' he said, indicating the remaining two taxis waiting.

'I just fancied a night in my own bed, alone,' said Erika, pulling out a packet of cigarettes and stripping off the cellophane.

'No, no, no, don't start smoking again,' said Peterson, reaching over to take the packet.

She pulled her arm back.

'Please, just leave me.'

'But you've done so well…'

'You think what happened in there tonight was me doing well?' she shouted.

He watched her with concern as she opened the packet and, pulling out the foil, put a cigarette in her mouth. She lit up and exhaled.

'I meant you'd done well giving up smoking for so long… And you couldn't have foreseen that we'd get the wrong address…'

'You should get home, James,' she said.

'I'm on your side,' he said, leaning towards her angrily. 'Don't forget that.'

'I know. I just want to be alone.'

'Yeah, maybe you should be,' he said.

He went to the waiting taxi and got in. Erika watched it drive away, then she smoked another two cigarettes. The building opposite was wrapped in scaffolding and a bright security light shone over it, casting a grid over the pavement around her. Like she was in a cage. It made her think of Ella Wilkinson, trapped somewhere.

Erika knew she would be hauled over the coals for what had happened. And the identity of the true killer was still unknown. She ground out her cigarette on the pavement, and got into the taxi for the journey back to her cold empty flat.

CHAPTER 47

Thirty-eight-year-old Martyn Lakersfield was a full-time carer for his wife, Shelia, who was living with multiple sclerosis. Just four years ago, they'd been living a happy life, with busy careers. Shelia had worked in advertising, and he had worked for Citibank. They'd often said they passed like ships in the night, but now they were both prisoners of their third floor flat in Beckenham, just a few miles from Lewisham. It was a decent enough area, and they were lucky to own the property, but this was not how they had seen their life together panning out. In recent months, Shelia had found sharing a bed difficult and stressful, so Martyn had taken the decision to sleep in the spare room. It had broken his heart.

On Tuesday morning, Martyn had woken at three, and had been unable to get back to sleep. After checking on Shelia, who was sleeping soundly, he went into the living room to watch TV. At three thirty, his eyes were scratchy, but he was still wide awake, so he decided to take out the rubbish, something he hadn't managed to do the day before.

He came out of the main entrance and stopped on the steps, breathing in the cold air. He walked over to the line of dumpsters which were at the front of the building, to the left of a paved car park overlooking the street. He was surprised to see what he thought was another neighbour at the black dumpster, but he didn't recognise the small figure, with its face obscured in the shadow of a baseball cap pulled down low. As he moved closer, the figure heard his feet on the gravel path and turned. It stood still for a moment, arms hanging down, feet braced and then darted away onto the street, passing under an orange streetlight before vanishing around the hedgerow.

There was something about the way they had behaved that made Martyn stop. The person had stared at him, almost weighing up what to do, *fight or flight*. Martyn gently placed the bag of rubbish down on the ground, and not taking his eyes off the entrance to the car park, he crouched down and picked up a large rock from the row lining the path. He moved swiftly to the entrance, with the rock braced in his hand, and stepped out onto the pavement. The road was empty and silent, pools of orange light stretching away in both directions. The windows of the surrounding flats were dark.

He was relieved whoever it was had chosen to flee. He came back and retrieved his rubbish bag, and keeping hold of the rock, he went to the dumpster.

The lid was open and what he saw inside made him cry out in shock. He stumbled back and fell onto the cold, hard ground.

CHAPTER 48

Erika was woken by her phone ringing in the darkness. She rolled over in bed, reaching out with her fingers. The space beside her was empty, and the mattress firm. She was at home. She'd been dreaming she was back in Manchester, as a Specialist Firearms Officer. It was a recurring dream she hadn't had in a long time; the ill-fated drug raid where she relived the death of her husband and five members of her team.

She was thankful the phone had woken her, until she saw who it was.

'Crane, what is it? It's five thirty in the morning,' she said. She sat up and flicked on the bedside lamp and winced at its brightness. She saw she'd fallen asleep wearing her clothes.

'Boss. The body of a young girl's just been found in Beckenham… She's got dark hair, and she's been left in a dumpster.'

Erika sat up. 'Is it Ella Wilkinson?'

'We don't know for sure, but everything points to it being her.'

Erika felt the floor under her feet fall away, and she had to steady herself on the edge of the mattress. 'I'll be there right away.'

It was just starting to get light as Erika pulled onto Copers Cope Road, in Beckenham, a long wide residential street dotted with large trees and a mixture of smart flats and older houses. She slowed past a couple of old houses, set back from the street with large polished bay windows, and then an apartment block came into view. Squad cars were lined up outside with their lights flashing, along with a large support vehicle, and the pathologist's van. Erika parked at the end of the row and got out.

It was a modern red-brick building, set back from the road with a sweeping brickwork driveway. The pavement out front was cordoned off, and two large floodlights were accompanied by the whir of a petrol generator. To the right of the driveway was a small patch of lawn with some plants, and to the left a huge white crime scene tent had been erected, where lights glowed from inside. Glancing up, Erika could see that this building was overlooked on both sides. Lights were on in several of the windows, and the pale faces of residents could be seen peering down at the crime scene.

Erika showed her warrant card and pulled on a pair of pale blue crime scene coveralls. She ducked under the police tape, and was met by Crane, who looked just as rough as she felt. There was very little talking as they went over to the large white tent.

It was hot and cramped inside, and brightly lit by two large lights, where three large plastic dumpsters were housed under a small awning with a wooden roof.

Isaac Strong wore overalls and a face mask; he had two assistants working with him. The smell of the dumpsters under the hot lights made Erika's stomach lurch.

'Morning,' he said softly. He indicated the middle dumpster, which was black. Its curved blue lid was pushed back.

Erika and Crane edged forward and looked over the edge and inside. A young girl lay on her back. She was filthy, and covered in dirt and dried blood. Her body was badly beaten, and her long dark hair was lank and greasy. As Lacey and Janelle had been, she was naked from the waist down. Her dark top was saturated with blood and it clung to her skin. Her forehead had a deep dent in it, and her left cheek had also collapsed. Crane looked away and put a hand to his mouth, but Erika forced herself to stare at the poor girl and take in what had been done.

'That's her,' she said. 'That's Ella Wilkinson.'

CHAPTER 49

Erika was glad of the cold air when they emerged from the tent and handed in their overalls.

'We've got Martyn Lakersfield, the guy who found her,' said Crane as they ducked back under the police tape.

An ambulance was parked further down the street, past the line of squad cars, with its back doors open. Martyn was sitting in the back dressed in jeans, a grubby Manchester United T-shirt, a denim jacket, and was wrapped in a red blanket. Erika thought how depressed he looked, with bags under his eyes and a bloated, unshaven face.

'I understand that you found the body?' said Erika, as she and Crane approached.

Martyn looked up at her and nodded. 'I was just putting out the rubbish, when I saw him,' he said.

'Saw him?' asked Erika, glancing at Crane.

'I don't sleep much. I always come out when it's quiet and put it in the right bins. I don't normally see anyone…'

'Who did you see?'

'A guy, I think, but he was wearing a baseball cap…'

'Was he tall or short?'

'Short. I think. A bit chubby. Although it happened so quickly. He had an odd stance.'

'What do you mean?' asked Erika.

'A stillness, a confidence. It was unnerving.'

'And you're *sure* you didn't see his face?'

'Positive. He ran off, but he looked like he was thinking whether he should stay and… I don't know, deck me.'

'Did he have a car?' asked Crane.

'He vanished around the corner. I think I heard an engine. He could have been parked round the hedge.'

'Did you see a car?'

'No.'

Erika ran her hands through her hair, not quite believing he'd managed to get away without being seen.

'Which flat do you live in?' she asked.

'We're the one there, third floor,' he said, pointing to a window on the left-hand side of the building.

'Is that window a bedroom or the kitchen?' asked Erika.

'Bathroom,' he said. 'All those windows at the front are bathrooms.'

Erika looked up and counted three floors with six windows.

'Do you know if all the flats overlooking this front drive are occupied?'

'There's a woman downstairs; she's old. I know they're still trying to rent out the flat above. I know that because we had some noisy bastards in there who moved out last month… She looked like a young girl,' he said, looking up at Erika and Crane. He started to heave and put a hand to his mouth.

'Thank you. Let's get you a cup of tea, and I'll have someone take a formal statement,' said Erika.

They moved away, back towards the crime scene.

'I want everyone who has a view out front over this car park interviewed, and I want a door-to-door of the surrounding flats. This whole courtyard is overlooked and someone must have seen *something*,' said Erika.

There were groups of people now filling up the pavement on the other side of the road, standing around and watching curiously.

'There's no CCTV cameras on the road,' said Crane. 'Further down, there's a private CCTV camera mounted outside a Fitness First gym and about four hundred yards along there's New Beckenham station, but the cameras don't cover the road, just the station approach.'

'If he drove off in that direction then they may have caught something,' said Erika. 'This guy either has incredible luck, or he's choosing the places where he dumps the bodies.'

CHAPTER 50

When Darryl had finished with Ella Wilkinson, she was unrecognisable, badly beaten and screaming like an animal. He'd broken her jaw, which had made her screams sound like she was drunk, but she still had some fight left in her, which was remarkable.

It was then that he took a scalpel and severed the artery in her leg. Watching the gouts of blood pour from her body gave him the biggest thrill, like an electric surge coursing through his veins. The light left her eyes and she was still.

He'd stumbled out of the Oast House into the darkness and the cold, his legs shaking uncontrollably, and he'd vomited into the snow by the frozen stream. When his stomach was empty he'd lain face down. The snow pressing against his hot face was delicious, and he lay there for a long time until his breathing slowed and he started to feel the cold seeping in through his clothes. The Oast House had a water supply, carried in a pipe under the soil, and it hadn't frozen. After Darryl stashed Ella's body in the car, he washed himself down in the furnace chamber, wincing at the snow-cold water from the hose. Then he drove across the field to the gate, and on to Beckenham to dump her body.

Darryl had returned to the farm just before five, cutting it fine with the early morning milking, but he hadn't run into any of the farm workers. He had parked the car, taken a long hot shower, and fallen into bed.

* * *

He woke just before one in the afternoon, his bedroom bathed in dim blue light shining through the closed curtains. His body ached, and his throat burned. He reached out to the bedside table for a glass, and took a long drink of water. A shaft of sunlight appeared through the crack in the curtains, and he watched the dust particles twirl in the weak sunlight which played a strip of white on the threadbare blue carpet.

A metallic twanging noise broke the silence, and he stiffened. It came again, like the soft tinny chime of a clock, but it was coming from inside the wardrobe. Darryl kicked off the bedcovers and stepped barefoot onto the carpet, moving over to the wardrobe. The furniture had been in this room for as long as he could remember, going back to when his paternal great-grandfather had built the farmhouse. Like the bed and desk, the wardrobe was antique, with heavy dark wood. It had double doors and was huge, seven feet tall, and almost reached the ceiling. The left door had a smoked glass mirror spotted with black, and in the right door a tiny tarnished key poked out from the keyhole with a Celtic-style pattern.

Ting, ting, came the noise again, like a metal coat hanger striking the inside of the wardrobe. He stopped at the door, and looked at his reflection. His pasty bare legs in boxer shorts, his pot belly with a fuzz of dark hair. And then he heard it: the creaking sound of a taut rope.

'No,' he whispered, taking a step back.

The creaking came again, followed by a choking, gagging sound. 'No. This isn't real, it's not real,' he said.

The little Celtic-patterned key rattled in the door, and then spun. The gagging sound came again, and the mirrored door slowly swung open.

Inside, nestled between old winter coats and his work shirt, his brother Joe hung from a noose. He wore the same blue jeans, white T-shirt and Nike trainers. Joe had been a handsome young man, but in death his face was grey and swollen, his eyes stared, bloodshot and criss-crossed with broken veins, and his mouth was fixed with a wide grin. Darryl closed his eyes, but when he opened them, Joe was still hanging there, the rope creaking slightly. His trainers swinging gently a few feet off the bottom of the wardrobe. A horrible laugh escaped from Joe's fixed grin, and Darryl felt something warm and wet splatter onto the front of his boxer shorts. He looked down. The flies on Joe's jeans were open, and he was holding his penis and peeing all over him.

Joe's face came alive, and he opened his mouth.

'Bed wetter, filthy little bed wetter!' he hissed, the grin widening.

Darryl woke with a jolt, and sat up. It was dark in his bedroom, and there was banging on his door. He stumbled up through the darkness and opened it.

His parents were out on the landing.

'It's half one in the fucking afternoon,' said John. 'What the hell are you doing in bed?'

'I called in sick for work,' said Darryl, rubbing his eyes.

'You didn't,' said his mother. 'I've just had some woman on the phone called Bryony, says she's your boss and she wanted to know where you are…'

'Work is what defines us,' said John, jabbing his finger at Darryl for emphasis. 'A job is a job, and there's millions out there who can't find work.'

'I'll sort it, Dad,' said Darryl.

John looked down at Darryl's crotch, and back up at his face. 'You've pissed yourself,' he said.

Darryl looked down and saw to his horror that the front of his boxer shorts were soaked.

'Oh, oh, no...'

'How old are you? Jesus Christ!' said John, shaking his head, and he walked off to the stairs.

'Mum... I didn't... I...' Darryl started blubbing, the nightmare still clinging to him.

Mary looked at him with concern, and then bent and pulled down his boxers.

'No!' cried Darryl, trying to step back, but she held on tight to the waistband.

'Come on, I need to get these in the wash...'

'Mum! Please!'

In the tussle, the wet boxer shorts tangled around his knees and he went crashing backwards into the bedroom.

Mary advanced on him. 'It's nothing I haven't seen before. I'll put them through the wash,' she said, reaching down and pulling them off his thrashing legs.

Darryl writhed around and covered his nakedness with his hands. She moved past him into the bedroom, holding his dripping boxers, and opened the curtains.

'Mum, leave me alone,' said Darryl, mortified.

She surveyed the room: his two computers on the desk, the huge laminated map of Greater London on the wall, and then she looked at the large yellow wet patch covering the bedsheet. Her eyes came back to him lying on the floor, with his hands covering his privates. 'Get yourself cleaned up. Looks like we're back to the plastic sheet again,' she said, walking out, swinging the wet boxers in her hand.

When she was gone, Darryl got up and grabbed for his towel on the back of the chair, feeling shame and embarrassment. He looked back at the wardrobe. He hadn't wet the bed since he was sixteen, when Joe had hanged himself.

CHAPTER 51

The door-to-door on Copers Cope Road in Beckenham had been extensive, but came up with nothing. No one, it seemed, had been taking in their surroundings or seen anything. The CCTV outside the gym and the train station further down the road didn't have a direct view of the road. Again, he'd been and gone, managing to stay in the shadows and leaving without a trace.

Erika returned home late on Tuesday afternoon and slumped onto the sofa, attempting to grab a few hours' sleep. She dozed fitfully: her dreams were filled with the battered faces of Janelle, Lacey and Ella, and then she found herself in a high-walled car park. It was night, and the car park was empty apart from a black dumpster in its far corner. A small man in a baseball cap was hunched over it. She ran at him, her feet slipping on the snow, and grabbed his shoulder, spinning him around, yanking off his baseball cap…

But he had no face. Where his face should have been was a blur of shadows. She stepped back and looked into the dumpster. She saw herself, lying battered and bloody amongst the bags and the eggshells and rotting food.

She woke with her phone ringing. It was dark, and she fumbled for it in her pocket. It was Isaac.

'I've finished the post-mortem on Ella Wilkinson,' he said.

'I'll be right there,' she replied.

There was a fine drizzle when she parked her car outside the mortuary in Penge, and she made a dash inside. The weather had warmed a little and rain was mingling with the melting snow. Isaac met her at the door and they went straight through to the mortuary. His team was just finishing up; a DI and a CSI, plus a photographer and an exhibits officer. They left, nodding at Erika on their way past. Ella Wilkinson's body lay on the steel mortuary table, covered in a clean white sheet to her neck.

Erika didn't know if she could do this again. She knew what was coming, knew that this girl had been tortured in the most gruesome fashion.

'I'll make this as swift as I can,' said Isaac softly, seeming to read her thoughts. He moved to the body and peeled back the sheet. 'As with Lacey Greene and Janelle Robinson, she suffered multiple incisions, some of which had started to heal. There are also tears to the left nipple which are consistent with her being bitten.'

'Bitten? He didn't bite the other victims?'

'No. Unfortunately there is not a clear impression to examine. The left cheekbone, cranium and the wrist in the right arm are broken, and she has three broken ribs to the left side of her body... There is an incision in the right upper thigh, which severed the femoral artery. As with the other victims, this would have been fatal.'

Erika closed her eyes and placed her hand to her forehead. When she opened them again, she looked at the y-shaped incision sewn neatly but crudely up the victim's sternum. She suddenly felt light-headed, and gripped hold of the edge of the mortuary table; her knees gave way a little and Isaac rushed around to support her.

'It's okay,' he said, hooking his hands under her arms. His two assistants looked up at her curiously.

'I'm fine,' she said. But as he let go, her knees buckled again.

'Come on, come to the office and let me get you a glass of water,' he said.

Isaac's office was warm and inviting in comparison to the cold mortuary, and Erika sat down on one of the cosy armchairs. He went to a small fridge and pulled out a bottle of water, handing it to her. She took a long gulp and sat back.

'You look pale.'

'I always look pale,' she joked.

He took her wrist and felt her pulse. 'What's your resting heart rate?'

'I don't know.'

'Do you exercise?'

'I rush about,' she said.

'When was your last health check?'

'Um, couple of years ago. Do you remember when that kid bit me at Lewisham Row? I had to have a screen, bloods, the works.'

'And?'

'And it was all clear.'

Isaac came and sat in the armchair opposite.

'Have you been sleeping?'

'A little, but with this case, sleep isn't something I have the luxury of doing.'

'That's no way to live.'

'That is how I live,' she snapped and took another swig of water. 'Sorry,' she added. To her horror she started to cry.

Isaac reached out and took her hand, and she let him hold it softly.

'As I said, this is no way to live, Erika.'

'I don't know how to live anymore. When I met Mark, I resisted him. Not that I didn't want to be with him, but I felt how easily we became a unit. There was always someone to come home to. Someone to go out with, to share things… I need it, but even then I could see it was a weakness, if that makes sense?'

'You thought being in love was a weakness?' said Isaac, raising one of his thin eyebrows.

Erika nodded. 'Isn't it easier in the long run to be alone? It's just you, there's no vulnerabilities, nothing can be taken from you.'

'That's a deeply depressing way of looking at life, Erika.'

'You know what it's like to lose someone. When Stephen died last year? Don't you feel vulnerable?'

Isaac straightened up a little; he looked as if he was feeling uncomfortable. 'I loved Stephen, but we were only together for a couple of years, and as you remember it was… tumultuous.'

'It doesn't matter how long you loved someone. It doesn't mean you miss them any less when they're gone.'

He nodded. Erika wiped a tear away.

'It's one of the reasons I resisted having kids with Mark. I kept putting it off… He wanted them.'

Isaac sat very still and just listened.

Erika went on: 'When Mark died… I tried to be practical. I thought that if I could get past one day, one week, month, a year, it would get easier, but it doesn't. And not only is there the loss to deal with, which threatens to crush you every single day, you're left with all this life left to lead. Alone. No one really talks about that, do they?'

Isaac nodded.

She went on: 'Getting over the loss, that bit people can sympathise with and understand, but moving on, trying to fill the gap the loss has left, is impossible… You know I've been seeing Peterson – James – since before Christmas.'

Isaac nodded. 'You like him, don't you?'

Erika nodded and got up, grabbing the box of tissues from the desk opposite.

'He just wants to be with me, and I keep pushing him away. He's such a good guy… Like Mark, he was the one everyone loved. I just don't know why Mark had to die and I'm still here. He was a great guy. I'm just a bitch.'

Isaac laughed.

'I am, it's not funny.'

'You're not a bitch, but you have to act like one sometimes. It helps you get the job done.'

'Isaac, this case, it's going to be the one that gets away. I know it. I have nothing. And I have to bring Ella Wilkinson's parents here later to formally identify her body… And I have to go to Sparks's funeral tomorrow… He's left behind a daughter.'

'Erika, you need to get a grip on all this. Do you want to come and stay at mine for a few days? You can come and go as you please, and it helps to have someone to come home to… I promise to keep my hands to myself.'

Erika laughed. 'No, thank you, but I just want to be alone.'

'No, you don't… Every day I have to do post-mortems on people, and so many of them had their whole lives ahead of them. They probably died wishing they could have done things differently, wishing they had been nicer, loved more, not stressed so much. Go and see James. You could be dead tomorrow, and lying on that slab in there.'

'Brutal, but true,' said Erika. 'You should give advice more.'

'I do, but most of the people I see at work can't do anything with it. They're dead.'

Erika held on to him again and gave him a long hug.

CHAPTER 52

Peterson was at home watching television when the doorbell rang. He checked the time and saw it was just before eight; he muted the sound and went to the front door. He was surprised to see Erika when he opened the door; she was completely drenched from the rain. Her hair flat against her head. They stood there in silence for a moment, just the sound of the rain drumming on the windows.

'Is it raining?' he asked.

'Just spitting,' she replied. They both burst out laughing.

'Come in, woman, before you freeze to death,' he said, standing to one side.

'I'm sorry about last night,' she said, going inside.

He closed the door, and she took his face in her hands and kissed him urgently. He hesitated, and then responded. They staggered to the bedroom, pulling at each other's clothes until they sank down onto the bed.

'You've got so much food in your cupboards,' said Erika, when they had dragged themselves out of bed a couple of hours later, now hungry.

They each had a beer; Erika was wearing one of his huge sleeping T-shirts with a faded picture of Scooby-Doo on the front.

'Have I?' he said, sitting on the countertop opposite her, wearing just a pair of boxer shorts.

'You have Kaffir Lime leaves… What the hell can you cook with those?'

'Curry. Noodle dishes. Loads.' He grinned, taking a sip of his beer.

'Seems a shame that we've ordered pizza.'

'I'll cook for you some other time,' he said, getting down and wrapping his hands around her waist.

She ran her hands down his smooth muscular back and felt the warmth of his skin pressed against hers.

'I'd like that,' she said, resting her chin on his shoulder. 'I wish I was shorter, there's something about resting your head on a guy's chest… It's comforting.'

'You want me to rest my head on yours instead?'

'Ha ha, very funny…'

They stood hugging in silence for a minute. Erika looked around his flat. It was a classic man pad with black leather furniture, and a giant television with a games console on the carpet in front. There was a picture of him, taken when he was a teenager with his parents and grandparents, and his sister. She remembered the story he'd told her, how his sister had killed herself when she was a teenager. She realised she wasn't the only person in the world who had lost someone.

'Mark was a little shorter than me. It really used to get to him. He hated me wearing heels, not that I did all that often, but sometimes I wanted to.'

'I'm not trying to replace him,' said Peterson, pulling back and looking her in the eyes. 'I know I could never do that.'

'I know you're not, but I need to move forward, and I like you, a lot. And I think Mark would have liked you.'

Peterson leaned in and gave her a kiss. The doorbell rang. 'That'll be the pizza,' he said.

* * *

They settled down in front of the late news with the hot pizza and a fresh beer each. The national news didn't mention the death of Ella Wilkinson, but the local London news ran it as their first story. They had footage of the crime scene in Beckenham; luckily the news reporters had arrived at the crime scene after the pathologist's work was complete, so all that they had to show was the police cordon across the car park entrance, and a lone police car. They did show a couple of short clips, interviews with concerned locals; a young woman with two small children and an old man in a flat cap.

'Makes me worry about letting the kids go out to play,' said the woman, holding on to her fidgeting young son and daughter.

'It's not the kind of thing you expect in these parts, terrible business,' said the old man, squinting at the camera through his thick glasses.

Then they cut to a woman outside a set of iron gates, with a house in the distance down a long driveway. The road was dark and windy, and she was bathed in the glare of a spotlight. Her hair whipped across her face, and she brushed it away with a gloved hand.

'Police last night raided this farm, just twenty miles away from the capital,' she intoned. 'No arrests were made, but concerned locals are asking if the death of Ella Wilkinson is linked to the deaths of Lacey Greene, a young woman from North London, and Janelle Robinson, a homeless woman whose body was found last summer. All victims were found in similar circumstances, dumped in refuse bins. We contacted the Met Police for further comment, but no one was available…'

The news report cut back to the studio, and the next story, about the lack of cycle paths in the borough of Islington.

'I hate local news,' said Erika. 'They always manage to sound clueless, but end up scaring the shit out of people.'

'Perhaps they should be scared,' said Peterson.

'And Melanie is inconsistent… We're talking as friends now, okay,' Erika added. Peterson nodded. 'She really stepped up, authorising the raid last night, but then she goes AWOL, and I can't get hold of her.'

On cue Erika's phone began to ring. She wiped her hands and went to her coat. 'Speak of the devil,' she said holding up the handset. She answered.

'Erika, have you seen the news?' snapped Melanie.

'I'm watching it.'

'Why did it say no one at the Met was available to comment?'

'Because no one was. I've tried to call you. Colleen is still working on follow-ups from the appeal, and Ella Wilkinson's parents only identified her body a couple of hours ago.'

Melanie huffed and puffed on the end of the phone. 'Well, we've been called into a meeting with the Assistant Commissioner tomorrow morning at nine. We need to be prepared.'

'I am prepared. You're the one who's been incommunicado for the last couple of days,' said Erika. She saw Peterson's face wincing as she said this.

'I am Acting Superintendent, Erika, and until you know what that entails keep your opinions to yourself. I will see you tomorrow at New Scotland Yard.'

With that she hung up the phone. Peterson was still shaking his head.

'Why did you just go off on her like that?'

'I'm pissed off!'

'And how did it help, having a go at your boss?'

'Hang on. I'm YOUR boss.'

'Not right now. You're just a fit bird eating pizza in my flat.' He smiled.

'*Fit bird?*'

'What? You're not fit?'

'Well. I'm certainly not a *bird*.'

'So you're my girlfriend?'

Erika took another slice of pizza from the box. 'Um. I suppose so... I'm not really a girl.'

'So you're not fit, you're not a bird or a girl... But you are pissed off with your boss. Can we at least agree on that?'

Erika laughed. 'Yes.'

'It gets in the way of what a good copper you are,' he said, his face serious. She stopped smiling and nodded.

'I don't endear myself to top brass, do I?'

'No. Now eat your pizza,' he said. 'Keep that foul mouth busy.'

She nodded and took a bite. 'Maybe I should go to this meeting tomorrow with a mouthful of pizza. It will keep me out of trouble.'

CHAPTER 53

Darryl had remained in his bedroom for the rest of the day, fearful of falling asleep, but wary of his parents. His head was mixed up. He'd had such courage when he took those women, but when they were dead and gone, it all drained away and he felt scared, insignificant, the weak little loser he'd always been. He spent the afternoon online, clicking through pictures of girls on Facebook, and profiles on Match.com. He was always looking: it was an addiction for him, a habit. He liked long dark hair, and he dragged a few pictures onto his desktop which took his fancy. He was just looking, that's what he kept telling himself.

He'd only ventured downstairs when he heard the creak of his parents climbing into bed. He found Grendel lying in her huge basket in the boot room, and her tail thumped when she saw him. He took a packet of honey roast ham from the fridge and split it with her, watching her huge white jaws as she chomped it down. He lay down, squashed in with her in the dog bed, and only then was he able to drift off to sleep.

He woke just before five, warm against her soft furry back and wondered if the only person he could feel close to was Grendel; of course, she wasn't a person. He was relieved to see the front of the tracksuit bottoms he wore were dry.

Darryl showered and took the early train into work the next morning. The dull routine of the office further comforted him, and the morning moved past unremarkably. He left for an early lunch, choosing to nip to the McDonald's by Guy's and St Thomas's Hospital. When he returned with his grease-spotted bag of food there were only a handful of people in the large open-plan office, and Bryony was the only one in their section, eating alone at her desk.

He sat down and started to unpack the contents of his food, and then looked up, feeling her eyes on him. She was chewing rhythmically, her eyes magnified and unblinking behind her grimy glasses. On closer inspection he could see, and smell, that she'd brought some leftover Indian food in a Tupperware container. He glanced up and smiled at her. A small piece of garlic clung to the top of her downy lip.

'You didn't fancy the pub with the others?' she asked.

'Yes, I'm there right now. This is merely a hologram,' he replied, sweeping his arm over his face. She looked back at him with her blank face. 'Bryony. That was a joke.'

'Oh,' she guffawed, ejecting a little of the chewed onion bhaji onto her chin. 'Oops, I'm such a pig.' She blushed, swiping it off with her finger and sucking it off the tip.

Darryl turned to his computer and started to eat his McDonald's. He logged onto the BBC website and was about to search for details of Ella Wilkinson when he heard her clear her throat behind him. He jumped.

'Onion bhaji?'

He looked around and Bryony stood behind him with her Tupperware container. It contained a neat row of dark bhajis nestling on a fold of paper towel. There was something childish about the way she held it out, as if she was offering him a crisp during playtime. They smelt good. He looked down at his McDonald's, which had sweated and gone cold on his way back to the office.

'Thanks,' he said, taking one. It was delicious.

'My dad always orders too much Indian,' she said, twirling her stubby fingers delicately over the box and picking one.

'I love Indian; we don't have a good one near where I live,' he said through a mouthful.

She nodded sheepishly, taking a big bite and chewing. 'You didn't have to worry about using the Internet, so long as you keep it to break times…'

'It's all doom and gloom, isn't it? The news.'

Bryony nodded. 'Do you want another one?' She pushed the Tupperware box up under his nose, thrilled that her playground friend wanted her to stick around. He took two.

'Is that your dog?' she asked, inclining her head to the photo of Grendel tacked to the bottom of his computer monitor.

'Yeah.'

'A he or a she?'

'She.'

'She's beautiful, in an odd kind of way.'

'Yes. She's a mix of Staffordshire Terrier and Dalmatian,' he said, unsticking the photo from the monitor. 'Her name's Grendel.'

Bryony wiped her hand on the seat of her jeans and took the photo. 'Grendel? Is that French?'

'No. Do you know the story of *Beowulf*?' he said, taking the photo out of her greasy grip.

'Sorry,' she said, watching him wipe it off carefully with a tissue. 'I saw the movie, *Beowulf*, you know, the cartoon.'

'It wasn't originally a movie. It's an epic poem, ancient… Grendel is the monster.'

'Why would you name your dog after a monster?'

'Well, not everyone thinks Grendel is a monster. One person's monster is another's friend…'

Bryony chewed thoughtfully for a moment and swallowed. She looked back to his computer and the *BBC News* page where there was a side piece about Ella Wilkinson.

'I've been following that story. Those girls who were killed. I live near Waterloo, close to where the first one went missing.'

'He wouldn't go for you,' said Darryl, taking a bite of his bhaji. Her face faltered. 'I mean, you're too clever to fall for some bloke on Internet dating.'

'I've tried Internet dating. Didn't have much luck,' she said bashfully. *Cos you probably used your own photo!* a voice shouted in his head, but he used the silence to shove the rest of the bhaji into his mouth. 'The first victim sold coffee, but the second one worked in an office job. She even had the same job title as me, *Administrator*,' she said, pulling her top down over her backside with a large yet dainty hand.

'You should keep your eyes peeled. Tell people where you'll be,' said Darryl. He imagined trying to kill her, the knife glancing off her blubbery thighs, and a guffaw escaped him. He clamped his hand over his mouth to fake a coughing fit. 'I'm fine,' he added, waving her away. 'Fine.'

Bryony thumped him on the back.

'Better?'

He nodded and took a sip of his Coke.

'Darryl...'

'Yeah?'

'I saw *Beowulf* when it was at the IMAX... I got a couple of tickets to the cinema, the IMAX, the one near Waterloo... They were a present for my birthday.'

'When was your birthday?' he asked.

'Today,' she said, looking down at her feet.

'Oh. Happy birthday.' He watched her for a moment, and she quickly seized another bhaji and bit into it.

The IMAX cinema at Waterloo was built on what used to be the Bullring roundabout, near the train station. You could only get to it by going down through one of four dank, dark concrete underpasses, and they were often filled with homeless people. He'd fantasised about abducting a homeless girl. There was something about their desperation when confronted with death... Darryl looked up and realised Bryony had said something else.

'So would you like to come, Darryl?'

'To?'

'The IMAX with me, tomorrow night. There's a showing of *Guardians of the Galaxy...*'

Darryl hesitated and then thought what a great opportunity it would be to look around, just look. It was a scratch that needed itching. It was a huge cinema, central, and Bryony could be a good cover.

'Okay,' he said.

'So it's a date?' she said, chewing and swallowing the last of her bhaji.

'Yeah. It's a date,' said Darryl. He kept the smile plastered to his face until she'd retreated back to her desk, her face flushed.

He wiped the photo of Grendel again, and stuck it back to the bottom of the computer monitor. The screen had gone into sleep mode and was blank, and he was reminded of his reflection. Inside he felt like a strong invincible warrior, like Beowulf, but the face which stared back at him was podgy and ordinary, with a weak chin and beady eyes.

He sat back in his chair and realised something; Bryony actually thought she had a chance with him. *Her* with him.

He found it difficult to concentrate for the rest of the day, especially with Bryony opposite constantly looking up and smiling, and just before four, she even brought him a cup of coffee from Starbucks.

He took it with a smile, but inside he was furious. He would show her. She would regret thinking they were in the same league.

CHAPTER 54

As instructed, Erika and Melanie met at the New Scotland Yard building. They waited for twenty minutes in silence outside the Assistant Commissioner's office until her secretary finally broke the heavy silence and they were shown through.

Camilla was dressed to kill, but looked determined to at least maim in an elegant black trouser suit with a white silk blouse. She sat at the head of the conference table in the corner of her office. To her right sat a neat little man with a stern cherubic face. And on her left, a handsome young male uniformed officer was ready to take minutes. Melanie sat at the opposite end of the table, and Erika beside her.

'Thank you for coming, ladies,' said Camilla. 'I've called this meeting to discuss the triple murder inquiry... Acting Commander Mason is joining us.'

The neat little man nodded. Camilla opened a folder on the desk with a light flourish, and slipped on her glasses from a gold chain around her neck. 'Acting Superintendent Hudson. Do you prefer Mel or Melanie?'

'It's Melanie, ma'am.'

'Good, that's very wise,' she said, scanning the papers in front of her. Melanie looked confused; Erika gave her a sideways glance. Camilla loved to confuse people during meetings with her off-the-cuff comments. Camilla went on. 'Melanie, I asked you along here with Erika to get a broad idea of the case. The parents of Ella Wilkinson are now pursuing a formal complaint against you and the Metropolitan Police through the Independent Police Complaints Commission, and along with Erika we'd just like to get your side of things. Informally, at this stage.'

'Ma'am. There isn't a side. There are facts. Would you like the facts?' said Erika.

Melanie didn't object to the interruption.

Camilla nodded.

'I've been briefing Melanie at every step during this case. We were in the process of finalising the media appeal into the deaths of Janelle Robinson and Lacey Greene when we heard that Ella Wilkinson was missing. I had less than ten minutes to make a decision whether or not to include her abduction in our appeal. At that stage, all I knew was that Ella was of a similar age and looks to Lacey and Janelle, and she'd been reported missing in broadly similar circumstances. I took the decision not to include her name in the appeal at that time so as not to distract from the victims we did have. I also didn't want to add fuel to rumours that we had a killer of multiple victims.'

'I wasn't kept fully updated with what was unfolding,' said Melanie.

Erika turned to her. 'Yes, you were. But you were away at a conference and we weren't able to speak.'

'It was a racial awareness conference, ma'am.'

Camilla held up her manicured hand. 'How is that relevant?' Melanie opened and closed her mouth, flummoxed. Camilla went on. 'If it had been a conference about the prevention of scrumping apples, would you have told me with such relish?'

'I'm just giving you the information, ma'am,' said Melanie, stung.

'I want useful information, not window dressing.'

'Yes, ma'am,' said Melanie, struggling with her composure.

Erika almost felt sorry for her.

Camilla glanced at her file again. 'Are you aware that a journalist from the national press visited Ella Wilkinson's parents, the retired Chief Superintendent Wilkinson and his wife, and enlightened them on the details of your Specialist Firearms Operation?'

'No,' said Melanie, looking at Erika, who also shook her head.

'They told him how you mobilised two Specialist Firearms Teams to raid the home of a Mr Darius O'Keefe and his recently widowed elderly mother. Mr O'Keefe, incidentally, also performs as a drag queen, "Crystal Balls" is his drag name...'

Camilla paused for effect, and Erika saw a smile flicker across the face of the young officer taking minutes. Acting Commander Mason remained stern, placing his small neat hands on the table.

Camilla continued: 'Mr O'Keefe also wishes to make a formal complaint, saying that whilst the police were courteous, a Heckler & Koch G36 assault rifle was discharged in his costume store, damaging a plastic mannequin, which was holding a fake plastic revolver, and wearing a Swarovski-encrusted tubular bodice worth seventeen thousand pounds... I'm expecting all of this to run in the national tabloids with the added coda that, hours later, former Chief Superintendent Wilkinson's daughter turned up dead.'

Erika looked to Melanie, but she had sunk down in her seat and was staring at the polished surface of the table.

'Ma'am, you must be aware that the press has twisted this to make us sound incompetent,' said Erika. 'We were acting on a tip-off from what we believed was a reliable source who came forward after seeing our appeal on television. I was aware that Ella Wilkinson had already been missing for three days, and time was running out. It was our duty to go in there and investigate what could have been a dangerous individual who had already abducted and killed two women. It's all very well to sit here and recount the story as if it's some amusing anecdote.'

'I don't find it amusing,' snapped Camilla.

'Careful decisions had to be made in a short time, ma'am, and I believe I did the best I could in a difficult and complex situation.'

There was a cold silence. Erika looked across at Melanie, hoping she would jump in, but she remained quiet.

'It's not about what we believe, Erika,' said Camilla. 'It's how public opinion is formed, and in this day and age much of what we do and the decisions we make are led by public opinion. Budgets are decided... policy... The press will now zone in on the targeting of a gay man, the damage to his livelihood, and the cost to the taxpayer of deploying two teams from the Specialist Firearms Unit at short notice!'

'Why are we even having this meeting?' snapped Erika. 'You've decided to take a rather blinkered view of the facts: you're looking at them through a tabloid lens.'

'Erika, watch your tone,' said Melanie.

'So now you decide to speak, and pull rank,' said Erika, unable to stop herself.

'Melanie is your Superintendent,' said Mason, speaking for the first time.

'Acting Superintendent,' said Erika. 'And forgive me, sir, but you were involved in our decision. Do you have anything to contribute?'

Mason shifted in his chair. 'I don't appreciate being placed on the spot,' he said.

'*Placed* on the spot!' cried Erika. 'This is a meeting about a Specialist Firearms Operation that was ultimately authorised by you, sir!'

'Could you please wait outside, Erika,' said Camilla.

Erika thought back to what Sparks had said, the night before he died, how he'd been unfairly hauled over the coals by Camilla, and she wished he were here. If only because he had balls. Melanie was sitting like a meek church mouse.

'Can I please add on the record that, whilst having the support of the public is essential to the job of policing, the public never have the full picture of what it takes to run a police investigation—'

'Erika.'

'Please don't let this investigation be dominated by the upset of one of the victims. My team has been working tirelessly to apprehend the killer of these three young women. That is our priority, ma'am.'

Camilla gave her a thin smile.

'Thank you, Erika, now please, that will be all,' she said.

Melanie merely stared ahead as Erika walked out of the room. Fuming.

CHAPTER 55

Erika was waiting for Melanie in an unmarked police car outside the New Scotland Yard building. It had been arranged before the meeting that they would travel together to Sparks's funeral. Melanie emerged ten minutes later, and got in beside her. There was a nasty atmosphere as the car set off.

'From now on I want to know *everything* that's going on,' she snapped. 'I want to be informed of every decision you make.'

'So I'll continue what I was doing, and it's up to you to make sure you answer your voicemails,' Erika shot back.

'I am your senior officer!' shouted Melanie, turning to her.

'Then act like it! Erika roared back. They stared at each other, then turned away and stared out at the buildings whipping past.

'Sorry, I just have to check – what time's the funeral?' asked the uniformed officer driving.

'It starts in an hour, so you better put your foot down,' said Erika.

'You have my authority to blue light it if necessary,' added Melanie. The driver eyed Erika in the mirror.

'You know that's unlawful. There's no justification for us to use blue lights to go to a funeral,' said Erika. Melanie looked at her and the driver.

'Of course. I just wanted to make sure we didn't miss our colleague's funeral.'

'I'll get you there as fast as I can,' said the driver.

'Thank you,' said Erika.

They passed the rest of the journey in silence.

Superintendent Sparks's funeral was held at a small church in Greenwich, high on the hill overlooking the Royal Naval College and the city. They arrived just as the service started and slipped into a pew at the back of the church. It was well attended, for a man who had been a bully and a divisive colleague. Erika wondered how many people had felt obliged to attend. Sparks's wife was on the front row with an elderly couple and a little girl in a sombre black velvet dress with a matching ribbon in her hair. His coffin shone under the bright lights of the church, and a large spray of red and white roses sat on top amongst a cloud of gypsophila.

Did Sparks like roses? thought Erika. *Was he religious? How many people in the congregation really knew him?* All of these thoughts went through her head. Funerals were a time to remember the dead, but very often they struggled to do just that. Erika thought back to Mark's funeral; of having to pick flowers and hymns, and who would say what. It all felt so alien, so unlike the youthful, vibrant man who had died.

The most poignant part of the service was when Sparks's childhood friend gave the eulogy and told how they had been close growing up, and had gone travelling for a year after high school.

'Andy was my buddy. He was a complex bloke, but he had a heart and he cared. Life and work got in the way of all that towards the end… I just wish we'd been able to talk more. Sleep well, mate,' he said.

Erika looked to Melanie beside her, and saw a tear running down her cheek. She grabbed her hand and squeezed it. Melanie nodded and Erika let go. When they stood for the next hymn,

Erika spied Marsh sitting a few rows forward with a few other senior police officers she recognised, but didn't know by name. She leaned forward in the hope of catching his eye, but the organ started to play, 'I Vow to Thee, My Country'.

An hour later, the service finished. Erika and Melanie left the church and hung around close to the entrance, as mourners filed out. There was an awkwardness between them, and Erika didn't know how to broach it.

'I'm going to give my condolences to Sparks's wife,' said Melanie, peering back through the church door to where she was surrounded by well-wishers.

'Look, Melanie, earlier I was out of order. Sorry.'

'It's okay. It's like Sparks's friend said back there. This job, it…' She looked like she was going to say more, then checked herself.

'It gets in the way sometimes of being decent,' said Erika, adding, 'I'm talking about myself here.'

'Let's try to touch base a couple of times a day. I'll make sure I'm available, when I'm not in the office.'

'Sure.' Erika nodded and smiled. Melanie went off back through the crowds, and she waited for a few more minutes as the church cleared out, and finally Marsh emerged. He looked exhausted, but still quite handsome. His short sandy hair was cropped close to his head and he'd lost some weight, emphasising his square jaw. He looked more like the officer she and Mark had trained with back in Manchester all those years ago, before his ambition had driven a wedge between them.

'Finally I get to talk to you,' she said. He leaned in and gave her a peck on the cheek.

'Why haven't you been answering your phone?'

'Sorry, Erika, things haven't been all that good.'

'I've heard. When were you going to tell me you've been suspended?'

He rolled his eyes. 'Can you keep your voice down?'

'Can you return my calls, and then I don't have to skulk around outside a funeral to get to talk to you.'

He ran a finger around the collar of his shirt. 'Are you going to the wake?'

'I don't know. I wasn't planning on it.'

They stepped out of the way as a large group emerged from the church to shake the priest's hand. They started to move off towards the gates.

'I heard you were there when he died?'

'I was in his office, having a go at him, when he collapsed,' said Erika.

'So you nagged him to death?' said Marsh, deadpan.

'Very funny.'

They got to the gates, and Erika saw the police car waiting to take her and Melanie back.

'Come on, I'm taking you for lunch,' she said, putting her arm through his. 'I want to hear everything, and I want to pick your brains about a case I'm working on.'

CHAPTER 56

They walked into the centre of Greenwich and found a smart little café. They ordered large coffees and a full English breakfast each.

'I know you're not a man for details, but I'm shocked you've been suspended,' said Erika when they were settled in a booth in the corner.

'Brutally honest as always,' he said, adjusting the cutlery awkwardly.

'What happened exactly?'

He took a deep breath. 'I've been suspended because the Met has suddenly decided to go after the Gadd family for money laundering on their import/export business. You remember the Gadd family when we were working over at Lewisham?'

'I remember being in hot water for crashing Paul Gadd's mother's funeral wake to track down a witness,' said Erika.

Marsh grinned ruefully. 'Yes. I haven't forgotten that. Took a lot of smoothing over.'

'So what is the deal with the family?' asked Erika.

'For the past twenty-five years, the Met has turned a blind eye to some of their *activities* in return for information. Officially, the Gadd family run the contracts for recycling paper and plastics in and around London. They also own a warehouse complex out at the Isle of Dogs, used for import/export.'

'So, they're mafia?' said Erika.

'They don't deal in drugs or weapons. It's mainly black market cigarettes, alcohol…'

'What about the recycling business?'

'That's a hundred per cent legit, and it's very lucrative. They take in collections London-wide from the council and they sort it before it's exported to China.'

They paused when their food arrived, a posh version of a full English breakfast, which came arranged artfully on the plate with the baked beans snug in their own little ramekin. They tucked into their food for a moment.

'Okay, so what are you accused of? Taking bribes from the Gadd family?' asked Erika, buttering some toast.

'No, no, no.' He took a sip of coffee and looked uncomfortable. 'Now, bear in mind that when I was promoted to Chief Superintendent, I inherited staff, infrastructure, budgets...'

'I know how it works...'

'I also inherited my predecessor's relationship with Paul Gadd. He's seventy now, but still very much active in the family business. There was an arrangement in place whereby certain deliveries would come into their warehouses which Customs and Excise would turn a blind eye to.'

'You don't work for Customs and Excise.'

'But I could have officers briefed to help, shall we say, disguise or divert attention, nothing dangerous, just to help to keep it away from prying eyes...'

'Okay.'

'Erika, everyone knew about this. It was an open secret. But as you know, things change, and when Camilla became Assistant Commissioner, she was eager to make her mark, curry favour with top civil servants and the government. Her husband is great pals with our Chancellor of the Exchequer, and Camilla saw an opportunity to claw back half a billion in unpaid tax duty from the Gadd family. An enquiry was launched, heads have rolled. My head is one of them.'

'Can the Gadd family afford half a billion?'

'They can afford a large chunk of it if they cut a deal with Her Majesty's Customs and Excise. And Camilla scores a high profile win for the police.'

'But, of course, it's not really a win, is it?' said Erika.

Marsh shook his head. 'The flip side of our agreement with the Gadd family is that we've been able to control what comes into London via the river. They've helped us keep the doors shut on billions of illegal drugs flooding into the city. Now that all stops, and the Met is going to be stretched to the limit both physically and financially to deal with it.'

'More than half a billion...' They chewed their food for a moment. 'Are you okay, Paul?'

'Not really. I'm on gardening leave, but I've got no bloody garden. Marcie has taken the twins to France with her mother. They're staying in our cottage. She can't bear the shame of being seen by the other women, locally.'

'She still wants a divorce?'

'Yeah.'

'Sorry,' said Erika. She took a large forkful of food. 'Where does Sparks fit in with all this?'

'Sparks?'

'Camilla was having him investigated too. Thought he was taking backhanders: Simon Douglas-Brown came up.'

'Bloody hell, it is a witch-hunt,' he said, shaking his head. 'What happens now?'

'I wait for a tribunal, which could take months.'

'I'm sorry.'

They ate for a moment, watching the traffic go past on the road. An idea dawned on Erika, and her heart began to race.

'When you worked with the Gadd family, you had a contact?'

'Yeah. Why?'

'Have you heard about the case I'm working on?'

'The girls found dead in the dumpsters?'

'Yes. I've been trying to find a link, something to tie the case together. The body of each victim has been left in an identical dumpster, and I'm wondering what if the killer works for the company which supplies the dumpsters? This could explain the random locations where he leaves them. What's the company called?'

'I don't know; the Gadds run umbrella companies...'

'Can you get me the info?'

'I can tell you now, but this is strictly off-the-record.'

'Okay, what will it cost me?'

'Give me your fried bread, and I'll call it quits.'

She smiled and passed it over to him. He smiled back at her, and thought, as he did often, that she was the one who'd got away.

CHAPTER 57

It had been an awkward day at work for Darryl. He had felt Bryony's attentions keenly. Every time he looked up from his work, he would see her, staring at him across the partition. She then left early for lunch, returning with sandwiches and coffee for them both. She'd bought him egg and cress, which he hated, and for herself cheese and onion, which didn't bode well for their 'date' later that evening.

When they had their weekly departmental meeting that afternoon, she'd saved him a seat next to her in the conference room. During the meeting, she'd slid a note across the table, which read:

Can't wait 4 2nite Bryony x

He'd glanced over at her, and her eyes behind her thick glasses had been feverish with desire. Darryl had smiled awkwardly and then looked away, catching two of the younger more popular lads across the desk smirking. When they finished work, he expected Bryony to ask him if he'd like to have something to eat, but much to his relief she didn't, saying that they should meet at the IMAX just before seven thirty.

He went for a walk along the South Bank next to the river, and then for a bite to eat in a modern Thai restaurant close to the Royal Festival Hall. It was half empty and he requested a seat at the end of one of the long benches looking out over the river. A slim dark-haired girl called 'Kayla' was his waitress, and when she seated him and took his order, she'd offered up a broad smile. When she brought his steaming bowl of Ramen noodles, she'd leaned across him and her tight T-shirt had ridden up to show a washboard stomach tattooed with a swirling mass, and two dragons engaged in combat. Darryl had felt his penis grow hard, and had inhaled her scent. She wore a heavy musky perfume. Slutty. It thrilled him. He couldn't keep his eyes off her as he ate, watching as she moved through the tables, seating customers and bringing out plates of steaming food. A few times she must have felt his gaze and she turned, but she didn't return his smile. When Darryl finished, it was a tall skinny waiter who came and took his plate.

'Any dessert?' he said coldly.

'No, just the bill...'

Kayla emerged from the kitchen at the other end of the restaurant and shot him a wary look. Then the waiter returned with the card payment terminal.

'I thought you all had your sections in the restaurant?' asked Darryl, handing over his credit card.

'We do,' said the waiter, slipping the card into the machine and keying in the details. He thrust it back at Darryl. 'Pin please.'

'So why didn't Kayla finish with me? I wanted to give her a tip.'

'You made her feel uncomfortable, sir. Here's your card,' he said, chucking it on the counter with the receipt and stalking off.

'Cunt,' Darryl muttered, picking it up.

'What did you just call me?' said the waiter, doubling back and standing over him.

'I CALLED YOU A CUNT!' shouted Darryl, rising to his feet. 'I'M THE CUSTOMER. I'M ALWAYS RIGHT!'

The restaurant fell silent. There was just a clatter of a fork in the kitchen.

'You need to go, before I call the police,' said the waiter, taking a step back. He was much taller than Darryl, but now looked afraid.

'I'm going. It was a shitty meal anyway,' he said, walking out.

He was furious as he walked back along the river, but the cold air soon began to calm his nerves. He wouldn't let a lowly waiter spoil his evening.

Darryl left the embankment near Waterloo station, and passed through the dank underpass. Sadly, it was empty of homeless people, and he emerged at the base of the huge circular IMAX cinema. He could see through the glass that it was crowded inside, and more people were pouring out of the other three underpasses.

He found Bryony waiting just inside the main entrance, by a small table where leaflets were laid out. He still wore his work clothes, and for a brief moment wondered if she had expected him to get changed. She wore a purple diaphanous dress which came down almost to the ground. The tips of a pair of silver shoes peeped out from under the layers of fabric. Wrapped around her doughy shoulders was a black pashmina. She'd also done something odd to her hair. It was still pulled back into a ponytail, but she'd added a sort of small beehive at the front, which, with her prominent nose, made him think of the alien from the Sigourney Weaver films.

'Hi, Darryl,' she said, her face lighting up.

She held a small silver bag on a chain in her right hand, and she hooked it up over the crook of her arm nervously. It felt quaint, this meeting, and he leaned over and gave her a peck on the cheek. He could smell alcohol on her breath, whisky or brandy. Had she taken a nip for Dutch courage? Yes, more than a nip. She swayed a little and put her arms around him. Over her shoulder he saw a group of teenagers waiting in the ticket line. One of the girls took a sly photo of their awkward embrace and they all laughed. He pulled away from her and smiled.

'Do I look alright?' she said, touching a hand to her hair.

'Yeah. Great.'

She beamed again, displaying an inch of gums above her teeth. 'I've got the tickets already. Would you like anything to eat, any snacks?'

'Popcorn?'

She nodded, smiling again.

It was a smile of complete... complete what? Adoration? Awe? Drunkenness? Or could she see into him; could she see the real person inhabiting this unremarkable shell? He suddenly felt strength from being with her. It was as if he cast a light and she was basking in it. For a brief moment he thought he might be able to tell her the things he couldn't tell anyone else, and that on hearing them, she wouldn't run.

When they'd bought popcorn, Bryony guided him to one of the lifts.

'We've got seats right at the top,' she said excitedly.

They came out of the lift and went into the auditorium. Darryl had never been to an IMAX cinema before; he'd only been to the cinema once, when he was nine, with his mother and Joe, but Joe had stuffed his face with popcorn and thrown up all over the place before the trailers had finished, and they'd had to leave.

The size of the screen and auditorium shocked him.

'It's as tall as five double-decker buses,' said Bryony, enjoying his awestruck face and leading him up to the back row, which was empty. They sat down, and he peered forward at the crowds of people stretching away below them. The lights dimmed and then the trailers started. They ate their popcorn for the first few minutes of the film, a box each on their laps, and they had the back row to themselves, save for a young boy at the far end.

Bryony placed her popcorn on the floor, and took his from his hands.

'What are you doing?' he whispered.

She leaned into his face, and he got another whiff of the booze on her breath.

'Just sit back and relax,' she said. She looked around, then put her hand down into his lap and started to rub his crotch.

'Bryony... What are you doing?' He flinched.

'Shush, you don't need to say anything,' she whispered. She started to rub harder, and he shifted in his seat awkwardly.

'You don't have to...' he started.

'Oh, I want to,' she crooned in a soft voice. 'Is this okay? Am I doing it right?'

She started to work at the outline of his penis with her fingers, then squeezing and cupping his balls. He looked around at the auditorium, at the backs of people's heads watching the huge screen. Kayla, the girl with the tattoo, swam into his thoughts, and he gave in and put his head back.

'Oh, I can feel it, you're getting hard,' whispered Bryony, then hiccupped. Darryl opened one eye. 'Sorry, I had a little drinky-poo before I met you,' she said, pulling her hand back.

'No. Don't stop, Bryony. It's good,' he said, taking her hand and placing it back.

She nodded and smiled. The light from the cinema screen was reflected in her huge glasses. He closed his eyes as Bryony started to rub again. His thoughts went back to Kayla. How she smelt, her dark skin with the tattoos. He unbuckled his trousers and pulled down the waistband of his boxer shorts. He felt the cold air on his hard penis and opened his eyes again.

'Go on. Put it in your mouth,' he said.

'Oh my,' said Bryony, looking down and breathing heavily, her eyes behind her glasses filled with awe.

Oh my God, she's never seen a penis before, thought Darryl. This turned him on even more.

'Your lips are so beautiful,' he said.

'Thank you,' she said, putting a hand to her mouth.

'Go on, put my big dick between those beautiful lips.'

Bryony nodded and eased off her chair awkwardly and onto her knees, taking him cautiously in her mouth. Darryl felt both thrilled and disgusted. He gripped the back of her head and pushed her down. She gagged and pulled back a little, but he held onto her ears and thrust in and out of her mouth. She made slurping squelching sounds for a couple of minutes, and then he climaxed, gripping the hair at the back of her head, as she made more gulping gagging sounds.

She sat back on the floor between the cinema seats, breathless, and looking a little shocked as he tucked himself back in, and did up his flies.

'Was that alright?' she asked, wiping her mouth.

'That. Was very good,' he said, giving her the thumbs up.

Her face lit up with a huge smile. 'Oh, I'm so pleased!' She started to heave herself back up into her seat, but knocked over their popcorn. 'Ow, I think I've got cramp,' she hissed.

'It's okay,' he said, getting up. 'You sit down.' He picked up the two boxes. 'I'll go and get us some more.'

'Thanks,' she said, sitting awkwardly and rubbing at her leg.

'Was it salty or sweet?'

'Salty… but I think now I fancy sweet,' she said, swallowing again. 'And can you get me something to drink?'

Darryl grinned and went off to the snack bar downstairs.

CHAPTER 58

After lunch with Marsh, Erika returned to West End Central. She'd been working with the team for the rest of the afternoon and early evening on the information Marsh had given her. At eight thirty, Melanie came back to the station, and she and Erika had a meeting in her office.

'I'm going to request specific data on the employees who live around Greater London, on the borders,' said Erika. 'Specifically, males aged between twenty-one and thirty-five.'

'And this is from the waste management company, Genesis?' asked Melanie, looking over the document Erika had prepared. 'What evidence do you have to back up a request like this?'

'We've spent a long time looking at the locations where the bodies were dumped, trying to find patterns, repeat behaviours. We know he goes for the same type of girl. The only other similarity is that they have all been dumped in general waste recycling bins specific to the Genesis recycling company.'

'Erika, do you think this can be classed as a similarity? Do you know how many households there are in Central London?'

'I would hazard a guess at—'

'This afternoon I sat through three meetings discussing crime statistics and burglaries. There are 886,000 people in Greater London who own their household but have a mortgage; some 862,000 people rent privately from a landlord; social housing accounts for 786,000 homes, and 690,000 people own their home outright.'

'You remembered those figures?'

'They were drummed into us repeatedly,' she said. 'But my point is, they have one thing in common. Their refuse needs, or should I say rubbish collection, is done by Genesis. That's 2.6 million homes. Add to that the millions of businesses that operate in London. And Genesis is one of the largest waste management companies in Europe with 400,000 employees. You think we can just go in there and request data on their staff?'

'We know that he drives a Citroën C3,' added Erika desperately.

'Oh, well, that narrows it down even more. It's only one of the most popular cars bought in the past five years. Do you think that Genesis would keep records of the cars their employees drive? Or shall we also go ahead and put in a general request from the DVLA for every driver of a Citroën C3 in the Greater London area?'

Erika paused.

'I've already done that, and we're working through a colossal list of names. We're first working through males who have previous criminal records.'

'But as far as we know, this guy isn't in the system?' said Melanie. 'We have his DNA but he's never been sampled, which leads me to think he's never been arrested.'

Erika sighed. 'Melanie. I have to start somewhere. We've tried tracing the car from the CCTV footage, following its progress through the CCTV network, but without a number plate and the amount of Citroën C3s there are on the roads, it's impossible.'

Melanie sat back and took a swig of her coffee.

'I know, Erika…Anything you do would have to stand up in court. There are data protection issues, manpower issues. Are you aware that, as well as our issues with the Gadd family who are shareholders in Genesis, two major shareholders sit on the board of the IPCC, who are already dealing with a complaint from the parents of Ella Wilkinson?'

Erika nodded. 'But it might lead to a breakthrough; we may have something in all that data that cracks this before he takes another young woman.'

'We don't know he's—' started Melanie.

'He's taken three, and the gaps between the abduction and murders are getting shorter. Melanie, I work on my gut instinct.'

'So do dictators, and megalomaniacs,' she said, not unkindly. 'Look, come to me with something more concrete, tailored and specific. Narrow down who you are looking for, a location where they might work. Genesis has seventeen offices in Central London. Another forty-six nationwide. I will, of course, turn over every resource I have at my disposal, but I can't write a blank cheque for you to cast a wide net and see what you can catch.'

Erika stared at her despondently, and then nodded. 'Keep me in the loop. Close the door on your way out.'

Peterson was waiting downstairs in the station foyer when Erika emerged from the lift. She relayed the conversation she'd just had with Melanie.

'What are you going to do?' he asked.

'I don't know. I need to think. I need to work out a way to find a needle in a haystack.'

'Would pizza and beer at my place help?' he said as they walked out and into the cold air.

'Yes,' she grinned. 'Yes it would.'

CHAPTER 59

When Darryl had returned with fresh popcorn, Bryony had been very clingy and had insisted they held hands throughout the rest of the film, which had creeped him out far more than the other thing she'd done to him.

As soon as the film ended, Darryl had leapt up and insisted on leaving. While they were waiting with a big group of people for the lift down to the foyer, he'd overheard one of the ushers, a pretty young girl with a cloud of Afro hair, talking excitedly about how she was meeting a casting director for a drink. From her conversation with another usher, it was clear she was an actress, didn't know the man she was meeting, and was prepared to flirt quite hard to get on his radar.

Darryl barely noticed what Bryony was saying as they rode down in the lift. When they emerged from the IMAX, Bryony stopped and turned to him.

'Let's go and have a drink, or walk together along the river,' she said.

'I better go, I have to get the train home,' he said.

'Oh. We could go back to my place,' she said. Her eyes shone hungrily.

'Sorry, I have to get home, to feed Grendel…'

'Oh,' she said, barely able to hide her disappointment. 'I'll see you at work though? We've got the conference tomorrow. It'll get us out of the office. Should be fun.'

'Yeah. See you then.'

Bryony leaned in to give him a hug, but he gave her a nod and moved off towards the underpass, leaving her standing under the coloured lights coming from the IMAX.

The next morning all the employees of the company Darryl and Bryony worked for were attending the annual staff conference. It was a big corporation, so lots of money had been spent on hiring the auditorium of the Royal Festival Hall. The staff from Darryl's building had first been bussed over to the South Bank.

Darryl avoided Bryony, walking past the seat she'd saved him on the coach. When they arrived at the Royal Festival Hall, he darted off the coach through the side door, then hung around in the toilets, only going through to the auditorium when the address was about to begin.

He found the dark wooden splendour of the 3,000 seat auditorium, with its high ceiling insulated and studded with lights, captivating. Almost three thousand employees from the twelve London offices of the Genesis corporation had convened to hear a series of presentations and an address from one of the CEOs.

Darryl sat on the end of a long row, next to a group of men and women he didn't know from another floor in his building. At lunchtime, he avoided the huge cafeteria and took a sandwich outside and ate it looking out over the river.

He realised he'd made a big mistake going on the date with Bryony. She was interested in him. She'd watch his every move. He had to nip things in the bud.

When it came to the afternoon address, Bryony wasn't having any of it. Back in the auditorium, she appeared out of nowhere and dashed to fill the seat next to him before he had a chance to move.

The lights went down and then the CEO, a tall bald man, started to speak.

'Hey. You okay?' whispered Bryony.

Her large thigh pressed against his, despite him trying to angle himself away from her.

'Fine,' he nodded, looking ahead.

The CEO droned on, under the misapprehension that their low-level employees actually gave a shit about quarterly results and write-downs. He talked of how every family in the UK used one of their products, and how the company had made an impact on renewable energy. As he droned on through the long list of company achievements, Darryl resisted the urge to stand up and announce at least three families had had their young daughters stuffed unceremoniously into a Genesis branded dumpster. He stifled a girlish giggle which had crawled up his throat.

'Why are you laughing?' asked Bryony. She reached out and put her hand on his.

'No reason,' he said, pulling his hand away.

'Did he say something funny?'

'No,' said Darryl. She was annoying him now, making him angry as she pawed at his arm and pressed herself against him.

'Why were you laughing?' she said coyly. 'I want you to tell me. I want to laugh too.'

He turned to her. 'You really want to know?'

'I do,' she grinned.

'Really?'

'Yes!'

He leaned into her ear. 'I was thinking fucking you might be a challenge. I'd probably have to roll you in flour… In fact, you disgust me. Last night was a mistake.'

The auditorium then erupted in applause as the CEO took his bow. The audience rose to their feet, and Darryl joined them clapping enthusiastically. He glanced down at Bryony and she looked destroyed, staring out in front, almost in a trance. The applause went on, and she stood unsteadily and pushed past him, tripping as she fought her way out along the row of people, knocking some of them back into their seats.

He followed her progress as she reached the end of the row and started down the steps. People looked after her, pulling faces, and he wondered if there would be consequences.

He pushed it to the back of his mind and focused on the young girl he was going to pursue next. The out-of-work actress he'd friended online.

CHAPTER 60

Beth Rose was in her second year of studying at the Drama Centre in West London. Ever since she was a little girl growing up in Suffolk, she had wanted to be an actress, and she'd decided if that didn't pan out, she was certainly going to be famous. Beth had long dark hair, large brown eyes and a tall, slim, almost gangly body. But she was beautiful, with a clumsiness which endeared her to her friends and peers. Beth stayed with her aunt during term time, exchanging the bedroom she shared with two sisters in a small seaside town for a large bedroom at the top of a town house in Central London. Aunt Marie had been married three times, but was childless, by choice, she always said.

'You're so much more interesting now you're an adult,' Marie had told her when she arrived eighteen months previously to start her Drama course. Marie's third marriage had been to an investment banker, and as part of her divorce settlement she now lived in Tyburn Road, in a gorgeous house in an exclusive row of terraces on New Oxford Street.

On Thursday evening, Beth was relaxing upstairs in her bedroom after a long day at school, painting her fingernails Peacock Green. Aunt Marie was downstairs watching *Poldark*, again.

The horny cow, Beth chuckled to herself. She was studying her nails, admiring her handiwork, when her phone pinged. She blew on them and picked it up, carefully swiping the screen. She saw she had a Facebook friend request from a casting director called Robert Baker. She quickly accepted, for fear that he'd done it by mistake. She hurriedly blew on her nails again, and then googled him.

'Fuck a duck,' she said, eyes wide as she scrolled through the search results. He was a *known* casting director. He was Robert Baker CDG. She couldn't quite remember what the 'CDG' stood for; she wanted to say 'Casting Director General', but that wasn't right. Either way he was part of some union; he was legit. She saw that he did casting for films and TV and he worked out of the Cochrane Street Studios near Tottenham Court Road.

Beth's Facebook profile clearly stated she was an actress; she'd uploaded showreel on there, several professional headshots, and it said that she was studying at one of the best drama schools in the country.

Why else would he friend me?

Beth believed her life was at the beginning of an exciting journey. A journey filled with infinite possibilities stretching ahead. Bad things happened to other people. She was destined for something life-changing. She always liked to remember where she was when something *life-changing* happened, and this had to be life-changing. Beth minimised the screen and placed a call to her friend, Heather.

'You'll never *guess* who I'm now friends with on Facebook,' she said.

CHAPTER 61

The next day was Friday, and Darryl found himself in the evening rush hour traffic, driving slowly into Central London. He was astonished that Beth Rose had taken the bait so fast, and so enthusiastically.

He'd had a Facebook profile he'd been working on for several months in the name of Robert Carter, and all it had taken was changing the name and photo, and he'd become Robert Baker CDG, a casting director. Robert Baker was real, and he even had his own Facebook profile, but his profile photo was of a black Labrador. As always, it was risky, but Darryl had downloaded Robert Baker's headshot from the casting studios website, all the time covering his tracks with his VPN software.

He'd found Beth Rose almost at random, clicking through the *Student Spotlight Directory*. Actors subscribed to the *Directory* so that casting directors could look them up, and a typical directory entry gave you the actor's headshot, their eye colour, weight, height, and vital statistics. With some of the entries there was even a voice sample and a short showreel. He'd liked Beth very much, and her showreel was a scene recorded with a tall dark lad where she'd played a battered wife. It wasn't from a stage show or a television programme, it looked like it had been made by a showreel service for actors. The production values were low, and Beth was far too well-groomed to play a victim of domestic violence, but she gave it her best shot, and Darryl had enjoyed her fake screams and tears. It was something he could work with.

She'd taken the bait so fast, responding to the friend request within two minutes. Messages had pinged back and forth all evening, and they'd even spoken on the phone. Now, this evening, he was due to meet her.

After seeing footage of his red Citroën splashed across the news, Darryl had decided to take Morris's car, a blue Ford. It had been sitting in the carport since Morris had been arrested and then bailed. His father said Morris was probably too embarrassed to come and get it, so he'd been taking care of it until he showed up, starting the engine each week, and checking the oil. He never did it with Darryl's car, *but then again*, thought Darryl bitterly, *Morris was a good milker.*

He reached the outskirts of South London just after 7 p.m. The interior of Morris's car had a whiff of horse and straw. It mingled in with the fresh scents of his shower gel and aftershave. Even though he knew this date wouldn't end romantically, he still liked to pretend. He stuck to the speed limit. He could now drive into Central London without paying the congestion charge, but he tried not to think about the cameras which could scan each number plate, and wondered if they still scanned cars as they came into the capital during the evenings. He'd spent time poring over maps detailing the CCTV coverage, and whilst he couldn't avoid them, he could certainly dodge the areas with the heaviest coverage.

His phone rang on the dashboard and he saw it was Beth. He was just driving through Camberwell, and looked to see if he could pull over, but it was a busy road with no stopping points. He checked for police cars, and answered.

'Hey you,' he said, his voice almost curling around the receiver. He'd decided that Robert Baker CDG had a deep confident voice with a transatlantic twang; after all, he did do castings for American productions.

'Hi. Sorry! I'm just calling to say I might be a few minutes late,' she said, flustered. But it was a confident flustered.

He gritted his teeth and forced a smile. 'No worries. So what're we looking at, 8.15?'

'Yeah, I'm having a bit of a hair crisis…'

'Hair on your head?'

There was silence. He cursed himself for using a bit of Darryl humour, and apologised. She laughed awkwardly and said she'd see him later, then rang off. He chucked the phone back on the dashboard.

'Stupid, stupid IDIOT!' he said, slapping the steering wheel. He glanced to one side and saw a man and a woman in a car on the opposite side, the woman in the passenger seat staring. He gave her the finger and put his foot down, accelerating past them.

He'd arranged to meet Beth outside the casting studio where the real Robert Baker worked. It was in Latimer Road, a quiet street in Southwark, next to a huge glass office block. Risky, but meeting her outside here was essential for her to buy into the lie.

He made his way slowly into Central London, and he reached Latimer Road just after eight. He saw the large, long glass office block, which dwarfed the casting studio of smart red brick beside it. A few dribs and drabs of office workers were coming out of the office block, and when he looked up he could see that the offices were empty. He carried on and turned off into the next street, where he found a parking space in front of a boarded-up row of shops.

Darryl breathed slowly in and out. As the minutes ticked by the inside windows of the car fogged up, his rhythmic breathing coming out in short bursts of vapour. He wiggled his toes and stretched, not wanting his muscles to seize up.

He was glad she said she'd be late. He thought of her long hair, how her skin and body might feel. Images of what he was going to do to her flashed into his mind.

At ten past eight he switched on the engine, and the hot air began to flow, clearing the condensation from the windows. He checked that he had his map and the leather sap in the glove compartment. He checked his reflection in the mirror. He was drooling. He wiped his mouth on his sleeve, and drove off around the block and back to Latimer Street. He passed the entrance to the office block, and saw Beth waiting outside the casting studio.

She was leaning on a small iron bollard. She wore a long tailored grey coat, black high heels, and her long dark hair was loose. She had her head down engrossed in her phone. He pulled past her, and parked by the kerb. She was now just a few metres from the boot of the car. The road was empty.

He leaned down and pulled up the handle to release the lock on the boot. He then got out, holding the sap concealed in his right hand. He made a show of tucking in his shirt and moving to a parking sign, peering, Mister Magoo-like, up at it and stepping back, checking his watch.

'Sorry, I'm blind as a bat,' he said over his shoulder to Beth. 'Is this residents' parking?'

Beth looked up from her phone and shrugged. She checked behind her, looking at the dark casting office and frowned, then went back to her phone.

Suddenly, Darryl's phone began to ring in his pocket. He looked over, and Beth had her phone to her ear. She was trying to call Robert Baker. He scanned the road: there were no cars and no people.

Just as she looked up in confusion at Darryl's phone ringing, he moved lightning fast, swooping over and bringing the leather sap down on the back of her head. He caught her as she crumpled, dragging her to the boot of the car. There was an awkward tussle as he tried to get it open with his foot and keep hold of her, and her phone clattered against the back of the car, swinging from its earphones. Just as he got her inside and shoved her phone in on top of her, a woman emerged further down from the main entrance of the office building and began to walk along the pavement towards him.

He'd wanted to subdue Beth, bind her wrists and her feet, but there was no time. He closed the boot. The woman was moving closer with a clip clip of heels. Darryl knew he had to keep moving, to look like part of the street furniture. With his head down, he went to the driver's side and got in.

The woman walked past, deep in thought. She had her hands thrust deep into her trench coat; she was elegant and middle-aged with short greying hair. He relaxed a little. She hadn't noticed him. Darryl started the engine and pulled away from the kerb.

CHAPTER 62

Darryl drove through the back streets behind Southwark Bridge. He'd worked out a route he could take to avoid the CCTV cameras as much as possible, and at least making it hard for anyone to piece together his movements, but he was flustered and he saw he'd taken a wrong turn. Had that woman coming out of the office seen him? And the road he'd just pulled into, was there a bank of CCTV cameras at the end here? He took a series of turns, and office blocks and coffee shops streaked past in a blur. He found himself on London Bridge, feeling the wind from the river buffeting the car.

'Shit!' he cried, thumping the steering wheel. He was approaching the junction by the train station which would be chock-a-block with CCTV cameras.

He had to find somewhere quiet where he could pull over and bind her arms and legs. As he left the bridge, he saw there was a diversion where the construction was happening around the Shard, and instead of being able to turn left he was taken on a looping detour away from the train station.

He found himself sandwiched between two vans, and either side were temporary rows of plastic barriers. He had no choice but to keep driving. Several minutes went by, and the diversion took him down streets he didn't recognise. It was all poorly lit; a building encased in scaffolding and green netting, which then turned into abandoned offices, the windows whitewashed, and then the road curved around sharply to the right, spitting him out in a shabby-looking area of houses and betting shops around Bermondsey.

He drove on, and was going to pull over onto what looked like a piece of wasteland, when a bus suddenly appeared behind him, lights blaring, and so he kept moving. The road took him past a bus depot, which again he was going to pull into but another bus rounded the corner from the opposite direction. He closed his eyes against the headlights and had to slam on his brakes as it cut him up, pulling across him and into the depot.

He sat for a moment; his hands were now shaking. He was lost. He couldn't work out how to get back to the Old Kent Road, which would then take him on through New Cross and to the South Circular.

He put the car in gear and drove on for a couple more minutes until he approached a set of traffic lights, and his heart leapt when he saw it was signposted straight ahead for New Cross. The lights changed to amber then red, so he stopped the car and took some deep breaths. Peering through the windscreen he saw a mixture of flats and office blocks, and next to the traffic lights was a Costcutter food shop and off-licence.

A couple of people had been waiting at the crossing, and as the green man started to flash, they stepped off the kerb and began to move across the road in front of him. Something about one of the pedestrians' gait was familiar, but he was too occupied with getting going. He looked in his rear-view mirror, scanning the road behind him, then looked down to check that he had stowed the sap back in the glove compartment. When he looked up again, he nearly yelled out in shock. Standing in the beam of his headlights, and staring through his window, was a familiar figure clutching two full carrier bags of shopping.

It was Bryony.

CHAPTER 63

It was dark and cold when Beth began to regain consciousness. The rocking of the moving car reached the edge of her consciousness, along with the sounds and sensations: the tangy warm smell of engine oil, and dusty old carpet.

She lay on a lumpy hard surface, and she had a thumping headache, but her throat didn't feel parched. Had it been a big night out? Her body still smelt freshly showered. She flexed her fingers, and her nail polish was still tacky. For a moment, she worked backwards. She was waiting outside the casting studio for Robert. He was so handsome in his photo. *In his prime*, Aunt Marie had described him. But something odd had happened: he'd said he'd be at the casting studios working late, but the windows had been dark. She'd phoned him. There had been a funny little man outside, making a meal of peering at a road sign. He'd asked her something...

And then she realised where she was. Her head was in agony, and even moving caused a jolt of pain. She tried not to panic and shifted her body. Had she been tied up? No, she could move her legs and arms in the cramped space. A thin wire lay trapped under her left side, and she realised it was the headphones plugged into her iPhone. She groped around, reaching under herself with her free hand, feeling for the wire and taking up the slack. It seemed to go on for ever and ever. Had the earphone jack come loose? But the wire finally went taut and as she felt down her hand closed around her phone handset. In the darkness, she swiped at the phone with a shaking finger, and again. Was it broken? No. She had it the wrong way up. When she twisted it round, the screen light activated, illuminating the interior of the car boot: a carpet; a pair of jump leads; a roll of electrical tape. What looked like several pairs of women's underwear.

'Oh Jesus,' she said, and she almost screamed. She gulped it back, pain shooting up her jaw to her temple. Her vision was blurred and it took a few attempts to remember the pin code for her phone and key it in. It seemed to take her an age to navigate through the phone; where she had been hit was affecting her balance and vision. Finally, she found the contact of her friend, Heather, and pressed call. The sound of the phone ringing set off even greater pain through her head, and when Heather's chipper little voicemail message kicked in she thought she might throw up it was so bad. Beth left a babbling message, trying to articulate what had happened.

Then the car came to a stop. She held the phone away from her ear and strained to hear what was going on.

CHAPTER 64

Before Darryl could put the car in gear and move off, Bryony lurched round the front of the car to the passenger door, and pulled it open. She threw her shopping bags into the footwell and climbed in, slamming the door shut.

He was lost for words. Her eyes behind her glasses were wild and unhinged; her face had a sheen of sweat. She pushed back wisps of hair from her face.

'Tell me you didn't mean it,' she said without preamble. 'Tell me you were doing a joke that I didn't understand…about you and me and the flour… or that you made a mistake…' She jabbed her finger into his chest. 'Please, say it now, Darryl, or God help me, I'll—'

'Bryony, what the hell?' he shrilled.

There was a honk from behind and he saw there was now a line of cars waiting, and the lights were green.

'What you said to me was vicious. I invited you for my special birthday at the cinema. I did things to make you happy. Don't men like that kind of thing?'

'Bryony, you need to get out of my car.'

The cars behind honked and revved their engines; an elderly couple waiting on the pavement stared into the car curiously.

'I'm not going anywhere until you tell me why!' she shouted, locking her door. Her eyes burned with anger, and for a moment it scared him.

Don't be stupid, it's Bryony, the stupid lump from work, he thought. *Take her home, get her out of the car.* Reluctantly, he pulled away from the traffic lights, and the curious eyes on the pavement.

'Where do you live?' he snapped.

'What?' she asked.

'I said where do you live? I'll take you home, and we can talk there… I take it you live close by?' he said.

She wiped spittle from her mouth, and nodded, looking hopeful. 'I'm on Druid Street, it's about a quarter of a mile along here…'

Darryl accelerated, the shops and takeaways flying past. Then without warning Bryony started to hit him, landing blows on the side of his head and neck.

'Why? It was a perfect date, wasn't it? I bought us popcorn! You were nice to me, I was nice to you, and then without warning you were so nasty… WHY? WHY? WHY?' She thumped the dashboard so hard that her knuckle began to bleed. She put it to her mouth and sucked at it.

'I didn't mean it… I was just… You've hurt your hand,' he said, trying to soothe her. He put out a hand to make sure she remained at arm's length, whilst attempting to keep an eye on the road.

'You didn't mean it? Really?' she said, tears now running down her cheeks.

'Really. I'm sorry,' he said.

He saw a right turn for Druid Street, and took it in fourth gear. Bryony wasn't strapped in and was thrown against the window, hitting her head against the plastic handle above.

'Ow!' she whined. Druid Street was a cul-de-sac of small new-build homes.

'Which house?' he asked.

'The third one,' she said, clutching her head and looking at him.

He pulled the car to a stop by the kerb. Most of the street was in darkness, and only one of the streetlights was working at the dead end. Darryl slowed his breathing, working out how to get rid of her.

'Bryony, you go ahead inside and make us some tea…'

'Darryl, please. I love you,' she said, launching herself at him. He turned, and her mouth glanced off his cheek. She sat back.

'I love you, Darryl, I love you so much…' Blood was oozing from her knuckle, and she squeezed the skin hard and sucked up a little more of the blood.

'And I love you, but I need to talk to you about something,' he said.

'You love me?' she said, clasping her hands under her chin.

A horrible trickling feeling started to run through Darryl: *was this normal? Is this how women in love behave?*

'What if you go ahead indoors. I can bring the shopping bags,' he said, looking out at the empty street.

'Yes. I've bought food. We could have dinner.' She smiled. 'Do you like Viennetta?'

Darryl nodded. She smiled.

'It's mint chocolate. Is that okay? I know some people don't like…'

A thumping sound from the boot silenced her. She turned to Darryl. 'What was that?'

'I didn't hear anything,' said Darryl. There was another thump, and the car rocked.

'Is there someone in the back?' asked Bryony, looking out of the back window at the boot.

'Course not!' He grinned.

'Help! Help me! Someone, please! He attacked me!' cried Beth's muffled voice, and there was a volley of kicks which shook the car.

Bryony slowly turned back to face Darryl, and it was as if the face she knew had fallen away. The kicks and screams continued from the boot.

'Why did you have to get into my car?' he said calmly. 'Now I have to kill you.'

Bryony lunged for the door, unlocked it, and got it open. But as she made a dash for it, her foot caught in the seat belt and she tripped, landing on the tarmac and hitting her head.

Darryl opened his door and walked around the back of the car, scanning the road. The whole car was now shaking, and Beth was loud. He was torn about what to do.

Then he saw Bryony lying dazed in the road, reaching out for her phone, which had skittered across the tarmac. He went to her and kicked her in the face, then picked up her phone and dropped it down a drain behind the back wheel of the car.

At the end of the road, cars continued to whip past, and a man stepped off the pavement and crossed over, but he was engrossed in his phone, the wire hanging down from his earbuds. Darryl retrieved the leather sap from inside the car, and went to the boot.

When he opened it, Beth lashed out blindly. Her nose was bloody, but her eyes were wild, and she tried to fight him. He swung the sap at her head, and there was a nasty cracking sound, and then she was still. He looked up, and Bryony was now lurching blindly across the road towards her house, without her glasses, searching in her bag for her keys.

He slammed the boot shut, and ran after her, but she was already through the gate and had managed to get her key in the front door. As she got it open, he charged in behind her and they went crashing down on the floor in the hallway. He kicked the front door shut, and there was a strange sweaty fumble as Bryony tried to push him off, but he climbed on top of her.

His hands found her throat and he gripped hard, pressing down with his thumbs and squeezing. She grabbed at his hands, scratching his arms, then shoved her knee upwards, crushing his balls. He crumpled over and Bryony heaved herself up, pushing him against the wall as she ran off up the dark hallway.

Darryl lay curled up in pain, trying to catch his breath. His eyes were getting used to the dark, and he could see he was lying near the bottom of a staircase. Bryony was making strange whimpering sounds, and he heard her fumbling about, opening a drawer. She was in the kitchen, and she was looking for a knife.

Darryl staggered up, feeling around on the wall, and found a light switch. As he turned it on, Bryony came charging towards him with a kitchen knife, her eyes wide. He stood his ground, leapt to one side and, almost comically, she ploughed into the front door. He moved behind her and slammed her against it, seizing the wrist holding the knife, and banging it against the doorframe until she dropped it. He grabbed the back of her hair and slammed her face into the door: once, twice. She slid down onto her backside, and was still.

He stood, sweating and shaking, and then spied the landline phone sitting in its dock on a low table. He yanked the cord out of the wall and dragged Bryony back by her hair to the base of the stairs. There was a bloody gash on her forehead where he'd kicked her, and her nose was broken. He started to wind the cord around her neck. She opened her eyes and began to struggle, but he kneeled on her stomach and pulled back, holding the two ends of the cord like reins, pressing his knees into her stomach and pulling his arms up, tightening the cord around her neck. She made some gurgling screeching noises, and her hands scrabbled at the cord. He kneeled harder, felt her ribs crack, and yanked the cord upwards. Her face went purple, she gagged and her feet flailed, and finally, she was still.

Darryl got up and threw down the ends of the telephone cord. He stood back, breathless. Still in the hallway, he caught sight of himself in a large mirror on the wall: wild-eyed and dishevelled. A clock ticked above the doorway leading off towards a living room, and he saw that it was now 9 p.m. He checked he hadn't dropped anything, and wiped down the phone cord with the corner of his shirt. He picked up Bryony's limp arms, dragged her body through to the living room, and left it behind a large sofa. Now if anyone looked through the front door, or the living room window, they wouldn't see anything amiss.

Darryl emerged from Bryony's flat into the empty cul-de-sac. He was now certain his DNA was all over the hallway, but there was nothing he could do. He had no criminal record, and as far as he could tell, without his DNA, the police had nothing to link him to the dead girls. This was bad. He'd killed her; he'd killed Bryony. The woman he sat opposite at work... His colleagues had seen them together.

He went to the car and got in. He drove away and kept to the speed limit all the way home, stopping once in a lay-by where he threw up. He held out his hands as a car passed bathing him in bright light and he saw he had Bryony's blood on his left hand. He wiped it on the seat of his trousers.

Then another thought came to him: Beth had had a phone when he'd taken her! He went to the boot of the car and opened it. She lay still, her nose bloody. He rummaged around under her leg and found it. Car headlights appeared again and he slammed the boot shut, keeping his head down. When it had passed, he dropped the phone and ground it into the tarmac until the screen splintered. He then wiped it down and threw it far into a bank of trees. He got back in the car and concentrated on driving the rest of the way back to the farm.

CHAPTER 65

Heather Cochrane was woken at seven thirty by her alarm clock. She could make out the row of leotards she'd hung on the radiator, and the small window of her box room was steamed up, the blue light of dawn filtering through. She pulled back the covers and looked down at the ankle she'd sprained in her dance class the previous afternoon. It was resting on a pile of text books she'd placed at the bottom of the mattress.

She gingerly pulled her leg towards her, and peeled off the tight support sock, wincing at the pain. There was a dark bruise across the ankle bone.

'Shit,' she said, lying back on her pillow. She would have to see the doctor, or if she couldn't get an appointment at the surgery, she would have to get to A & E. She heard the sound of her housemates laughing downstairs, accompanied by the radio, and the water ran through the pipes behind her head in the bathroom. Sitting on the edge of the bed she practised putting her weight on the sprain, but even the smallest amount caused a shooting pain. It looked like her weekend job was out of the question too.

She reached for her phone on the bedside table and waited whilst it switched on. She saw she had a voicemail, and pressed to listen. It was strange and muffled, with what sounded like the roar of an engine in the background.

'Heather, it's Beth…' came her friend's voice. 'This man. He took me. When I was waiting for Robert… He took me from

the street. Dark hair, short and fat, piggy eyes… I'm in his—'
There was a creak and the sound of traffic got louder. 'I'm in the
back of his—' There was interference, and then just the noise of
the engine.

Heather sat on the edge of the bed for another two minutes,
listening to the ambient sounds; traffic, a horn honking, but
nothing more from her friend. She took the phone from her
ear and saw on the screen that the missed call was at 8.51 p.m
the day before. She put it back to her ear as the message finally
clicked off, and a recorded voice asked if she wanted to 'press 1'
to return the call.

She did, but got a recorded message saying that Beth's number was unavailable.

CHAPTER 66

Just before nine a.m., Erika and Peterson were on the way to West End Central in Peterson's car. They'd stayed at Erika's flat in Forest Hill. Peterson was driving, and she lay back against the headrest, her eyes half closed. The snow had now all but melted, but it was cold and grey with a light drizzle.

'You didn't sleep?' he asked, looking over at her.

'Not much. Did you?'

'I got a few hours, but you were tossing and turning.'

'You should have said. I'd have moved to the sofa.' A sign for a McDonald's loomed ahead, and Erika checked her watch. 'Can you stop at the drive-in? I need grease and coffee.'

'That sounds good,' he said, indicating and pulling in. They joined a queue of five cars, and then a van pulled in behind them. They'd placed their order and were inching toward the drive-thru window, when Erika's phone rang. She scrabbled in her bag for it and saw it was Moss.

'Boss, where are you?' she said.

'Camberwell, just grabbing some takeaway breakfast.'

'We've had a call come through from a young girl called Heather Cochrane, a student. She says her friend, Beth Rose, was due to meet a bloke for a blind date last night near Southwark. She's just woken up to find a message on her phone which indicates the friend was abducted and stashed in the boot of a car—'

'Hang on, the friend phoned the girl?'

'Yeah, Heather has a voicemail from Beth, actually saying that she was abducted by a funny little short guy, with dark hair… Crane is just on the phone with her; we're asking more questions.'

'Okay, we'll be there asap,' said Erika. She put the phone down and saw they were sandwiched in-between cars in front and the van behind.

'You need to get us out of here, there's been another girl abducted,' she said.

Peterson put the blue lights on, but no one moved. There were two cars behind the van and they were boxed in. He drove up on the small verge, managed to squeeze past the line of cars and they left the car park with a squeal of rubber and pulled out into the road with their siren blaring.

When they reached the incident room at West End Central, the officers from her team were starting to arrive, and Moss, Crane and John were huddled around a laptop.

'Is Melanie in yet?' asked Erika, as she and Peterson came into the incident room.

'She's got meetings this morning,' said John.

'Call her, get her in,' said Erika.

'Boss, we've just had the voicemail come in,' said Moss.

They moved over to join them at the laptop.

'We need to get a location on that phone,' asked Erika.

'I've just put in an urgent request with telecoms,' said Crane. Moss pressed 'play' as they listened to the message. There was a lot of background noise, and the girl's voice sounded drunk and slurring.

'Heather, it's Beth… This man. He took me. When I was waiting for Robert… He took me from the street. Dark hair, short and fat, weird piggy eyes… I'm in his—' There was interference. 'I'm in his—' More interference, and then just the noise of the car engine.

Erika paced up and down as the audio continued playing. They heard cars approach and then pass, and a scratching as if something were pressed against the phone's mouthpiece. The message finally cut out and the recorded voice kicked in.

Erika's team were silent for a moment.

'Boss—' started John.

'I know. This could be our breakthrough,' said Erika. 'But we need to do this by the book. I want the phone location. I want you to pull CCTV from where she was due to meet this guy. We'll need to contact her next of kin.'

'Yes, boss.'

'Now I want to hear that message again. There could be something in there which tells us where he was taking her.'

CHAPTER 67

Darryl hung his head over the toilet and threw up for the third time. His guts burned, and he brought up nothing more than bile. He wiped his mouth and stood flushing the toilet, and looked at his reflection. His face was grey and he had huge bags under his eyes. He hadn't slept; he kept having the same dream of discovering his brother, Joe, hanging in his wardrobe. He looked down at his boxer shorts, where the wet patch spread across the front. He pulled them down, balled them up and dropped them in the old clothes hamper by the bath. There was a knock at the door.

'What?'

'You alright?' came his mother's voice.

'I'm fine…' he said. 'Just something I ate.'

'What?' came his mother's voice.

'Something I ate!' he shouted. He went to the sink and splashed his face with cold water and looked out the window. A low mist was rolling over the fields towards the house, and the sky was an ominous grey. He turned off the water and realised he hadn't heard the creak of the floorboards as his mother retreated.

'What is it?'

'I need to go shopping, but Morris's car is blocking my way,' she said.

Darryl dried his face, put a towel round his waist and yanked the door open. His mother was standing in her 'going to town' outfit: a smart purple trouser suit and black patent leather court shoes. She had her white handbag over her arm.

'They keys are in the ignition. Can't you move it?'

She peered at his face.

'You know I can only drive my automatic. His car has gears.'

'All cars have gears, Mother.'

'You know what I mean. Now can you move it for me, please?'

He went to his room and pulled on an old tracksuit, then came out to the carport. His mother was peering into Morris's car, her handbag over her arm. When he came close, she was looking at a large smear of blood on the passenger doorhandle. She turned and regarded him.

'You look ill.'

'I'm not going into work today. Tummy upset.'

'It's Saturday,' she said.

'Oh yeah…'

She looked at the smear of blood again.

'One of the farm lads must have cut themselves,' said Darryl, moving round to get into the driver's side.

'Which one? They have to come to me if they do, and fill in the accident book.'

He ignored her and got in. Mary moved to her car and unlocked it. He reversed Morris's car and noticed his mother staring at him as she backed out in the large Jag, then pulled off with a spray of gravel. He put Morris's car back, and looked at the blood. It was Bryony's. He'd had her blood on his hand when he'd left last night. He took some tissues and scrubbed the smear of blood until it was gone.

When Darryl came back into the house, he stood in the boot room, shaking all over. Grendel padded over and licked his hand, and the house creaked around him. Familiar noises. He suddenly thought of the future: what if he didn't live at the farm? If he got caught? What would happen? He tried to work out the best thing to do. If he went into work on Monday, it could be crawling with police, that's if they'd found Bryony's body. But as far as he knew, she lived alone. She wouldn't officially have to be back at work until Monday, and then people might think she was sick. Her body might not be found for days. He just needed time, time to think. They didn't have an ID on the car, and as far as he could tell no one had seen him; he wished he'd looked around when Bryony had got into the car. Was there an ATM? It would have a camera. Did all traffic lights have cameras on them? He'd used Morris's car. He wished he'd worn gloves; his DNA would be in her house. He'd panicked…

Then a flooding calm came over him. He and Bryony had been on a date together. This linked him to her, but he could say that he went back to hers for a cup of coffee so, technically, his DNA *would* be there.

He suddenly felt euphoric and light. He patted Grendel on the head and went upstairs to run himself a bath. Then he would have some breakfast and walk down to the Oast House to visit his new captive.

CHAPTER 68

It was a few hours later. Melanie Hudson had now arrived, and she was working with Erika and her team in the incident room. The lights had been dimmed, and they were watching CCTV footage projected onto the whiteboards.

'This is CCTV footage from inside the reception area of the large glass office block, the Purcell building on Latimer Street. It's next to the casting studio where Beth had arranged to meet Robert Baker at 8.15 p.m. This CCTV footage from the reception desk inside the building is the closest footage to the abduction site that we've been able to find. There's nothing on Latimer Street.'

'I thought Beth was due to meet Robert Baker at eight?' asked Erika.

'Beth had texted her friend, Heather, to say she was running late because she couldn't decide what to wear, and how to do her hair,' said Crane.

'Have we had any luck chasing up the real Robert Baker?'

'He's in Scotland visiting his brother. The casting studio is closed until the middle of February,' said John.

'Good, so we know for sure she wasn't really meeting him,' said Erika. 'So we're working on the timeline that she met our man at or just after 8.15 p.m.'

The image showed the inside of the reception area, behind two security guards sitting at the front desk. In one corner was a bank of three lifts.

'Here we are, at 8.09 p.m. last night,' said Crane. 'You can see that, as it's dark outside, the interior is reflected in the glass, but the automatic doors are floodlit and you can see through them out onto the street. Beth also activated the automatic doors when she passed.'

He froze on an image of Beth walking past as the doors opened. Erika looked at the faces of her team, bathed in the pale light from the projector. John put up another image beside it: this time is was Beth's driving licence and her acting headshot.

'So, everyone, we're in agreement that this shows Beth Rose walking past?' asked Erika.

The team nodded.

'I'm not happy about us just guessing,' said Melanie.

'Maybe a guess is all we have?' said Erika, turning to her.

'That's not all we have,' said Crane. 'I emailed pictures of Beth over to the security desk when I requested the tapes. The two guys who were working on the front desk last night say they remember her, commenting on what a knockout she was.'

'So sexism is working in our favour for once,' quipped Moss.

Melanie smiled and nodded. Crane went on: 'We took a look at the footage from 7.30 p.m. through to 8.25 p.m., and the only cars which go past the front entrance are a lorry, a motor-bike, two white vans and a blue car.'

Erika's heart sank. 'No red Citroën?'

'No, boss,' said Crane.

A look passed between Melanie and Erika. Murmurs went around the incident room.

'Can we see the footage please?' asked Melanie.

'You bet,' said Crane. He loaded up the footage and ran it at speed, slowing and going back as each vehicle passed the front entrance. 'And finally, there's the blue car; we think it's an older Ford model…' The footage carried on. Just before 8.15 p.m. on the timestamp, a woman with short grey hair and a long coat darted out of the lifts into the reception area. She zipped over to the front desk.

'Hang on, slow it down,' said Erika.

Crane slowed the video to normal speed, and they watched as the woman went through the main doors and turned to the left, walking out of shot.

'That woman,' said Erika. 'When she leaves she walks to the left, which would take her past the casting studios.'

'At the same time when Beth was due to meet Robert Baker,' said Peterson.

'Crane. Get back in contact with the security team. Find out who she is. I want to talk to her,' said Erika.

CHAPTER 69

After Mary had gone shopping, Darryl took Grendel for a walk down to the Oast House. When he pulled back the large steel door, it took a moment for his eyes to adjust. He saw Grendel's large flat nose move up and sniff the air near to the metal door housing the large furnace, and he slipped his finger under her thick leather collar. Using his free hand, he switched on the light and pulled the metal door shut. He opened the door to the furnace chamber, and it smelt rank. Beth was crouched in one corner of the large metal cage. Like the other girls, her neck was chained to one side of the cage, and her hands were bound with chains and fastened to the other. Darryl had also taped up her mouth.

He let go of Grendel, and she padded over to the edge of the cage and sniffed at her. Beth's eyes grew wide, and she tried to pull her head away from where she was chained to the bars. Grendel launched herself at the cage, barking and growling, flecks of spittle flying.

Beth lurched from side to side, screaming under the gag, as the huge dog galloped round the cage, bashing into it, trying to get her teeth through the wire mesh.

Darryl watched for a few minutes, smiling.

'Okay, okay, shush girl,' he said. He pulled out a knuckle of beef bone, and chucked it by the curved brick wall at the side of the furnace. She bounded after it and settled down on her haunches to chew.

Darryl went up close to the cage, and smiled.

'It's okay. I won't hurt you,' he said softly. Tears poured down Beth's face and she gave a muffled yell from under the tape. 'I can take off the tape. Just promise not to yell.' He crouched down beside her, still smiling. Beth looked at his teeth and shuddered. They were small and crooked, so small, almost like milk teeth. 'Do you promise?' She nodded.

'You need to put your face close to the bars,' he said. 'Or I can't reach the tape… Come on, good girl… put your head back against the bars.'

Beth was now trembling, and with one eye on Grendel chewing her bone in the corner, she sat back and turned her face up to him through the bars. Darryl pushed his fingers through and plucked at the tape, peeling it away from her mouth, rubbing his finger over her lips.

'There. Now spit it out, go on,' he said.

Beth didn't let her eyes leave him and spat out the bundled-up rag he'd shoved in her mouth. She swallowed and took several deep breaths. He took a bottle of water out of his pocket and removed the lid, pushing it through the bars.

'This is water, look,' he said, taking a sip and offering it back to her. She kept her eyes on him as she drank. 'Goodness you are thirsty,' he said, tipping the bottle up as she drank. 'Just bear in mind, you'll have to do your business in there. There's a grate under the rug. You won't drown.' He stifled a girlish giggle, and Beth's eyes widened and she stopped drinking. She swallowed and took some deep breaths.

'Who are you?' she croaked.

Her eyes were so brown, so inquisitive, and her voice had a rich tone. Nice to listen to.

'Just a guy. Joe Public.'

'Is that your name, Joe?'

'No. Joe was my brother's name.'

'Was?'

'Yes, he died,' said Darryl, matter-of-factly screwing the lid back on the plastic bottle. 'Well, I killed him if we're being frank… and that's another name, Frank.' He giggled again. 'Why is it "Joe Public" and not "Frank Public"? Have you never heard of the phrase "Joe Public"? To describe the ordinary man on the street.'

Beth shook her head, tears filling her eyes.

'Well, that's me. I'm an ordinary Joe. Ordinary, but with so much to give, and girls like you… Like YOU,' he shouted angrily, jabbing a finger at her accusingly. 'Bitches like YOU who are so shallow, you want looks and money and someone who you THINK is right for you. But how do you know I'm not right?' Beth stared up at him, and even in her fear and horror could see the irony in what he was saying. Then it dawned on her that he really was crazy. 'Bitches like YOU always give me this fucking snooty look. So fucking snooty!' Darryl was getting really worked up now, spittle was flying from his mouth and he was slamming his hand down on the top of the cage.

'I'm sorry. I'm sorry, so sorry, I'm sure you're lovely,' she gulped, and winced, knowing she'd chosen the wrong words. 'Not lovely, handsome, and sexy.'

'Oh, NOW I'm sexy, am I? Well you know what, bitch? It's too late! I saw how you looked at me last night. It took one second and you JUDGED ME! You know, if you'd just smiled back and been nice to me… then this, THIS, wouldn't have had to happen!'

Grendel barked and came trotting over to the cage. He seized her by the scruff of the neck and pushed her towards the bars. She gave a deep growl and bared a set of glistening white teeth.

'No! Please!' cried Beth.

'Yes. You should meet my dog properly,' he said, dragging Grendel by the scruff of her neck around to the gate of the cage.

'What are you doing? I'll do anything, I'll do anything, please!' cried Beth, shrinking back as Grendel began to bark and growl, her lips curled back.

Taking one hand off Grendel, Darryl unlocked the cage, and opened the door. Grendel was snarling, and trying to bite his hand. He twisted the fur on her neck and he pushed her inside the cage.

Beth screamed as the dog pounced on her.

CHAPTER 70

Mary had been shopping, and was driving back up to the farm when she saw the road ahead was blocked by a skittish herd of sheep. She recognised the yellow dye mark on their backs, and knew that they belonged to their neighbour, Jim Murphy. Her husband and Jim had a respectful rivalry, and she hadn't seen Jim for a long time. She sat patiently as the sheep flooded out of an open gate to the side of the lane, and then moments later, Jim followed. He walked with a stoop, and wore a pair of trousers and jacket that looked to be disintegrating. He dug in his crook as he walked, and turned. He was about to pass her car off as belonging to one of the villagers, then clocked who she was. He stopped and lifted a hand. Mary pulled forward and came level.

'Afternoon,' he said. His face was weather-beaten, and he had a scar running across his temple.

Mary nodded and smiled. 'Spring will be here soon,' she said, looking at the sheep skittering away down the lane.

He nodded sagely. 'What you up to?'

'I've been shopping, for the week,' she said, then noticed that the back seat was covered with boxes of wine and several bottles of vodka. She liked that he didn't bat an eyelid.

'I miss having someone shop for me,' he said sadly. His wife had died two years before.

'You know,' said Mary, gripping the wheel, 'you should come over sometime for supper.'

He waved her away. 'I can't think of anything worse than being stuck opposite John, watching him slop his food.'

Mary laughed.

'Say,' he added, leaning on the roof of her car. 'Have you got a new lad working for you?'

'No.'

'It's just that bottom gate has been left open a couple of times when I've come past. I know it only leads up to the old Oast House, but the padlock's been left open.'

Mary stared back at him.

'Course, I just closed it and locked it back up, but I thought you'd want to know, in case someone you don't want has got hold of the key... I know you probably steer clear of there, after...'

He looked at the ground. *After your Joe hanged himself down there,* he was going to say. Mary bit her lip to compose herself.

'Thanks, Jim. I'll mention it to John,' she said.

Jim nodded, still looking at the ground. Just then a car came up behind them.

'I'd best be off,' she said. He nodded and touched the brim of his cap and, with a smile, she drove away.

The last of the sheep were just vanishing through a gate further up, on the opposite side of the road, and one of Jim's young farmhands raised a hand in greeting as she passed. Mary waved back and then drove on, her brow furrowed. No one who worked for them had a key to that gate. The only keys were in the office at home.

When Mary got home, she called out to Darryl to help her with the shopping, but he wasn't in, nor was Grendel. She went to the office and checked the board where all the keys were hung up. The set for the gate was hanging on its hook. She reached out to take them, and hesitated. She pulled her hand back and went to fetch in the shopping, and pour herself a large drink.

CHAPTER 71

When Grendel had pounced into the cage, barking and snarling, Beth had closed her eyes, expecting to be savaged. In the back of her mind she'd hoped that the dog would do it quick and fast. She'd squeezed them shut tighter and braced herself, but there was nothing. Just some odd gulping noises, and then she'd flinched as she felt something rough and warm. The dog had started to lick her face. She remained very still, wincing with fear as it continued to lick, and then she realised it was cleaning the wound on her forehead, licking the dried crusted blood from around her nose. It finished, and Beth opened her eyes. The huge white face loomed close, staring at her with small beady eyes. Then it turned, and trotted out of the cage.

Darryl was silent. He closed the door of the cage and fed a large silver padlock through, and he snapped it shut. Beth shifted, feeling the pull of the chain circling her neck. Grendel moved to the door, and flopped down onto the uneven brick floor of the furnace.

'Grendel likes you,' he said.

'What?' she croaked.

'The dog is called Grendel. She usually hates women…'

'She's… She's sweet.'

'You don't think that,' said Darryl, watching her. He was deciding what to do next.

Beth thought Darryl was strange to look at. His eyes were soft and brown, but deep-set and small, giving them a piggy quality. He had a round little face, thin lips, and no real chin, just a slope of podgy flesh from his bottom lip to neck. It was those baby teeth which disturbed her the most, so small and sharp.

Beth watched as he left through the low door of the furnace and returned a moment later with a black backpack, which he placed on the floor. Keeping his back to her, he rummaged in it. She wanted to shout out and ask what he was doing.

He came close to the cage, a sharp little baby-toothed smile on his face, his hands behind his back.

She shrank away. 'Please. No,' she said.

'You don't know what I'm doing. How can you say "no" to something when you don't know what it is? I could have a treat behind my back,' he said.

'A treat?'

'Yes. Now choose. Left or right?' He leaned closer: 'Left or right.' She closed her eyes, feeling a hot tear escaping her left eye. 'I said, left or right, now CHOOSE!'

'No.'

'If you don't pick, it will be worse for you. I promise. CHOOSE.'

She opened her eyes. His face held a smile so dark and full of malevolence that her stomach contracted.

'Choose, or you'll die!' he screamed.

'Left, I choose left,' she stuttered.

He swiftly brought his left hand round. In it he held a small silver scalpel. He brought out his right hand, and it held an identical scalpel. He giggled and pushed the left-hand one through the bars and dragged it across her forearm. She looked down in shock, the feeling of pain delayed for a moment. And then it felt as if her arm was on fire, and blood began to ooze and then pour. She tried to pull away, but her hands were chained together, and he sliced through her flailing arm several times. She

landed a blow to his hand, and he dropped the scalpel. Quick as
lightning, she picked it up and held it out.

'You come any closer, you sick fuck, and I'll slash you!' she
cried. Grendel lifted her head and growled. 'And your dog too.'

Darryl laughed and walked back over to the backpack. He
returned with something in his hand, watching impassively as
the blood poured from her wounds.

'You'll want this,' he said, holding up a roll of gauze bandage.
'Throw out the scalpel and I'll give you this.' She gripped the
scalpel in her hands as a stream of blood dripped down on to her
legs. 'You can use the bandage to stem the bleeding. I'm serious,
Beth. Give it back and this will be forgotten.'

'No.'

'Beth, I'm sorry, take the bandage. I have another scalpel. I
have a boxful in that bag, and I could take them all out now and
go to town on your body, and on that pretty, pretty face. Who
would want to hire an actress with a messed-up face?'

Beth yelled in pain and despair and threw it outside the cage.
It landed with a clink on the brick floor. He picked it up, and
dropped the packet of gauze bandage through one of the mesh
holes above her head.

'Such a stupid bitch,' he said, holding up the bloody scalpel.
'If you'd kept hold of this, it would have given you leverage.
Now all you have is a packet of bandages. I used this on the
other girls. I cut them out of their underwear, along the seam
between their legs. It was tricky without nicking them.'

He picked up the backpack and left, Grendel following.

The door to the furnace clanged shut, and she was in darkness. She heard the outer door open and close.

Beth scrabbled at the bandage, using her teeth to tear the plastic open. Twisting her hands in opposite directions where they

were bound and using her teeth, she crudely wrapped the material around the cuts on her forearm. It felt better not to have them open to the air, but her blood rapidly soaked through. Just as she wound the last of the bandage around her arm, she felt something small and hard. It was a little safety pin attached to the very end. She quickly unfastened it from the material. It was small but sturdily made. She held it between her fingers for a moment. His words echoed in her head... *other girls...* and then she knew for sure who had taken her.

CHAPTER 72

Erika called her team in for 10 a.m. on Sunday morning, and again the day started slowly. Just before 3 p.m., Moss knocked on her office door and poked her head round. Erika looked up from the pile of paperwork on her desk.

'Boss, I've managed to track down the grey-haired woman seen leaving the office on Latimer Road. Her name's Lynn Holbrook, and she's on line one.'

'Great, come in. I'll put her on loudspeaker,' said Erika.

Moss came in, closed the door and sat opposite.

'Hello, Lynn, this is Detective Chief Inspector Erika Foster. Can I call you Lynn?'

'No, I prefer Ms Holbrook,' said a snooty voice through the loudspeaker. Moss rolled her eyes. 'Why have I been pulled out of a meeting to speak to you?'

'You've been pulled out of a meeting because we believe, on Friday night, you may have witnessed the abduction of a young girl,' said Erika.

'You must be mistaken.'

'We believe the girl was abducted outside your office as you were leaving work.'

'What?' she cried.

'We have CCTV footage of you leaving the office building at Latimer Road on Friday night at 8.13 p.m. Is that correct?'

There was a pause. 'I don't know the time I left to-the-minute, but if the CCTV footage shows it...'

'It does, Mrs Holbrook…'

'It's Ms, if you don't mind.'

Moss shook her head and twirled her finger in the air. Erika nodded.

'Ms Holbrook, you left via the main entrance at 8.13 p.m. and you turned right into Latimer Road… Did you see a young white girl with long brown hair waiting by the kerb?'

There was a pause.

'No… I don't think so.'

'You don't think so? Or you're sure you didn't see a young white girl with long brown hair? She was wearing a long brown coat and black high heels'

'No,' she said, more certain. 'No, there definitely wasn't a girl waiting on either side of the road. It was almost empty.'

Erika sat back in her chair and ran her hands through her hair.

'What do you mean it was almost empty?'

'There was a chap, fiddling at the boot of his car…'

Moss's head snapped up, and Erika sat forward. 'What did he look like?'

Moss scribbled on a piece of paper and held it up:

WHAT COLOUR WAS THE CAR?

Erika nodded.

'Funny-looking; I suppose I'd say geeky. Climbed into his car and drove off.'

Erika scrabbled through the papers on her desk and found the photo of the blue Ford.

'What colour was the car, Ms Holbrook?'

'Erm, blue. It was blue…'

Moss punched the air and started to jump up and down.

'Can you remember what kind of car it was?' asked Erika.

'I don't own a car. I don't tend to think about the make...'

'Could it have been a Ford?'

'Yes. It could have been, it was a little old and grimy ...'

Moss was doing a funny shrugging little dance, and Erika waved at her to sit down.

'Thank you, Ms Holbrook, I think you may be the only witness I have right now who could identify the man who has been abducting women in South London.'

'Good lord,' she said. 'Really?'

'What else can you tell us about this man? What did he look like?'

'Well, I did see him. But only from behind and the side. And my mind was on other things... He was quite dumpy; he had dark hair. Mid-length.'

'You didn't happen to see the number plate of the car?'

'No, sorry. I'm not in the habit of remembering those.'

'What exactly did this man do as you walked past?'

'He looked as if he was moving around from the boot of the car; he hitched up his trousers – I remember they had a brown stain on the rear – the fabric was a sort of tweedy green. He went to the driver's door and got in.'

Moss wrote another note:

WAS THERE A GIRL WALKING AWAY FROM CAR?

'Did you see a girl up ahead of you, walking away from the car?' asked Erika.

There was a pause on the line.

'No. No. Latimer Road is a long straight street, and you can't turn off it until you get down to the bottom, where a train track runs along behind the buildings. The buildings on the opposite side of the street are all being refurbished, and they're covered in scaffold.'

Erika gripped the phone. 'How long does it take to walk down to the bottom of the street?'

'I don't know. Four, five minutes.'

'Okay, thank you.'

Erika put down the phone.

Moss gave a yelp of glee and jumped up and down again. 'A blue Ford! He's using a different bloody car!' she cried.

'Yes. We've got him. Now we have to find him,' said Erika.

CHAPTER 73

After confirmation of the blue car, the atmosphere in the incident room became energised, and the team began their search afresh, looking to trace the journey of the car. Finally, just before 9 p.m., CCTV footage came through which led to another breakthrough.

'Look!' cried Crane, jabbing his finger at his computer screen. 'We've got him. We've got him! This is footage from the next building along the block, before the Latimer Road offices. It's from a block of private apartments which have a doorman and security.'

Erika and the rest of the room crowded around Crane at his computer.

'At 8.11 p.m. our blue Ford passed, which ties in with him passing the security cameras on the Latimer Road offices, twelve seconds later!'

He played the footage again through the projector on the whiteboard.

'Go back to just when he crosses the image and pause it,' said Erika, moving over to stand next to where the picture was now huge on the wall. Moss joined her. Crane ran the footage back and paused. They peered at the car.

'Shit, we have a partial plate, J892,' read Moss. 'Half of it is grimy, but we've got a partial number plate! We've got a partial!' She hugged Erika. 'Sorry, I must stink,' she added. 'All day in a cramped hot office.'

Erika grinned. 'Okay, this is really good, everyone, and thank you for coming in this weekend. I know it's been a slog, but now we have a partial, I need to ask a little more from you all. We need to keep working to trace the journey he took after abducting Beth. We need to work our contacts,' she said, checking her watch. 'Let's get on to TfL. Now we have a partial number plate it should speed things up with their image recognition.'

Two hours later, a batch of video files came through from Transport for London.

'Okay let's see what we have,' said Crane, downloading the files. Everyone gathered round his computer. He clicked on the first. 'Here he is, 8.28 p.m.,' he said, as a time-lapse image on the screen showed a blurry side-on image of the blue car moving past a petrol station forecourt. Crane minimised the screen and pulled up the next video file. This time the car was pictured head-on and passing some traffic lights; they could even make out a white face through the windscreen, but the whole image was blurry.

'So he goes past here at 8.30 p.m., and again cha-ching, we've got that partial number plate: J892,' said Crane, grinning up at Erika.

'So he's obscured the number plate again.'

'But not well enough this time,' said Peterson.

'Crane. Where does he go next?' asked Erika.

Crane clicked on the third video file, which showed the blue car from behind, moving past a traffic camera mounted high above the road, and away until the image became blurred.

'Where does he go? Did he turn right?' asked Peterson.

'Or is he going over the brow of the hill?' asked Moss.

'There isn't a hill,' said Erika. 'Look, at the next car, it signals right.' They played the footage a couple more times.

'Is this still Tower Bridge Road?' asked Erika.

'Yes,' said Crane.

Moss went to a nearby computer.

'Where does that right turn-off lead to?' asked Peterson.

'Tower Bridge Road turns off to Druid Street, and it's a dead end,' said Moss, working on her keyboard.

'How much footage did they send through of each file?' asked Erika.

'They only sent two minutes of each,' said Crane.

'If Druid Street is a dead end, then he would have had to come back out at some point,' said Erika.

'Unless the car's still parked there,' said Peterson.

'I want someone from uniform to go over and check out Druid Street,' said Erika. 'It's a long shot, but we need to see if the car is still there. In the meantime, I want CCTV footage from this Tower Bridge Road camera for the twenty-four-hour period afterwards. Just in case.'

'Hang on, boss. We don't need to send uniform division over to Druid Street,' said Moss, looking up from her computer.

'Why not?' asked Erika.

'They're already there. The body of a young woman has been found. Police are on the scene.'

It was just after 2.30 a.m., when Erika, Moss, and Peterson turned off the main road into Druid Street. They were waved through the first police cordon, and parked behind two squad cars and a support van lining the pavement. The streetlights were out on the cul-de-sac, and Erika counted six houses. Number four was busy with officers moving in and out, and bright lights shone from the open door. The rest of the houses on the cul-de-sac were dark, apart from one at the end, where a young couple stood in the light of their porch, watching.

Erika and the team approached the police tape with their warrants, and explained that the murder scene may be part of their investigation. They were given crime scene overalls, and suited up before they ducked under the tape and made their way to the front door. They were then met in the cramped hallway by DCI Mortimer, a grey-haired man Erika had never met. He was friendly but a little wary.

'We're not trying to crash your case,' she explained. 'I just want to know if you have an ID on the victim. We're investigating the abduction of a nineteen-year-old girl called Beth Rose.'

'We need to formally ID this one, but it's not Beth Rose,' said Mortimer. 'We believe it's a thirty-seven-year-old white female called Bryony Wilson. At least that's what we've got from the ID on her.'

He led them down the hallway and through the first door on the left into a small living room. A sofa had been pulled out and behind it lay the body of an obese young woman with a length of telephone cord tight around her neck. Her face was bloated and purple.

Two CSIs were crouching down and taking swabs from under the victim's fingernails, which were black.

'Tommy, can you get me a close-up of the face and neck,' said a voice Erika recognised. The crime scene photographer leaned over and took a shot and then stood back, revealing Isaac.

'Hello,' he said. 'I didn't think this was part of your investigation.'

Erika quickly explained why they were there.

'This poor girl was strangled,' said Isaac. 'I don't think she was killed in here. This carpet is fairly new and can you see there are marks where she was dragged. There are also carpet burns on the backs of her thighs, which would indicate that she was still alive when she was dragged through, although only just... There's bruising to her face, and the wrists; there are fingermarks just below the right hand.'

The crime scene photographer leaned in and took another shot. The flash dazzled Erika, and the small white light swam in her vision for a few seconds. She smiled at Isaac. He nodded. They came back out in to the hallway with DCI Mortimer.

'Who found her?' asked Peterson.

'Her cleaner,' he said. 'There was also a carving knife on the floor here, but no blood. Which leads me to think she was trying to defend herself. We need to check it for prints.' He indicated the kitchen, and they followed him down the hall. 'She was found with her handbag; all the cash and cards were in there, so I'd rule out this being burglary.'

The kitchen was small and cosy, with a view out over a tiny dark yard. A row of orange streetlights illuminated four large gas towers. Laid out on a small kitchen table with two chairs were the contents of Bryony's handbag.

'The cleaner did the living room last,' said Mortimer.

'So she cleaned up the dirt and the forensic evidence?' added Moss. Mortimer nodded.

Erika went to the contents of the handbag laid out and labelled in clear plastic bags. Bryony Wilson's work ID caught her eye. She picked up the evidence bag and stared at it, turning it over in her hand.

'What is it?' asked Moss.

'This ID. Look. Bryony Wilson worked for Genesis,' said Erika.

'If she works for them, then that's the connection,' said Peterson.

'But what the hell *is* the connection?' asked Moss.

CHAPTER 75

Erika, Moss, and Peterson left the crime scene and removed their crime scene overalls, depositing them in bags for the crime scene manager.

DCI Mortimer accompanied them out, and one of his officers met them at the front gate.

'You need to see this, sir.'

They all moved across the road, to where a police support van was parked with the headlights on full beam. Just in front of it, a uniformed officer stood beside a drain, the cover removed, and was training a torch down to where another officer wore blue crime scene overalls and was lying on her side on the tarmac, with her arm deep in the drain. Just as they reached her, she pulled out her arm, her sleeve black and grimy, and in her gloved hand she held a muddy cracked mobile phone. She placed it in a clear evidence bag.

'This is getting weirder by the minute,' said Peterson. 'If the blue Ford pulled into this street, or when it pulled in, it would have been on this side of the street.'

'We need to find out who that phone belongs to,' said Erika.

'If it's Beth's it counts out us knowing where he took her, if he dumped the phone here,' said Moss.

'But what has Bryony Wilson got to do with all this?' asked Peterson.

'If that's all, I need to get back into my crime scene. Let's keep in contact by phone,' said DCI Mortimer.

They thanked him and went back to their car parked at the entrance to the street.

Erika put on the heaters, and they sat in silence for a moment. The glowing clock on the display showed it was coming up to 4 a.m.

'What do we make of all this?' asked Erika, turning to face Moss, who was sitting in the back. Peterson turned also, hooking a long arm over the back of his seat.

'Okay. Bryony Wilson worked for Genesis. All our victims have been found in dumpsters owned and managed by Genesis. She's the obvious link to the killer,' said Moss.

'You think she was involved?' added Peterson.

'Beth Rose was abducted just after 8.15 p.m. Twenty minutes later, the car comes here. Bryony could have been involved,' said Erika.

'We're looking at a couple who kill?' asked Moss.

Erika drummed her fingers on the window. 'We need to have her house pulled apart. Check for anything suspicious, computers, forensics, people who knew her. I also want to pay a visit to the office where she worked. There are seventeen Genesis offices in London alone. We now have this one office where she worked. What time do you think it will be open?'

'I wouldn't expect people to start arriving for work until eight thirty, nine a.m.,' said Peterson. 'So that's four, five hours.'

'What's the chances of us getting home and back in time? There's rush hour to take into account…'

'Maybe we should find somewhere to bunk down for a couple of hours, get some sleep,' said Moss.

Peterson nodded. Erika looked out into the darkness and a fine sheen of rain began to fall.

'Thank you, both of you,' she said. 'I know we've been on the go for hours, but we're getting closer. How long since Beth was abducted?'

'Coming up to fifty-seven hours,' said Moss.

'Shit,' said Erika. 'What if we're too late?'

CHAPTER 76

Beth had lain on the cold floor of the cage, drifted in and out of sleep, and lost track of time. The cold and the lack of food sapped her energy. Despite the bandage on her arm, the blood continued to seep through the crepe material. Her jeans were wet, but it was dark and she couldn't be sure if she'd wet herself, or if it was blood.

She now knew who was keeping her captive, but she cursed herself for not paying attention to the news. She'd heard her friends at drama school talking about girls who had been abducted and then left in dumpsters. She'd been through stages of blind panic, screaming the place down, and then calm resolution. At one point she'd started to cry, thinking that her dream of fame would now come true – but it would be as a murder victim.

In the darkness she had felt around several times at the padlock which fastened the chain behind her neck, but lifting her bound hands stretched the cuts on her arms and made her hands slippery with blood.

Once or twice she'd thought he was coming back, when there were some bangs and shudders, but then she heard a terrible wailing sound. Was he keeping another girl here?

'Hello?' she yelled. 'Hello who's there?'

The scream came again.

'It's okay. I'm here! My name's Beth… What's yours, can you speak?'

The scream came again, and it was long and low. It went on for a minute, and then Beth realised it was the wind. It was the wind blowing through something. A metallic clanking noise coming from above, like something metal flapping.

'It's a vent, some kind of air vent,' said Beth, hope rising in her chest. She listened to the moaning of the wind as it increased in pitch, and the bash, bash, bash of the metal.

She scrabbled around on the damp rug, running her hands over it until she found the edge where she had tucked the small safety pin. Her fingers were cold and stiff and it took several attempts with the tiny clasp. She finally opened it out, finding it hard to grip it in her bloody fingers. She put her hands up to the back of her head. There was a little slack in the chain, and she pulled the padlock up and, after a few tries, rested it upside down in the crook of her neck. She found the keyhole, and pushed the pointed tip of the safety pin inside.

'Now what?' she said. She gave a dry laugh, which sounded nothing like her. She pushed in the pin and twiddled it about, jiggling it harder when nothing happened. 'Come on,' she hissed. Suddenly the safety pin snapped, and she was left with just a short piece of metal, and the safety head.

'NO!' she cried. 'No, no, no!' She felt around the padlock but the rest of the pin wasn't in the lock. Then carefully she ran her fingers over the lock and down the chain, but there was nothing. She scooted around, and put her hands by the edge of the cage to feel if the pin had fallen out onto the floor. She hadn't heard it fall, but where the hell was it? What if he found it when he came back?

Her feelings of despair and panic had risen as she'd spent the next few hours trying to find the small piece of safety pin, but there was nothing. Her hands were numb and she felt faint. She was going to die here. She was going to die. Beth shivered and pulled at the thin blanket folded under her. It was damp, and her legs were starting to cramp at being forced to sit upright with her neck chained against the mesh. She curled herself up into a ball as best she could to stay warm.

To stay warm, and wait for death.

CHAPTER 77

Just as Beth fell into a disturbed sleep, Erika and Moss were sitting in the front of the car. It was just after five thirty in the morning, and they were parked on the ground floor of a multi-storey car park on Tooley Street, opposite London Bridge train station. Their parking space looked out over the Thames, which was a churning brown colour under the lights from the buildings lining the embankment. A large tugboat rolled past on the water, shining a bright light and spewing out thick smoke from its funnel. A long, flat barge was dragging behind it, churning up the water. Peterson was laid out on the back seat, snoring.

'Does he always snore like that?' said Moss, shifting uncomfortably in the passenger seat and looking back. Erika nodded and sipped her coffee, resting the cup on the steering wheel.

'Moss. Are you on Facebook?'

'Yeah. Why?'

'I've never really done social media...'

'I'm on it, cos Celia's on it. And Celia's on it because her brother lives in Canada, and we can see pictures of their kids, and they can see our pics of Jacob. Although I've told Celia to stop uploading so many.'

'Why don't you like her uploading so many pictures?' asked Erika.

Moss shrugged. 'I know she's proud of our little son, I am too, but it's not his choice, is it? And you never know who is lifting off the pictures.'

'That's the thing,' said Erika. 'People don't realise what the word "sharing" means.'

'It's not a difficult word, boss.'

'No, but the dictionary definition of "sharing" is, "a part or portion of a larger amount which is divided among a number of people, or to which a number of people contribute".'

'That sounds about right.'

'But when you "share" on social media, don't you give away something of yourself? Your privacy. Information. Social networks are free, aren't they?'

'Yeah. That's another reason we're on it: we can talk to Celia's brother, my mother, well, Celia talks to that old bag more than I do.'

'And that ability to communicate is a good thing, but in return for a free service, don't they want to find out everything they can about us? Our killer probably didn't have to leave his house or his bedroom until he was about to grab the victims. He found out everything about them online. Where they were going; what they liked to do; their habits. And people don't realise they're giving it away. If a stranger came up to you on the street and wanted to know where you were going next, or what kind of films you like, if you're married or single, where you went to school, or where you work, you'd be a bit freaked out… The same if they wanted to have your phone for a few minutes to scroll through the photos. But the same people blithely stick it all online for everyone to see.'

'Course, people don't see it like that,' said Moss. 'They put things on social media to show off. Look at my new car; look at my house.'

'Look at my little boy,' finished Erika. Moss nodded ruefully.

'No wonder famous people sue to have their kids' faces blurred out… I don't think it's people being stupid though. I think most people find their lives boring, and uploading their achievements, things they're proud of, it validates them.'

'They don't think who might be watching them,' said Erika. 'I wonder if Janelle and Lacey, Ella and Beth knew?'

'Jesus, when you put their names together, that's heavy. Four girls.'

'Three. We're going to get the fourth. She's not going to die,' said Erika. They sat in silence for a moment, then another tug-boat pulled past, and its horn blared out twice.

'Christ on a motorbike! What was that?' cried Peterson, waking up and banging his head on the inside of the door.

'Snoring beauty is finally awake,' said Moss. 'Actually, snoring and farting beauty.'

'Piss off, Moss, you're the farter. I've spent plenty of long car journeys with you.'

'Ha ha,' she said, reaching back and slapping him on the backside.

He rubbed his eyes and sat up.

'What time is it?'

'Quarter to six,' said Erika.

'It'll be light soon,' said Moss. 'Who wants another coffee before the office opens?'

Just before eight, they left the car and walked through Borough High Street to the offices of Genesis, where Bryony Wilson had worked. It was a tall brown brick building about three hundred yards down from the market. They joined a group of bleary-eyed office workers trudging up the steps to the main entrance. They went to the front desk and had to deal with an overzealous head of security, but when they produced their warrant cards and explained that they were investigating the murder of one of the company's employees, she called the manager of Human Resources.

They were instructed to go up to the sixth floor, but mistakenly came out onto the fifth floor with a group of office workers. When they saw the floor number written on the wall, they were about to go back to the lifts when Moss noticed a collage of staff photos on the wall. Under some of their names were gold stars. Bryony was pictured with hunched shoulders and a manic gummy smile. Under the photo were three gold stars.

'Excuse me,' said Erika to a dark-haired girl about to go into the office. 'What do the stars mean?'

'Commendations,' she said, pulling a security pass from her bag. 'Overtime you get one; the company emails you a twenty-five quid iTunes voucher.'

'Does Bryony Wilson work on this floor?' asked Erika.

Moss and Peterson gave her a look; they were supposed to be going up to meet the head of Human Resources.

'She's my Team Leader,' said the girl.

She put her pass on a sensor and opened the door. They followed her inside and along the large open-plan office. She stopped at a desk towards the end divided into partitions.

'This is her desk, if you want to wait for her…'

Bryony's partition was tidy with a pot of pens topped with Trolls of varying coloured fuzzy hair. On one side of her computer was a plastic M&M Yellow figure, smiling with a thumb up, and under her desk was a footrest and a spare pair of smart court shoes.

'She walked to work,' said the girl, following Erika's eyes to the shoes. 'Sorry, who are you?'

Erika took out her warrant card and introduced them all.

'Why are you looking for Bryony?' asked the girl, sitting in her chair warily.

'We'll need a warrant if they don't want to play ball with the computer,' said Peterson, peering at Bryony's desk.

'This was Bryony's permanent workstation?' asked Moss. The girl nodded. 'What's your name?'

'Katrina Ballard,' she said, tucking a long strand of hair behind her ear.

Erika, Moss and Peterson moved around the desks, adorned with mess, paperwork and family photos. Erika came to a stop at a desk where a photo of a large white-faced dog was pinned below a computer monitor. It was an unusual breed. With the wide face of a Staffordshire bull terrier, but with black spots like a Dalmatian.

'Excuse me,' came a shrill female voice. 'EXCUSE ME, officers?'

They looked up, and a small woman with poker-straight dark hair and a pinafore dress was striding towards them.

'I'm Mina Anwar, I'm HR manager.' She reached them and her eyes darted around them, attempting to work out what they were doing.

'Thank you. We must have come out on the wrong floor,' said Erika, giving her a disarming smile.

'If you'd like to come up to my office,' she said, putting out a small arm to scoop them up and away. Other members of staff were arriving and had noticed the commotion.

'Lead the way,' said Erika.

When they came out onto the communal corridor by the lifts, Erika's phone rang. The lift doors pinged and opened. It was John on the phone.

'Boss, we've been working through the night following up the CCTV. We managed to get more footage of the blue car from a traffic camera near the South Circular, and we have a full number plate: J892 FZD.'

Erika held up her hand, and they all stopped outside the lifts.

'That's fantastic, John!'

'The car is registered to a thirty-seven-year-old white male called Morris Cartwright. He's a farm labourer, and he has two convictions for assaulting women, in 2011 and 2013. And, get this, he lives in a village on the outskirts of London called Dunton Green. It's near Sevenoaks.'

Erika quickly relayed the information to Moss and Peterson. Moss punched the air, and Peterson put his hands to his head and closed his eyes.

'Yes!' he cried.

Mina waited by the lifts, her hand being buffeted by the doors as they kept trying to close.

'Officers, I have a lot to do this morning, can you please explain what is happening here?' she asked.

'Boss, you and Peterson go,' said Moss. 'I'll stay here and get as much info as I can about Bryony.'

Erika and Peterson took the waiting lift and, just before the doors closed, Moss gave them a smile.

'Good luck and stay safe,' she said.

As it started to descend to the ground floor, Erika hoped that they weren't too late. That Beth was still alive.

CHAPTER 78

Darryl had started throwing up in the early hours of Sunday morning, and then a dull headache had crept up from the base of his neck to a stabbing pain in his temple. At lunchtime, his mother had made him a sandwich, but when he'd taken a small bite, it had come straight back up again. The pain and a sense of doom continued, until he came down to the living room in the evening. John and Mary were watching an episode of *Inspector Morse*.

'Mum, I don't feel well,' he said.

'You must be coming down with something, just get a good night's sleep,' said Mary, studying him over the top of her drink.

'You should get the hell out of here, is what you should do,' said John, not taking his eyes off the television. 'I have to get up for work in the morning, and I don't want to catch whatever it is.'

Darryl had left the living room, and as he'd started upstairs he'd had to grab the bannister, feeling dizzy, and a tingling sensation had begun down his left arm. He went to bed, and as he lay there the pain increased.

He drifted off to sleep in the early hours of the morning, and began a cycle of dreams which repeated over and over.

In the dream, he would wake on a bright sunny day still in his bedroom, with the light streaming through the curtains. He'd get up and be relieved to see that the bed sheets were dry. Then he would hear it: the ting ting sound coming from the wardrobe, a hanger lightly brushing the wood. Then a tight creak of taut rope, and as he approached the wardrobe door, the key would begin to spin, until the door swung open to reveal Joe hanging inside, his feet swinging in mid-air, trembling.

'You've pissed the bed, baby,' Joe's voice would say, but his lips weren't moving. His purple bloated face was fixed in a smile with the eyes open.

Finally, Darryl would feel the warm liquid splashing on his legs.

The dreams seemed to go round in circles, over and over, and every time he thought he was awake, the same would happen over again. The sunny room, the ting ting sound of a hanger in the wardrobe…

The pain grew intense in his side throughout these dreams, and the final time he'd come to, the room was dark. He'd climbed out of bed and felt the sheets. They were dry. He'd moved to the curtain and seen that it was dark outside: a large bright moon hung in the clear sky.

I'm awake, he'd thought. *I have to be awake.*

Then a ragged breathing came from the wardrobe. It seemed to loom bigger in the room. The door slowly opened and a large figure stepped out and into the light cast by the moon. It was Bryony, her face wide and now almost blackened. The telephone cord was wound tight around her neck, and she was advancing on him. Darryl had turned to get out of bed, but lying beside him, with her bloody battered head on the pillow, was the coffee bike girl, Janelle, and next to her lay Lacey and Ella. They tried to open their beaten eyes; they reached out for him with their arms… Bryony started to unwind the cord from around her neck…

Darryl woke, finally. It was pouring with rain outside, and he was drenched in sweat. He gingerly pulled back the cover and incredible pain shot down his left side. His stomach and chest were covered in clusters of yellow pustules. There were scores of them, and just moving sent pain shooting through his body. His mattress was soaked in urine.

'Darryl,' came a voice through the door. 'Darryl, are you alright? You were shouting; you were shouting about Joe?'

His mother opened the door and came in.

'What's happening to me?' he said, wincing in pain.

His mother went to him and stared down at the terrible rash and pustules.

'Shingles. You've got shingles,' she said incredulously. 'Why were you shouting about your brother?'

CHAPTER 79

Beth drifted out of a disturbed sleep. A faint light came through the thick iron grate in the ceiling, and the metal vents banged in the wind, accompanied by a low moaning howl.

She was so cold, she flexed her frozen fingers bound by the chain. She touched her tongue to her arm. The bandage felt dry and a little tacky. How long had she been here? Had that freak been back when she was asleep? What if he was here, now, crouching in the shadows?

'Hello?' she said. Her voice echoed in the darkness and sounded strangely polite. Then despite everything she laughed. 'Come on, Beth, he's a complete psycho, and it's not as if he's going to say hello back…'

It must be morning, she thought; there was light coming from above, and there was a definite sliver of white light filtering through under the door. She remembered the last morning before she was abducted. She'd come downstairs to the kitchen, and her aunt had been on the phone with one of her friends.

'You don't want to get into threesomes quite yet, Derek,' she'd said. 'Why don't you both try taking up a hobby, see if that brings you closer together? I've always wanted to learn bridge.' Aunt Marie had smiled, and indicated that there was coffee in the pot. She'd sat on the stool, drank coffee and eaten hot buttered toast with jam, listening, laughing, as her aunt gossiped on the phone. She wondered what Aunt Marie was doing right now and missed her like crazy.

Beth tried to sit up straighter so that the chain wouldn't dig into her neck, and she felt a strange tickling sensation in her hair. She felt her head, thinking it was a spider or a fly, when something fell from her hair and landed on her leg. She picked it up. It was the other half of the safety pin. Her hands had been above her head when she was trying to unpick the padlock. It must have fallen into her hair when it broke, and become tangled during her frantic search. She lifted the corner of the blanket beside her feet and found the other piece of the pin.

She now had a long thin piece of metal making up the sharp pin, ending in a twisted loop, and she had the remainder of the safety pin; the curved safety head which was attached to a long piece of metal.

She remembered something she had seen in one of the *CSI* TV shows Aunt Marie loved to watch. The character had been locked in a cupboard under the stairs, and had used a bobby pin to pick a lock: snapping it in half and using the two pieces of metal, one piece was slipped into the top part of the lock, and then another in the bottom. She still wasn't sure how the hell it would work but this had to mean something, didn't it?

Of course, the captive woman in *CSI* had broken out of the cupboard with remarkably sleek hair, and even though she'd been in there for two days, her light blue slacks were devoid of piss stains… Beth could only imagine what she looked like, and she laughed. A laugh which then turned into tears. She cursed the lack of light, and that her hands were bound together. She turned the two pieces of metal over between each of her fingers, but her hands were numb. Beth blew on her hands to warm them up.

If she could manage this, then she might have a chance to escape.

CHAPTER 80

Erika drove fast through London, blue lights and siren blaring all the way. Peterson called in for backup, giving the address for Morris Cartwright. As they reached the South Circular, it began to pelt with torrential rain. It hammered down on the roof, and the windscreen wipers could barely keep up with the deluge, but Erika pressed on.

They reached the outskirts of Dunton Green forty minutes later, just after ten a.m. It was a tiny village and very quiet. They drove through it in a matter of minutes, past a church and then the train station, a pub, and a small supermarket before the houses thinned back out to a country lane surrounded by fields. The rain continued to pound on the roof of the car, and as the road banked sharply down, Erika sped through a deep flooded patch.

'That's deep water there, whoa…' said Peterson, grabbing the dashboard, and as they sped through it a spray of water engulfed the car and spilled up and over the bonnet.

Erika thought the engine might cut out but, miraculously, it didn't.

They approached a couple of houses surrounded by fields, and Erika pulled up in the small driveway of the first. It was two semi-detached houses, and they sat in a dip amongst a vast field. A chain fence surrounded the back garden, but there was no shed, no outbuildings. It was open.

'This is it?' said Erika, when she turned off the engine.

'This is the address. Confirmed by control,' said Peterson.

'This is a shitty little two-up-two-down,' she said.

They got out of the car as the rain continued to pelt down, and they had to avoid a huge muddy puddle on their way to the front door.

A young messy-haired woman in tracksuit bottoms and a grubby T-shirt answered the door, with a podgy pale baby on her hip. It reminded Erika of the Stay Puft Marshmallow Man from the *Ghostbusters* films. The baby turned to look at them with big blue eyes, along with the woman whose eyes were tiny, and a little too far apart.

'What?' she said.

'Are you Mrs Cartwright?' asked Erika.

'Who wants to know?'

'I'm Detective Chief Inspector Erika Foster; this is Detective Inspector Peterson,' said Erika, blinking in the heavy rain as they held up their warrant cards. 'We're looking for Morris Cartwright.'

The woman rolled her eyes, tipped her head back and yelled: 'Morris! It's the pigs again!'

Morris came into the hallway wearing jeans, a T-shirt and in bare feet. He was holding a yoghurt pot and had the spoon in his mouth.

'I ain't done nothing,' he said, taking it out. Erika saw his front two teeth were missing.

Just then two police cars pulled into the drive behind their car, the blue lights rolling above. Morris took one look at them and bolted back down the hallway. Erika and Peterson dashed past the woman and the pudgy baby. The hallway led past a tatty living room, to a grubby kitchen. The back door was already open, and they could see Morris running barefoot across the waterlogged garden. He dodged a small plastic swing set, and went to vault the chain fence, but slipped and landed in the mud.

Erika and Peterson bundled over to him, just as two uniformed officers appeared out of the back door.

They all slipped around in the mud, the rain still pelting down, and Morris still resisted as Erika tried to handcuff him and read him his rights.

'Where are you trying to go with no shoes?' shouted Peterson, himself slipping over. He got up and slammed Morris against the fence, pulling his arms behind his back.

Erika put him in cuffs.

'I'm arresting you on suspicion of the kidnap, false imprisonment, and murder of Janelle Robinson, Lacey Greene, and Ella Wilkinson, and the kidnap and false imprisonment of Beth Rose…' Peterson turned him round, and he spat at Erika. They handed him over to the uniformed officers, who dragged him away.

'That's him? You can't be serious,' said Peterson, wiping his face.

'I know, he's an idiot,' said Erika, running her hands through her hair. They were both drenched.

CHAPTER 81

The rain had started to fall harder, roaring on the roof of the Oast House. Below, in the brick furnace chamber, Beth was sitting with both hands tucked between her thighs. She had made an attempt to pick the padlock, but her hands were bound together and her fingers had gone numb and it was as if she'd been holding the tiny pieces of the safety pin wearing boxing gloves. They'd warmed up a little, because she felt a dull ache with pins and needles, as the sensation came back into her fingers.

'Okay, come on, come on, let's do this,' she said, lifting her hands and flexing them. She was worried he'd soon be coming back. She took the two pieces of the broken safety pin, one in each hand. Now to make the key, or something that would mimic a key. The padlock was behind her head, and she couldn't see what she was doing.

She took several deep breaths and then shifted her body down, so that the padlock rested against the nape of her neck, upside down. Her hands were bound together, and chained, but there was just enough slack in the chain so she could lift her hands behind her head. Gripping the two pieces of safety pin, she found the lock and inserted the longer piece with the safety head in at the top, pressing it into place and holding it fast. Then with her other hand she pushed in the straight piece of metal with the pointed end.

With her arms in the air behind her head she gripped the padlock with her free fingers.

'Shit, what the hell do I do now, turn it? Yes, stay calm…
Think *CSI*… You're going to get out of this and you're going
to be on *CSI*.' She smiled at the thought. 'Or even if not, you'll
have a great story to tell.'

Clasping the two pieces of metal in place and holding them
between her thumbs and forefingers, she started to twist. It was
awkward and fiddly, and wouldn't budge. She pushed the two
halves of the safety pin into the lock harder and twisted again.

Suddenly the padlock sprang open and landed on the concrete floor with a loud clatter. Beth gasped in shock and pulled
her head forward, quickly un-looping the chains from around
her neck. She flexed her body, feeling a sense of joy and ela-
tion. Her hands were still chained together, and the chain was
padlocked to the opposite side of the cage, but she could move
around; she flexed her stiff neck and body and moved to the
padlock where the chain around her wrists was locked to the
opposite side of the cage.

Then she realised that she was only holding one piece of the
safety pin. The bent end was still lodged in the open padlock lying outside the cage. She tried to fit her fingers through the bars.
It was out of her reach.

'The chain! Use the chain!' shouted a voice in her head.

It took several attempts, but Beth managed to use the chain
as a lasso to grab the padlock and pull it back towards the bars.
The wounds on her arms had now reopened, and the exertion
had caused her to start bleeding. The bandages were sopping
wet. She wiped her hands on her unrecognisable T-shirt and
grabbed the padlock. She retrieved the piece of her key from its
lock and started to work on the second padlock. It took three
attempts and then the lock sprang open. She quickly unwound
the chains around her wrists, gingerly shaking out her arms.

The padlock on the door of the cage took a lot longer, but
eventually she managed it, and it sprang open.

Beth laughed in delight, quickly unhooked it, and opened the cage. The feeling of freedom was immense, and she moved around quickly, shaking out her numb legs, willing the blood into her feet. She pushed open the door of the furnace, and the roaring of the rain grew louder as she stepped out into the outer room of the Oast House tower. It was gloomy, but she could see up through slatted beams to the funnel-shaped roof above. A cool breeze and some flecks of rain fell against her face, but despite the cold she welcomed it. She found a light switch and flicked it on.

In the corner was a small table with the black backpack, and a small plastic box. She went to it and fumbled with the catch. Inside was a syringe, some small glass bottles filled with liquid drugs, and a selection of razor-sharp scalpels.

'Oh my god,' she whispered.

It was a stupid to stay there any longer. There were two doors; straight ahead was a large metal sliding door and behind her a small wooden door. She tried the metal door first, heaving it with all the strength she could summon, but it wouldn't budge. She tried the other door, and it opened out into a huge barn-like structure with what looked like three floors. However, there were just bare beams where the floors should be, and she could see right up to the roof tiles. There was no door, no way out. Just some tiny windows high above the third level of beams.

CHAPTER 82

Erika and Peterson rode in their car behind the police van carrying Morris Cartwright. They bumped along country lanes on their way to Sevenoaks Police Station, where they would be conducting their interview.

As Peterson drove, Erika had John on speakerphone back at West End Central.

'We've pulled Morris Cartwright's criminal record. He was twice arrested and charged with assault and battery: first time in 2011 it was against his wife, but she decided not to press charges; the second time in 2013, the case never got to court. He was arrested a couple of weeks back after stealing and trying to flog some fertiliser from a local farm where he was working.'

'What about the car?'

'He bought the blue Ford S-Max back in 2007—' There was interference on the line.

They hit a rough patch of road leading up to another patch of flooding, and the van slowed in front as it went through.

'John, you still there?' said Erika.

There was more interference, and then John's voice came back. 'Yes, boss.'

Erika's phone beeped to say she had a call waiting. It was Moss. 'Hang on two seconds, John, I've just got to take this,' she answered.

'Boss, I'm in town still. I've had no joy on Genesis. They let me take a look at Bryony's work email; there was nothing suspicious, seems she was very diligent, didn't mix her work and private life. A team is now pulling her house apart; I'll keep you posted.'

'Thanks,' said Erika, and she went back to John.

'Boss,' he said, 'I've got more on Morris Cartwright. He rents a lock-up in the village, on Faraday Way in Dunton Green.'

'Good work, John. Can you call in local plod, just get them to check out the last employer where Morris worked.'

'Yes, boss.'

The van in front reached a junction, and they slowed behind it. The police van pulled out and turned right.

'Hang on, stop,' she said to Peterson as he went to follow. They watched the police van drive away.

'Erika. What are you doing? You're the arresting officer. We have to follow them and present Morris Cartwright to the custody sergeant.'

'I'll brief them over the radio, they can do it on my behalf. Time is ticking with Beth Rose, and I want to go to Morris Cartwright's lock-up.'

She looked over at Peterson, and he nodded. She keyed the address of the lock-up into the GPS. With a squeal of rubber, he did a U-turn, and they sped off, hoping they were not too late

CHAPTER 83

Darryl was in terrible pain, but relieved that he wasn't dying. His mother left him, and he managed to dry himself off and get dressed. The rain was pounding against his bedroom window, and when he looked out the sky was almost black. He switched on the light, sat at his computer gingerly and logged on to the news. His hands were shaking as he scrolled down. There was nothing on *BBC London* about the body of Bryony being found, but he still couldn't shake off the feeling of dread. Things were getting out of control. *Why hadn't his mother suggested calling the doctor?* He needed painkillers or antibiotics and then he'd go down to the Oast House.

He staggered downstairs, and found his mother in the living room. The television was on and showing interference.

'Mum…' he started.

'How do you get teletext?' she said, peering at the remote control in her hand, unconcerned by his ashen face.

'I'm in pain, Mum,' he groaned.

'I want to see the weather, and I can't seem to find teletext on here.'

'You've got a weather app, on your phone…'

'I don't know how to work that, Darryl,' she said. 'I like how they lay it out on teletext,' she added, indicating the white noise on the screen. It suddenly went black and the CCTV activated, showing the front gates.

Darryl gripped the wall and began to panic. There was a police car; he could see two uniformed police officers through the windscreen. His blood went cold, and he stood transfixed. His mother was looking at him. She got up and gave him the remote.

'Well, go on, press the button, and open the gates,' she said.

'You know what button it is,' he said.

'Press it. Then I'll call the doctor.'

'Please don't,' he said.

She pulled the remote control back to her and pressed the button which activated the front gates.

'Mum. You don't know what they want!'

'They probably have something to tell us about that intruder, or those gypsies we saw the other week, the ones who were hanging round the gate the other night... or do you know what they might want?'

She looked at him long and hard. He shook his head. She tucked the remote control into her housecoat and bustled off out of the room.

On the screen the police car moved forwards through the gate, its wheels crunching on the gravel.

CHAPTER 84

Darryl was hiding in the small toilet off the boot room and strained to hear what the police were saying to his mother in the farm office. They had knocked on the little-used front door, next to the living room, and when Mary had answered, Grendel had gone a little crazy, but she'd locked her into the living room and taken the police officers through to the office.

Darryl came out into the boot room and moved closer to the door. Their muffled voices carried on, and he held his breath. If they had come to arrest him, wouldn't they have done it by now?

The door opened a crack, and he shrank back. He could see through the gap his mother in the office with two young male police officers, and she was going all fluttery-eyed as she moved between two large filing cabinets where they kept all of the farm records.

'This is everything we have on Morris Cartwright,' she was saying. 'He was a good milker, but we had no choice but to let him go… He didn't have access to any of the farm buildings; we keep the keys in here on that board, and the office is always locked.'

Darryl tried to breathe.

What if the police wanted more? What if they wanted to go down the farm and look at some of the outbuildings? He suddenly made a decision. He had to kill Beth. Quick and easy. Kill her, dump her body and wash it down, and then he'd stop. He'd stop the craziness; he'd go back to work. He knew the farm better than the police, and didn't they need a warrant before they could go looking around? He had time. And there was a maze of buildings to search until they would get down to the Oast House.

Darryl forgot the pain as he pulled on his boots and coat, and then he went to the high shelf in the boot room where his father kept his shotgun. He took it down and opened it, pushing two cartridges in from the box of ammunition next to it.

'What are you doing?' said a voice.

He turned. Mary was standing in the doorway, staring at him. He closed the shotgun magazine and leant against the wall.

'What did the police want?' he said.

'They asked questions about Morris. They saw his car in London... But you were driving it, weren't you?'

'Did you say the car was here, parked out back?'

'No.'

Darryl swallowed, and picked up the shotgun.

'Mum, you need to let me go, please...' His voice sounded strange and distant.

She moved to him and put a hand across the back door.

'You knew I wouldn't go down there, didn't you?' she said, shaking her head. 'You knew that I would keep away, after what happened to... to... my beautiful boy.'

'Joe, Mum. JOE. You want to know something? Your beautiful Joe was a sadistic little bully.'

'No,' she said, shaking her head.

'Your son. Was no angel.'

'You!' she spat. 'You're no son of mine.'

Darryl leaned in close, and said in a low voice: 'Joe and the other boys would wait for me in the woods after school, then hold me down, and piss on me, and then Joe would make me do things to them...'

'NO!' cried Mary, and she put her hands to her ears like a small child.

'Yes! Yes, YES!' shouted Darryl, grabbing at her hands and pulling them away. 'Joe hanged himself because he was sick. He was evil. He told me he wanted to go.'

'You said you found him.'

Darryl shook his head.

'No. I watched him do it. I could have stopped him. But I didn't.'

Mary launched herself at him, clawing at his face. He swung the barrel of the shotgun up and round and hit her over the head. She went down on the floor and remained still.

Darryl stared at her, his heart pounding. He reached out to touch her face, then pulled his hand back.

He picked up the shotgun and left the house.

CHAPTER 85

It was still raining hard when Erika and Peterson drove up to Morris Cartwright's lock-up. It sat amongst fields at the end of a long bumpy track. The building was spread out and made up of four huge asbestos arches with a large wooden frame. It looked odd, like a piece of East London landscape had been plonked in a muddy field.

Peterson pulled up onto an overgrown concrete platform, and they got out of the car. The windows running along the top were dark. Peterson put a hand on her arm.

'Erika, if we go in, how do we link Morris to her? He could say it was nothing to do with him. That he didn't know anything about it. We have no proof.'

'Beth Rose could be in there. She'll be in a bad way; isn't this about saving someone's life?' Erika replied. Peterson looked over at her, her hair flat against her head in the pouring rain. He wiped his face and nodded. 'Call for backup: ambulance, police. We don't know what we are going to find.'

Peterson called in for backup, as Erika pulled a pair of bolt cutters from the boot of the car. They moved over to the row of doors.

'It was this one, the first?' she asked.

Peterson nodded. Erika snipped the chain easily, and they unwound it. The door pulled back with a squeal.

It was empty apart from a small pile of sacks in the middle of the concrete floor. The light shone through a window high above.

'Fertiliser,' said Peterson, kicking the pile.

'We need to move them; there could be a trapdoor...'

They shifted the small pile, but there was nothing. They moved along the line, opening the other three lockups, which were similarly full of gardening equipment, an old car, and the last lockup held a speedboat with its engine lying strewn across the floor.

They went back to the car and got in, just as three police cars arrived with sirens blaring, together with an ambulance and fire engine.

After an embarrassing exchange with the emergency services, Erika and Peterson set off back towards the police station in Sevenoaks. Their mood was dark in the car, and they listened to the police radio as it was communicated to control that it had been a false alarm.

They'd just reached the village of Dunton Green, and were passing the local pub, when one of the police officers came over the radio to say that they'd been to check out Morris Cartwright with his previous employer at Bradley Farm.

'Spoke to a funny old girl,' he was saying. 'They've got a bloody huge dog. It went ballistic.'

'You okay? Did you get bitten?' joked the police officer on control.

'Almost. And I wouldn't have fancied my chances. Weird breed it was, it had a big white face like a bull terrier, but spotty like a Dalmatian.'

A thunderbolt realisation hit Erika as they carried on chattering. A big white bull terrier with spots... Where had she seen it? That kind of breed. The photo in the Genesis office. It had been of a big wide-faced dog with spots.

'Stop the car!' she cried.

'I'm on a junction, at lights,' said Peterson.

'Reverse, pull in at the car park.'

They parked, and Erika got on the radio to Moss.

'It's me, officers have just been out to Bradley Farm in Dunton Green. Tell me who is registered as living there.'

Moss came back after a moment. 'There's a Mary, John, and Darryl Bradley.'

'Have you got the employee list from the HR woman at Genesis?'

'Yes. I'm just working through it.'

'Darryl Bradley, is he there?'

The wait seemed to go on forever as Erika sat in the car park with Peterson, the phone poised in her hand.

'Yes, Darryl Bradley. He lives at the farm, and he works for Genesis!' said Moss.

'It's there. That's where he's holding Beth Rose,' said Erika. She held onto the car dashboard, as Peterson roared out of the car park, hoping they were not too late.

CHAPTER 86

Darryl ran through the rain and the mud with the shotgun under his jacket. He passed several of the farmworkers sitting with his father, sheltering under the barn from the rain, drinking tea from a flask. They watched with their steaming plastic cups as he dashed past, oblivious to their gaze.

'He's not right up top,' said John, tapping his head.

They watched as Darryl reached the gate and vaulted it, almost slipping over as he landed on the other side and carried on running.

'You think 'e's, well, you know?' said one of the older farmhands, indicating a limp wrist. He was an old man with bristly grey hair poking out from under his flat cap.

'Oh lord, I hope not. I'd rather he was a murderer,' said John, taking the flask and filling up his cup.

The fields were waterlogged, but Darryl slipped and plunged on along the muddy track. When he came close to the Oast House, he heard the rain hammering on the top of the tower. He stood for a moment to catch his breath, and then he opened the large sliding door. He moved inside, staring at the lights – which were on – and at the open furnace door. The sight of the empty cage shocked him. The chains lay coiled in the centre of the grubby rug, with the three padlocks. He went to one and saw two halves of a safety pin protruding from the lock, which was streaked with blood. He moved back out of the furnace chamber, gripping the shotgun.

Then there was movement, and he saw Beth coming at him, a scalpel in her bloody hand. He managed to react in time, and deflect her with the barrel of the gun, and she crashed into the wall.

How the hell? What the hell?

He stood over her as she scrambled to her feet, blocking her from running to the sliding door.

'How did you? Where did you get it?' he said, lifting the shotgun and aiming it at her.

'The bandage you gave me, had a pin attached to it,' said Beth. She was filthy and shaking, but there was scorn in her voice. Then she tipped her head back and spat in his face. He blinked in shock, and she ran through the wooden door into the larger part of the Oast House.

CHAPTER 87

John had finished his tea with the farm workers, and they were just about to go back to work, when he heard the police sirens in the driveway. By the time he'd hurried back to the house, there were several cars in the driveway, and Grendel was going mad barking. He went to the back door, which was hanging open.

A tall blonde woman and a black man were in his kitchen, and Mary lay on the stone floor. She was still, and there was blood on her head.

'Who are you?' demanded the blonde officer. She held up her ID and identified herself as Detective Chief Inspector Erika Foster, and the other officer as Detective Inspector James Peterson.

'John… John Bradley. I own this farm… Mary, what's happened to Mary?' he said, moving to her and kneeling down.

'There a pulse, but she's got a nasty head injury,' said Erika. 'An ambulance is on its way.'

He looked bewildered, and took his wife's small hand in his, which was large and calloused.

'Mr Bradley. Your son. Where is he?' asked Erika.

'Down the field… I just saw him running down the field…' He looked back at Mary. 'Have we been burgled?'

Erika looked at Peterson.

'Where was your son going?'

'Down the field… I don't know.'

'What's down the field?' asked Peterson.

John was now in tears, his face red, and he was stroking Mary's face.

'The lake, erm, fields… the old Oast House.'

'Stay with them,' said Erika to one of the uniformed officers, and she and Peterson set off towards the Oast House.

It was still raining when Erika and Peterson rushed down the yard and past the outbuildings. They came to the gate and climbed over, landing in mud on the other side, which oozed up and over their shoes.

'DCI Foster, Erika, are you reading me?' came a voice over the radio.

'Yes, reading you!' shouted Erika over the roar of the rain.

'Suspect's father says his shotgun is missing from the house. I repeat, the shotgun is missing. Suspect could be armed. We are calling for backup. Do not proceed without backup. Do not proceed without backup."

Erika looked at Peterson.

'Acknowledged,' she said.

CHAPTER 88

Beth was backed into a corner in the main building of the Oast House. She was shivering and streaked with blood. The straw felt prickly under her bare feet and the wooden rafters stretching away above her. Darryl stood a few feet away from her, the shotgun trained at her head. They had been standing there for several minutes. At first she'd closed her eyes, expecting him to pull the trigger, but when it hadn't come she'd opened them again. She could see he was sweating, and his face was breaking out in a strange rash.

'Why don't you just do it?' she said hoarsely.

'Shut up. SHUT UP!' he cried. He gripped the shotgun on his shoulder, and stared at her down the barrel. His finger twitched on the trigger. The rain hammered down on the roof with a roar.

He had his back to the open door, and behind him, Beth saw Erika and Peterson appear. The rain masking the sound of their entrance. They were both soaked and covered in mud. Beth's eyes widened, and she forced herself not to react.

Erika saw the situation and looked at Peterson. They glanced around inside, then Erika put her finger to her lips and indicated that Beth should keep Darryl talking.

'What do you, um, what is this place used for?' asked Beth, saying the first thing which came into her head.

'What?' said Darryl, momentarily thrown.

Beth's eyes involuntarily flickered to where Peterson was about to move back through the door.

Darryl followed her gaze and turned with the gun. 'What the hell?' he shouted, and he fired the shotgun.

Peterson went down onto the straw clutching a rapidly growing red stain in his stomach.

'No!' cried Erika with horror, rushing over to him. Darryl kept the shotgun trained on her.

'Get away from him!' he shouted, and then he started to panic, turning it to Beth and then back to Erika. 'You stay there and you, do you hear me, get away from him!'

Erika kneeled over Peterson, who lay in the straw in shock. She looked down and saw the red stain on his white shirt was spreading

'Oh my god, the, the pain,' said Peterson, grimacing. He put his hands up to his stomach.

'No! This is not going to happen,' said Erika. Darryl was now moving towards her with his shotgun, but she didn't care. 'Here, press hard, down on here, you need to put pressure on the bleeding,' she said, taking his hand and pressing it against the wound.

He screamed in agony.

'You get away from him,' shouted Darryl, advancing on her and aiming the gun at her head.

Beth suddenly ran at him from behind, and managed to knock him off his feet.

Erika had tears in her eyes as she pressed down onto the top of Peterson's hand. Blood oozed between their fingers. She took out her radio. 'This is Erika Foster. I have an officer down; I repeat, I have an officer down. He's been shot and he's losing blood fast...'

Darryl was now back on his feet, and he had the gun aimed at Beth. 'Get over there, with them,' he said.

Beth moved towards Erika and Peterson.

Erika suddenly got a grip of the situation. 'Beth, I know you've been through so much, but please can you help?' she said.

Darryl trained the gun on them, as Beth, despite being hungry, cold and terrified, nodded and moved to Peterson and pressed her hands onto his wound.

'Pressure, it needs pressure, even if it hurts him,' she said.

Peterson was now in shock, lying back with wide eyes.

'Why are you all ignoring me!?' screamed Darryl. 'I have a gun!'

'Let them go,' said Erika, turning to him. 'Let them both go. I'll stay here with you.'

Darryl shook his head and trained the gun at them, unsure who to concentrate on. Peterson was moaning as Beth pressed her hands, slick with blood, onto his stomach. An incredible calm came over Erika, and she stood.

'It's over, Darryl,' she said, moving toward him with an out-stretched hand. 'We know about them all: Janelle, Lacey, Ella, your mother...'

Darryl shook his head. 'My mother? No.'

'Yes, your own mother... Darryl, where is there left to go?'

Erika heard the far-off sound of helicopter blades. Backup was almost there. She looked over at Peterson, who was fading fast.

'Beth, I need you to keep pressure on his stomach,' she said, trying to keep her voice even. 'Keep on the pressure.' Beth nodded and pressed her hands into his stomach, but he had gone quiet and still. She turned back to Darryl still holding the gun, 'You need to let us go. If you let us all go, I can make sure you're treated well...'

'You shut up! SHUT UP you stupid BITCH!' cried Darryl, and he advanced on Erika with the gun, pushing its barrel close to her face.

She stood her ground and stared at him.

'Darryl. It's over. What kind of future have you got? Turn yourself in; if you come quietly we can cut you a deal. You'll be treated fairly,' she said.

Darryl shook his head, and pushed his finger against the trigger.

CHAPTER 89

Back in the incident room at West End Central, John, Crane and Moss were listening with horror at the audio coming in from control at Maidstone Police Station. They heard that two helicopters were now approaching the Oast House: the Air Ambulance and an Armed Police Response Team. Melanie joined them, having heard what was happening.

'Erika and Peterson entered the Oast House without authorisation,' said John with tears in his eyes. 'They found Beth Rose, but the suspect, Darryl Bradley, shot Peterson… We don't know if he's alive or…' His voice tailed off.

'Then he's still alive,' said Moss, struggling to stay composed. 'Until we hear otherwise, he's alive. Do you hear?'

John nodded. Melanie reached out and took Moss's hand. A voice came over the radio, saying that the Air Ambulance would try to land but the ground was soft. The Armed Response Team said it would be standing by.

'Suspect is armed and dangerous,' said a voice. 'I repeat, suspect is still armed and dangerous.'

'Come on,' said Moss under her breath. 'Please, don't let this end badly.'

CHAPTER 90

The hum of the helicopter grew close, but Erika couldn't see anything out of the small high windows of the Oast House. Darryl still had the gun trained on her. A red rash now covered half of his face.

Erika glanced at Beth, who was now crying, her arms covered in blood. Peterson was still. The sound of the helicopter grew louder.

'Darryl. Please. It's over,' she said.

'No, no, no, NO, NO, NO!' he said, shaking his head. He suddenly flipped the gun around and stuffed the double barrel into his mouth. His lips stretched wide, and he closed his eyes tight.

'Darryl! NO!' shouted Erika.

There was a deafening bang; the glass on one of the windows imploded, and Darryl hit the floor. Erika rushed over to him and saw a gunshot wound in his left shoulder. She looked up and out through the window, and saw the helicopter hovering – the silhouette of an officer holding a rifle. She grabbed the shotgun and cracked it open, taking out the remaining cartridge. Darryl lay dazed and covered in blood, but still very much alive. Erika grabbed her radio.

'Suspect is down; I have his gun. We are clear. I repeat, we are clear.'

Suddenly there was a crash and a team of three Specialist Firearms officers rushed in. They were followed by four paramedics, who fanned out between Peterson, Beth and Darryl.

'He's still alive, but only just,' one of the paramedics shouted, kneeling down on the ground beside Peterson. 'James, James, can you hear me?'

He started to work on him, putting in an IV line.

Erika turned back to Darryl and stood over him as a paramedic placed a pressure bandage over his injured shoulder. His face was wet with sweat and drops of blood, and he looked bewildered.

'Darryl Bradley,' said Erika, as the paramedic quickly unwrapped an IV line and pushed it into a vein in his arm. 'I'm arresting you on suspicion of the murder of Janelle Robinson, Lacey Greene, Ella Wilkinson, Bryony Wilson, and the abduction and attempted murder of Beth Rose, and the assault of your mother, Mary Bradley. You do not have to say anything, but it may harm your defence if you do not mention when questioned something which you later rely on in court. Anything you do say may be given in evidence.'

He stared up at her as the paramedics got him on to a stretcher and lifted it up.

'I got you,' she said.

For the rest of her life, Erika would remember the look Darryl Bradley gave her as he was stretchered away. It was as if she had come face to face with pure evil.

Erika stood outside the Oast House, wrapped in a blanket, and holding on to Beth as Peterson and Darryl were stretchered over the grass, still covered in patches of melting snow, and loaded into the Air Ambulance helicopter. They watched in silence as it lifted off and slowly moved away in the sky until it was a tiny speck and then vanished.

'Oh my God, thank you, thank you,' said Beth, finally breaking down.

Erika looked down at the girl who was pale and filthy and took her gently in her arms and they hugged. Moments later, a group of police cars came ploughing over the brow of the hill towards them, lights flashing and sirens blaring.

CHAPTER 91

It was late in the evening by the time Erika arrived back at West End Central. She caught sight of her reflection in the mirror of the lift as she rode up to the top floor, and the woman staring back frightened her. It reminded her of how she'd looked when Mark had died, her face devoid of colour and emotion. She was muddy and sleep-deprived, wearing days-old clothes, and without realising it, she was in shock. When she came out of the lift she hesitated at the door marked MURDER INVESTIGATION TEAM and then went inside.

The floor was empty, and the lights were out, all the officers having gone home hours before. There was one light still on, down the far end of the office, a door was ajar, and Erika walked towards it. She knocked and went inside. Melanie looked up at her, and for a moment they were silent.

'Come in, take a seat,' she said. 'Drink?'

Erika nodded. Melanie pulled out a bottle of whisky from her desk drawer and found a couple of mugs.

Erika sat down in the chair opposite the desk as Melanie poured them each a large measure and then passed her one of the mugs. They took a long drink.

'He came through surgery,' said Melanie.

'Darryl?'

'Darryl did, it was only a wound to the shoulder. I'm talking about Peterson. He came through the surgery. I just heard.'

Erika froze with the mug at her lips.

'I thought... I thought...'

'He lost a lot of blood, and they had to remove a large piece of his stomach and, of course, there's a risk of infection... but saying all of that, the doctors are hopeful. He has a high chance of pulling through,' said Melanie with a weak smile.

'Oh, oh my god,' said Erika. She dropped the mug down on the desk with a clatter and put a hand to her mouth and started to cry.

Melanie came over and put an arm around her, rubbing her shoulder hard.

'It was amazing what you did today, Erika.'

'No, it wasn't,' she said, wiping her face and trying to regain her composure. 'I should never have gone in there without backup. Peterson...'

'You shouldn't have gone in. But you'll be judged more on the outcome. I'll make sure I emphasise this when I submit my report.' Erika nodded. Melanie went back to her side of the desk and sat down. 'They've retrieved two computers from Darryl Bradley's bedroom, maps and plans he'd downloaded of the CCTV network in London. We have the cars: the red Citroën and the blue Ford which was parked at the rear of the house, and forensics have been working on the Oast House...' Melanie paused and took another sip of her whisky. 'They found human teeth, skin, and hair samples in the furnace where he kept the women.'

Erika shook her head. 'What about his mother?'

'She's still in Maidstone General with a concussion, but she'll be released in the next twenty-four hours. We'll want to question both her and the father.'

'I don't think the father knew,' said Erika.

'How can you be sure?'

'I don't know. There was something so innocent about him when he saw his wife lying there. Maybe innocent isn't the right word. He seemed sheltered from life. In his own world... Maybe the mother knew. We'll have to see what she says when questioned… Darryl Bradley. He's not on the same hospital ward as Peterson, is he?'

Melanie shook her head. 'When Darryl Bradley recovers, which should be soon, he'll be transferred into custody.'

'Where?'

'He'll need to be evaluated.'

Erika shook her head. 'I'm sure as we speak there's an expensive lawyer and doctor hovering around. He'll plead insanity… He'll end up in some cushy fucking psychiatric institution.'

Melanie put her hand on Erika's arm.

'You got him, Erika. You caught him. He would have kept on doing it, I'm sure. You saved lives. Take that home with you tonight. The rest we can worry about later.'

Erika downed the dregs of her whisky.

'Thanks.' She went to get up and go, then stopped. 'Look. I'm sorry if I gave you a hard time when you took on acting superintendent.'

'I won't be for much longer. I'm not going to take the job when it's made official.'

'No?' said Erika, surprised.

'No. I've got two kids, a husband. Life's too short, and I found myself forced to pick. I chose my family.'

'I didn't know you had a family.'

Melanie nodded. 'Twin boys.'

'Good for you.'

'I've recommended that you get it, the promotion to superintendent,' said Melanie. 'I don't know how much my word will sway things, but in light of what has happened, and if they don't drag you over the coals for going in without backup, you could be in with a chance.' She picked up her coat. 'I'm going to head off. Why don't you stay for a moment, have another drink? Or get a feel for the office.'

She nodded, and Melanie left.

Erika got up and went to the window, looking out over the rooftops, and then back at the office. The neat shelves stuffed with paperwork. A large dry marker board with cases written up in small grids. She went around the desk and sat in the chair, and her eye fell on the patch of carpet where Sparks had collapsed. She'd always had a dream, to get ahead, to succeed in the force. Was it all worth it?

EPILOGUE

A week later, Peterson was well enough to be transferred from intensive care to a regular ward, and Erika went to visit. She'd already been to see him a couple of times, but he had been unconscious.

She was nervous about seeing him, and had spent a long time choosing what to wear, and trying to work out what best to take him as a gift. She'd settled on a book.

When she arrived at his room, on the top floor of the UCL Hospital in Central London, Moss was sitting beside his bed. He looked thin, but bright, and he was sitting up in bed.

'Hey, boss,' said Moss, getting up and moving over to give her a hug. 'We were just wondering where you were.'

'I got held up... I got held up trying to work out what to wear,' she said sheepishly, deciding to be honest. They looked at her jeans and cream jumper, and she followed their gaze. 'I know; it doesn't exactly look like I've chosen anything exciting.'

'I like it,' said Moss. There was silence. 'Peterson was just telling me his exciting news. His catheter was taken out.'

He rolled his eyes.

'Not something I would like to experience again,' he said.

'How are you doing?' asked Erika, moving around to him and gently taking his hand. She looked down and saw the ID bracelet on his wrist, and that there were two IV lines in the back of his hand.

'It's going to be slow,' he said, 'but they're saying I'll make a full recovery. Who'd have thought that you can live without forty per cent of your stomach?' He shifted awkwardly in the bed and grimaced.

'I would kill to have forty per cent of my stomach removed. Have you seen the size of my arse!' said Moss. There was another awkward silence. 'Sorry,' she said. 'But you're my best friend, and I'm just relieved you're going to be okay, and I make jokes cos I don't know what else to say.' She pulled out a tissue and wiped her eyes.

Erika reached over and took Moss's hand. 'It's okay,' she said. Moss grinned.

'Stop it, I'm fine,' she said. 'Now, what did you bring him? I was told no grapes, now he has less room for stomach acid.'

'I brought my favourite book,' she said, taking the copy of *Wuthering Heights* from her handbag and giving it to Peterson.

'Thanks,' he said.

'I know it might seem an odd choice, but it was the first proper book I read when I learned to speak English, and it blew me away. The love story, the atmosphere. I thought you could do with a little escapism. I know I could. I was thinking of rereading it.'

'Then I don't want to take your copy,' he said, going to hand it back.

'No, that's new. I bought it for you.'

'Maybe we should read it together, at the same time,' he said. 'Sort of like a convalescent book club.'

'Sounds good.' She smiled.

When Peterson grew tired, Erika and Moss said goodbye, promising to visit him the following day. When they emerged from the hospital into Goodge Street it was busy with traffic, and they decided to walk down to Charing Cross.

'I've been formally offered superintendent,' said Erika, as they passed a coffee shop where several women sat shivering outside at tables smoking cigarettes.

'Bloody hell! That's great,' said Moss.

'Is it? I don't know.'

'You don't know!? You quit in protest the last time you were overlooked for promotion, and now you don't know?'

'Of course I want it, but what about life?'

'What *about* life? Life is what happens when you're making other plans. Take the promotion. You'll be the first non-arsehole that gets to that rank for a long time.'

Erika laughed. 'What if I turn into an arsehole?'

'Then I'll tell you.'

'Okay. Deal,' said Erika.

'Right, now we've got that sorted, let's have a drink. A big fat bloody drink. We've certainly earned it.' Moss took Erika by the arm and led her into the first pub, adding: 'And as my new superintendent, you're buying the first round.'

A NOTE FROM ROB

First of all, I want to say a big thank you to you for choosing to read *Last Breath*. If you did enjoy Erika's latest adventure, I would be very grateful if you could write a short review. It needn't be long, just a few words, but it makes such a difference and helps new readers to discover one of my books for the first time. As with all stories, I started this with only a vague idea of how things would pan out. I didn't intend to write about social media, but I think it's changed the world in so many ways that it's something that will always fuel my imagination. So much of social media is great: we can keep in touch with relatives and friends thousands of miles away, it forms opinion, and it's often an outlet for how we are feeling. But there's a dark side, which I think we are all still trying to understand. Just be very careful what you put out there for people to see. You don't always know who's watching…

Now, speaking of social media, you can get in touch on my Facebook page, through Instagram, Twitter, Goodreads or my website, which you'll find at www.robertbryndza.com. What do you think should happen next? Do you want Erika and Peterson to settle down and live happily ever after? And what about Erika's past, surely that should come back to haunt her in future books? There's still some unresolved stuff going on there, don't you think? I love hearing your thoughts, and read every message and will always reply, but I promise not to snoop around your social media profile… Well, I'll try not to :)

Robert Bryndza

P.S. If you would like to get an email informing you when my next book will be released, you can sign up to my mailing list using the link below. Your email address will never be shared and you can unsubscribe at any time.

www.bookouture.com/robert-bryndza

ACKNOWLEDGMENTS

Thank you to Oliver Rhodes and the fantastic team at Bookouture, you are all such a joy to work with. Thank you to Kim Nash for all your amazing hard work promoting our books, and for being there for all us authors, with your love, kindness and good humour. Special thanks to my brilliant editor, Claire Bord. I love working with you, and your notes and ideas always take my work to the next level, and help make it the best it can be.

Thank you to Henry Steadman for another incredible cover, and special thanks as ever to former Chief Superintendent Graham Bartlett at www.policeadvisor.co.uk, for advising me on police procedure, and for ensuring I tread the fine line between fact and fiction. Any liberties taken with fact are mine.

Thank you to Maminko Vierka for all the love and support and lots of laughs, and a mahoosive thank you to my husband, Ján, who keeps the wheels turning so I can concentrate on writing, and to Ricky and Lola for keeping my feet on the ground, and toasty warm. I couldn't do any of this without your love and support.

And lastly, a great big massive thank you to all my wonderful readers, all the incredible book groups, book bloggers and reviewers. I always say this, but it's true, word of mouth is such a powerful thing, and without all your hard work and passion, talking up and blogging about my books, I would have far fewer readers.